DAYS OF THE DEAD

Also by Agnes Bushell

Shadowdance
Local Deities
Death By Crystal

Days of the Dead

Agnes Bushell

John Brown Books

Salem, Oregon

For more information contact: John Brown Books, P.O. Box 5683, Salem, OR 97304.

"I Just Walked Away From Myself," by José María Cuéllar from *On the Front Line: Guerrilla Poems of El Salvador*, Claribel Alegría and Darwin J. Flakoll, eds. (Curbstone Press 1989). Copyright 1989 by Claribel Alegría and Darwin Flakoll. Distributed by InBook. Printed with permission of Curbstone Press.

Excerpts from *Popol Vuh*, translated by Dennis Tedlock, copyright 1985 by Dennis Tedlock. Reprinted by permission of Simon & Schuster, Inc.

The author and publishers thank the Guatemala Working Group, 1 Amwell Street, London, for permission to use their design "Guatemala: The Eternal Struggle" for the cover of this book.

The overall design for the cover was provided by Mohammed Smith.

Excerpts from *Days of the Dead* appeared in somewhat different form under the title "Geographies of Desire," in *The Underground Forest/La Selva Subterraneo*, Spring 1990.

The map of Central America was done by John Boring.

The photo of the author is courtesy of Marilou Townes.

PUBLISHER'S CATALOGING-IN-PUBLICATION DATA

Bushell, Agnes, 1949-
   Days of the dead
   I. Title
PS3552.U8244D39   1995
813'.54--dc20   94-068038

ISBN 0-9639050-8-2

Printed in U.S.A. by Gilliland, Arkansas City, Kansas

First Edition 1995

For Jim

Traveller, there is no road.
You make the road as you go.

—Popular Revolutionary Song.

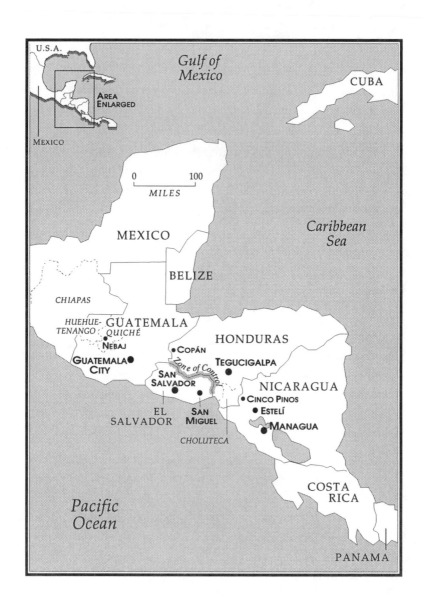

Zones of Control

July to October 1989

ONE

Guatemala City, Guatemala

The General and his young man left the club at half past nine. In the backseat of the limousine, the General handcuffed his companion and ran his hand several times through the other's sun-bleached hair.

"I will hurt you tonight," the General said. "You understand?"

"Yes, General," the young man whispered. "It's what I want."

"Of course it is," the General said. "You're a good boy."

The limo moved smoothly down the streets of Guatemala City. Outside it was hot, humid; inside the cool air raised bumps on the young man's skin.

"You are very beautiful, David," the General said. "After a few hours with me, you will look even more beautiful—to my eyes, anyway."

"Thank you, General," the other answered.

"You know, I spent quite a long time in your country," the General continued. "In Boston I studied how to control people and governments, and in the sex clubs in New York, I learned how to control boys like you."

The younger man sat quietly and listened.

"Thinking of Boston," the General continued, absently stroking the young man's thigh, "I am reminded of another young American, blond too, from what I hear. He lives with the *guerrilleros* in the mountains. The stupid Indians think he is Cucumatz, the white god returned to lead them to victory. I will ask him about this when I meet him. I will ask him questions about MIT. He went to MIT, believe it or not. I will ask him what bars he frequented in Cambridge while I am choosing the tools I will use to remove his

5

testicles. It will be interesting to see how long it takes a god to die, and what kind of sounds he makes while he is doing it."

The young man closed his eyes and tried to keep his breathing steady.

"Does this excite you, David? Do you want me to tell you exactly what I will do to him when I get him? Shall I tell you everything? Yes, it excites you. I can see that it does. . . ."

The General was never so talkative. It was he who was excited, the young man realized as the General pulled him toward him, down onto his knees in the back of the limousine. The sex part of the evening was going to begin sooner than he had expected.

In between beating his companion, the General took cocaine.

He would use his belt on David's back or legs or thighs or chest until the skin was covered all over with red welts, until the sounds the young man made changed from rapid breathing to sobs. Then he would stop to admire his work, and prepare and snort a few lines. He would then adjust the position of his companion's body on the suspension frame so a new section of smooth flesh was exposed. He was precise about where his belt left its marks, so his companion could only assume that he was equally precise about the cocaine, about the lines, about the time.

Cocaine, the General had told him earlier in the evening with a certain amount of satisfaction, came to him through Nicaragua. Directly through. Sandinista snow, special delivery, he said. The General spoke good idiomatic English, thanks to those years at Harvard.

"Easy to buy them," the General said. "Easy to buy any of them." And then to David. "Even you. I can buy even you." And he had.

Finally the General was aroused enough for intercourse. He released first the ankle, then the wrist restraints, and the young man's lanky body collapsed into his arms. He carried the body to his bed and laid it down, still admiring it. He turned around toward the table where, along with a tube of lubricant, his cocaine and its accoutrements also lay, a mirror, a razor blade. But the instant his back was turned, the younger man sprang forward, gripped the General's head with one hand, seized the razor blade from the table with the other and in one powerful stroke sliced through the artery in the General's neck.

It took General Garcia Fuentes more than a little time to die. In that time the young man held him in his arms and whispered in his ear, "This is your death, *maricón*. It is sent to you from the Maya, for the three hundred and sixty you slaughtered in the village of San Francisco. Remember them, *maricón*, as you go to hell."

When the General was dead, the young man pulled his body onto the bed. Then, seeing on one of the General's shelves an obsidian blade of the sort the Maya once used for sacrifice, he took it, cut the genitals from the General's body and stuck them into the dead man's mouth.

"And this," he said, "this is from me, and Cucumatz."

He went to the bathroom, washed the General's blood off his body, gingerly put on his clothes. He returned to the bedroom and sat down at the General's computer. It was only eleven o'clock.

Relaxing because he had time, he searched through the General's files. Garcia Fuentes was head of State Security, but the feudal model had never gone out of date in Guatemala, and so the General kept the Ministry's most sensitive documents to himself, in the security of his own compound. But the compound wasn't impregnable, and neither were the General's files. The young man duplicated, memorized, and erased file after file: names of government informers and infiltrators, names of suspected Unity collaborators, secure communications codes. He stumbled upon other interesting bits of information, for example cash payments in dollars made to certain ministers in certain ministries in other countries. As the General had bragged, Nicaragua was one of them.

At precisely one a.m. he had to leave. The last thing he did was study the photographs displayed in the General's room. Some of the cruelest men on the isthmus were smiling down on him from the walls. Several he knew on sight: Roberto D'Aubuisson, mastermind of the Salvadoran death squads, for one. Several he recognized, but could not place. One in particular, the face of a man so familiar to him, a man he had seen in a different context entirely, a place that was intimate, personal. It frightened him that he should find anything familiar here. He glanced at Garcia Fuentes one last time, recalled exactly Alejandro's mutilated body at the moment they pulled it out of the earth, and dashed into the bathroom to vomit into the bowl. He let the water run in the sink for a long time, washed his face in it, watched it flow down the drain. He looked like shit, but they would expect that. How else would he look?

The only way out of the General's compound was the way he had come in. He opened the bedroom door, closed it behind him, and walked down the corridor. At the front door, the driver was waiting for him. He was punctual; it was one a.m.

He was finding it hard to walk; his body was stiffening up from the beating. He noticed the guards watching him, smirking to each other as he climbed into the limo. His legs wouldn't bend without aching anyway, so he let himself groan a little. It pleased him to see the smirks on their faces and the other expression he caught, bordering somewhere between pity and disgust.

Pity and disgust would do just fine.

TWO

Cinco Pinos, Nicaragua

Three men were sitting around a wooden table in the room at the end of the corridor. There were tall glasses of dark brown cola in front of them, a few bottles of rum, a bowl of ice, slices of lime, packs of cigarettes. Wooden blinds were half open letting in some air, some light, a line of blue which was the mountains. It was that blue he saw before he saw anything else.

The two soldiers who had guided him through the cool parlors of the house, along the corridor and past the flagstone patio to this room hadn't said a word to him, as though he were a deaf mute or a foreigner. The house chilly as a crypt, and these stony-faced little bastards staring through him like he was a ghost. So he wondered what the three men would see when they stood up to greet him, whether it would be a tall, blond, privileged North American with an earring in his ear, or something better. Or something worse.

Three of them. The oldest, Luis, about fifty, a skinny, hawk-faced priest with a *campesino's* roughened hand. The smallest, Victor Zapeta, a Maya, whose name was familiar to him. Of the three he knew only one, the tallest and biggest, the one who stood first to greet him before introducing the others, who took him in his arms and held him in a strong embrace. Carlos.

From the patio came a wild chirping of birds. Somewhere a dog barked. Ice popped in one of the glasses with a sound as sharp as gunfire.

"Have a drink with us, Patricio," the priest said, gesturing to a chair, as though the popping ice had brought him out of a trance. "Or would you prefer that I call you Patrice? It is always interesting to me, how a man chooses his *nom de guerre.* For example, I hear that in the mountains you are known as Patrice, so naturally I think of Comrade Patrice Lumumba. The hero of Africa, they called him, but only after he was murdered. Ironic, isn't it, *com-*

9

pañero, that there can be such a thing as a hero who fails. So. Sit, please. You must be thirsty. Tell us, how long have you been traveling?"

Patrick helped himself to a glass of cola, tried to read the underlying tone of the priest's voice, the levels of tension around the table, signs of what was to come.

"Five days out of the Zone. Except for the last hundred kilometers I traveled slowly."

"And carefully I see, since you are here. Crossing the frontier was not difficult?"

"No. I hitched a ride over with an Israeli. He'd just finished a little stint in Guatemala, advising the military. He was very interesting to listen to, I must say. Quite forthcoming about the terrible situation there, with the subversives and all. He had been in El Salvador for a vacation. The beaches, I imagine."

"This was crossing from Salvador to Honduras, I take it?"

"That's right."

"And entering Nicaragua, there was no problem?"

"No. No problem at all."

"Well, Carlos," Luis said. "We are your guests. How do you wish to proceed?"

"As a good host. And as such I think we should give Patrice some time to rest. Let's meet back here in three hours."

There was agreement. Shown to his room Patrick glanced at himself in the mirror, saw a man he did not recognize as himself, knew Carlos would soon come to his door, and understood why.

The knock came sooner than he had expected. The knock and the opening of the door. Carlos was never one for standing on ceremony or in front of a closed door. Even the knock was an uncharacteristic courtesy.

He lumbered in, his fatigues sweat-darkened, a pack of cigarettes bulging in his breast pocket, the cigarettes probably as damp as his clothes. His beard was showing a few traces of gray. He had had an interesting mouth, Carlos, before he covered it up with hair.

10

"You look like the walking dead, Patrice. Do you want to eat? I'll have the woman bring something up."

"What woman is that?"

"The housekeeper. I don't know her name. Why? Do you want a woman?"

"And if I did, could you get me one? Excuse me. I thought I was in Nicaragua Libre not Guatemala City."

Carlos snorted. "You never change, do you, Patrice? Politics, always correct. Well, let me tell you, no ideology ever changed human nature."

"A woman might object strongly to such arrogance, Carlos—taking your own nature and making it universal. Anyway, I don't want a woman, but thank you for offering. Especially since I didn't detect any sarcasm in your voice. No, what I want right now is a shower and a shave. There's no hot water, I bet."

"There's plenty of hot water."

"Sounds like paradise."

They were standing in the middle of the room, which had in it only a bed and a wardrobe. It was a small room, made for small people. Neither of them was small.

"So, tell me. Is it true? Everything went smoothly? The mission was successful?"

"Yes."

"But you—you aren't ill are you?"

"No. I'm fine, Carlos. Just tired and dirty and a little sore. I have a few moral problems to deal with, but I'm sure I'll manage. And that's not your province anyway, is it? Maybe you should send up the priest."

"Maybe you should tell me."

Patrick sat down heavily on the bed. He was more than tired and more than sore and he didn't trust anyone, not even Carlos. He hadn't realized it before, but now that the thought existed he had to acknowledge it as true. He didn't trust anyone down here.

"It doesn't matter, Carlos. I wanted that son of a bitch and I got him. The rest of it doesn't matter."

"I will tell you something, Patrice. If I had been offered this mission, and given the choice, I would have refused."

The bed was exerting its force on him. He stretched out on the mattress. Too short, of course. A musty dampness rising from it. The room itself was cool, almost chilly. He could sleep here, wrap up in a blanket and disappear into sleep.

"Since when are we given choices, Carlos?"

"North Americans always have the choice."

Patrick closed his eyes and let that sentence cut into him.

"But look, it was well done, Patrice. You did a great service for us."

"Yes. I did a great service for you. For *you*. That's what you mean, isn't it? I did a service for *you*. And what's wrong with me, I wonder, that I keep thinking this revolution belongs to me, too? I must be a very sick man, Carlos, to think such a thing."

Carlos sighed, took a few steps to the window, set so high in the wall, like a window in a prison cell, that only a tall man could see out of it onto the tile roofs and the blue sky, azure, cloud-flecked.

"You are too sensitive to words, Patrice. Words are not so important as deeds."

"No. Words are deeds. And words dictate deeds. What you call me is what I become. We've had this conversation before. The power of words. Don't you remember? The difference between being called a terrorist or a liberation fighter, a nigger or an Afro-American, a faggot or a gay man—"

"Yes. We have had this conversation before. But some things cannot be changed by changing the words."

"Like the color of my skin? Like the place of my birth? Things like that, Carlos? Or how about the definition of the *us*? How about that word, Carlos? Who is this *we*, Carlos, this *us*? What if we change the definition of *us*, Carlos? What happens then?"

"You are angry, Patrice, and there is no need for it. Has anyone insulted you? Have you been deprived of anything? Do we undervalue your experience, does your advice go unheeded? Aren't you always consulted up there, don't you have men under your command? I don't see what you have to complain about. For a North American you are in a very important position of authority and responsibility. Some might say too important."

12

"You might say too important."

"I might, yes, if I did not know you so well."

"When you knew me well I was a different man. And that man didn't know shit about anything."

Carlos sighed again and started walking toward the door, but he paused at the foot of the bed. "The debriefing may be long. Rest now. And anything you want—"

"Just win the damn war, Carlos. That's all I want from you."

He saw the briefest of smiles pass over Carlos's face and then he was left alone.

Streams of afternoon sunlight slanted into the room through the wooden blinds, long rays, tangible as bars. Dust in the air. Patrick took his place at the table facing the inquisition. From his seat the room had an uncanny feel to it, as though they had stumbled into a painting by Vermeer: the stream of light, the surfaces of polished wood, the cases of leather-bound books, the blue pitcher of water on the table. Stepping into another time . . . Carlos asked him to begin and he began.

"My name is Patrick Day and I am a combatant with Guatemala Unity, assigned to a squad operating in the highlands of Huehuetenango. Early in May my commander gave me orders for this mission. I left the highlands on May 13th and joined one of our intelligence cadres, received my identity papers and briefing. The goal was the termination of General José Garcia Fuentes, whose war crimes, for those of you who may not be familiar with recent Guatemalan history, include the organizing and training of the Guatemalan Army's so-called Special Forces Unit, the Kaibiles, and direct responsibility for dozens of massacres of Indian peasants in the highlands, the slaughter of three hundred and sixty *campesinos* at Finca San Francisco in July 1982 being perhaps the most dramatic. My orders were to terminate him however I could. That was the first priority. The second priority was to get into his data files and pull out certain documents: communication codes, names of informers, whatever I could get hold of.

13

"I had been warned that much of this was going to be improvisational, and though I had contacts in Guatemala City, they proved to be elusive. Several of them were already disappeared by the time I got there. I was pretty much on my own, with a strategy that I wasn't entirely comfortable with—"

"You were unhappy with the strategy?" Luis interrupted. "Perhaps it would be clearer for all of us if you were to be specific. So tell us, Patrice. This strategy—what was it?"

Victor had been sitting with his eyes half-closed, but now he slid his pack of cigarettes across the table as though he had read Patrick's thought. He chose one from the pack and lit it, slowly, stretching out the seconds.

"Yes, I was unhappy with the strategy from the beginning, though I understand why it was necessary. And since it worked I guess I can't really complain, can I?"

"The strategy, Patrice? You will explain it to us. Please." A tempting, honey-smooth voice. The priest's.

"Carlos," he said, "I find it difficult to believe that you haven't received information about this mission from the *compañeros* in the Zone of Control. Could you tell me why I am being debriefed again?"

"If I may answer, Carlos." Luis's smooth voice, his hard face, hawk eyes, his scrutiny. "You see, Patrice, there are still some difficulties that we have, some problems. For example, there is the woman with whom you were seen, a woman who is a member of the diplomatic staff of the United States Embassy in Guatemala. Now we understand that as a North American you have access to people and places that we do not. If you took advantage of that access on our behalf, that is perfectly correct. Only tell us so we know, so there is no doubt. We do not wish to doubt you. You must help us with our doubt."

"The woman you are speaking of is Lucia Mendoza. She is an assistant to an assistant of the ambassador, yes. But seeing her was a personal matter. We had been very close at one time. Besides that, it turned out to be helpful to be seen with her. Our spies weren't the only people watching me."

14

"All right. Say we accept that explanation. There is still a second difficulty, the bruises on your body that were treated in the Zone. How you came by them . . . well, your explanation was not credible to everyone."

"What does that mean, Luis—'not credible'? Does that mean you think I'm lying to you?"

"That is what we intend to find out, Patrice. Because, you see, the report from the medical workers in the Zone is quite specific. They identified your wounds as indicating the use of torture. Now, please, put yourself in our place. Say you are in the highlands and you send one of your combatants on such a mission. You do send men out on missions, yes? You order your men to—"

"They aren't my men, Luis. And I don't order anybody to do anything."

"Patrice," Luis said, "you must tell us the truth here. The truth is you are a squadron commander. And unless the reports we have received are inaccurate, it was a squadron under your command that took six garrisons in Huehuetenango. According to our information, you are second in command of the Unity divisions in that department."

"We have one hundred and eighty combatants in the entire department, Luis. I wonder how you can make such a number into divisions."

"You are avoiding my question, Patrice."

"I can't remember your question."

"Do you not command men in Huehuetenango?"

"I command men in Huehuetenango the way the morning calls of birds command the sun to rise. There may be coincidence, but there is no causality."

"Which is to say that the Unity does not honor rank?"

"Which is to say that a squad of the Unity is an organism. And acts as an organism. With one mind."

"Very well, then. You hold no rank, you are not a squad commander, you are merely a cell in an organism. Let us return to the point. It is necessary that you put yourself in the leadership's place. They send a man on a mission and he returns claiming success. Yet upon examination it appears quite obvious that he has

15

been tortured. Is it not reasonable to conclude that his mission has been discovered, he himself interrogated, his release conditioned upon his cooperation with his captors? Would you yourself not at least entertain such a supposition? And if such a man told you that the bruises on his body came, not from interrogation, but from a sexual encounter, would you not find such an explanation extremely difficult to believe?"

"Indeed I would, if I had been so derelict in my duty that I hadn't bothered to review the details of the mission before I debriefed the commando. But if you had reviewed the documents, *padre*, you would see that I was recruited for this mission because our informants had discovered that Garcia Fuentes was actively engaging male prostitutes in Guatemala, and was particularly interested in men who fitted my physical description. The General also had a reputation for playing it rough, though I only discovered that after I had arrived and began talking to people. His perversions are fairly well known among certain elements in the city. It only required stepping inside any bar within a certain sector of the city and asking the first *pasivo* who sidled up to you. Which is how I found out about it. You could do the same, Luis. If you're that interested."

But he knew what was really going on here, and it seemed pointless to say any more. After years of trying, and failing, to terminate the General, and losing good men in the attempt, they had finally found a man willing to get down on his knees for the privilege of slitting José Garcia's throat and now his existence was an embarrassment to them. A *maricón,* after all, could hardly be a hero of the revolution. Certainly not a revolution Carlos was part of. Maybe only the ancient Maya might acknowledge what he had done as an honorable sacrifice, those warriors who would maintain strict celibacy for months before cutting into their penises with blades.

"Anyway, Luis," he said, "I don't understand your logic here. You think the mission was discovered and under torture I betrayed you? How then do you explain the fact that Garcia Fuentes is dead and you have the communication codes and the names of government agents working within the popular movement—"

"Yes. But the codes could be bogus and the names could be of innocent men."

"I see. And I suppose you're going to tell me that the General could be alive?"

"Indeed. Slipped out of the country, clandestinely, to aid in this deception. Or simply retiring for some time in the country. The funeral was private, a closed coffin, very little publicity. . . . And you yourself, Patrice, you may have bought your life dearly. There is a great deal you know, yes, but a great deal more you could find out. How are we to know you are not now an informer yourself? What assurances can you give us?"

Smoke from Luis's cigarette blurred the air. The ice, slender, only a film, floated in a bowl of water.The silence was deep, shadows played on the wall. He glanced across the table at Victor. In his face with its smooth skin the color of copper, its strong cheekbones and aquiline nose, its lustrous dark eyes he saw the faces of other men. He was home again, friends sitting around him, the smoke from their fire rising up into the vines, rising up to join the slow movement of cloud, mist, smoke, circling hawks. *What assurances can you give us?* A question Martín Azitzip never asked him when they went out together on night patrol. Not anything Anselmo Xec would have to ask him, or Andres Tzampop or any of the other men in his squad. But he was not in the highlands. Oh, he had been warned, he had been well warned. First the daykeeper's words, *Death waits for you in the city*, then the quetzal dying at his feet, both unquestionable heraldings of disaster. That he had not died in Guatemala meant very little. There were other cities; death could be waiting for him in any one of them. Death could be waiting right here.

The Maya will never trust you again, he thought. *If you kill me they will turn against you. You will kill your alliance with Guatemalan Unity, Luis, with the same bullet you use on me.* Not that they'd be stupid enough to make his execution public. Eliminating traitors was easy work with death squads operating all around them. The method was tried and true: dump the body and blame the enemy, mourn the loss, account to no one.

"You think we are entirely unjustified in questioning you? You think we do not have the right? Or are we to imagine, Patrice, that you would have us simply believe you? That your word alone should be enough for us?"

The priest's voice was cool, detached, without malice. Men who sat on tribunals in the highlands had voices pitched like his, men who were about to sentence other men to death. Impersonal, without rancor. He himself could never kill like that. He had to hate. And so did Carlos. The old Carlos anyway would not be able to sit and watch him die without feeling some hate.

They were still, silent, waiting.

"I'm afraid," he said finally, "that all I have is my word. I have no other assurance to offer you."

"Nothing but your word," Luis said in an unnervingly soft voice. "So. And do you know the price for betrayal?"

"I have fought with the Unity for four years, Luis. I know the cost of betrayal as well as the price."

"And you have nothing more to say to us?"

He did not answer. He did not look at Victor or Carlos. He looked at no one but Luis.

"So," Luis said after a few seconds, "you will not speak in your own defense. *Bueno.* I will consider everything you have said. I ought to order you to remain under guard until this matter can be resolved, but your *compañero* from the Unity has persuaded me to release you to his custody. Victor, you understand that I am holding you personally responsible for Patrice until you return to the Zone. Carlos, thank you again for your hospitality."

Luis rose from the table, shook hands with Victor and Carlos, and left the room. As he did, a phrase from the *Popol Vuh* went through Patrick's mind. Odd he should think of this now, these subtle words of the god Tohil which seemed on first hearing to be words of tenderness, but which really announced the god's wish to have men bound and cut open before him and their hearts removed from their chests: *Don't they want to be suckled? Isn't it their heart's desire to embrace me?*

18

THREE

The cantina where Carlos took Patrice and Victor for dinner was thatched like a Mayan house, though without walls. There was music coming from a crackling sound system, and many people sitting around wooden tables, drinking, eating, laughing. Soon the band of Rasta musicians from the Atlantic coast would begin to play, perhaps couples would dance. Victor wondered if Patrice liked to dance, if the music they played would be music he liked.

There was much about Patrice he did not know.

They sat beside each other and ate and drank. The beer was cold here and there was no shortage of rice and chicken and beans. Victor made sure to stay very close to Patrice. He wanted to act as a buffer between him and Carlos, who was unable to sense the pain Patrice was in, was perhaps too close to him to see him, whose sight was always focused on the horizon, always on the future, never on the place where he was. Victor wanted to give Patrice as a gift this evening of lightheartedness, of freedom from worry and fear. After all, they were in Nicaragua Libre, and in several days it would be the tenth anniversary of the Triumph. He wondered if anyone had bothered to inform Patrice of that fact.

After they had eaten Patrice left the table and stood at the bar talking to one of the Rastas. When the two men left together and made their way into the darkness outside, Victor's first inclination was to join them. But he did not. He was a guardian, not a jailer. He waited twenty minutes until the Rasta returned alone and then he went out in search.

He found Patrice stretched out on a low limb of a giant banyon, almost entirely concealed by the tree's massive vines.

"It's a little cooler out here," Patrice called down to him in Quiché. "Want to come up?"

Victor smiled and climbed up. He sat on the limb with his back against the trunk and lit a cigarette for each of them. The night was filled with wild, familiar sound, discordant, rhythmic, the music of insects, of frogs and birds, and the air around them was thick with the heavy, aromatic smell of marijuana smoke.

"In all the world there is only one thing I know to be absolutely true," Patrice said.

"Is this a truth you will share?"

"Of course, *compañero*. It is this: where there is a Rasta, there will be ganja also."

From inside the cantina came the first strains of a droning reggae beat.

"What is the song they are playing, Patrice?"

" 'Four hundred years. It's been four hundred years and the people they still can't see.' Bob Marley, Victor. Remember him?"

Victor could see his long shape on the bough, the shape only, and at the end, like a dragon's breath seen at a great distance, the burning end of the cigarette and the white tail of smoke.

"You are hurt, Patrice. But how deep is the wound?"

"Why do you ask? Are you a *curandero*? Can you heal me by the laying on of hands? Would you dare? Call on all those winds? Blow the whole goddam town down."

Victor called upon a zephyr wind. His heart called it. The leaves rustled slightly, a small breeze. Sitting like this with his knees drawn up, he felt like a bird, tight and small, perched on the bough beside a languorous though ever crafty and vigilant snake.

So the image returned and the daykeeper's words: *You will meet him in the land of Death, for that is the place to which he goes. And you will not leave him, for you are his brother. . . .*

The smoke from their cigarettes was rising like burning *copal*. And they were two brothers up in a tree, they were the twin brothers, Hunahpu and Xbalanque. The words of the story came to him and he began to recite:

"This is the tree of Seven Macaw, a nance, and this is the food of Seven Macaw. In order to eat the fruit of the nance, he goes up the tree every day. Since Hunahpu and Xbalanque have seen where he feeds, they are now hiding beneath the tree of Seven

Macaw, they are keeping quiet here, the two boys are in the leaves of the tree. And when Seven Macaw arrived, perching over his meal, it was then that he was shot by Hunahpu. The blowgun shot went right to his jaw, breaking his mouth."

Patrice laughed. "Poor old Seven Macaw, thinking he was the sun and the moon, dressing himself in jewels. I feel sorry for the old guy, up against those two daredevils. He breaks off Hunahpu's arm, doesn't he, and runs away with it to roast it. The boys go back to get the arm disguised as *curanderos* and say they can fix his teeth, but instead they pull them all out, beginning a tradition Guatemalan dentists have been following ever since. But those last lines, Victor: 'Just as they had wished the death of Seven Macaw, so they brought it about. After this the two boys went on. What they did was simply the word of the Heart of Sky.' I love that sentence.'What they did was simply the word of the Heart of Sky.'"

"It is what you do as well, Patrice."

"Try telling that to Carlos and Luis."

"They know it, though they call it by a different name."

"Then, *curandero*, tell me this. How did they know about Lucia Mendoza, unless they were watching me all that time? Watching me, but not doing a fucking thing to help me."

"They were not watching you. That information was in a report we obtained from G-2, Guatemalan Intelligence. The embassy was a little embarrassed, but not much. *Señora* Mendoza evidently had met you through a mutual friend, or you had friends in the States in common, or excellent letters of reference, or a charming smile. . . . Patrice, do not bother yourself about it. She is a professional diplomat, and if nothing else professional diplomats know how to get out of a tight place."

"Lucia and I lived together when we were students," he said, without emotion. "At one point we were even engaged to be married. So she did me a great favor and introduced me to General Garcia Fuentes. What do you think about that, Victor?"

"And did you tell her why you wanted to meet the general?"

"I told her that some Mayan friends had asked me to settle a bit of unfinished business with the general. Diplomats, I find, appreciate ambiguity. But I didn't want her to be left with a mess on her hands and no forewarning. I still care about her a great deal."

"Then I think you acted honorably toward her, and she toward you."

"Well then, at least there was some honorable activity going on during that mission. . . .Victor, I want to thank you for . . . taking me into your custody. I don't much like jails."

"It was the least I could do. Besides, I have a mission of my own here. To guide you back to the highlands. To help you to return."

"I have the sense that it will be difficult."

"I have that sense as well. There is a reason why they ordered you to come here, rather than return at once to the highlands. You are very far from the Maya now. There is a reason for that. The man who killed that devil in Guatemala City, such a man might be thought to have slain Seven Macaw himself. For him to return with such a victory. . . . Well, why do you think Luis was so interested in the chain of command in Huehuetenango? Why did he ask you about your position there? Why does he threaten to keep you down here?"

"I don't understand, Victor."

"Not too long ago, ten years maybe, the commander of Guatemalan liberation forces was fair, like you."

"Fair, perhaps, but he was Guatemalan."

"He was not Mayan."

"Nor am I."

"Exactly."

"I don't understand. What do you mean to say to me?"

"That the leadership is wary. They will not allow a North American to gain power among the indigenous people."

"Someone should inform the leadership that the indigenous people are perfectly capable themselves of preventing that from happening."

Victor laughed. "Indeed, Patrice, I did point that out to them. I also told them that if we chose to offer one of our combatants a position of command that was our business, not theirs. A ladino in command of Mayas, a *criollo*, this is nothing to them. But let them

22

see a gringo in the highlands. . . . And do you know why? Because they think all Indians are waiting for Quetzalcoatl, or in our case, Cucumatz, to return."

"That's ridiculous."

"I am only telling you what they fear."

In the pause between their words the cacophony of the night swelled up around them: from the trees, the hums, whizzes, shrieks and calls of insect, animal and bird; from the cantina, a shelter made of trees, the music, songs and voices of men.

"I myself," Victor said very softly, "have experienced that fear." He lit two more cigarettes and passed one to Patrice. Then he leaned back against the trunk and closed his eyes. The image of the fear returned to him: a quetzal, bleeding, plummeting into a lake of blood.

"You should give your own people more credit, Victor. Nobody I've ever met in Huehuetenango has ever once taken me for a god. Maybe they figure a god would dress better. Anyway, it doesn't matter. I'm not there now and chances are I won't be going back there again. So nobody has to be afraid of anything."

"I took my fear up Patohil, Patrice. I laid it before a daykeeper of my own lineage, a mother-father. These are the words he said to me: You will meet him in the land of Death, for that is the place to which he goes. And you will not leave him, for you are his brother, his twin, Hunahpu. You are one body, he the left, you the right. His hunger is your hunger. He will read your heart, you will understand his. And the bird that died in his hand you will return to him, living."

As he spoke the daykeeper's words, Victor felt his mouth go dry, felt a dizziness begin to descend on him, and so he knew that he had said enough, and that the rest of the announcing was for himself alone.

The deafening, raucous sounds of the night closed over them like the rushing of a waterfall, and for a long time Victor heard nothing else. Then Patrice said, "What does it mean?"

"For me, it means I have no need to fear you because your desire is the same as mine. What it means for you I cannot say. But

23

if it is the desire of your heart to return, then I will help you. As for the rest, it is in the hands of the gods."

"Where it belongs. Well, Victor, all I desire is to be set down on the Green Path and given the strength to stay on it. So let's hope the daykeeper spoke truly. I don't have a brother, but I have felt his absence all my life."

"You will feel his absence no longer, Patrice."

"Then, brother, I think we should go inside and buy each other a beer. I'm dying of thirst."

Victor smiled into the darkness. He was thirsty too.

FOUR

Patrick sat smoking on the patio, the house encircling him, breathing in its dark, empty sleep. The patio was dark too, shadowy, its dry reflecting pool and dry fountain illuminated only by moonlight. Running along the east side of the patio, under the verandah, was the corridor with its hammocks, ornately fringed and tasseled but shabby now and frayed, and its shrines, statues under glass bells, the Bleeding Heart of Jesus, the Madonna and Child, each statue dressed in clothing richly decorated but gray with age, bouquets of long dead flowers still resting at their feet. Hung along the corridor's walls were photographs, faces of the dead in happier times.

The whole house felt dead to him. It wasn't the same house that had existed in Alejandro's memory. Everything beautiful was gone from it now, stolen by the Guardia, expropriated by the Revolution, gone either way. Everything was disappeared: the paintings Alejandro had described to him and the wood carvings and the goldfish in the reflecting pool, the good smell of soup cooking in the kitchen, the horses in the stables, tonight even the stars themselves were disappeared, the stars Alejandro had wished on, even then wishing for a prince, or so he always said, wishing for the very prince he finally found much later in another country thousands of miles away. All of it disappeared as Alejandro himself had been disappeared, all but the stone angels dancing hand in hand around the fountain, only that small testimony left to the past and to Alejandro's memories which had become his own.

He had been sitting there for some time when Carlos joined him. They sat side by side in rocking chairs beside the empty pool, smoking, but they had nothing to say to each other. Finally Patrick broke the silence.

"How odd it feels, Carlos," he said, "to be a guest in one of your houses again."

"You make me sound like an oligarch, Patrice. This is not my house. It belonged to a branch of my family once. It belongs to the Nicaraguan government now."

"Yes. But I could swear this is the exact rocking chair I sat in on the patio of your family's house in San Miguel. Different patio, though. Hibiscus there, not bougainvillea. Banana trees, not palms. I remember that dry sound the leaves make. And it wasn't an enclosed patio, as I remember. I could sit there and watch the street."

"And I still remember driving up in the car, there were two *compas* with me, all of us had rifles. . . . God, what a chance we took! And finding you there. Just sitting there with that damn .22 in your lap. And I had searched all over the damn town for you. I thought they'd found you already. I thought you were already dead. But what balls! Son of a bitch, Patrice. You had balls."

Patrick closed his eyes. He didn't want to remember it again, but the memories came back to him as they always did. The heat, like standing in front of an open oven. The men, digging, wearing kerchiefs over their noses and mouths. Red ones. Black ones. And straw hats. All of them wearing straw hats. The dirt was newly packed over the spot. That was how they knew. That, and the *zopilotes* and the flies. One thrust with the shovels, two, and they hit something and then first a hand, an arm, and then a leg and already the stench and the maggots and the color was wrong and the shape. . . .

"You were rocking in a rocking chair just like this. And to tell you the truth, Patrice, you looked insane."

. . . Everything was wrong and so for one single final moment he had hope because this could not be Alejandro, nor the next one, nor the third, stiff and dirty, bloated, torn like something had ripped it apart. But beside him Maria Dolores began to wail and gripped hold of his arm and he looked again but all he could see of Alejandro was his long, straight, beautiful, black hair. . . .

"So I said to you, Get up, Patrice. Get up and get in the car. Believe me, I thought you were going to shoot me, too. Ha. What

26

a dumb gringo move, Patrice. But, son of a bitch, you got away with it! The only man I've ever heard of to hunt down an *escuadron de la muerte* and live to tell about it. . . . But what a fool you were to do it! Like the fool he was to go out alone at night in San Miguel."

"I'm glad to see you're not blaming yourself, Carlos."

"How is it my fault, Patrice? Tell me that."

"You never warned us, never told us you had joined the guerrillas, that the death squads were hunting you, your whole family was in danger. You let him walk into that—"

"And you never read the papers, I guess? You had no idea there was a war going on, a repression? He was my brother, remember. I loved him, too. But men die, Patrice. This happens. When are you going to bury him? When are you going to let him rest?"

Patrick pulled hard on his cigarette and let it pass. Alejandro was already dead and buried, and nothing would change that, no matter how long he himself lived and carried Alejandro's memory in his heart. Nothing would change it. It was done.

"See, I worry about you," Carlos said. "You're like a brother to me and I worry."

"If I were you then, I'd be worrying about Luis."

"Luis? You know what this is about, Patrice. The leadership doesn't doubt you. They just want to flex their muscle. The more punishment you can take, the more they give you. You succeed at killing one man, next they send you to kill ten. I'm just reminding you, OK? Next time say no. You can always say no."

"Maybe I don't want to say no. Maybe I enjoyed it. Maybe all I'm good for now is killing the bastards. But since I'm like a brother to you, maybe you could do me a great favor and tell me why I'm here and when I'm going back to Guatemala. The truth, please."

"The truth. All right. You are here because it's safe to be here and because it's time to celebrate the tenth anniversary of the Sandinista victory. As for going back . . . you are burned, Patrice."

"I see. So I'm not going back, is that it?"

"You will come with me into the Zone. From there we'll see. See what Guatemalan Security does. Wait awhile."

Carlos offered his pack and Patrick took another cigarette, accepted a light. There were many kinds of truth. Many kinds of lies, too. Lies of commission and lies of omission. Partial lies and partial truths.

"Tell me about Luis. If he's a real priest I'm a Black Muslim."

"Try cardinal, the one closest to the Pope."

"Really? I suppose I should be flattered. And what does the leadership want with me?"

Carlos shrugged. A lie of omission.

"And Victor, my guardian. What about him?"

"He's represented the Unity before at meetings on this level. He's intelligent, cool-headed. Separatist leanings. But the Mayas are all like that. Anarchists in their own way. That's probably why you get along with them so well."

"Probably. Do you trust him?"

"I've never had reason not to. Why?"

"Because he told me something tonight I wanted very much to believe and so I distrusted everything he said."

"You are deeply perverted, Patrice."

"I am deeply cynical if that's what you mean, yes."

Carlos sighed. "You are going to be angry with me for saying this to you, but I love you so I'm going to say it anyway. Patrice, why don't you go back? Why do you stay? Go home. Make a life for yourself. Get that damn Ph.D. Go home to the States, go back to MIT, fall in love again. You are getting too hard, Patrice. You frighten me sometimes. Today you frightened me very much."

"Did I? That's funny, Carlos, because for years you were the one who frightened me. The night you came at me with a broken bottle in front of the Plough and Stars, saying you were going to cut me into pieces because I was fucking your brother. The time you came to visit us and ended up smashing the furniture. You scared the shit out of me, man. Now I scare you. Well, you know, sometimes I scare myself. I slit a man's throat two weeks ago, Carlos. And you think I can just waltz back to Boston, back to MIT, back into the philosophy department? Get another apartment in the south end, buy another ten speed, get another pair of running shoes? Just pick up where I left off, minus a lover, but, well, I'm not alone, right, lots of men have lost their lovers. . . . Carlos, I don't know what the fuck you've been doing for the past four years, but do you know what I've been doing? Do you have any fucking idea? No, I didn't enjoy sucking off that son of a bitch, but I don't enjoy burying castrated bodies either. I don't enjoy sleeping in a man's house one night and going back a week later to find the house burned to a cinder along with everybody who used to live in it. I don't enjoy pulling dead women and their dead babies out of wells and I don't enjoy putting bullets in my friends' heads because they're too far gone to carry off a battlefield. Compared to my usual routine, Carlos, that night with Garcia was goddam pleasant because I knew exactly how it was going to end. I knew every second how it was going to end. So please, Carlos, don't talk to me about getting hard. I'm not half as hard as I need to be. I have a long way to go yet."

He leaned back in the rocking chair until all he could see was sky. Cloudy, starless. Not the sort of sky he could find his way home by. Maybe he'd never find his way home again, or if he ever did, maybe he'd be such a different man that no one would recognize him. He'd be a stranger again.

"I only wonder one thing. I wonder who I should thank for recommending me to Vladimir for this mission. Oh, give me some credit, Carlos, and don't start denying it. Who else but Vladimir could have dreamt up something like this? So who recommended me to him? Who mentioned my name? Who near the leadership even knows me, Carlos? Only you."

"They asked me, yes. They asked if I trusted you and I said I did. They did not tell me anything about the mission, though. I knew none of the details."

"No, of course you didn't know. I was just curious. Anyway they probably have dossiers on all of us complete with sexual preferences and current HIV status. And God knows we poor beleaguered bisexuals in our dwindling numbers are becoming as rare as the quetzal. . . .You know, Carlos, the more I think about it the less I want to go to Estelí."

"You'll enjoy yourself. They'll be many internationalists. Who knows, maybe even some gays. The Nicaraguan Revolution is very liberal about these things."

Patrick sucked on his cigarette and let it go, the remark and the disdain in Carlos's voice that went with it. None of it mattered, none of it was worth arguing about now. Every revolution wound up throwing men like him into prisons and labor camps, the Soviets, the Chinese, the Cubans, now even the Senderistas in Peru were said to be murdering any homosexual they found. He wasn't in it for the revolution anyway. He was here to settle old scores, a Fury enacting vengeance for the murder of Alejandro. That was all he was doing here. The rest of it didn't matter.

"Yes, I think you will enjoy Estelí," Carlos continued. "You need some rest and you deserve it. Besides I understand Marta will be there. You haven't seen her in a long time, but she always asks for you. You are like a son to her, you know. So don't even think about not coming, understand?"

"I can't think about not coming. I'm in custody, I believe. I have to go wherever my custodian takes me."

"Ah, Patrice," Carlos said, getting up. "Don't worry so much. We'll go, we'll have fun. It's the Triumph, time to celebrate. Sleep well, and tomorrow everything will look brighter."

But before he retired to his room, Patrick took a walk along the corridor that enclosed the patio. He wanted to find Alejandro's face among the many family photographs and portraits that hung on the walls. He knew the photographs would be there because Alejandro had told him about this house, and in Alejandro's mind's eye there were photographs hanging along the corridor. All of Alejandro's memories were vivid, and he had a way of describing people and things so that Patrick could see them perfectly. It was the way he had described his relatives, his friends, his life. It was the way, slowly and painfully, he had described how at ten years of age he had been taken by one of his uncles into a certain room and what had happened to him there. Every detail of that time, and all the other times. He had remembered everything.

And now it seemed that he was looking for someone else, no longer Alejandro but another face. They were indeed a family of oligarchs, coffee-growers, land owners, diplomats, and politicians. All of them without exception until, from a branch of the family that had generations ago fled Nicaragua for the relative stability of El Salvador, there had come two exceptional brothers, one a revolutionary, and one a homosexual.

Searching the faces, but he already knew the face he was looking for. He would be twenty years younger in these photographs, of course, but evidently he hadn't changed much over the years, or else his image had been so carved in Patrick's mind that he would recognize him no matter how many years had passed.

And the night Alejandro had told him, that night was carved in his mind, too. He had made promises to Alejandro that night: to love him, to protect him and care for him, never to hurt him, never to leave him, never refuse to accompany him down dangerous streets, never let him walk to his death alone.

The photograph was there, as he knew it would be. The man and the boy, sitting together on a bench. Beneath someone had written in a clear hand: Alejandro, age 11, with Uncle Emilio, Five Pines, Nicaragua, 1972.

Emilio Castillo. Maternal uncle of Alejandro and Carlos Martínez, staunch supporter of the ARENA party, plantation owner, *patrón*.

The same man who had posed smiling in Guatemala with General Garcia Fuentes.

31

FIVE

Estelí, Nicaragua

They drove through the mountains to Estelí in a Sandinista Army jeep, Carlos at the wheel. Coffee at forty-five hundred feet, tobacco at three thousand . . . but Patrick was used to living at eight thousand feet, ten thousand, he was used to standing twelve thousand feet above sea level deep inside the Cuchumatanes and seeing before him the summits of thirty-two volcanoes. Counting volcanoes, as exalted and lonely as a god. But this was man's country, not god's. This was rolling, soft, fertile, husbanded land, a geography of desire, and here in a landscape of houses and fields and gardens, he felt such longings, he could hardly bear them, for tenderness, for the ordinary, for a garden, a house, children, where it was not impossible to think of time opening up before you, not impossible to expect to die of old age. No walking into a village here and finding naked men hanging castrated from trees, children. . . .

Victor, sitting beside him in the back of the jeep, touched his arm. "Cigarette?"

Patrick accepted a light and inhaled deeply. Carlos had his hand on the horn, was passing the troop carrier in front of them though they were heading into a curve. Machismo.

"Your family, Patrice," Victor said softly, "they must miss you, being away so long. It would be possible to call them from Estelí."

"If we live that long," Patrick said.

"You think the contra will be active so near to Estelí?"

"No, it's Carlos's driving I was referring to."

"You want to drive, Patrice?" Carlos called back over his shoulder. "You don't like my driving, just say so, son of a bitch. You can deal with the potholes and the fucking cows in the road. And watch for land mines while you're at it. This road isn't safe."

"What irony," Patrick said in a low voice only Victor could hear, "if we die on a back road in Nicaragua Libre."

"En route to the tenth anniversary celebration," Victor whispered back. "Bad luck, ten. A death number."

But Victor was smiling and so Patrick smiled too, leaned back and smoked and watched the scenery go by.

Estelí, the cradle of the Revolution. The sun so bright it blinds. Streets, hot and dusty; buildings, white, pink and azure; flags and banners hanging from every street lamp and strung together between buildings, and paper streamers already littering the streets, red and black for Sandino, blue and white for Nicaragua. The cradle of the Revolution celebrating its birthday.

Ten years ago the city had seen some of the fiercest street combat of the war. Walls were still pock-marked with bullet holes, SANDINO LIVES scrawled in red paint over them, and plaques were set into the walls memorializing the names of the fallen. Many walls were covered completely with murals: students teaching *campesinos* to read; doctors vaccinating children. Images of what the Revolution had sought to accomplish, and might have if the counter-revolution hadn't interfered, backed by dollars and supplied by the arms network of the greatest military power on earth.

HERE, the official graffiti announced in bold red letters, WE DO NOT SELL OUT OR SURRENDER.

Carlos drove the jeep slowly through the streets toward the army barracks where they would be put up. Slowly and carefully, there were so many people crowding around, so many children running, so many men and women in uniform, so many internationalists with cameras and clean clothes. So many people, so much activity and noise: radios blasting North American rock 'n roll, and voices of kids hawking newspapers and *chicles* and *refrescos*, and smoke rising from food venders' fires, the sweet smell of baked meat and ripe fruit and the thick, sweet scent of tobacco from the drying sheds.

33

But Patrick looked into face after face, Indian and mestizo, woman, man, child, and saw only grief.

"Something's happened," he said. "Stop, Carlos! Ask!"

"What are you talking about?"

"Something's wrong. Just ask."

"Ask what's wrong? Are you crazy?"

"Hey!" he called to a group of *campesinos*. "What's going on?"

One man shrugged, the others turned away.

"Let's buy a paper. Carlos, I'm telling you. Something bad's happened."

He called to a kid selling papers and bought a copy of *Barricada*. All about the Triumph, the celebration tomorrow, representatives of governments coming from all around the world to honor the people of Nicaragua on this anniversary of ten years of freedom and revolution. Even a presidential candidate from Honduras, the peace party candidate, Gabriel Aguilar, was expected.

"But look at everybody!" he said.

"Indians," Carlos said over his shoulder. *Indígenas*, at least, not the insulting *indios*, but it was spoken in the same tone of voice.

"They are mourning," Victor said in his softest voice. "As when the birthday comes of a dead child."

That evening a message was radioed to Carlos from inside the Zone of Control, but it was meant for Victor, and for Patrick. It was from the Unity command in Quiché: a squadron of guerrillas coming out of the mountains had been ambushed near the town of Nebaj in the department of Quiché. Sixty men had died in the massacre. There had been no survivors.

The Guatemalan Army does not take prisoners of war.

What they do take: eyes, ears, tongues, testicles, skin.

Several hours later Martha came to the barracks looking for him. "Surprised to see me?" she laughed, embracing him. "But of course I knew you were here. There are no secrets in Nicaragua. Come along. I'm buying you dinner."

She took him to the one restaurant in town that always had cold beer and usually had steak to go with it. He ate and drank inattentively, drank until the center of the table was filled with empty bottles, though the beer was so weak it had no effect on him. He listened to her, but he said very little and she didn't press him but let him eat in peace.

She told him about the Christian-base communities, about the cooperatives and the schools, about the growth of the popular movement in El Salvador. And he ate as though he hadn't had a meal in months, because he had to eat and drink and not think about those sixty men in Nebaj. And then he was finished eating and he lit a cigarette. She had finished, too. She waited.

"So," he said, and he smiled at her, this tiny, white-haired, North American woman, an exile like himself, and for the same reason. "You've been busy."

"And you too, I expect. But all of it *classified*."

"No one's told me it's *classified*. But it's not very nice. I'm afraid I've grown a few extra skins since I saw you last."

"I have seen you more vulnerable, yes. But I don't feel that you've become hard. Stronger, yes. But no happier."

"Happiness isn't on my agenda for this lifetime. Next one maybe."

"You haven't yet forgiven yourself?"

"I don't believe it's possible to forgive oneself. I think it's a contradiction in terms. Besides, it's not a question of forgiveness. I'm like you, Marta. You can't have another son. I can't have another husband. Some things you get one of. If you're lucky. So I was lucky for six years. I'm not complaining. And truly if you'd caught me on another day I would have been a lot cheerier. But we just got some bad news from Guatemala. As though there's ever good news from Guatemala."

35

"But I've just heard some good news from Guatemala. Rumors anyway. You must already know about this. If there's any truth to it anyway."

"What?"

"Garcia Fuentes. Dead. True or not?"

"I believe it's true. But what have you heard?"

"There are many versions, as usual. Some say he was murdered by a mistress. Others suggest it was more sordid than that, that a young man was involved, a male prostitute. A crime of passion, either way." They exchanged smiles at this small irony. The term "crime of passion" was often used by the Guatemalan government when the mutilated bodies of labor organizers or peasant leaders were found by the side of the road. "Of course," she added, "the official story is that he died in his sleep."

"*A saber*, as we say in Guatemala. Who knows. Maybe the Nicaraguans will claim responsibility."

"God forbid, no! Even if they had done it, they'd never admit to it. We are abiding by the terms of the Esquipulos agreement, remember? No military, financial or logistical support for irregular armies or insurrectionist movements. Of course the greatest offender against this provision is not a party to the agreement."

"Oh well, Marta. The United States doesn't abide by its agreements anyway. Why should it? Who's going to make it? But I'm surprised to hear you say that Nicaragua is taking that bullshit seriously. So much for international revolution, eh? Well, let's see how long they stand all alone, these Nicas. None of them look too happy about their anniversary party. I've seen more animated faces in coffins."

"Estelí is Sandinista, one hundred per cent Sandinista. The rest of this region, though . . . you'd be surprised the support the contra have around here. It's the draft and . . . well, other things. The Sandinistas are not universally loved. Of course, men who have power over others often misuse it, no matter what their political ideology. I've even heard stories of disappearances up here. It scares me, to tell you the truth."

He knew how scared they must have been, those sixty men in Nebaj. You can get so scared you can't think. Aerial bombardment, when the earth shakes under you and you want to crawl into yourself, become small and hard like a seed, burrow yourself into the ground. Or when it comes out of the blue, scares you so much, you piss all over yourself. One second there's a man walking in front of you, next second he's bursting open, blown to bits and the bits coming at you, all over you, limbs that can kill you, splinters of bone that can take out an eye. Or entering a village where you'd just been a week, two weeks before, and you see them lying on the ground or hanging from posts, butchered, crawling with maggots, people you knew, children you played ball with, and you see what life is worth to the enemy and the horror of it eats into your heart.

"Every Maya in Guatemala has lost someone too. But we still remember how to smile when we're at a birthday party."

"There is a sense of despair in this country. Everything is falling apart. Even in Managua nothing works, buses, telephones, the electricity, the water pumps, nothing. Nobody even knows how much anything should cost because the value of the *córdoba* fluctuates so from day to day. What is money worth? Nobody knows. Is ten thousand *córdobas* for a bottle of Coke a bargain or a form of theft? To what do you compare the price when electricity costs next to nothing but a roll of toilet paper costs a week's wage? The latest joke is, How are Nicaraguan salaries like menstruation? They come once a month and last a couple of days. . . ."

Capture though—they can keep you alive for days, slow torture, men working you over with their knives. What could you hold onto then? Close your eyes and think of the cloud forest, of walking a narrow green path under the canopy, the hanging vines, the mosses and ferns, shafts of light filtering through the leaves, monkeys in the trees? Close your eyes and feel yourself walking with the gods, breathing with them, touching them, so the knife's first cut might be the mouth of the god, suckling, and as they strip the skin from your body your scream might be the cry of Heart of Earth to Heart of Sky? Not a death he'd stick around for. He always kept a bullet in reserve. He'd blow his head off before he'd ever let them take him alive.

"Patrick?"

"Forgive me. I'm still here. Really."

37

"Yes. But even I can see that the economic woes of Nicaragua are not of great interest to you tonight. And now that your plate is empty . . . do you want some fruit? No? Then it's your turn to talk to me. Something's bothering you. What is it?"

"Ah, what's bothering me? Only my life. I've been wondering lately what happens to men who lose their ability to judge between right and wrong. I think it's happened to me. Not that I care except that I don't want to die being somebody Alejandro wouldn't recognize. If he happened to be looking."

"What was it they asked you to do?"

Her voice was serene. As always, she generated a space around her which was safe, loving. Once long ago he had opened his heart to her, sensing that compassion in her. Just after Alejandro's death. She was the last person he had trusted with his heart.

Her son had been a doctor. He had come down after the Revolution and worked in a small clinic near the Honduran border. The contra had captured him and shot him. He was North American, but they didn't care. The United States government didn't care either. She came to bury him and she never left.

"I believe it's called an extra-judicial execution. Or that's what we call it anyway. . . . Comandante Vladimir isn't in Estelí by any chance, is he?"

"I hear that he is expected to attend the celebration as the representative of the Frente, yes."

"So Liberated El Salvador will be represented. On the platform or not, do we think?"

"Depends on who among the leadership wins the power play. I'd guess not, myself. I'd expect that it would be far too risky now for the Sandinistas to acknowledge their support for the Frente. Even if it's only moral support. But you're fighting in Guatemala, Patrick. What does Vladimir have to do with you?"

"Nothing. Except to get back to the highlands I need a safe-conduct through the Zone of Control, and I'm not sure the Salvadorans are going to cooperate. I thought if I could talk to Vladimir—"

"Yes, he'd be the one, of course. Maybe the most powerful man in the FMLN. A genius, I'm told. But dangerous. He turns men into martyrs, Patrick. Be careful of him."

What's wrong with a being a martyr? he wanted to ask her. Your son was one. There were many questions he wanted to ask her, like, When you think of Stephen, where is he? Where did he go? Instead he asked about Stephen's clinic.

"It's doing very well. Considering how hard it is to get medicines and supplies here at all. But the Minister of Health has made a personal commitment to keep it opened. It is highly symbolic, that clinic. I wish you could come up to Santo Tomás and see for yourself."

"I'd like that," he said. For a split second he saw himself living in a community like Santo Tomás, working in a medical clinic or teaching kids how to read. For a split second he saw himself there and he saw himself happy. A fantasy of course. He was way beyond planting vegetable gardens in a Christian-base community. He was way out somewhere where men cut off each other's balls and slit each other's throats.

He walked Martha to the door of the community house in which she was staying, but he did not return to the barracks. Instead he walked through the sweet, soft, Nicaraguan night, the safe Nicaraguan night, and thought about the dead. He was still thinking about them when he met Victor by the river, standing alone by the flowing water, watching the moon.

"This is a good death for them," Victor whispered in Quiché, reciting the passage from the *Popol Vuh* as though he were not speaking to Patrick but chanting a prayer to the spirits of the night, "to dump their bodies in the river. And it will also be good to grind their bones on a stone, just as corn is refined into flour. And then spill them into the river, sprinkle them on the water's way among the mountains great and small. And when it was done, Hunahpu and Xbalanque became handsome boys. They looked just the same as before when they reappeared."

Victor stopped speaking and the night settled around them again. Yes, just sprinkle their bones into the river and they will return again as handsome boys. But the Twins were gods, Patrick thought bitterly, not ordinary men.

"There were to be no reprisals this time, Victor," he said, hearing an anger in his voice he wished he could disguise. "The entire action was designed so that there would be no reprisals."

"You are speaking of the massacre in Nebaj?"

"Sixty men. And were they really *guerrilleros* or just *campesinos* the army rounded up and murdered?"

He wanted to stop himself there. After all, the mathematics in Guatemala were as well known to Victor as they were to him: for every soldier the guerrillas killed, a dozen Indians slaughtered; for every garrison taken, a village burned; for every word spoken against the civil patrols, a woman raped, a child slit open with a bayonet. But they had never killed a general before. If the Unity's involvement in Garcia's death were known, Nebaj might only be the beginning.

It was impossible to fight a war like this. They didn't have the guns. They didn't have the men. Even if they had the men and the arms it wouldn't make much difference. The army never tried to engage them in battle. Why bother? To the army, all Mayas were subversives, the sea in which the *guerrilleros* swam. Dry up the sea, that was the army's aim in the highlands. For what little the Unity had accomplished—and what had it accomplished anyway?—the toll was fifty thousand Mayas dead, a million displaced, half a million in exile, five hundred villages burned. Already some of this blood was on his hands, and now there was more.

"No reprisals, Victor. This action was clandestine. A gringo, a *maricón*, was going to kill Garcia. No link to the Unity. Nobody was ever going to know. Well, what happened? Tell me that."

Victor did not reply, but the answer was clear enough. Nebaj had not been a reprisal; it had been a betrayal.

He glanced at Victor's face, as inscrutable as any Mayan face, as impossible to read. "I think you'd better lock me up in that cell in the barracks now," he said. "Because I know damn well they'll arrest me the minute I set foot in the Zone. And since I know it, I may just take off on you."

"And why do you think such a thing, Patrice?"

Why did he think it? He had lived with the Maya long enough to know that fatalism was bred in their bones. Madness in the blood, violence, massacre, none of it was unexpected. Heart of Earth, the god who created men, was also Mundo, the god who devoured them. The Maya were prepared for the worst because the worst was all they had experienced for five hundred years. And so if sixty men died in Nebaj two weeks after he returned from Guatemala City, then he had betrayed them there. The logic was obvious.

"You believe that Vladimir will use Nebaj as an excuse to detain you in the Zone?"

"Detain me? I think Vladimir will bury me in the Zone. And in his position I'm not sure I wouldn't do the same. What about you, Victor?"

"I, Patrice? I feel no desire to accuse you or suspect you. I'm holding nothing against you in my heart."

"You don't suspect me, Victor? You have no fear of me? Is this true? Because of what a daykeeper announced to you?"

Victor closed his eyes. The image of his fear returned: a dying quetzal plunging into a lake of blood.

How many years it had haunted him, how many years while he heard the tales, rumors, omens, about this golden one who fought in Huehuetenango. *Balam*, they called him. Jaguar. *Balam Kin*, because his surname was Day. But *kin*, day, also means sun. And when he first heard this his blood ran cold. The Quiché had called Pedro de Alvarado "Sun" too, when he came in 1524 and conquered them. Sun, Golden One. So it was with a relief like joy that he heard the news that the Jaguar had left the highlands, had gone down, and at a time that was not auspicious, that he had been sent and, some said, to his death. But his feelings had been wrong. All signs pointed to pain, grief, loss. Wild animals entered people's houses and when diviners read what such invasions announced it went back time and again to the loss of this man who, they said, had been protecting the people, who was, or so others said, the spirit-familiar of Tepeucucumatz, Sovereign Plumed Serpent. And these rumors were fueled by the story that came out of the mountains, that on the morning of the day the Jaguar was to leave a quetzal flew into his hands and died there. The last time such a story was told was at the death in battle of the resistance hero of the Quiché, Tecún Umán.

He remembered how his fear had turned to black terror. That lords returned, he knew. But in such form? And if the signs spoke truly and he had been sent down and died there, what then?

How long he traveled to consult the daykeeper who could tell this text for him. He climbed high into the cloud forest. The mountains unfolded for him, at four thousand feet, the pines, at five thousand, the clouds, from summer to fog-bound cold, to fog that smokes, to the place where it cannot be told whether mountain emerges from mist or mist from mountain. And there, in the cloud forest that was the Jaguar's home, he found the daykeeper for whom he searched.

Upon request he presented dreams and feelings, fears, he presented the sightings of certain animals and birds, and still the daykeeper hesitated and still he burnt more *pom*, lit more candles, counted out the stones, over and over, until in the white clarity the saying, the announcing, came: *Don't they want to be suckled? Isn't it their hearts' desire to embrace me?*

The mountain had become silent, still, like the silence, the stillness, as thunderheads gather. The daykeeper asked for his *mebil* which he carried in a pouch around his neck to protect him. He demanded it, so what could Victor do but show it to him, though in showing it he surrendered all of its power. The daykeeper took the stone in his palm and closed his hand around it and closed his eyes and out of the tension gathered inside himself he spoke the remaining words of the announcing.

"Yes, because of what the daykeeper told me, those things I have said to you and other things as well which I cannot say to you, because of this I trust you, Patrice. But trust is a burden, and sometimes a heavy one to bear."

He heard Patrice sigh in the darkness beside him, and he knew his words had touched him, as he had hoped they would.

"I also sought out a daykeeper before I left the highlands," Patrice said in his beautiful Quiché, accented so slightly it almost sounded like his native tongue. "He told me that death waited for me in the city. Then he said, But you are to go. You are to wander, entering and departing from strange villages. Perhaps you will achieve nothing anywhere. Do not turn back, keep a firm step. Something you will achieve. Something the Lord of the Universe will assign to you. . . . But you know, Victor, I don't want to believe those words and I don't want to obey them. All I want is to go home."

Home. The *altiplano*. Sunlight slanting through the clouds over the summits of the mountains. The smell of *copal* and pine, the sound of the rain on the canopy. Walking through a verdant landscape shimmering with sunlight or glistening with night frost, stopping in a village to play ball with the kids, drink with the men, whisper at a shrine the *guerrillero's* prayer to the gods:

Wait! thou Maker, Modeler,
Mother-Father of life, of humankind,
Giver of breath, giver of heart,
Bearer, upbringer in the light that lasts,
Don't let us fall, don't leave us aside. . . .

"You will have your heart's desire," Victor said softly. "This announcing has been made."

43

Six

Patrick had walked off the stands during the President's speech that morning and he wasn't sure he'd be staying long at the President's party that night. Carlos had found him sleeping in the barracks and dragged him to this event, telling him he had to make an appearance, he was expected to shake hands with the President and the Vice President and beautiful women and great poets, several great poets who were also beautiful women. It was his duty.

He did all that but everything at the party seemed pathetic to him: the waiters in their white jackets, the trays of food, the music, the candlelight, the gaiety. Everyone was worried sick and trying to hide it. Everyone was putting on a brave front for the visiting dignitaries, of which there were a pathetic few, and for the internationalists, those friendly North Americans and Europeans who were given the red carpet treatment so they would go home and speak well of Nicaragua. Every Sandinista was willing to kiss a little ass for the Revolution; every ministry was in need; every gringo had been targeted. He had been mistakenly identified several times, once for a Californian who was thinking of setting up a bicycle repair school in the city, once for a famous apiarist who might be persuaded to work with beekeepers to increase their yield. . . . No need to send in the Marines; it was cheaper and easier to starve them out. Any day now.

He had wandered around the two patios of the hacienda, no doubt expropriated by the government from a rich landowner, and tried to imagine what Alejandro would think of this, what he might say. At least he could see Alejandro in a place like this; he couldn't see him in most of the other places he found himself. He strolled through the clusters of people, catching bits of conversation, and past the long tables set up by the pool where people were sitting and eating, and somehow it reminded him of his cousin's wedding, how he had come out blazing to his entire family just by bringing Alejandro to that wedding. And all the other social events after that one, coming out with Alejandro, life just one debutante ball after another. How everything became an undertaking, not just weddings and funerals, but parties, dinners, basketball games, walking down the street at night. It wasn't just the hassle of being gay in a straight world, it was living with the real danger, the constant fear, of being a dark-skinned man in a white world, of loving a dark-skinned man in a white world. Fag bashers and racists, he'd never known that Boston was so full of them, that the whole country was so full of them. It had been such a relief to come down here.

Getting off the plane in San Salvador: that was as far as the film went. It stopped right there.

He was being watched. He felt it, couldn't isolate it. Plain-clothes security men were staked out along the walls, by the doors, along the periphery, but it wasn't any of them. This was subtle, rather like being stalked.

Or like being cruised.

He was about thirty, give or take a few years, small, slim, attractive as Nicas were, mestizos all of them, but some more Indian than others. This one had Indian features, but was built rapier-lean like a Spaniard, with a Spaniard's bearing and quick, engaging eye. Besides, Indians didn't flirt.

It was a mistake to make even the most furtive eye contact. It was taken as an invitation.

He sighed and looked around the patio for Carlos, who might come and save him from yet another pathetic encounter.

"Excuse me," the man said, coming up to him, and standing just a centimeter closer than another might, which was already for a North American far too close. "I have noticed that you are without a drink." He motioned to a passing waiter, who came over immediately and offered his tray. "Inexcusable on such a night. There's rum and . . . rum. Which do you prefer?"

"Rum, thank you."

"It is a fine party, don't you think?"

"Very fine. Like an Irish wake."

He glanced over the man's head, couldn't find Carlos anywhere. Victor was supposed to be at this party too, but he couldn't locate him in the crowd. Instead his eyes found every white face, so many white faces; he wasn't used to it. He was usually the only white, the only one who didn't belong. Except in the highlands, where he did belong. Where, at least, they let him believe he belonged.

Those who didn't fear him, anyway.

Though even Victor had experienced that fear.

The man standing in front of him had not gone away. His mustache was *de rigueur*, of course, like the loose-fitting, white *guayabera* shirt and the tight jeans, for a Sandinista the alternative uniform to fatigues. But on him it looked natural, as though he had invented the style. Maybe he had; someone had to.

"Do you have a cigarette?" he asked, since the man was still there.

"Of course. Please." He offered his pack.

"I haven't seen Marlboros in a while."

"Really? But you were recently in Guatemala City, weren't you? Couldn't you find American cigarettes there?"

It was like someone had doused him with cold water. "Well, I see my reputation has preceded me. If you'll excuse me. . . ."

But the man was too close to him, and gripped hold of his arm. "Forgive me, please. I did not mean to offend you. But do you really think that no one here knows who you are?"

"Just half an hour ago I was taken for a beekeeper."

The man laughed. His laugh broke through all the bullshit of the evening; it was the first thing he had heard all night that was real. "Well, let us toast to mistaken identities. My name is Julio."

"Charmed," he said, extending his hand. "Mine is Patrice. As you already know."

"Yes, I do already know that. Also I know that you are not enjoying yourself. I have been watching you."

Julio smiled at him with the warmth and attentiveness of the skilled predator moving in for the kill. Every word, every move and gesture, the ever-so-slight, nearly imperceptible extension of their handshake, promised intimacy. Patrick recognized it and it both impressed and sickened him. It was the same technique he had used to come on to Garcia Fuentes.

"I guess I don't feel much like celebrating tonight. There was a defeat several days ago. In Guatemala."

"Yes, I heard. Unfortunate. They were your *compañeros*?"

"I thought we were all *compañeros*. They were not members of my unit, if that's what you mean."

"Perhaps I might make a suggestion, then, if the party does not please you. The gardens of this house are very beautiful. The river flows through them, just a little way beyond the house. Perhaps you would like to take a walk with me. I would very much like the opportunity of speaking privately with you. And this is not the most conducive place."

A dozen different replies entered his mind, tempted him, each one nastier, crueler than the last. Part of him was horrified that he could even think of saying such things to anyone, but part of him had turned. He knew it now: Guatemala City had turned him, he was damaged, there was something in him that had not been there before, something vicious and sadistic that at times like this he could only just control.

Julio took his arm. "Come," he said. "The air will do you good. Sometimes these small decisions are harder to make than the big ones. So I will assist you. We are going outside to walk. Very simple, my friend. You agree?"

Someone was singing as Julio led him past groups of people toward the corridor and the open doors, and the song made him smile. He wasn't used to rum; he was already feeling the lightness of being just a little drunk. He started to sing along: *"Caminando, caminando, voy buscando libertad. Ojala encuentre camino, para seguir caminando."*

"You like Victor Jara?"

47

"I *love* Victor Jara. . . . Why do you smile? Is that funny?"

"No. It is only that sometimes I forget how intense North Americans can be. You have intense emotions. When you are angry, for example, you are very angry. I heard that you walked out in the middle of the President's speech today."

"Word travels fast around here. Yes, I did. I admire him very much, your president, but I don't have any patience left for political speeches. I just wish that some day somewhere somebody would have the guts to say in public that none of us is going to live to see the revolution triumph. I mean the big one, the real one. No offense to yours, of course."

"I take no offense. I am also an internationalist."

"Ah, yes. Well, there are so many tendencies in the world it's hard to keep track, isn't it?"

"So you left before the President announced the death of General José Garcia Fuentes. A crime of passion, they say. And yet the people know differently. Too bad you missed the applause."

"I'll live," he said.

They were walking down a narrow path lined with night-blooming jasmine and draping hibiscus. The flowers were hardly visible in the moonlight, but the scent was heady, intoxicating. Ahead of them the river, watered by mountain brooks and months of rain, stretched wide, struck by rippling, golden moonlight.

"I have a friend," Julio was saying, "who claims there are only two tendencies in the world. Freudian and Jungian."

"My conscious ego versus the collective unconscious. I like that."

"Fear of merger versus desire for merger. That also." Julio's voice was gentle, like a caress. Patrick was gazing out at the river, but even with his eyes averted he could sense Julio moving closer to him, because, after all, these things were choreographed, and every dancer knew the steps of the dance.

They were walking along the Charles on the Cambridge side, gazing across at the lights of Boston. It was a warm, fragrant night, Alejandro's first night in Boston. This was a cruising spot, but that wasn't why they were there, they were just walking along the river, looking at the lights. (Why wasn't he with Carlos? Ah, Carlos had a class, an exam, something. "Take care of him for me, Patrick. Take him to dinner, go to the movies. . . .") And first Alejandro had taken his arm, walking very close to him, but that was how Latin men walked. (Was he crazy? Did he really hope to convince himself that this was just how Latin men walked?) And then they had stopped and it was dark and, yes, he knew, of course he knew what Alejandro wanted, it was so clear what he wanted, and he felt he could do it, just this once, just to see, but he wasn't sure, not totally sure, until Alejandro turned to him, and lifted his face to him and they were kissing each other. . . . But how had it happened? Like beginning to swim, taking the first stroke, laying your body on the water and pushing off. Yes, as natural as swimming once you start. And Alejandro had wanted it, love at first sight, this one man, this one night. And he had thought, This is Carlos's brother. And then, But it will only be this once. Carlos will never know. And then, Watch out. This one is going to break your heart. But already his heart was lost, gone, disappeared. It went into Alejandro that first night and was never seen again.

He glanced at Julio and he wanted to say, *Don't come a step closer, faggot.* He wanted to say, *I hope Carlos is paying you a lot for this.* He wanted to push him away, to say all the things a man says to a fag. Or maybe what he wanted was to fuck him right there, turn him around against the tree and fuck his ass, or get him down on his knees. . . .

He didn't say anything; he didn't move. He let Julio come closer and closer, he let him put his arms around him, he kept thinking that any second he would say no, that he would push him back, but Julio was so close to him, touching him, and he couldn't bear not to be touched, he couldn't stop him, not yet, in a minute maybe, but for this minute, for only this one minute, he closed his eyes and surrendered.

The room Julio brought him to was in a building on the hacienda grounds. Moonlight and a cool breeze came in through the balcony

49

door. That it had a balcony door was significant. That there was a mattress on the bed and sheets on the mattress. That there was a lock on the door, and the lock worked.

It was altogether far too nice a room.

"Shall I get you a drink?" Julio asked, turning the key in the lock.

"No, thanks. . . . I think it's only fair to tell you that I killed the last man I went to bed with."

"Should I be frightened?"

"Maybe."

Julio took a few steps into the room and switched on a lamp. In the lamplight the room's furnishings looked even more impressive, the linen on the bed freshly pressed, a quilt, a telephone on the night table, a leather briefcase, a real wooden desk. Seeing the layout of the room, he wasn't sure which of them should be more frightened.

"Listen, Patrice. There is only one question now. Do you want to be with me tonight or not? Only that. Nothing about what happened yesterday or what will happen tomorrow. Just tonight. Will you stay here with me—yes or no?"

And then, as though the question had already been answered, Julio walked up to Patrick and began to unbutton his shirt.

Alejandro was the only man he had ever made love to, the only man he knew how to make love to. He didn't even know how to ask this man what he wanted, and all he could think of was what it meant in English, *to have sex.* What that expression *meant.* And the Spanish *coger.* To get, to grab, to take, to fuck. But he couldn't think for long. They were naked and he was already giddy with it, the lusciousness of the touch of another man's skin, the taste of another man's mouth, feeling another man's erection in his hand. He was like someone coming off a desert, wanting only a sip of water, being offered an entire lake. And then Julio whispered, "Come to bed now," and he heard experience in the voice, and warmth and confidence, and he knew they would be all right.

The pallor of the light just before dawn, a mountain chill in the air, colors slowly emerging in the room. The briefcase bothered him. The telephone and the wooden desk. The location of the room in a building on these grounds. Being a guest in this country, he should obey the rules, but he didn't know what the rules were. He was in a government-owned house, in bed with a strange man. His instinct was to get up and get out and do it fast.

But he didn't want to get up. He felt languid, and Julio's body was wrapped around his, or his around Julio's, and it felt so good to hold someone, he had made himself forget how good it felt.

"I should go now," he said.

"There is no need for you to go. Unless you wish to, of course. But it seems too soon for us to thank each other and say goodbye."

"It's almost dawn," he said, as though he were speaking to the blind. It hardly mattered what he said now, what either of them said now. He could go or stay a little longer; he could enter him again or take him in his mouth or simply stroke him and hold him a little longer. It hardly mattered. It was over.

"Patrice, there is something we have to discuss. Now or later. But before you leave."

"Well, we might as well discuss it now. I suppose I should wonder how you knew who I was. Who I was and how receptive I was likely to be to you. Another man might have punched you in the face back there at the river."

"Another man, yes, of course. But I think you would have found a less extreme method of declining my offer. As for knowing who you are, Patrice, you were pointed out to me at the party. You are somewhat famous now, you know."

"And the person who pointed me out to you, did he also inform you that I might be likely to accept your offer? Or am I wearing a pink triangle these days. . . ? Not that it matters, Julio. I'm glad you approached me. I'm glad this happened. Truly. So, what do you want to discuss?"

51

"I'd like a cigarette, please. If you can reach them."

Patrick loosened himself from Julio's arms and sat up. The cigarettes were on the night table by the phone. It was the phone that disturbed him more than anything else.

"It's that bad, is it? You're going to tell me you're an agent of the counterrevolution?"

"And what if I were?"

"And what if I were a Green Beret? U.S. Army, Special Forces. Direct from Fort Bragg, via Jacaltenango." He lit two cigarettes and passed one to Julio. "Just as possible, isn't it?"

"Just as possible, yes. But I have been less than candid with you tonight, and I'm afraid you're going to be angry. The truth is I wanted you. I wanted to spend this night with you, and I didn't know how you would take it if you knew more about me. I didn't want anything to stand between us, you understand? But it was unfair of me. I hope you can forgive me."

"Listen, Julio," he said. "I know everything about you that I need to know. I know you are fearless and generous in love, and warmhearted and gracious, and if you can be all those things in bed with a stranger then I can only imagine what a pleasure it would be to be your friend. So please don't apologize for anything. And don't worry about anything. I'll be leaving Nicaragua soon. And I won't say anything about this to anyone. I would never expose you, believe me. So if that's your concern, please—"

"No, Patrice, that is not my concern. Only that you don't feel that you have been used."

"If this is your idea of being used, Julio," he said, smiling at him, "then we have had very different life experiences."

Desire was growing in him again, desire tugging at him. He put their cigarettes out and took Julio in his arms. All he wanted was to be inside him, he didn't care about anything else. He wanted to slip into his body and into his embrace, he wanted to hold on to him, hold on tight. He couldn't bear the thought of going back to being alone. "Don't say anything," he whispered. "Please, don't tell me anything. Not yet."

He had suspected something like it, of course. The room, the telephone, the leather briefcase. But it could have been someone else's room, borrowed for the occasion. Could have been, but probably not. Still he wasn't quite prepared for the woman who brought in the breakfast tray and greeted Julio as *'comandante.'* Or for the young soldier who came in next and was given orders to keep everyone else out except whoever brought up another tray of food.

"I'm sorry, Patrice. I tried to tell you," Julio said.

"I should have left hours ago."

"Why? It's no problem. Except we have to share a cup until she brings another."

They were sitting on the balcony overlooking the gardens, the river, the mountains on the horizon. The sky looked freshly washed, and the air, though warming even as they sat drinking their coffee, still carried with it a memory of the coolness of the hills.

"So," Patrick said, trying to negotiate his way by feel now, but uncertain even of what his feelings were, "you are Azul."

"Yes."

"Julio Ibarra Cruz. Comandante Azul. Youngest of the commandos who took the National Palace, August 22, 1978. One of the liberators of León. Fought with Vladimir during the battle for San Salvador. A doctor of medicine. For the past five years, Minister of Health."

Julio laughed and again Patrick was at first stunned, then instantly reassured, charmed, by the sound of it. It was so natural, that laughter, so secure, so centered. Had it been that long since he had been around men who, when something struck them as funny, could simply laugh? "Well, Patrice," Julio said, "it sounds like you've just been through my dossier."

"No. It's just that there aren't many heroes of the revolution who are *gay* and only one who is *out*." He had to use the English words; there were no Spanish equivalents. "Only Azul."

53

"Well, it was either that or . . . what? Live as a celibate or live as a liar? Why fight and bleed, Patrice, if not for freedom?"

"Freedom's a pretty big word. Big and slippery. Sometimes I think Victor Jara got it right in that song. We're always walking to freedom but we never get there. So you better just learn to enjoy the walk."

"Like in the mountains, all we ever did was walk. But I can't say I ever learned to enjoy it."

In the sunlight, Julio's hair was blue-black and his eyes were dark as Alejandro's. The bones in his face were strong and he had beautiful hands, long-fingered. A pianist's hands. A healer's hands. But Patrick couldn't let himself think about Julio's body, because they were having breakfast and then saying goodbye. There was no point talking, no point going any further in. It was time to disengage.

"So maybe you're right. Maybe freedom is too big a word. Maybe we fought and bled for something more modest, Patrice. Look, there's something I want to tell you about myself, something you would not read in my dossier. I expect by now that information has been expurgated. Cigarette?" Julio took one from his pack, lit it from the end of his own and passed it to Patrick. It was wet on his lips, like a kiss. "I joined the Frente when I was fourteen. That was in the early days, back in '74. The *compañero* who recruited me . . . you know where he found me? In the old cathedral in Managua, the one that was destroyed in the earthquake of '72, and is still in ruins. It was where men went to engage boy prostitutes. That was how I supported my family, Patrice. By prostitution. Seven of us, and I was the oldest, my father was dead. . . . Well, it was easy money so long as you didn't think about it too much. Anyway he came there and talked to me about Sandino and the struggle and I was a romantic even then and I said, OK, I'm in. And so my first job for the revolution was to get certain information from two particular men who often came to the cathedral to buy boys. Men I had serviced before, men I already knew. It was no more dangerous than doing it just for money. I would be doing it anyway, so what difference? Still, you know, this *compañero* was so concerned, almost horrified —well, he was of the bourgeois class himself and did not know much about how the poor lived— that he gave me his word that after I got this information he'd see to it I never had to go back to the cathedral again. And that man kept his word. He pulled me out after only a few more weeks, and the Frente gave me work and they made sure I went to school. I remember I asked him why he trusted me. I was a dirty barrio kid, a whore, and I could have sold him to the Guardia as easily as I sold my ass to those piece of shit bankers, you understand? You know what he said to me? 'We have to trust each other, Julio. If we cannot trust each other, who are we going to trust?' So maybe you are correct. Maybe it isn't freedom we fight for after all, but each other's trust. For someone like me, earning other men's trust was very difficult. For example, I studied for one year in Cuba. There it didn't matter who you were or what you had done for the revolution, if you were a faggot, a hole, prison was the only place for you. In Cuba now if you test positive for SIDA they put you in quarantine, nicer than prison perhaps, but from that life sentence there is no appeal. I learned an important lesson in Cuba, Patrice, and it is this: when your own *compañeros* doubt you, when they distrust you simply for being who you are, then you yourself begin to doubt. Your strength leaves you, you lose faith in the entire enterprise, and you sink into despair and cannot save yourself. Someone else must save you, simply by trusting you again. So we struggle with our own doubts, our own vulnerability, even while we make the revolution, and that struggle also becomes part of what the revolution is. Which is only to say that I have to live openly, I have to force myself to take these risks. I have no choice. But you must know that wonderful line of Nietzsche's, 'What does not kill me makes me stronger.' It is a line we use a great deal in Nicaragua. . . . I suppose that you have plans for today?"

I suppose I could fall in love with you today, he thought. But he said, "I don't know, to tell you the truth. I may be called back to active duty—"

"Not today, Patrice. Everyone is too hung over today to call anyone to active duty."

"Well, then, Azul," he said, smiling back (*Azul*, Carlos had said to him once, there's the man to watch in Nicaragua. Give him a few years, he'll be president of the Republic), "I don't suppose I do have plans. Why do you ask?"

"Because if you are not busy and if the idea appeals to you I thought we might spend the day together. I really was serious last night when I said I wanted to talk with you. But, I don't know, the opportunity for talking didn't seem to arise."

Patrick laughed. He laughed and at the same moment realized that he was happy, and the realization came as a shock, palpable as a slight electric current passing through him. There was a knock at the door, the woman delivering the second breakfast tray; Julio followed her to the door and locked it and took his phone off the hook. Patrick stood at the balcony door and watched him.

"So, are we beginning the interrogation now, *comandante*?"

Julio turned to him. His face was serious, almost solemn, but there was something about him that was luminous, pellucid, that made Patrick's heart beat faster, made his blood pound. Lust, he thought. Only lust. "Would that all interrogations were like this one," Julio said softly. "Or that all combats were like ours last night, that ended so successfully in mutual surrender."

Patrick stood in the doorway with the hot sun shining at his back, shining into the room on Julio, a long ray of sunshine falling at Julio's feet, and he felt that slight but fleeting shock of recognition, the flashlight beam in the dark that sweeps over the lost object and then sweeps back, searching to find it again.

He had been dreaming. In his dream there were buildings all around him burning, or lying in charred ruins, jet fighters flying low overhead, bombs dropping, masses of people in lines trying to escape, trains broken down, machinery abandoned on the roadsides. And he was frantic, wandering through this wreckage, this chaos, searching for someone or something that he knew in his heart he would never find. And that had been his life. Four years of his life. And now was he waking up? Was it possible that he could wake up here, in this room, with this man, and find that he was home?

SEVEN

Julio Ibarra sat up in the bed in the deepening twilight and watched Patrice sleep. He could not tell whether at this moment he was supremely happy or in the deepest despair. As long as he could stay right where he was, as long as nothing moved, neither he nor Patrice nor time itself, his heart would remain full. But the moment anything changed, his heart would be stricken. He should have taken precautions. Too late now.

He could not keep the world at bay much longer. He had managed to stretch a single night out into a day and another night, and another day, and now this third night which was fast approaching. But the hounds were on the scent, Managua on the one side, Vladimir on the other. Because they didn't know what Patrice was up to. Because they didn't trust him. Vladimir would use him, yes; trust him, no. And Managua? He could imagine the scandal. No, it was impossible for him to consider returning to Managua with a white, North American lover. And yet, as absurd a notion as that was, it was even more absurd a notion to think that tomorrow morning they would part forever.

He lay down next to Patrice and propped himself up on his elbow. The bed was damp with their sweat, the air itself exuding the musky sweet scent of sex and sleep, exuding the lassitude of desire satisfied over and over again. Slowly he let his hand caress Patrice's body: his face, very lightly, pushing back the hair from his cheek and his neck; his chest, nipples, rib cage, diaphragm, feeling the smoothness of skin, the ripple of muscle, the ridge of bone; his sex, small now, and soft, sleeping under his fingers, but easily awakened.

Patrice stirred slightly, rolled over onto his side. The bruises that had covered his whole body were still visible, but healing. Julio ran his hand down his side, over the line where his color

57

changed from brown to white, over his flank, hip, thigh. He had never known such desire and it appalled him. It was overpowering, pulling him down, threatening to erase everything else. Patrice was all he wanted, to take him again in his hand and in his mouth and inside his body, Managua be damned. And not for today only or for two more days, but for as long as this desire between them lasted, or for as long as whatever might grow out of this desire lasted. But it was an impossible wish. Even if Patrice were simply a Guatemalan *guerrillero* and not a Yankee on top of it, the liaison would be unacceptable. Anyway too many people knew it was he who had killed Garcia Fuentes.

Twilight would give way to evening, evening to night, night to dawn. As banal as it was inevitable. Banal, yes, but if he didn't wake Patrice soon, he might go mad thinking about it.

It would pass of course. There was work waiting for him in Managua, enough to keep his mind engaged. He would forget Patrice's body; pleasure was easy to forget. What would he remember in a year or two? Maybe only the stories Patrice told him about his life in the States, about his lover, how his voice changed when he spoke of him, how his voice broke. Maybe only what he told him about Garcia Fuentes. Or maybe only what he told him about the drugs.

Patrice had told him that the cartel was shipping drugs through Nicaragua. Garcia Fuentes was handling some of the financial dealings, since there was a close and well-known connection between the work of the Guatemalan security forces and the growing of poppies. But that there should be Nicaraguans involved with the likes of the cartel and the Kaibiles, that was a different story.

"And what did they say about this in the Zone?" he had asked.

"I didn't tell them about it in the Zone."

"You withheld this information from them? Why?"

Patrice was lying on his back staring up at the ceiling. It was afternoon, very hot. Too hot really to be so close, skin to skin. So hot that they stuck together, sweating all over each other, into each other's mouths and eyes. "Why? I was pissed off, that's why. I just answered questions. I didn't offer them anything. If they asked me, I answered. If not. . . . Shit, Julio, the bastards treated me like I was some fucking mercenary, some hired gun. Like I wasn't a member of their club, you know? Better to tell you than them anyway. They can't do anything about it. You can."

Clearly the information had scandalized Patrice. Combatants were notoriously naive about the realities of maintaining political power.

"The cartel is a fact of life, Patrice. One deals with it as one would deal with the empire itself if the Americans were willing to deal at all. By negotiation. What else can we do? We are in a vise—the empire to the north, the cartel to the south. So some of the cartel's money found its way into some Nicaraguan hands. I would not worry too much."

"So," Patrice had said, his cat's eyes narrowing, "in other words you've made a deal with the cartel with the stipulation that your own people are off-limits, the hell with anybody else. You give them some airstrips and some land to set up processing plants—"

"I did not say that, Patrice. We would never make that sort of agreement. But the cartel is not our enemy. It has never harmed us. And we are a beggar nation. We cannot cross-examine those who drop pennies in our cup. I am sorry this comes as a shock to you."

"No, I'm not shocked, Julio. Nothing shocks me. Nicaragua Libre, where nobody sells out or surrenders, free country or death, a little feudal duchy under the lordship of the prince of Medellín—doesn't shock me at all."

Julio felt a surge of anger rise in him. "All right then, why don't you procure a nuclear bomb for us? Give us that capability, Patrice. Make us a world power, give us an air force. Do that if you can. But don't preach to us. Whose fault is it that we are forced to make pacts with the devil?"

Patrice got up from the bed, strode the length of the room and turned around to face Julio. He was naked, magnificent, enraged. "Mine. It's mine, right? I did it to you. My people, my country, me. I'm the one, right, Julio? Go ahead, say it. Say it."

What Garcia Fuentes had said to him as he was beating him with his belt, what he had repeated with every blow: I am going to

59

fuck you now. Say you want it. Say, I am your hole. Say, Fuck me, general. Say it.

They were the same men after all: the generals and the Kaibiles and the Treasury Police and the *narcos* of the cartel. All the same.

"All right, Patrice," he had said. "Write down the names, all the names you remember, everything you remember. I will see to it. If there is corruption in the ministries, I will deal with it. It is the sort of thing I am good at."

Patrice had come over to him then and just touched his cheek with his hand. The simplest of caresses, and yet it was possible that no one had stroked his face like that since he was a child.

It was at that moment that Julio realized he was in love.

The twilight was turning into night. Julio stretched out on the bed and put his arms around Patrice. For a moment he imagined sleeping every night for the remainder of his life with his arms around Patrice. And just as he was feeling the horrible loss of this life which he would never have, nor had ever before imagined, Patrice turned toward him in his sleep, wrapped himself around him, and held him tight.

Midday. The small guest house, no longer either a fortress or a seraglio, returned to a state of normalcy, and its occupants—the Minister's secretary, assistant, and bodyguards, the household staff, even the groundskeepers— reverted to their usual schedules. Julio had days of mail to go through, appointments to reschedule, phone calls to return; at eleven he would meet with a delegation of medical workers who had been waiting in Estelí for two days to see him, at twelve-thirty he would lunch with a friend, at two-thirty he would leave for the capital.

For days and nights he hadn't slept, but by midday he was no longer feeling immortal. He could barely remember joy and youth. By the time Ileana arrived to lunch with him, he felt he would have to take the existence of happiness itself on faith alone.

He greeted her on the small patio downstairs, to which Patrice had never come, a patio shaded by a wall covered with blood-red bougainvillea. She was as beautiful to him as ever, though he noticed the streaks of white in her hair, the age in her hands, how the skin puckered, showed its texture. He noticed the circles beneath her eyes, the lines being chiseled onto her face. But the beauty of that face for him lay in something other, for at one time she had been his salvation, the living embodiment of those saints to whom he had prayed as a child. He remembered sitting in her office in Havana, opening his heart. How he dared do it because her poems had moved him so, and she had smiled at him and said, 'You fought in Salvador beside my *compañero*. I am in your debt.' And how she had repaid what she perceived to be a debt, though there was no debt owing. She had offered him a way to escape from the Island: she had arranged for him to continue his medical studies in Spain.

They were meeting today to continue their discussion about the national elections which were scheduled to take place in February. Or more precisely, to continue their argument.

"I am glad you could receive me before you return to Managua, Julio," she said, taking her place at the small, round table. She sat while he remained standing, and smiled up at him. "I was afraid I was going to miss you this time."

"I admit I have been incommunicado for several days, Ileana. But I certainly wouldn't leave Estelí without seeing you."

"Incommunicado with a certain handsome North American. Or so I've heard."

Julio laughed and lit a cigarette. "All right, Ileana. And have you come to talk with me about my taste in men, or something less important?"

Again she smiled at him. "Well, I am glad to see that this was not a serious liaison. Sometimes you worry me, Julio."

Julio pulled a chair out from the table and sat down. "Why? You didn't think for a minute that I'd keep him, did you? Still it was a very enjoyable few days. I wonder how Vladimir ever found him."

"If you are speaking of the death of Garcia Fuentes, I understood that Patrice was acting for the Unity. What would Vladimir have to do with it?"

"Please don't insult my intelligence, Ileana. I know Vladimir, too, remember. As for the Unity organizing that operation, only a gringo would be naive enough to believe that."

She nodded slightly and said, "Well, I don't know who recommended him. Luis does not tell me everything."

"Come now, Ileana. Don't expect me to believe that your husband does not tell you everything. Not that it matters except that I am indebted to the man who procured him for Vladimir since he inadvertently procured him for me as well."

She sighed and gazed steadily at him for a long moment. He resisted her gaze. "You surprise me sometimes, Julio."

"Ah, Ileana, sometimes I surprise even myself. But Vladimir should thank me at least for not luring him away with me to the capital. I suspected that Patrice was valuable to the Frente and I wouldn't think of disturbing Vladimir's plans for him. I expect Vladimir does have further plans for him? He's certainly not going to let such talent go to waste."

He could see that this remark pained her. The recoil was very slight, and occurred only in her eyes. He pressed on. "Vladimir must know him as well as I do now, to have planned that operation in Guatemala for him. How is it that I have to live with a man to know him that well, and Vladimir. . . . Well, perhaps I can give him some insights into Patrice that he might find useful. Is he still in Estelí, or has he gone back to the Zone?"

"He left yesterday. He wanted to speak to you himself about Patrice, but I dissuaded him. I assumed that you would be unreceptive. I underestimated you, Julio."

"Too bad. Because I do think that Patrice is emotionally unstable, and therefore dangerous. I would not recommend another commando mission for him. But, of course, I am not as willing to take risks as Vladimir is. And if I know Vladimir, he already has the next operation planned. The target, the method, the time and place."

She did not answer him, and in her silence he read affirmation.

He glanced at his watch. "Excuse me a moment," he said. "I have to return a phone call."

He went upstairs to the bedroom and sat on the bed. It had been made up and the entire room cleaned; there was no trace of Patrice anywhere.

Perhaps it was because they had become so intimate with each other that their parting in this room had been almost painfully formal. They had awakened that morning to find urgent telexes from Managua for the Minister, and for his guest, a strongly worded "request" that he report to army headquarters in Estelí immediately. It was dated July 20th; it had taken them two days to track him down.

"Are your intelligence agents kind, or just slow?" Patrick mumbled, reading it.

"It is your people who want you at army headquarters, Patrice," he said. "Not mine."

"And who are my people going to be this month, I wonder." And then he tried to smile, a half-smile. "Oh, well, Julio, I guess we have to put our clothes back on today."

Who are my people going to be this month?

Patrice was no fool. He suspected that the Guatemala operation was too complex to have been coordinated entirely by the Unity. He had met Luis and had taken him to be an agent of Vladimir's. He knew Luis wanted to prevent him from returning to the highlands, though he did not know why. He had not put the puzzle together completely, but he had all the pieces. But now it was clear to Julio that Guatemala had been merely a dress rehearsal, that Vladimir had found a perfect instrument in Patrice and was not about to let him go.

Who are my people going to be this month? He might have told him. Not Mayas, Patrice. Not Nicas, either. This month your people are going to be the militants of the Zone of Control, Vladimir's own cadres.

Julio knew these militants from the Zone; he knew Vladimir; he knew Patrice. Vladimir had the power to seduce men into defying death for him; Patrice was susceptible to seduction; appeal to him, phrase it correctly, give him the right image, and he would

63

fall. Vladimir would offer him an impossible mission, a suicide mission, and Patrice would accept it. Maybe he would succeed again; then he would be used again. He would be used over and over until there was nothing left of him to use and then he would be tossed away. For Vladimir and his kind, the struggle itself was the only important thing. And the struggle continues, irrespective of who is left behind.

Only now, sitting on his bed, did he realize the terrible mistake he had made.

They had gotten dressed, hardly speaking to each other, and, clothed again, they embraced like acquaintances and separated. But it was too painful that way, too inhuman, to let him leave without saying anything at all. So as Patrice was about to open the door, Julio said the formulaic words, words that seem empty only because they carry more meaning than either speaker or hearer is willing to admit. "Perhaps we will see each other again." And Patrice had given the proper ritualistic response. *Claro.* Of course. And that was how they had parted.

That even then he did not break the silence and speak from his heart was a mistake he might never have the power to correct.

He made four phone calls from this desolate room, trying to track down Patrice. Finally he spoke with Paco Ruiz of State Security. Find him, he said. I don't care what you have to do, but find him and bring him to me. Under no circumstances is he to cross the border. See to it.

But it was already five hours since Patrice had left this room, and Vladimir was clever and quick and could have him in Choluteca by now, out of reach of even Paco Ruiz's long arm.

Plates filled with chicken and rice, tortilla and salad were placed on the table as soon as he returned. Instead of eating he smoked another cigarette and tried to attend to Ileana's analysis of the celebration, of the significance of who accepted their invitations to attend, and who declined. Julio mentioned his disappointment that the Honduran presidential candidate, Gabriel Aguilar, had canceled his visit.

"But you really didn't expect him to come, did you? Just because he calls himself the peace candidate? Really, Julio! People are sick of the war in Honduras, too, so of course the candidates adopt a certain rhetoric. That's what elections are about: deceiving the people in order to win."

"That is one interpretation, yes."

"You think me too cynical? Listen, Julio, Aguilar talks about restricting the U.S. presence at Palmerola. But do you mean to tell me you actually believe that if he were to win the election he would kick the Americans out? Do you think the empire would ever permit such a thing to happen? They've got twelve hundred men there, their Special Forces unit, their Green Berets—"

"I know, Ileana."

"It's there they train Salvadoran pilots and launch their air attacks against the zones of control. It's there they train the contra who attack us here. It's there they train their interrogators, their torturers, their infiltrators and spies. It's the center of all their counterinsurgency activities, their command base for the whole region. No Honduran politician would ever consider closing Palmerola, no matter what platform he runs on. Even if he wanted to, he would never be able to do it, not with his own military fully staffed with American advisers and getting all their money and weaponry from the States. And the proof is that Aguilar did not come here for the Victory Celebration, Julio. Because for him to come here would be too much of a provocation. He's an oligarch anyway. A liar, like the rest of them."

"And our election, Ileana? I suppose you think when it comes to our election, we are all liars, too."

"Not liars, Julio. Fools. But you may eat in peace. I have conceded on the subject of the election. If Fidel himself cannot make any of you see reason, I doubt very much that I can."

"His arguments found some receptive ears. And there are some among us who are wary enough as it is and don't need Fidel to give them guidance."

65

"You are not one of the wary ones, however. You are very young, Julio."

"Please, Ileana—"

"No. Listen to me. I am an old woman and I am giving you the benefit of a lifetime of experience. So just be quiet and listen."

So, she had not conceded entirely after all.

"You are asking people to do more than they have ever done before: go to school, go to meetings, join the army. And even when you explain to them that a drafted army is far preferable to a professional one, they resent going. You want people to act like adults, but for four hundred years they have been treated as children. And they don't wish to grow up, not overnight. Fidel understands this, so he carries much of the burden himself, he along with the Party. But elections, Julio! Elections are dangerous. An election gives people the opportunity to regress to childhood, to give their power back to parental figures, to hand it back in exchange for promises, for the simplest gratifications. The revolution is not old enough, the people are not mature enough to take that risk."

"I see that, Ileana. But tell me, How long does it take for a people to grow up? Thirty years of revolution in Cuba and still the people are not old enough to vote? I was born the same year as the Cuban Revolution, and I feel very much like an adult. I have killed men in war, and saved their lives on the operating table. I think I might be qualified to cast a ballot. Yes, Fidel is a father who will not let go of his children, but we are better than that. The people of Nicaragua are not our children. They are our sisters and brothers and they are perfectly capable—"

"Of betraying you. Yes, they are perfectly capable of it. Don't deceive yourself. The North Americans have been subverting revolutions for a century. They are experts at it. Give them an opening and they will bring you down. You will wake up one morning and it will be Santiago again, September 1973. You will be herded into the stadium—"

"For God's sakes, Ileana! We're going to win the damn election. It is impossible to think that we could lose."

"What is the statistic, Julio? As Minister of Health you should know it better than I. One in every hundred Nicaraguans dead because of this war the Yankees are waging against you. Dead. I am not going to mention the wounded, the orphaned, the displaced—"

"Thank you for not mentioning them, Ileana."

"All right. So now the Yankees stop killing and start buying. They are going to show the world something and it is going to turn the blood of every revolutionary cold in his veins. They are going to show the world that what they cannot do with guns they can do with dollars. They can bring an established revolutionary government to its knees."

"It is no use getting angry at me. The decision has already been made."

"But the damage has not yet been done. Use your influence, Azul. Keep control. Don't let the Americans set the terms. Don't let them finance the opposition."

"You are so sure the people can be bought?"

"You are so young, Julio."

"Yes, but I am getting older by the minute."

Finally she smiled across the table at him. "You Sandinistas always were crazy."

"And you love us because of it."

"Yes, I love you. All of you. But I don't particularly want to see all of you living in Havana."

"I will never live in Havana. I would let them shoot me first."

"I hope with all my heart it will never come to that. So, these are my last words on the subject of the election—"

"I would not talk about last words so soon, *compañera*. This is only July." And he returned her smile, but he was not thinking about what might happen between now and February. He was thinking about Paco Ruiz and Patrice, and what he would do if Patrice was already in Honduras en route to Salvador.

EIGHT

The Zone of Control, El Salvador

Choluteca and Valle, bordering on the Gulf of Fonseca, formed a relatively narrow land bridge across Honduras between Nicaragua to the south and El Salvador to the north, and through them ran clandestine but well-guarded supply routes connecting Salvador's liberated Zone of Control, governed by the Farabundi Marti Front for National Liberation, with the only other liberated nation on the isthmus, Nicaragua. These supply routes were protected not only by cadres of the Frente, but by Honduran guerrillas known as Cinchoneros. But Patrick wondered, as they marched along these footpaths day after day through the sweltering heat, who exactly the Cinchoneros were protecting them from. The Honduran government certainly didn't want to make waves in Choluteca; the North Americans were hardly likely to send a Light Infantry Division into Honduras to stop a few guerrillas from passing through the territory. Anyway Carlos didn't seem to have much trust in the Cinchoneros' ability to keep the roads safe: he kept his men on combat status, and every night he posted guards.

One of the last villages they came to before crossing the border was typical of the rest of the countryside. It was small, squalid, nothing but banana trees and wooden shacks, dirt streets, mangy dogs, scrawny chickens. A dozen men were standing around outside the store in their old straw hats and their worn clothes, staring out at nothing, or shuffling their feet in the dust. They might have been half-drunk already, or half-asleep, the way they just stood, vacant, never looking directly at any of the guerrillas. They were skinny and weathered and of indeterminate age. The ones who had the faces of sixty-year-olds could have been forty; the ones who had the bodies of adolescents could have been grown men.

Poor and insignificant as this village was, it was situated close enough to the Salvadoran border —and the southern-most point of the Zone of Control— for its people to find themselves always in danger of being attacked by the army for harboring guerrillas. Yet they could not help but harbor guerrillas since some of them were members of their own families and in any case they came armed, as this squad came, armed, loitering in the street, inquiring about Cinchoneros and jeeps.

Patrick sat on a step and shut his eyes. He'd been looking at the same scene for days now; he just couldn't look at it any more—the dirt and the grim faces and children and animals starving and everything broken and impossible to fix. In the highlands villages were poor, yes, but there was always something beautiful, the work of the women's looms, their bright clothing, striped or checked or embroidered depending on the village, but always there were colors, every color of the rainbow, and beautiful Indian faces, children with dark, luminous eyes. Not so here. And it was so hot, so humid, just the act of breathing made him sweat, and he smelt bad and he couldn't walk another foot, he would lie down and die here before he would walk another foot.

He was being watched. A child. Ten maybe, though he looked years younger in size if not in expression. He was wearing a pair of dirty shorts, no shirt, no shoes. His face was narrow, pinched, and his hair was light, a sure sign of malnutrition. His eyes were big, more curious than afraid.

Patrick forced himself to smile at the boy, expecting nothing in return. So it pleased him that the boy smiled back.

They began to play.

It was an ancient game, peek-a-boo. Like war, Patrick thought, as he hid his face behind the post beside him, peeked out, caught the boy's face peeking out at him, made him laugh. Like war. Hide and seek. Seek and destroy.

Escalation. The boy ran away, hid behind a mango tree, peeked out. He wanted to be pursued, but Patrick felt that if he tried to move he would keel over. Still, this was the best thing that had happened to him all day. Play.

He got up and crossed the dirt yard. The boy was still behind the tree; Patrick ducked behind the outhouse. He peeked out in time to catch sight of the boy scuttling across the yard to the side of the house. So, he was planning to attack from the rear.

Patrick recrossed the yard and flattened himself against the house. Soon he heard the boy creeping along the adjoining wall. Quiet, but not quiet enough.

He was playing. He forgot his size, his color. He was just playing. So when he knew the boy had reached the corner, he simply stepped out from hiding to tag him.

He had lived in liberated zones for too long.

The boy's body stiffened up under his hand. His eyes swelled, his mouth trembled. Patrick, towering over him, gripping his arm, felt the boy's fear enter him like a venom, as though instead of a child he had reached out and touched a scorpion.

Men who looked like him killed children who looked like this.

He knelt down in the dirt in front of the boy. Even kneeling he was taller, so he squatted back on his heels, holding the boy tight by both arms, looking up at his face. The boy was crying, his face streaked with dirt. There was dirt on his chest, his legs. His shorts were too small, filthy, the fly open.

He had to say it several times. When he was sure his words were understood, he released the boy's arms to let him wipe the tears away with his hand.

"I'm your friend," he kept saying. "I'm not going to hurt you."

But he was torn, because maybe it was better for the boy to fear white men in uniforms. Maybe it was better for him to learn to flee.

"I'm not going to hurt you."

The boy stared down at his face, examined him. He had never been subjected to such severe scrutiny.

"You are a Yankee?"

"No, I am Guatemalan."

70

The boy put out his hand and touched Patrick's hair. Curly, blond hair—perhaps he had never touched hair like that before. He let the boy put his fingers into his hair and remembered what it felt like to touch his friend's hair for the first time, his first black friend. Only children can do this, he thought, bearing up under the boy's unblinking examination of his eyes and his earring. Only children can touch your hair or your skin, only they can be so honest. How he had touched William Maxwell's hair, his skin, amazed. He remembered because some adult had pulled him away, some adult had been embarrassed. So they had touched each other in secret, in a corner of the nursery school's playground, touched each other's hair, each other's skin. They were so different, even their penises were different. They had touched those too. It made him smile to think of it, those long discussions about penises he had had with his friend William Maxwell at age five. Are they the same or are they different? Are we the same or are we different? How are we different? Why are we?

The boy had both hands in Patrick's hair and was smiling down at him.

"Are we friends now?"

"Yes."

They heard sounds behind them, Carlos's voice.

"I have to go now," Patrick said, and he ran his hand through the boy's hair. "OK?"

The boy released his hold and ran off, a little urchin running home to a one room shack. He thought of Julio at that age, of Alejandro, of the boys he saw in Guatemala City, of all the things he had put away in Nicaragua Libre where children aren't afraid of strangers. Though maybe children should always be afraid. Maybe what he had just done was wrong.

He got up and turned around. Carlos was staring at him, glaring at him, something on his face that was both ferocity and disgust.

Or maybe not. He was too hot to judge anything, Carlos least of all.

71

That night Patrick and Victor sat up at the campfire after the others had left for their hammocks or their posts. The fire was still burning low; Victor smoked. To entertain each other over the long march, and through hours of the long watches at night, they had been taking turns telling each other stories. Victor had just fin-ished telling the tale of the Twins, Hunahpu and Xbalanque, and how they outwitted the Lords of Death in Xibalba, the Mayan hell. They were put into the houses of death: Dark House, Razor House, Cold House, Jaguar House, Fire House, Bat House; they escaped from each one. They played ball with the Xibalbans and won, but the Lords of Xibalba wanted to kill them anyway. "And here it is," Victor had whispered to him in the close, tropical night, "the Epitaph, the death of Hunahpu and Xbalanque. They did whatever they were instructed to do, going through all the dangers, the troubles that were made for them, but they did not die from the tests. The boys went running and arrived at the mouth of the oven. 'Don't we know what our death is, you lords? Watch!' Then they faced each other. They grabbed each other by the arms and went head first into the oven. And there they died together."

But the story didn't end there. Their bones were ground on a stone like corn and thrown into the river. Then on the fifth day the two boys reappeared. As dancers they returned to the Lords of Death and as dancers they seduced the Lords of Death into allow-ing them to cut out their hearts and return them to their bodies. Hunahpu and Xbalanque demonstrated this trick on each other first, and the Lords begged them to do it to them as well. The boys performed heart sacrifice on the Lords of Death, but they did not return the hearts of the Lords of Death to their bodies. "Such was the defeat of the rulers of Xibalba," the tale ends. "The boys accomplished it only through wonders, only through self-transfor-mation."

Now Victor sat beside him very still and stared into the fire. Finally he said, "You will not stay in the Zone. You will come back with me to the highlands."

"If they let me, Victor. I don't know. I'm afraid I'm just letting Carlos lead me by the nose right into a detention cell. Or worse."

"Atanasio Tzul was killed in Nebaj, Patrice. May his soul ascend."

"Atanasio is dead? When did you hear this?"

"A courier brought me the news in Estelí. It is a great loss. Of course, Atanasio's life was hidden, so his death must be hidden. But this is a sad time for us, and a time of change for the Unity. Who knows, Patrice, what will happen. We are needed there, both of us. The Green Path, Patrice. Remember. It passes through the center of all the others. We who travel on it must be willing to go down to Xibalba as well as up to heaven. Patrice, because of Nebaj we are without leadership. Many would welcome your return. . . . Look into the flame. There you will see things being hidden and things becoming light."

Patrick stared into the smoldering fire. What he saw forming there, out of the red and gold and out of the blue, and something green as well, a distinct image rising out of the fire, and it rose out and toward him, it reached out to him and it was hot and strong, red and gold, green and blue, a serpent and a bird.

"Victor, stop!"

"I am doing nothing, Patrice." But it was in his voice, in the rhythm of the Quiché, the deliberate pauses, the way he had spoken as though in prayer, half-chanting, speaking until his breath ran out. Victor was a sender, and Patrick was so receptive that the sound of his voice alone had made him see the image in the flame.

"It is a lie," he said, very softly.

"Is it, Patrice? Are you sure, very sure. Deep in your heart, Xbalanque . . . are you very sure?"

"Sure I'm not Cucumatz returned, another Quetzalcoatl? Are you serious, Victor?"

"Very serious, Patrice."

"All right, I'll answer you, very seriously. I am quite sure, in my heart, that I am not Cucumatz. Is that clear enough? Would you like me to swear to it in blood?"

"It is not necessary. I believe you, Patrice."

73

"Are there others who think differently?"

"I don't know what others think, and it is of no consequence to me, to us. Let me tell you what's in my heart. I can guide you safely back to Huehuetenango. You are needed there. You have four years' combat experience and you know how to get things done, how to recruit, how to train, how to route supplies. You have these skills to give us and all this we need from you. But, my brother, listen to me. You also need us. We also have something to give you there. There, in the sky, on the earth, the four sides, the four corners, there is something for you, my brother. Your place, your destiny. . . . Patrice, look into your heart."

Patrick studied Victor's face. Something made him reach over and touch it. Victor's cheek was burning, his whole face. And as soon as Patrick's hand touched him, Victor began to tremble. "Your heart," he whispered, "it is *euaxibal zaquiribal*." Place of shadow, place of light. He said the words as though it were an announcing, and immediately his face became cool again, the fever went out of him as quickly as it had come.

"Enough," Patrick said. "It's time to sleep." And he took Victor by the arm, and led him to their hammock.

By dusk the next day they were in jeeps driving toward the Salvadoran border. Cinchoneros were riding with them. At the frontier they exchanged one guerrilla guard for another. They were in the Zone. Patrick wrapped himself up in a blanket in the back of a jeep and slept.

When he woke they were passing through darkness, steep darkness. Climbing. He dozed and woke again, got a whiff of pine, for a moment thought he was home.

Not quite dawn. They were in the mountains, though not his mountains. Banana trees and evergreens, heat, a town of adobe houses, a church. They passed through gates and climbed a steeper road to the guerrilla base. High above them was the old coffee finca, now the headquarters of the liberation army. Nestled in those hills were training fields, barracks, an airstrip. He could already feel the excitement, the tension: they had reached the innermost place within the Zone of Control, so secret, so concealed, not even satellite surveillance has been able to pinpoint it. Or so they hoped.

This was the heart of the Zone. Maybe they thought they had brought him here against his will, but they were wrong. This was Vladimir's territory, the man who had sent him into the arms of General Garcia Fuentes. Vladimir owed him something for that, and he was here to collect.

NINE

Moonset. Morning. Carlos stood at the edge of the training field and watched one hundred combatants practice the Viet Nam step. They trained in the darkness through the dawn, the Special Commando Unit who rule the night. They see in the dark. They are creatures of the dark. Invisible.

There was no other unit like this in the world. Each one of them could do anything, everything. Each one of them was a skilled technician, a marksman, a strategist; each one could command his own army. Each one was a revolutionary, and each one was willing to die.

They moved as one being, slowly, silently. Each man naked, camouflaged by dirt, only the eyes burning, catching the morning light. Each one of them was mightily strong, inside and out, unbreakable, indomitable. A year's work had made them into this hundred-headed being that could not know defeat.

The Ninja, Patrice called them.

Patrice.

He shook the name away, shook the image from his mind. Patrice was not his responsibility. He was not his brother's keeper. Nor was Patrice his brother.

The Ninja. Yes, and any one of them could fulfill the mission Vladimir had planned, any one of them could do it and do it better than Patrice. Only one thing prevented it: the color of his skin.

But Vladimir was sadly mistaken if he thought this plan would succeed. It would not succeed because he did not know Patrice, though Carlos had tried to tell him. Not last time, no, but this time he had told Vladimir the truth: Patrice is undisciplined, uncommitted; he knows too much and has not been trained to withstand torture; he is rebellious by nature and weak, cannot force his will. And even if Vladimir was skeptical, even if he didn't believe this

76

analysis, it hardly mattered. Patrice was many things, but he was not a fool. He would not accept the mission and so they would fall back on the general assault. They would have to.

He watched the unit fan out into formation: intelligent, precise, accurate, pure. He could not look anymore. It was for this that he had sold Patrice to Vladimir, for this weapon. He could have told him anything then. When Vladimir first asked about the gringo in Huehuetenango he could have said, I know the man. Do not trust him. Choose another to send to Guatemala City. And Vladimir would have believed him and looked elsewhere.

But they had been standing right on this very spot watching the unit train and Vladimir had said, Tell me what you know about this North American, Patrick Day. Can I use him or not? Help me, Carlos, and if we are successful, this unit will need a field commander by November. It could not have been clearer. Even Patrice had seen it. *Who near the leadership knows me, Carlos? Only you.*

Something close beside him made him jump: Victor, appearing as though out of the air.

"Excuse me, *comandante*," Victor said in his low voice. "I would like a word with you about Patrice."

He had expected this conversation. He muttered an agreement and began walking along the side of the field with Victor, head and shoulders shorter, padding along beside him. The sun was already breaking through the morning mists; it would be a hot day.

"Vladimir arrived here two days ago," Victor said at last in so low a voice Carlos had to bend his head to hear him. "He has met with you, but evidently he does not wish to meet with us. Guatemala holds no interest for him anymore. Or perhaps Patrice holds no interest for him."

"We were discussing the offensive."

"Yes. I understand. And of course neither Patrice nor I have anything to do with the Frente's offensive, so the sooner we are on our way home the better for everyone."

"Patrice can't return to Guatemala now, Victor. He'd be picked up the minute—"

"We appreciate your concern, of course. But, Carlos, we really are quite capable of entering and leaving our own country—"

77

"The risk is too—"

". . .With the same ease that you enter and leave the Zone of Control. Neither of us has any intention of falling into the hands of the Kaibiles, I assure you. I must leave for Guatemala, Carlos. We both must. This is not our war down here. This is not our struggle. Patrice is a member of the Guatemala Unity, not the FMLN. You must release him and let us go on our way."

"I'm afraid you are going to have to leave without him," Carlos said. "He'll be perfectly safe here until this thing with Garcia blows over."

"I have a difficult time thinking it is simply for his own protection that you are keeping Patrice in a detention cell. I have been unable to see him or even to speak to him for the past week. As for Garcia, do you think they will forget about his murder, Carlos? In one month or two, or twelve or thirty-six? Better Patrice goes now, before they get photographs up in every border post. . . . Or are you telling me that you will not permit him to leave?"

"It is not up to me."

"Vladimir, then. Vladimir will not allow him to leave."

"For his own safety Vladimir has decided to invite him to remain on the base."

"To confine him to this base. To imprison him on this base."

"Those are your words, Victor, not mine."

"That's right. And since Spanish is not my native tongue, I may have chosen the words incorrectly. But as far as I understand your language, Carlos, an invitation one cannot refuse is usually called an order, and a room one cannot leave is generally considered a prison cell. But we can call them anything we choose, can't we, Carlos?"

They walked past a bush, past a tree, to the spot where the path to the hospital branched off from the main path, and Victor halted there and, looking directly up into Carlos's eyes, said, "So I am curious, what do you call betrayal, Carlos? What word do you use?"

Carlos went to his office in the main building. He was angry but he didn't know who it was he was angriest at, Victor or Vladimir or Patrice.

Carlos was not a philosophical man, and he knew it. When he was a student, discussions of ideas, principles, theories, the things that Patrice loved so much, none of them meant anything to him. What he loved were tools, machines, hardware. He loved making things and he loved making them work. He loved that moment when what he made worked. He had expected to spend his life designing hydroelectric plants or factories. To create. The first thing they asked him to do when he joined the *guerrilla* was to blow something up.

He knew all about blowing things up. He could blow up anything. He was a genius at it. He could blow just the right power line to knock out electricity to an entire district. He could blow transmitters, railway lines, roads, bridges. After he had blown up half of El Salvador, they gave him a command. And then a bigger one. And then they asked him to design a plan for blowing the empire right off the isthmus.

He paced the room, back and forth. Like a cell. The size of a cell. Though a cell would be smaller, and dark, and in a real cell he would be chained.

He could see Patrice in such a cell.

Carlos sat down finally. In front of him was everything he needed. If he were given the signal tomorrow, he could mobilize thirty thousand combatants, an air force, a navy, Dunkirk-style, but functional, two established governments, three liberation fronts, a popular movement of unions, workers, teachers, and students, and solidarity organizations all over the world. But Vladimir, that bastard, that motherfucking son of a bitch, Vladimir was right: they needed a feint, a diversion, an unsuspected move, to give them the opening and the victory. And then he closed his eyes and he saw Patrice lying in the street with fifteen, twenty, bullets in him, and he knew that for what they would accomplish, not even Patrice himself would judge it too high a price.

Dusk. He thought of lighting the lamp, but didn't. He read until he couldn't see anymore and then he glanced up from his desk. The man sitting in the other chair was watching him.

He could feel his throat closing, the pounding of his blood in his fingertips.

"Don't be afraid, Carlos," the man said. His voice was very low, very gentle. "Have a cigarette. Relax. I just want to talk to you."

"It is not possible."

"Yes it is. And necessary, Carlos. You need to talk to someone, so I am here."

"What do we talk about?"

"You. Patrick. Can you see me clearly?"

"Yes."

"Good. And him, Carlos? Can you see him? Can you see him when the sun is on him? When the sun is low in the sky and he is sitting across from you facing the light? Have you ever looked at him then, how his eyes become so green, like emeralds, Carlos, and his hair like gold? Ah, Carlos, how beautiful he is then!"

"That is you seeing him, Alejandro, not I."

"Of course. Yet it is odd, Carlos, how you are thinking about this. If it were any other man Vladimir wanted for this mission, oh, you would object so strongly! You find the mission itself so distasteful, Carlos. And yet because it is Patrick you don't object at all. Now don't you wonder why?"

Carlos couldn't answer. He was filled with terror, and with something else. Alejandro looked at him with those eyes of his. Such a narrow face he had, long and narrow, the hair hanging straight and loose, long, to his shoulders, and then those eyes, almond-shaped, lustrous, a woman's eyes. Feminine, everything about him.

"How could you let him?"

"Let him what, Carlos?"

"You are a man. How could you let him use you like a woman? All those years, Alejandro. How could you let him do that to you?"

"Do that to me. What does it seem like to you, Carlos? Like burning a cooperative farm, is that it? Like bombing a health clinic or a school, with all the little children inside too, eh? Or worse? Is it worse? Like bayoneting babies perhaps? It's Roque Dalton, isn't it, our great poet of liberation, who can think of no worse insult to hurl at reactionaries than to call them homosexuals. Well, Carlos, face it. Your brother is a hole. There you are. I could tell you that I loved him. I could tell you that before I met him I didn't know what it meant to be happy, and afterwards I couldn't remember what it was like to be unhappy. I could tell you that, but what difference would it make to you? He still must be punished."

"Punished? We are fighting a war, Alejandro."

"Ah, yes. A war. It gives one ample opportunity to punish, doesn't it? A good setting for it. Far better than Boston, for example."

"What are you talking about?"

"You know very well what I'm talking about. Crime and punishment. I'm talking about enacting vengeance. Wasn't it enough to break off your friendship with him, wasn't it enough to make him pay that price? Maybe not. But *this*, Carlos, this is going too far."

"You don't understand anything. When Patrick joined this struggle he swore to carry out whatever tasks he was assigned. This is a task he is fit for."

"You turn your best friend into a killer and then say it is what he is fit for. Well done, Carlos."

"I didn't ask him to come here and I didn't ask him to stay."

"You didn't tell him not to come and you didn't tell him he couldn't stay. You didn't tell us you had taken up arms, Carlos. We thought you were teaching at the National University, remember? You never bothered to inform us. . . . Carlos, you were so close, you and Patrick. He missed you so much. Tell me, didn't you miss him as well?"

81

"Ten years ago, Alejandro, how can I remember? Perhaps for a little while. But I made other friends."

"Yes. And then, of course, you committed yourself to this struggle. Very admirable of you."

"Damn you! Sometimes I wonder how you and I could have come from the same mother. How the oppression of our people could never have touched you. All you ever cared about was yourself."

Alejandro smiled at him. The angrier he became, the more serene Alejandro seemed to him. His eyes shone and his hair, his skin, the white cloth of his shirt, everything seemed to radiate light. "Listen to me, Carlos," he said, and his voice was so gentle, like the voice one uses to soothe children at night. "You are the son of privilege, and it is altruism that motivates you. But for me, Carlos—do you really think that oppression never touched me? While you were away in the States, thinking about labor unions—though you must admit you never labored in your life—and thinking about land reform, and, yes, how to blow up bridges and power lines, what do you think was happening to me, Carlos? Do you think I hid in the house all those years while the repression happened all around me? And do you think the repression was directed only against the political activists, do you think they were that selective, Carlos? Yes, we came from the same mother, you and I, but there was a vast difference between us and no amount of family privilege counts against that difference. When I walked down the street, day or night, Carlos, I was not a Martínez, I was a *maricón*. It's like the color of your skin, you can't hide it. Oh, yes, you can see oppression, Carlos, but you have never felt it, never in your life. If you had you would be more forgiving to those who flee from it, more charitable. And while we are on the subject of charity, Carlos, I have to speak to you about Patrick. I want you to listen to me."

Carlos buried his face in his two hands. "This is crazy. I am sitting here talking to myself. When I look up again, this will all be gone."

"So. You think you are imagining me? Of course, a good materialist like you can only believe I am a figment of your imagination. Perhaps your diet is faulty, Carlos. Perhaps you need more vitamins, eh? Nevertheless you will hear what I have to say. You will remember something, Carlos. It was long ago, just before you left Boston to return here. You had come over to the house to say goodbye to us and you and Patrick got into an argument. Because you wanted it, Carlos. You wanted to leave angry. Anger has the virtue of erasing all other emotions. So you attacked him for studying Quiché. You said, 'Go ahead. Study our languages! Study our culture!' (Not that Mayan is your language or your culture, Carlos, but of course you were speaking as a representative of the entire Third World at the time.) 'Go into anthropology, why don't you?' This is what you said to him. 'The world needs another gringo anthropologist, just like it needs another white leftist. But don't think we'll ever let you close to us. Don't think we'll ever let you close enough to fuck with us. Alejandro's as close as you'll ever get.' Oh, yes, Carlos, you always knew how to go for the balls. But I want to ask you this. Who's doing the fucking now? Who's fucking who? Think about that, Carlos. And think how you loved him once, how he loved you. Remember that friendship you had, Carlos. You must not forget."

"I am asleep and dreaming this."

"Of course you are. So, I'll leave you now. But think about what I've said. It doesn't matter to Patrick. His destiny is written inside him. He writes his own script as he has always done and nothing you do will change it. But I worry about your soul, Carlos, the soul you deny you have. I hate to tell you this, Carlos, but there is an error in your thinking. You say you are imagining me, but, Carlos, you know very well that you do not have the imagination to imagine me.

"Listen to me, my brother. You are a good man, but you are on the brink now. Be careful! I beg you to be careful."

Carlos, hearing this, took his hands away from his face and looked across the desk to the chair where Alejandro was sitting. The chair was empty.

TEN

Patrick woke in the middle of the night convinced someone or something was in the room with him. It had no shape. He felt it as an infusion of heat, like the way an injection of iodine spreads heat throughout the body. He smelt it, too—a sweetness, flowers in a garden, summertime. Fragrance and warmth washed over him like the ripples of a tepid sea. Lying beside Alejandro, feeling the warmth of his hands caressing him. He thought that, and then he fell back into sleep.

He was awakened abruptly by someone shaking him by the arm, Carlos, who looked like he had just come in from field operations, grungy and weary and smelling of old sweat and mud. It was just getting light.

"Wake up, you son of a bitch," Carlos growled. Patrick sat up, Carlos tossed an envelope onto his lap. "Open it!"

It was a U.S. passport, his own passport, his own photograph, his own signature. "Where did this come from?"

"We don't throw them away, Patrice. You give it to us to hold for you. For when you need it. You need it now. So. Passport. Tickets. You are flying out of Managua, it's the only safe way. We doctored your passport a bit. See, you have only been here three weeks. Three weeks, Patrice. Seems like forever, doesn't it?"

"Flying out of Managua . . . to where?"

"Miami. Back home, Patrice. Where you belong."

"But I—"

"But nothing. You are out of this war. It's over for you. Now get up, get ready. You're leaving in half an hour."

"You can't just ship me off to Miami, Carlos. I'm not a piece of freight—"

"Shut up! Now listen, asshole. I can do whatever the fuck I want with you. I can have you disappeared, Patrice, and that might be the safest thing for all of us. But I have some reason to care about you, so I'm giving you an opportunity to leave now while you still can. Alive. But don't push me, Patrice. Don't push me or I'll wash my hands of this whole business, get it? All I do is tell them I don't want to see you again, and no one will see you again. Understand?"

"But why?"

"*Why*? You ask me *why*? Are you blind or just stupid? Nobody trusts you and nobody wants you here. You're a liability, Patrice. You're trouble. A gringo faggot . . . that's all you are. I didn't see it for a long time. I didn't see what you really are, not until I caught you with that boy just before we crossed into the Zone. I should have reported that, but I didn't. I've been protecting you for too long, and I'm sick of it. Now it's time for you to go. You have a passport, a ticket. They'll have money and clothes for you in Managua. Everything's arranged. The jeep will be waiting outside. Now get ready."

"What boy? What are you talking about?"

"The boy you were molesting, on your knees in front of him. . . . Don't think I didn't see—"

"You son of a bitch—" He started to stand up, but Carlos gripped him by the shoulder, pushed him backwards against the headboard, and pulled his pistol out of his belt. "I'll use it, Patrice. Believe me. It won't bother me in the least."

"Because men who do it with boys make you sick, right, Carlos?"

"That's right."

"They shouldn't be allowed to live, should they? No matter how close they are to you. Even if they're family, right, Carlos?"

"That's right, Patrice. Even if they're family. But I don't want to kill you. I just want you on that jeep, on your way out of here. Understand?"

"You know whose picture I saw hanging up in General Garcia's bedroom, Carlos? Your Uncle Emilio's. Interesting place for it, isn't it? Do you think Emilio gets off on boys by any chance, Carlos?"

"You motherfucker. No, Emilio is a decent man, Patrice. Emilio is not like you."

"But what if you're wrong? I guess I'd have your blessing to slit his throat if I ever got the chance. And maybe I will some day."

Carlos released Patrick's shoulder and backed away. He let his arm drop, though he didn't put the gun back in his belt.

"What the fuck has my uncle got to do with you?"

"I didn't like looking at his face, that's all, Carlos. It bothered me."

"I wouldn't talk much about Castillo around here. He's a very important man."

"A very important right-wing fascist pig, yes."

"No, a very important man. To us. Do you understand me?"

"No, I don't understand you. But you know how bad I am with pronouns, Carlos."

"Where do you think all the information about Garcia Fuentes came from? Who his friends were. Where he went for dinner. Where he went to find boys. Where he kept his security files."

"I don't believe you. I don't believe you'd use such a scumbag for intelligence work, that you'd trust anything he told you."

"Believe what you want. But I'm telling you, Castillo is important. . . . Anyway, you're out of this war. You're out of this country, out of my life. I'm serious, Patrice. Don't push me."

Carlos turned on his heel and strode to the door.

"Fifteen minutes," Carlos said at the door.

"Don't keep the engine running. I have a lot of things to do today."

"Don't defy me, Patrice."

"Stuff it up your ass, Carlos. You want to blow my head off, go ahead, or have one of your thugs do it for you. But the only way you're getting me to Miami is in a body bag."

"If that's the way you want it," Carlos said, and left the room.

He held the passport tight in his hand. Carlos's words had shaken him, but nothing Carlos could say would have half the force of reading his own name on his passport. He hadn't used it in four years, he had almost forgotten that it was his official name, that it was on his passport and his checkbook and his driver's license and his insurance policies and even his doctoral thesis: Patrick Martínez-Day.

The night they decided to hyphenate their names came back to him in its entirety. So what if it was corny and romantic, Alejandro loved it, loved every symbol, every sign, wedding bands and hyphenated names. They would have gotten married, after all, if they could have. They were married anyway, they didn't need the blessing of the state. They didn't need anyone's blessing but each other's.

He closed his eyes and imagined Alejandro coming toward him across the room. His black hair was loose, hanging to his shoulders. He was naked, smooth, beautiful. Just thinking it aroused him, just the picture inside his mind. But he felt that he was being watched. The assassin at the door. He opened his eyes. Alejandro was standing at the foot of his bed.

He pulled himself up straight, felt the coolness of the wall behind him. Eveything else seemed real except what was right in front of him.

"Patrick," the illusion said to him in Alejandro's voice.

"Alejandro," he said, expecting his voice to dispel the apparition. But the image of Alejandro remained before him, so like Alejandro himself that it was almost unbearable.

"I came before, but you couldn't see me. It's difficult and I was afraid to hurt you. I'm not hurting you now, am I?"

Patrick tried to swallow; his throat was dry and tight. "No, you aren't hurting me," he said.

"Good. But you are afraid, Patrick. Look, think of this merely as an example of the activity of the fourth dimension. You told me all about it once, remember? Complete with equations. It's mathematically correct. See?"

Alejandro laughed, a sound he had almost forgotten. And love swelled up in him, love and desire and awful loss. *Oh, Alejandro*, he thought. *I love you.*

Alejandro smiled at him, so clearly, his memory was so clear. "I know you do. But there is time, *querido*. Time and space. So much room. Life is very confining, have you noticed? Confining and filled with either/or. Every step, either/or. A zone of control, the whole fucking thing. But don't worry. Don't worry too much. I know you, remember. You love first, rationalize later. You let your heart lead you, then you think up reasons why. So El Che says the Revolution is love. Maybe he's right. Maybe the revolution is love and revolutionaries are lovers and desire directs them. Anyway this is what you are now, *querido*. This is what you have become. A revolutionary, a *guerrillero*. Not because of reason, but because of love. That's why you're here."

"Carlos wants me to leave."

"Yes. Carlos is trying his best, but he can't help sounding like a bad Clint Eastwood movie. He thinks if he insults you enough you will go away. Then he won't have to be responsible for what happens to you. In his own way, he is trying to shield you, though unfortunately Carlos is a man who never learned how to touch without bruising. So don't listen to him. Only trust your heart, as you have always done. Perhaps it will take you at last to Tepeucucumatz, to that god who is both serpent and bird. How beautiful and terrible he is, strange and fierce, monstrous, himself a marriage of the two. Like you and I were monstrous, Patrick, from a certain perspective."

"You are going to leave me," he whispered, moving down the bed toward him. "Alejandro, please don't leave me again!" He reached out with his arms but he couldn't take him. The apparition blurred and faded like vapor, leaving behind it nothing but air.

Several hours later there was another knock on his door and a young soldier entered and informed him that *Comandante* Vladimir wanted to see him immediately at the training field. The soldier was accompanied by three others; it was evidently an order, not a request.

But he was in a good mood despite the way the morning had started, Carlos's visit, his anger, his threats. He had gone back to sleep afterwards and had a marvelous dream, a dream that left him feeling unreasonably happy, as though his mind had been cleared and his heart lightened. He couldn't remember any specific images, only that it had been filled with the most amazing light.

So he was going to meet Vladimir at last. The man who had singlehandedly reconstructed the Frente from its own rubble, who had brought the revolution out of the zones of control and into every one of the fourteen provinces of the country, who had masterminded the spectacular attacks against army garrisons in La Union, El Paraiso and San Miguel, the man at whose call other men willingly gave up their lives. That man, Vladimir, the Lord of Life and Death, had finally come calling for him.

ELEVEN

He walked between two of the soldiers down the path toward the training fields. He didn't know them and they didn't try to make conversation with him, or even with each other. They seemed very young, but then everyone here seemed very young. Vladimir wouldn't be young, at least.

They passed the barracks and the depot, where some mechanics were working on a lame troop carrier. They passed the turn-off for the commissary and went up a slight rise to the stand of trees that separated the training fields from the rest of the compound. There the soldiers halted abruptly and nodded in the direction of the field. He was on his own.

He followed the path through the trees, the cicadas humming crazily to the morning, and emerged at the edge of the field. A man was standing there, but it was not Vladimir.

"Well, Luis," he said as the padre turned toward him. "Are you my new custodian, or are you going to offer me the sacraments before I meet Vladimir? Or are you here to shoot me?"

"Shoot you? I didn't realize you were so paranoid, Patrice."

"I am. Very paranoid. The climate down here doesn't agree with me either. I need higher altitudes."

"I understand your desire for the mountains. Well, there's some shade here at least. Come and sit down over here with me. Let's have a smoke and talk for a few minutes, OK?"

Reluctantly, because it didn't seem that he had much choice, Patrick walked with the priest to a bench beneath a stand of trees and offered him a cigarette.

"I am curious, Patrice," Luis said, accepting a light. "If you were to leave here, today or tomorrow, where would you choose to go?"

"To Guatemala. Huehuetenango. The highlands."

"Indeed? And you have a woman back there, eh, Patrice? It is to her that you wish to return."

"No, I don't have a woman in Guatemala."

"But how is that possible? You are a young and attractive man and four years in the mountains is a very long time. Indian women are loving and devoted companions and love and devotion are comforts all men need. And men need children, a home, a place to return to. Surely you have such a place up there in the highlands and that is where you wish to be. It is perfectly understandable, my friend."

"You're talking to the wrong gringo, *padre*. You have me confused with someone else."

"Do I? You know, I have been thinking about you quite a bit. I have been thinking how clever the empire would be to send us someone like you, just like you, Patrice. Smart like you, trained like you, with all your skills. But how to make such a man believable, make it so that we would trust him, so that we would never suspect him to be a member of SOF? Well, what is the one characteristic of a man that makes it impossible for him to serve in the United States military? What is that one thing, Patrice, that would convince us that you could not be a Green Beret?

"Then I thought how odd it is that your dossier contains the information it does. You see, in our experience, homosexuals are at pains to conceal that information from others. But not you. You want us to believe you are a homosexual. You tell us, and you go out of your way to convince us, and yet there is nothing in your behavior to give these words any credibility. So we ask ourselves why a man who was not homosexual, or at least, not overtly so, would want us to believe he was. Then we are reminded of the fact that the United States Army does not permit homosexuals in its ranks. So you are announcing to us your disqualification from membership in your own army while fighting quite successfully in ours.

"Then there are five years of your life that we cannot account for. Between the time Carlos left you in Boston and the time he recruited you in San Miguel. Five years. Long enough to be quite properly trained at Fort Bragg. You see, for all it contains so much information in some areas, your dossier is incomplete."

"Carlos knows where I was those five years."

"There is no proof."

"Carlos's word. Isn't that worth anything?"

"He gives us no facts."

"What can I tell you, Luis? I was in Boston those five years. Write to the Registrar at MIT, get my transcript. Though I suppose the Special Forces could even forge an MIT transcript if they wanted to."

"What is it that Carlos knows that he is not telling us?"

"Ask Carlos."

Luis smiled, a half-smile that passed fleetingly across his face. "You are a stubborn man, Patrice. Why won't you tell me the truth? You were living in Boston with Alejandro Martínez, Carlos's brother. All right, it's out. Now why is this such a secret? Because Carlos does not want to admit that he had a homosexual brother? Because of this we lose five years of your life?"

"Tell me, Luis, is Vladimir coming or am I going to get jerked around by you all morning?"

"Just let me finish this line of thought, Patrice. Let's say for the sake of argument that you were working for the intelligence services even then. MIT has defense contracts, doesn't it? There are probably operatives working there, trying to recruit people like you, mathematicians, logicians, computer geniuses, engineers."

"Even when? When I first met Carlos? When I started living with Alejandro? So you're thinking my entire life was a lie, my whole relationship with Alejandro was a lie? You think this little fucking war of yours is so important that anyone would put in six years pretending to be queer just to infiltrate it? Ever hear of megalomania, Luis?"

"But you are not queer, Patrice. Men live with boys from time to time. We understand this. It is the role one assumes that matters."

"Oh, yes, we understand this. We understand this so well. But since you never met Alejandro Martínez, how do you know which of us was the man and which was the *maricón*?"

"You are angry."

"No, I'm not angry. It's just that sometimes you people make me want to puke."

"Then there is the report from your commander in Guatemala. What are we to make of this? Four years in the mountains, not one incident of sexual misconduct, not even a hint of homosexual behavior. Then, too, you come to us already a marksman, a fighter. You come to us having shot and killed three members of a UGB death squad, the White Warriors who operate under the direct command of D'Aubuisson himself. That act, bold as it was reckless, forced us to come to your aid, to hide you, protect you. On the basis of that act, that extraordinary act, we brought you into the Zone and allowed you to train as a combatant. At your own request you left the Zone and took up arms as a volunteer in Guatemala. Once in the mountains you adapt yourself completely. You are commended over and over for valor, for tactical brilliance. You speak not only Spanish but Quiché, so you become an indispensable member of the communications cadre. Communications is a very sensitive area. Now do you see how all this could lead to certain suspicions?"

"I can see that."

"Then there was the capture of the Unity squad in El Quiché a few weeks after your encounter with Garcia Fuentes—"

"I said I can see, Luis. I can also hear. I've got it, all right? So let's cut the crap, OK? You still suspect me. What are you going to do about it?"

"No, I don't suspect you. Not at all. I am simply explaining to you how such suspicions might arise among some people, how it could happen that you were not trusted completely. As for myself, however, I have nothing but the greatest admiration for you. And I am not alone. There are many of us who appreciate what it means that a white man should come here and fight side by side with us—"

"This is bullshit, Luis."

"No bullshit, *hombre.* I'm being frank with you, OK? You are a white man. Forget that you are also North American. Just being

93

a white man, that alone. Everywhere on the face of the earth you have power. Everywhere on the face of the earth white men rule."

"And I can't tell you how proud and happy that makes me, Luis."

"As it should. Don't ignore reality, my friend. They had to preach that black is beautiful. But nobody has ever had to mention that white is beautiful. And tall, blond and white . . . this is the ideal, perfection. It is a fact, not an arguable point . . . Does it disturb you that I say these things? But this is reality, Patrice. Ask anyone. Go to Mexico. Go to Brazil. Yes, go to Cuba. You'll hear the same thing. The most beautiful has the lightest skin. The most beautiful has the lightest eyes. The most beautiful straightens her hair if it's too kinky and colors it . . . blond if possible. And in Japan, in China . . . who do they hate the most? Black men. They have no history of Africans as slaves there, Patrice. But still black skin is bad, bad, very bad. And why? Because where white skin is superior, its opposite must be inferior. This is what is real, Patrice. Do you object to reality? Why do you do that?"

"What are you getting at, Luis?"

"Only perspective, Patrice. Only understanding. Let's take you, for example. You come here for awhile and fight with us. And we are grateful to you. When the time comes for you to leave, you go back home to the States, back to your family, back to your position in society . . . and what an adventure you've had, isn't that right? You can become an authority on guerrilla movements in Central America. You can tell wonderful stories of your courage and our . . . gratitude to you. You can talk about the brotherhood between you and us, testimonial accounts of how there is no racism on the battlefield. But you will always be a white man, Patrice. You will always have the safety net of white privilege beneath you. Nothing can ever take that away from you. Your skin is your passport and it will take you wherever you want to go. And our skin . . . in this world it takes us one place only, Patrice. The gutter. If we want to get out of the gutter we have to fight all our lives. You may want to love us, but love requires equality. What love can exist, Patrice, between masters and slaves?"

"Well, Luis, I think that right now I am going to exercise my white privilege and walk away from this conversation. I have to hand it to you though. You won. You're the noble warrior struggling against oppression and I'm still trucking around with the white man's burden. And now I'm going to look for Vladimir so I can resign from this fucking little war and leave all you fucking little assholes in your fucking gutters where, if you don't mind my saying so, some of you belong."

"You don't have to look for him, Patrice," Luis said very softly. "He is right here."

Patrick stared at the priest. It didn't even surprise him. What was he expecting anyway? Someone exactly like this, someone exactly this good, part fox, part spider. He wet his lips; his whole mouth had gone dry. "One of the things I love about this part of the world," he said, hoping his voice was steady. "Everybody's got so many goddam names."

"Many names. Many jobs. Only one heart. I like you, Patrice. I like your spunk. You don't take shit from anyone. That's good. Because this was shit I was giving you, to see how much you'd take. You took enough, not too much. You're OK, *hombre*. Now, you still want to resign, or will you listen a little longer? I have a proposition to make to you. If you are willing to hear me out."

"I'm willing to listen," he said.

Vladimir smiled at him. "Good. Now let us both acknowledge agreement on several points: one, that white privilege exists; two, that for those with white skin it is inescapable; and three, let me admit to you that if I had it I would not want to escape it. But you, you say, Take your white privilege and shove it up your ass, and I admire that in you. Truly. But when it comes to these essential things—race, ethnicity, sex, class—we have no choice but to take what we get. In your case, what you have got is privilege on every possible level. Well, you're stuck with it, my friend. What is the solution? You remember the story of Prometheus, don't you? He is a god, isn't that right? But what does he do? He steals fire from his own kind and gives it to men. He breaks the code of his class and his race. He is a traitor to his own kind out of love for those

95

who are not his kind. He knows what power he has. He does not deny it or renounce it. He cannot renounce it. He *uses* it."

"I have the feeling that there is something terrible you want from me."

"That is true. But remember this, Patrice. You may say no. It will not mean you are a coward. You say no to me now, there will be no hard feelings between us, I will release you from custody, you can go anywhere you want: Nicaragua, Guatemala, back to the States if you want, anywhere. Just because you are the only man who can do this for us, does not mean that you therefore must do it for us. And by us I mean all of us, Patrice. Because in this struggle we are all *compañeros.*"

"Tell me what you want."

"I want you to assassinate Gabriel Aguilar."

They got up and walked through the trees to a small rise. From that point they could look down on the field where the commandos were training, their lines moving across the field in slow motion, hunters stalking their prey.

"The Viet Nam step," Patrick said, pausing to watch them. "It is like a dance."

"The dance of life. So they can cross open fields and live. They will be crossing many such fields soon. We are moving down."

The day had an uncanny clarity. Above their heads in the boughs of the trees birds fluttered and whistled; below them, a hundred men moved so slowly that they seemed not to be moving at all, each man, skin blackened, crouching on one bent leg, the other raised as though to step forward, frozen in space and time.

"I would think you would be moving west, not east."

"So would the Salvadoran military command. So would their U.S. advisers. So we move both west and east."

"You expect an uprising in Honduras?"

"Indeed. It needs only a single spark."

"Aguilar? The peace candidate, Luis?"

"Yes, my friend. Aguilar is a peace candidate the way Duarte was a peace candidate. He is the U.S. candidate, a moderate, a man of compromise, a businessman, popular among the bourgeoisie, of whom in Honduras there are precious few, but each one extremely powerful. In short he is a perfect puppet, a perfect tool. Around him the Americans would focus a so-called 'democratic opening' in order to balance the strength of the military, a strength which they have themselves created over the past ten years. There are now death squads operating in Honduras, and there is a liberation movement—two things that did not exist before the Americans began fighting a counterrevolution from Honduran soil. Now they have an overbearing military, an indigenous guerrilla movement and the contra as well—a big mess, Patrice. The solution? Aguilar. Not a true solution, of course, but like any American solution, one that will merely delay the inevitable.

"But Aguilar is much smarter than Duarte, much smarter than the Americans know. He is playing a very clever game with them. While publicly he denounces the military, privately he embraces them. And why? Power? Oh, yes. Also money. Aguilar, Patrice, is a businessman, and he knows where the money is. And who is engaged in the biggest business venture in Central America? The cartel.

"Oh, it is a fine *ménage à trois* Aguilar has created: a civilian government, compliant, eminently presentable; a fat but seemingly docile military; and the cartel. It is nothing less than brilliant.

"I don't need to tell you what it would mean for the revolution to have the cartel expand its operations into Honduras. We know that the Guatemalan military is already involved in drug trafficking. But borders do not confine the drug trade, nothing controls it, not even the strength of an entire people. Naturally, the Americans know very well what's going on. The cartel is infiltrated top to bottom. But what is important for them of course is not controlling the drug trade but undermining revolutionary movements."

"So you want me to kill Aguilar."

"Yes. And it must be done publicly. Dramatically. He must be assassinated by a North American carrying CIA identification. The assassin must allow himself to be captured. When questioned he must tell a certain story linking Aguilar with the cartel. This story will simultaneously appear in the North American press. Of course no one in Honduras will believe it. They will think it a slander, merely a pretext for the U.S. to take action on the military's behalf against the democratic opposition. There will be a great deal of anger among the population. This anger will manifest itself in street actions against the U.S. Embassy. Street actions will lead to demonstrations and demonstrations to uprising. As for you, Patrice, the military will believe your story because they will know it is true. In any case they will not dare to harm you since they will believe that you are an agent of the United States. By the time they realize their error, we will have gotten you out."

"And what happens if you can't get me out?"

"We can get you out, Patrice."

"No, Luis. Think about it. I could give them Guatemala. The whole of the Unity, everyone. I've seen what they do to people—"

"Not to you. You are white, you are North American, you will be carrying CIA identification. They will not take the risk."

"How long will it be before they realize it's all a sham?"

"Of course the CIA will deny any connection with you, but they will expect that. They will also not believe it. And they will remember that the President of the United States swore vengeance against any government that held captive or physically harmed a citizen of the United States."

"Sabre rattling."

"In some places, yes. In Honduras, no. And we will get you out before they have a chance to think about it too much. Three days, Patrice. I swear to you. We will get you out in three days."

A golden-green parrot darted into the tree beside them and began to chirp. From another tree and another, birds answered him. Soon the air was filled with a cacophony of chirping birds, deafening. Nothing could be said over the din. They had to wait and while they waited Patrick thought about those three days.

"Listen, Patrice," Luis said after the parrots rose up out of the trees in a single great rush of wings and took to the air. "In battle, men have trusted you with their lives. But I trust you with more. I trust you with everything. It is what you want, isn't it? To be trusted with everything?"

"My God, you are a spider, Vladimir."

The older man shrugged. "So. What do you say?"

He had been watching the sky, the clouds. Now he turned and looked at Vladimir/Luis. A small, wiry, tough peasant with a face like a hawk, hawk eyes, hawk nose, gray hair, bad teeth. The Lord of Life and Death.

"A lot of people believe in Gabriel Aguilar. A lot of people will be very angry when I kill him. Don't you think it's possible that Aguilar's bodyguards will shoot me dead on the street the minute I pull the trigger?"

"Yes, Patrice, there is that possibility. Every time you go into combat there is that possibility. You must look at this as just another armed engagement."

"And if I survive the engagement, and if you get me out before I break and tell them everything I know, and if I'm still sane when you do it, then I don't owe you anything anymore and you send me back to Guatemala, right, *comandante*? Will you give me your word?"

"You have my word, Patrice. I will send you back to Guatemala. I promise you."

"I'd like half an hour to think."

"Take all the time you need. I will wait for you back there."

Vladimir gripped Patrick's shoulder for a moment and then turned and walked away. Patrick watched him disappear through the trees. Wily old bastard. It was true. He did want to be trusted with everything. And if he were tested and if he survived, then he would be done with it, finished. It would be the final proof, simple, elegant, irrefutable.

Below him, the commandos were still moving across the field as slowly as Alejandro would move when he practiced T'ai Chi.

The flock of parrots was circling overhead, about to alight on other trees. The birds reminded him of Julio, he didn't know why.

He didn't know why he was going to say yes to Vladimir. He just knew he was.

And if he survived he would go to Managua. He would go there like a pilgrim, looking for a living man. He would find Julio again. And then he would see.

TWELVE

Managua, Nicaragua

Heat and misery: for him this was and always had been the essence of Managua. Even here on the expansive, banyon-shaded patio of the Ministry of Culture, tonight filled with poets, writers, dancers, actors, musicians, a gathering of international cultural brigades, even here in this cool, candlelit space, he felt its misery in his mouth, its dryness on his tongue.

He stood by the pool and watched them dance. He watched Mauricio in his tight black pants and purple shirt, his cornrows swaying around his face as he moved, hips swaying, the gold chain bracelet at his wrist. So extravagant a gift, and, of course, he had been bragging about it. *A present from my* comandante. With that coy smile of his. *Azul has good taste, no?*

Julio lit a cigarette, kept an eye on Mauricio's sexy black body. Sent special delivery from the Island. The irony of it alone could choke him. That was it exactly: he was choking on irony.

Mauricio caught his eye and drifted across the dance floor toward him, halting a few meters away within earshot of several groups of important members of various ministries. In fact, he had found the perfect center of the party. He had a gift for central locations.

"It's time to go," Julio said, coming up to him.

"I don't want to go," Mauricio replied. He was slightly drunk so his voice was louder than necessary and sounded extremely petulant.

"I do."

"Well I don't!"

"We are leaving now," Julio said evenly.

"You can leave whenever you like. I'm not your slave, *comandante*. You haven't bought me. Don't think you have. You can't afford to buy me."

101

"You're drunk and you're coming home with me now, Mauricio. Now. Do you understand?"

Mauricio swung his cornrows away from his face with a defiant toss of his head. But there was a wounded look in his eyes, wounded and submissive. In the tension they had generated around themselves that submissiveness had not gone unnoticed. Julio waited a few seconds and then took Mauricio by the arm. "Come," he said.

"You'll put me to bed, will you?"

"Come."

Mauricio smiled at him, a smile of conquest. "Yes, my *comandante*," he said.

Even driving fast along these ghostly roads created no breeze. The nights were becoming as unbearable as the days. Suffocating.

Mauricio sat leaning against the passenger door and smoked. "Well, how did it go?"

"You're very good at what you do. By tomorrow morning everyone in the capital should be talking."

"This capital and several others, I imagine. And those actors, did you see them all? Did you happen to notice how our little conflict attracted their attention?"

Julio laughed. "And to think you are *Cubano!*"

"What's being *Cubano* got to do with it? So I take a professional interest in these things. Anyway, Julio, we *Cubanos* are the best. At everything."

"Of course you are. You are the best at getting people into untenable situations. I only hope to God you are also the best at getting them out again."

"I'll get you out. Don't worry."

"I'm not worried. Things take care of themselves. This thing of ours, it has its own momentum now. What happens, happens."

"How eccentrically are you behaving?"

"I don't believe I'm behaving eccentrically in the least. If I ever had to hit you, well, that would be a bit out of my range."

"You will, you know."

"Yes. If you keep acting like this I certainly shall."

Mauricio laughed. "They will be surprised, in the end."

"Let's hope it is they who end up being surprised, and not we."

Julio's house was in a quiet and comfortable neighborhood, on a block of similar houses, small, enclosed by low walls with gardens in the back. Geraldo was still awake when they arrived. He had spent the day securing the house. There were new locks, new gadgets, new alarms. He had wanted to embed glass in the enclosing wall and string barbed wire along the top, but there Julio had drawn the line. "I refuse to allow my house to look like an oligarch's," he had said. "Enough is enough."

"Tomorrow, Geraldo," he said after a cursory look at the security system, "I am having a dinner guest. I want you to prepare a good meal and then I want you to disappear. Understand?"

Mauricio smirked at Geraldo. "I told him that we *Cubanos* are the best at everything. That includes making soup."

Julio sat down heavily in his favorite chair and looked around. Two more men in his house, everything seemed cluttered, disorganized. They liked loud music and TV. They left things around. The breakfast dishes weren't washed; the beds weren't made.

"Geraldo, I dismissed my housekeeper. You are supposed to be keeping house for me. Is this your idea of housekeeping? By tomorrow this all has to be clean. Hire day help if you need to."

Geraldo, who reminded Julio of a walking weed, about thirty, olive-colored, stalk-thin, sunken-cheeked, taciturn, said, "Believe me. By tomorrow you won't know this place."

"I already don't know this place," Julio said, and got up to go to his room.

"Wait!" Mauricio called after him. "I'm going to give you a massage and Geraldo is going to run you a hot bath. You can't go to bed like this. You are too distressed. You won't sleep."

"I don't intend to sleep. I have work to do. And, Mauricio, when I am distressed you will know it."

But he was distressed. He went into his room and shut the door. He knew he would be as unable to work as to sleep. It wasn't just this situation. It had been like this since he returned to Managua, since he left Estelí, since Patrice.

They had made no promises to each other. On the contrary, they had barely even mentioned the possibility of seeing one another again. Yet there were other words spoken and unspoken, said in gestures and in the passionate exchanges of love. . . . And he would get that far and stop short, damning himself for a romantic fool, an idiot, naive, like a lovesick boy who had no experience in the world. And that was the track, and back and forth went the car, from hope and desire to despair, and it was intolerable, the banality of it, the tedium, back and forth, like a man caught in some infernal repetition, or one under torture, being compelled to dig a trench and then fill it up again, hour after hour, day after day.

He had sent Patrice a letter, months ago now. Sent it so he would be sure to receive it. *Information has come into my hands that is of vital importance to you. As you loved me, now trust me, Patrice. You must return to Nicaragua. It is imperative that you return at once.* There was no reason to think that this letter had been intercepted; he had sent it up in the diplomatic pouch. So Patrice must have received it, and ignored it. Misunderstood it, or perhaps was disgusted by it. There had been more in it, of course. On paper he could open his heart. And foolishly he had. *Never put anything in writing.* The *Cubanos* had taught him that, but, like all Cuba's lessons, it was one he resisted, one he defiantly refused to learn.

Leave it, Julio. Leave it behind. Yes, leave it behind. Like a body. Like the corpse of a friend. You must leave it behind you. You cannot drag it along. You cannot bury it. You cannot even weep over it. You must leave it behind.

You cannot weep over it, Julio.

104

He didn't. He sat on the edge of his bed and stared into the dark.

It was the morning of the day he had been preparing many weeks for. He showered and dressed by rote, without enthusiasm. Glancing into the bathroom mirror, he was not even startled by the new face that stared back at him, as sunken-cheeked as Geraldo's with eyes that seemed too large, too lustrous, not his own. There were rumors about his health. SIDA, the word no one dared to say, though it crept about the edges of everyone's mind. He had the look of it, skeletal features with those deep, wounded eyes. Well, it was a different sort of plague he was suffering from, a different infection, a virus of the heart, eating at him with the same relentlessness as HIV, coming from the same source, a man's love.

He had to stop thinking like this.

Geraldo had made coffee and breakfast. Mauricio was eating with a gusto Julio envied. He sipped his coffee standing at the window, watching the tree outside move gently in what might be a breeze.

"The bars are going up today," Geraldo said in his flat, matter-of-fact voice.

"What bars?"

"Window bars."

"Sit down, Julio," Mauricio said in a stern voice. "Sit and eat."

"I'm not hungry."

"I don't give a damn if you're hungry or not. You are going to eat. Son of a bitch. I'm not supposed to have to play nurse to you."

Julio grimaced and sat down and swallowed some food. They both smiled at him, satisfied, triumphant. They had cowed him into submission again.

"Eat it all," Mauricio commanded.

He ate it all.

It began at ten-thirty precisely. Eduardo Flores was ushered into Julio's office at the Ministry. Like his two colleagues who were to follow him onto the carpet, Flores was a deputy of hospital and clinical administration in one of the southwestern departments. Normally he would be at his duties in the regional office, but he had been recalled to Managua for this short interview with the Minister.

Julio spoke with dispatch. He had already distanced himself from the process. He had only to say what had to be said, first to one, then to the other, finally to the third: that in the course of a routine investigation by the Ministry of the Interior certain information had come to his attention requiring him to suspend his deputy from his position of trust and service, etc. etc.; that he could only hope the deputy would see fit to cooperate with the investigation; that the deputy must now accompany the *compañeros* from Interior . . . at which point he would press a button on his desk, the security officers would enter, the man sitting before him would realize that cold, stern justice had found him out, that the playacting was over, that all artifice had been revealed.

Within an hour it was over. Paco Ruiz trailed in behind the last of his agents, watched them take the last, quivering deputy away. Watched them keenly, always on the look-out for bad form. Paco was a stickler for form, personal and political. He was a lady's man, a dapper dresser, or as dapper a dresser as one could be given the economic conditions of the country, savvy, street-smart. He and Julio had grown up in the same barrio; it made them like brothers. So when Paco pulled up a chair and pulled a bottle of rum out of his back pocket, it only meant they were going to have a brotherly chat. Julio sighed and sat down behind his desk.

"Any glasses in this joint?"

Julio lifted the phone, asked his secretary to bring in two glasses and some ice. Her voice shook a little. It was to be expected; Health had never been purged before. He lit a cigarette and leaned back in his chair. "It went smoothly, Paco. Thank you."

"It could have been done more smoothly still. We could have picked them up right in their own homes."

"I wanted to dismiss them first. This way they are *former* deputies of Health, a rather important distinction, for me if for no one else."

"Listen, man, I hear a rumor that you are planning to speak to the press about this."

"That's right."

"And you're going to reveal the charges?"

"That's the idea, Paco. You arrest men and then you tell the people what they did. It's supposed to deter others, I understand."

Paco sighed and shook a cigarette out of Julio's pack. "You don't mention the cartel, everything's cool. But you embarrass them in public, they may feel the need to retaliate."

Julio shrugged.

"The cartel has been helpful to us in the past. Hardware, software, all gratis, you understand."

"No one is accusing you—"

"I'm not just talking about myself personally. The whole of Intelligence relies on them from time to time."

"The leadership has declared that time over and done. It was not all as gratis as it seemed."

"No. But this much I know about them. You fuck with them, they fuck with you."

His secretary entered the office with a tray of glasses, lime, cola and ice. She was unnaturally quiet, did not look at either man, set the tray down and asked if there was anything else they needed. There was nothing else.

Paco kept his eyes glued to her as she walked back to the door. "What a waste!" he sighed, the moment the door shut behind her.

"Her *compañera* would disagree."

"What has Health become these days, the official homosexual enclave?"

"Our hiring policies—"

"Oh, fuck, Julio, I'm only giving you shit. I can't tolerate rejection, you know."

107

"Well, there's a young man in clerical who might be receptive. . . ."

Paco laughed and poured them each a half glass of rum, topping it off with a dash of cola. "I would not think of stepping on your toes, man. This is your territory. I stay out. *Salud!*"

Julio smiled though his heart was not in it, and listened to Paco's plan for the next wave of arrests. Patrice's information had been sound: each man he had named, each man who had been paid off by Garcia Fuentes, each one of those men whom nobody would ever have suspected of trafficking in drugs, each one was going down. They had begun with Health, but they weren't finished, not by a long shot.

Paco drained his glass and got up to shake Julio's hand. "As for that source of yours, Julio, he's excellent. Keep in touch with him. Treat him good. Anything else he's got, we want."

Julio sat for a long while after Paco had left, spinning his glass in his hand, smoking. There were some very intelligent men in Managua. Some were clever enough to have noticed the change in his style of living over the past two months. Some must be wondering how it was that the Minister of Health did not know what his deputies were doing one day and knew exactly what they were doing the next. And some must surely be smart enough to read the signals he was sending to the cartel, sending loud and clear. He was asking for it, begging for it: *plomo o plata*, lead or silver.

"I feel like I'm under house arrest," he said. He was standing in the middle of the living room of his immaculately clean house secured by gate and door alarms, triple locks and now iron bars on the windows. He tossed his newspaper onto the table.

"This place is turning into a goddam prison."

"Not a prison, *comandante*," Geraldo said, coming out of the kitchen. He was wearing a white apron over his jeans and he looked as mournful as ever. "Its purpose is not to keep people in, but to keep people out."

"It adds up to the same thing: locks on my doors, bars on my windows. Are we eating dinner tonight?"

"Yes. Would you like to see?"

"No, I would not like to see. I want to a shower. I want a drink. And I want Mauricio. Where is he?"

Geraldo nodded in the direction of the bedroom and went back to his stove.

Mauricio's skin was nightblack against the white sheet. Everything in the room was black and white, though he hadn't paid attention to the color scheme in years. Even the TV was black and white.

But Mauricio's skin against the sheets, his skin in contrast to the bright whiteness of his undershorts, his skin with its sheen, lustrous, like his hair in those tight braids was lustrous, and fragrant, the sweetness of his hair and his skin. . . .

He had to stop this.

"Hey, Julio! I just saw you on the news. But it's not in the paper. Why didn't they hold the presses for you? In Cuba they would have. . . ." But he was grinning at Julio while he said it. "Anyway, my friend, it begins." He got up from the bed and came over to Julio. Clothed he gave the impression of softness, femininity; naked he was all muscle.

"We'll see. Be very careful tonight."

"The news conference . . . superb." He kissed the tips of his fingers, and then, to Julio's immense surprise, took Julio in his arms and kissed his cheeks. "You looked good up there. I was proud of you."

This was too much. "Let go of me, you slut," Julio said, and Mauricio released him with a laugh. "Now get serious and listen to me. There is a pistol in the glove compartment. Loaded. The key is the small one on the chain."

"I won't need it tonight. They'll try silver first. There's no point killing me."

"Of course there is. It would serve me with a warning. And they might enjoy it."

Mauricio shrugged. "We'll see," he said.

By eight Mauricio had left for the club, Geraldo had laid out the food and taken up his position somewhere outside the house to keep watch. Julio turned on a single lamp and sat down to wait. He thought how it was like keeping a vigil, sitting alone before a single lamp, waiting for a stranger to come to his door. Wait and pray, Jesus had said. But Julio could not pray. Though there was something in his heart, some great desire, some yearning he dared not name, something that were he able to give it voice, might come out as a wild cry, the cry of a wolf perhaps, or of some great cat, some solitary beast, some animal who is the last of his species, the last one alive on the earth, crying out into the emptiness for his mate.

THIRTEEN

The man entered so quietly he seemed to take form in the dusky foyer like an apparition.

"How is this?" he said very softly, emerging into the light of the room "You do not lock your doors, *comandante?* Many locks, but none of them fastened."

Julio rose from his chair and extended his hand. "I was expecting you, Father."

"Yes. And were you expecting me to be fleeing bullets as I was last time we met? Well, let me embrace you, Azul. It's good to see you again."

The priest, who was taller than he, but skinny, all bone, held him tight and for a long time. The embrace of those in struggle is always tight and warm, always, potentially, the last embrace.

"Thank you for coming to my house."

"Thank you for inviting me."

They sat at the table spread with platters of meat and vegetables and Julio served Geraldo's soup. But everything had a strange quality to it: his own table, his own plates and bowls, this common enough food. Everything seemed more significant: the priest in his house, this meal, the bars on the windows, the mere act of pouring water from a pitcher into a glass. Was this betrayal?

Everything about the meeting spoke of betrayal: the clandestinity of their communication, the care which had to be taken, the secrecy, the threat of scandal if their relationship should be discovered. Furtiveness and stealth, as though there was something intrinsically shameful about this meeting, as though it were a sexual tryst. And all around it a sense of doom, of doubt. He felt that he was standing on the edge of a precipice and someone was urging him to step out, some voice, seductive, whispering, like a lover's voice, telling him to step out, telling him not to be afraid, there was a parachute strapped to his back, he would float to safety if only he would take the step. The voice was so beguiling, he wanted so much to believe it, but his body, his blood, the soles of his feet told him that if he once stepped off solid ground nothing would stop his plunge.

The priest glanced up from his bowl. "You are not joining me in this feast, Julio? Am I to eat all this alone?"

"No," he replied, but he could barely even speak that single word. There was another presence in the room with them now, palpable, standing right beside his chair, holding a hand over his mouth. It was his younger self, a combatant, a Kalashnikov slung over his shoulder, a boy filled with arrogance and bravado, or with courage and hope, he did not now know which. "I wish to confess to you, Father," he said.

It had its effect: bafflement, surprise.

"If it is absolution you desire, there are many other priests."

"You are the only one who can absolve me of this sin. And you are right here."

"That I am here, this much is true. But that I am the only one capable of absolving you, Julio. . . . Perhaps it is not in fact absolution that you require from me."

"Here in this country," he began, because he could not think of any other way to begin, "do you know how we find out about each other? Say you want to know about this one or that one, what do you do? You go and ask your mother. Your grandmother. Uncle, aunt. And soon you know everything: marriages back four, five generations, family tragedies, births, deaths, love affairs, murders, eccentricities of every sort. Then finally, after hours of these stories, someone will say, But remember he took three bullets in León and kept fighting. A brave man. Or, Yes, but remember that bastard cheated his brother of half his land in '62. A thief. And he'll spit in the dirt. OK. That's the end. Judgment has been rendered. This man could be twenty years dead or hale and hearty living three kilometers away, but nevertheless he has been judged. This is how history is recorded among the poor and the bourgeoisie alike. Nothing is forgotten. Everything is weighed. Judgment is rendered.

"But you live and work in Salvador, and you were born in Spain, your family is from Seville, no? So what I know about you

I had to find out a different way. I read your articles, your books. I asked my *compañeros*, tactfully, of course. I listened. But mostly I read your work, because that was most like being in your heart. This last one, last month, filled me with great hope for peace and dialogue in Salvador. It impressed me most because of its unbearable fairness. I say unbearable because I could hardly bear to read it, you took such pains to be just to men who do not know the meaning of the word. Inhumanly just, that is what I learned about you reading that article, Father. That you are a man who is inhumanly just. How else can one explain your ability to commend ARENA, the Salvadoran militarists, even D'Aubuisson himself for their restraint, for their attempt at negotiation, for their permitting a democratic opening in Salvador? How else explain it except to say that you are not like other men, like myself, for example, who cannot forgive, who do not possess the charity even to be able to begin to forgive. But you see glimmers of hope and you are strong enough to acknowledge them. So I know you are a just man, and I know also that you are a brave man. Your kindness I witnessed in Salvador with my own eyes. So I can make this judgment about you: a man worthy of trust. As for myself, up until recently everything in my life has been open to view. I have hidden nothing because I was ashamed of nothing, not my political loyalties, not my sexual desires, nothing. A faggot, but a good revolutionary. If they were to say that about me, well, it's the truth. But now I am about to embark on something that might change that judgment, something that fills me with the gravest doubts. Are you willing to hear this confession, Father?"

"You cannot be absolved of a sin you have not yet committed."

Julio leaned back in his chair. He had still not touched the food on his plate. He had not so much as dipped a spoon into his soup. *So. It begins.*

"Soon it will be the anniversary of Tet. The Frente plans to honor this occasion by launching a full scale offensive in Salvador. There will be a heavy assault on the capital, as well as armed attacks on army garrisons in every department. Nicaragua has made some commitments and will undoubtedly be swept up in this adventure. It may well trigger the North American invasion we have been keeping at bay for so many years. If not in Salvador or Nicaragua, in some other spot on the isthmus. But the Frente has decided that there will be a military victory, that it will occur before Christmas, that it will be victory or death. . . . Now there was a time when it would have taken a very skilled interrogator to get that information out of me and I would have prayed to die before I divulged it. I have just broken every rule by which I have lived my life. And I believe the deliberate breaking of confidence is still a sin."

"And do you repent?"

"Despair of its nature does not allow of repentance."

"Men cannot give each other hope, Julio. But I do not believe you are in despair, nor do I believe it is absolution that you wish from me."

"What I would ask of you is guidance."

"Yes. And you are El Zorro, my friend, binding me to the secret of the confessional and then casting before me the pearls of Nicaraguan intelligence. . . . So the fox comes to the shepherd for guidance. What would they say if they knew you were being advised by the opposition?"

"The center is not the opposition."

"To Vladimir the center is as much the opposition as ARENA itself."

"But I am not Vladimir."

"I know that, Julio. Vladimir would not bother to ask my guidance. Well, my friend, whatever help I can give you is yours."

"This help may take the form of information."

"Of course."

Julio pushed his plate back and pulled an ashtray closer. He didn't take a cigarette from his pack, though. Not yet. He played with the ashtray while he spoke.

"The situation is grim here. We are being pushed into holding elections early next year, pushed from both sides, the Yankees and our Russian friends both, and with equal pressure. Because we are being pushed, we resist. I believe in these elections, but I am becoming more and more a solitary voice. People are suffering in this country, you understand, and they blame us. The economy is in rapid decline, nothing works, not the electricity, not the telephones, not the currency. There is nothing to buy and nothing to buy it with. Perhaps the people are correct to blame us. An unarmed man should not stand in front of a tank. But we stood and bragged to the world about it and now the tank is upon us. The election on one side, this offensive on the other. . . . We can be destroyed by ballots or we can be destroyed by bullets. This is the choice. Unless we re-define the 'we.'"

The priest, who had been sipping soup while Julio spoke, pushed his chair back from the table and lit a cigarette. Julio took one out of his own pack, but only held it between his fingers. The priest held his match out to him, but he shook his head. Not yet.

The priest smoked. Julio waited. He could hear the bones in his body settling, the creaking of the chair as he breathed in and out, the sound his saliva made as he swallowed, his heart thudding and the beat of his pulse. Finally the priest spoke.

"There are caches of weapons buried all over San Salvador. We know, of course, that guns do not fire themselves. So I must ask you, Azul, what you offer in exchange."

Julio lit a match and for a second watched it burn. Then he lit the cigarette. *Now it happens. Right now.*

"Exact dates as soon as I know them. Exact locations. And my word that I will put my body in front of our tanks before I see them cross the border. I will see to it that no arms are shipped to Vladimir. I will throw all my weight, what there is of it, behind this election, and all the terms the Americans set. But I must have your assurance that the center will hold."

"You know, Julio, the real revolution happens in the center. It happens in men's hearts. And they are strong, Julio. They will hold. But I will need another promise from you. It is not enough to hold an election. The only way peace will ever come to our countries is if somewhere there is an example set of a peaceful transition from one governing party to another, smoothly, legally, a change of government without the winners slaughtering the losers or the losers refusing to give up their control. Perhaps the greatest thing the Sandinistas could do for us, for all of us, you understand, is to lose this election and graciously, gallantly, heroically, give up power to the opposition. It would be the most difficult thing. It would take courageous and just men. It would take patriots."

"I would gladly surrender my Ministry to the victors. They are welcome to the hospitals without medicines, the bombed clinics, the amputees, the children still dying of amebic dysentery. They are welcome to all they have wrought, every wound, every orphan, every corpse! I tell you I cannot speak a sentence about those people that does not reek of venom and you ask me to hand the government over to them *gallantly* if the Yankees buy them this election? Father, this is a penance that might better be reserved for the murderers of Christ."

"It was you yourself who said it was necessary to re-define the 'we'."

"I am only one man. I am not one of the Nine. I do not control the army or the police."

"Nor do I control the urban cadres. But I will use my influence, Julio, if I have your word that you will use yours."

"I only wish I knew whether this is a conspiracy born out of hope or out of despair."

"Look, Julio. I want to show you something." The priest searched in his satchel and removed from it a small patch of cloth, a round patchwork of five colors. "This is the *quintuplo*. It is the creation of a collective of cultural workers of the popular movement. One sees it pinned to the shirts of students and workers when they march in the streets. One sees it painted on walls. You notice the colors? Red, black, white and blue around a center of green. What is the significance? Red and black for revolution. Black and white for harmony between races. White and blue for all our national flags. And if you complete the circle around, red, white and blue for those North Americans of goodwill who are struggling with us down here as well as up there. In the center, green. Green for the Maya and green for hope. When you see young people wearing this little *quintuplo* on their shirts, you see intelligence, you see unity, but most of all, you see hope. Here, I will give this one to you. A small gift, Julio. A pledge."

Julio took the scrap of cloth in his hand. He noticed how carefully the pieces were trimmed and sewn, how precisely the five small swatches were fitted together, with someone's patient care. Ten years ago he was holding a rifle in his hand, now he was holding a piece of cloth. What had happened to him? And why was he still incapable of deciding? What was he waiting for?

The priest was waiting, too.

"There are some who will never forgive me for this," Julio said.

"The judgment of men is not the only judgment, Julio."

He looked up from the *quintuplo* to the priest's face, the white skin, blue eyes and chiseled features of a pure bred *peninsular*. A haggard face, yes, but one filled with intelligence. How much he himself would give to believe in that other judgment, how much he would give for the gift of faith. But he was alone on the brink. They were all of them, *peninsular* and mestizo alike, each one of them alone.

"I give you my word," he said.

FOURTEEN

"Silver," Mauricio announced. "Silver, silver and more silver. Where is the golden Flor de Caña and Geraldo? Where is that son of a bitch?"

Julio had been sitting still for so long he had to will his body to move out of the chair. He glanced down at his watch. Twelve-twenty.

"He's in the kitchen. Washing dishes."

"What a good wife! I'll get him and we'll talk in the bedroom."

Julio went into the bedroom and stretched himself out on the bed. A fatal move; he would never be able to get up again. So. Silver. Silver, silver and more silver.

A few minutes later Mauricio and Geraldo came in with cigarettes and a bottle of rum, pulled up chairs, one on each side of Julio's bed. He felt as though he was dying, a doctor on one side of him, a priest on the other. He was completely enervated, listless, as though he had just been drained of several pints of blood.

"Geraldo, how about surveillance from the streets?"

"The house is completely secure."

"Then, Mauricio, let's hear it."

He lay still and listened. Mauricio's report of his evening was detailed: images emerged, pictures clear as photographs, conversations as distinct as recordings. Julio could see the two men approaching Mauricio at the club, announcing themselves by the gold chains around their necks and their designer jeans. Mauricio noticed these things. He could feel Mauricio's apprehension as they tightened their grip on his arms, led him out into the darkness behind the building. He could hear their voices, the one who says, *Listen, faggot, your man Azul is treading on sensitive toes;* the other who gives him a kidney punch that knocks him down and then a kick in the ribs. *What if we teach him a lesson and leave your stinking corpse on his doorstep?* He could hear the third voice too, Mauricio's, begging, promising anything, everything. *He's crazy for me. He'll do anything I ask. And I'll tell you something. I'll tell you his secret. He's skimming money from the European donations to the Ministry. No one oversees what he does. He's been selling medicines on the black market. He needs dollars. You can buy him easily.*

Is this the truth, faggot? Because if it's a lie, if you're lying to us—

No. You'll see. He's getting me a car. He's crazy in love, I'm telling you. Give me a time and place. He'll come.

"Was it so easy then?" Julio sighed, watching the smoke from their cigarettes curl up to the ceiling.

"Except that they practically broke my ribs, yes."

"Get into the tub or you'll be sore tomorrow."

"I'll be sore anyway. When am I getting the car?"

"Anytime. You decide." He got off the bed with some effort of will. "Stand up and let me see you." He pulled up Mauricio's shirt, studied the rising bruises on his side, touched them, fingered the bone.

"You have gentle hands," Mauricio said.

"We've been lovers all these weeks and this is the first you've noticed it?" The smile they exchanged seemed to Julio to acknowledge everything, tension and tenderness and most of all the terrible irony. The smile made the night almost bearable after all.

"Tell me you're proud of me, Julio."

"I am very proud of you. Now into hot water with you!"

"Yes, doctor."

Days and nights passed. Julio sent several messages north. He attended private meetings with the leadership, individually and in groups, planning campaign strategies, always taking the most conciliatory position. Whenever the discussion turned to the Salvadoran situation, he supported total non-intervention. He came home mentally exhausted.

The sports car arrived from Panama, a classic Mercedes SL 190. Mauricio drove it around town, to the Hotel Inter-Continental, where he lounged around the pool, to cafes where he parked it ostentatiously in front so he could watch it being admired and where speculation as to its cost became a central and heated topic of debate.

Julio took to sleeping with a pistol under his pillow and a rifle beside his bed, lying in the dark with ears stretched out like feelers, stretching the length of the block, searching out rooftops and garden walls, his whole body becoming a sensor for sound. And the nights were never quiet, not in Managua. If on any one night any two of them slept, they did knowing the third would be keeping watch.

A Friday night. Mauricio drove the Mercedes to the club. Julio waited at home until eleven and then went out to get him. He knew Mauricio would be dancing. He knew there would be a scene. And it seemed so futile to him, as true as anything in his life: dirty, shameful, futile.

He left his house and drove across the city to the district of distractions.

Managua. It was a city that reminded him of hell. Sometimes he dreamt of the city, always it was a nightmare. His worst experiences had been here, not in the mountains, not even on the Island. Whenever he drove through it, even in daytime, even under blue, sunny skies, even then he felt that he was asleep and dreaming this, this horror from which he could not awaken.

Nightmare repetition: nothing had changed. A revolution later, and nothing had changed. If anything it had gotten worse. The earthquake might have happened yesterday, for all that it had changed. The great empty spaces where buildings had once stood were still empty, fields where a solitary cow or horse might graze, or covered over completely with shacks people had built of cardboard or scraps of wood, the same sort of shacks he had grown up in, the same misery. Along the lakefront there were the same shells of high rises, and the same cathedral, that same roofless skeleton where once he had serviced men he despised. It was all the same, all the same, the same potholes in the streets, the same burnt-out streetlights, the same children begging, the same boys selling themselves in the same places, the same darkness, the same secrets, the same pain.

He drove through nightmare, a city populated by ghosts. He drove blindly until he almost drove past the small club squatting all alone on an otherwise dark street surrounded by a vaster darkness, one of those sprawls of wooden shacks with their lean-to outhouses, their pathetic dirt yards, their barrels of water hauled from the public pump, their scrawny chickens and mangy dogs. . . . But the pulsing lights of the club stopped him and the sound, and the people, men and women, lined up outside to get in. Why a club in this district should have become so popular was one of those mysteries of nightmare he did not wish to fathom.

He had barely turned from locking his car when a man stepped out in front of him, blocking his way. Big, middle-aged, gold chains around his throat. "Looking for your . . . *friend, comandante?* Perhaps it is time for us to talk."

The man tried to take his arm, unsuccessfully. "Where is he?" Julio said, shaking the man's hand away.

"He is inside. Safe. He is simply being observed. Please, let's just stroll a bit and talk, you and I."

"I am going to light a cigarette. I will walk with you for the time it takes me to smoke it. Now what is it you want?"

"It is not so much what we want as what you want, *comandante.*"

"Really? You understand it is a crime in this country to threaten or attempt to bribe a public official?"

"Let's drop the pretense, Azul. You've fucked up with this black faggot of yours. You can't afford him, you can't control him, and you've already screwed around with Ministry funds. That too is a crime in this country, or so I understand. But it's how you discovered Hidalgo and Flores, isn't it? You wanted a little extra on your own and the fools gave you trouble about it? Well, we can take care of you, *comandante*, but you have to play by our rules, understand? It's very simple: you deal with us, or we deal with you."

"What sort of deal do you have in mind?"

"You could be very useful to us. And for the right measure of cooperation, six million per annum, American. You could keep a stable of boys with that, eh? You could get some pretty white boys with clean, tight holes instead of that black slut. . . ." Julio flicked his cigarette into the street and turned around. "That or you're a dead man, Azul."

The only light came from a single street lamp near the club entrance. Even in the semi-darkness, however, Julio sensed the presence of the barrio to his left, the newly burnt grass along its border, the dark shapes of the shacks, the occasional bare bulb shining out to light the rutted pathways. He had grown up in a place like this. It was hard to remember what it was like to know that everything your family owned in the world could fit into a few coffee sacks. He knew that eyes would be watching them from those hovels. If he lived in such a place, if he were a boy again living in such a place, this club would be his Mecca, his one chance to make his way out.

"What do I have to do for this six million dollars?"

"Now you're making sense, *comandante*. I knew you'd come around."

"I haven't come around anywhere yet. What do I have to do?"

"Nothing at all. We do everything. You simply give us the space."

"Be more specific."

"Our needs are very simple. Occasionally we need to transport through Nicaragua into Honduras and El Salvador to the North American bases. We will require transport clearance, papers, and a few key people will need to be persuaded to look the other way."

"That sounds like Interior work."

"You have friends in Interior, *comandante*."

"Have I?"

"Our sources say yes. There is enough money, you understand. Money is never a problem among us. Anything you want or need, we get for you. We become partners, *compañeros*, yes? Share and share alike."

"That appeals to me."

"Of course it does. Look at us as you would a great redistribution program, *comandante*. We redistribute wealth. The North Americans' excess returns to us. They stole it, we acquire it back. We share it. We are keeping farmers alive and flourishing all over Latin America. We are financing businesses. We are better than the Alliance for Progress."

"So, my friend, what do I call you?"

"Raul."

"OK, Raul, when and with whom do I negotiate this agreement? I assume you will want something a bit more formal that this?"

"Indeed. Tomorrow night. Someone will telephone you at home."

"I need dollars, you understand."

"Everyone in this country needs dollars, *comandante*. Of course I understand. Would ten thousand cash be too conspicuous?"

"I have friends and there are certain things I need and can obtain readily with dollars. Five hundred thousand in cash. The rest in gold. You can arrange that?"

"Five and a half million in gold by tomorrow night? I don't think so. Let's say . . . one million, half in gold, half in dollars."

"Let's say one million in gold, and another half million in dollars. I think I am being reasonable. You've certainly had time to make your arrangements."

"You strike a hard bargain. Very well. Let's consider this million and a half the first of four quarterly payments of one and a half million each."

"And all further payments rendered in gold, correct?"

"Correct. In return you sign an agreement with us and deliver to us a dozen blank security clearance passes. You can arrange that?"

"Yes. Don't call my house before nine. I won't be there."

"All right."

"And don't fuck with me, Raul. I have friends."

"I understand, *comandante*. We all have friends."

"Good. Now I want Mauricio. Go in and get him for me. Let's see how good you really are at getting me what I want."

He waited by his car and smoked another cigarette.

Mauricio emerged looking loose and drunk, leaning against Raul whose arm was around his waist. Julio stepped up to him and slapped his face hard. "You piece of shit," he said. "Get in the fucking car." Then he turned to Raul. "Tomorrow," he said.

"Tomorow, *comandante*," Raul said, smirking. Julio suppressed the urge to break his neck.

"**J**esus, did you have to hit me so hard?"

"It was either you or him. That bastard insulted me beyond endurance. Next time I see him he's dead. I'll kill him if it's the last thing I do."

"Insulted you? Julio, I don't think you understand the honor you have been accorded. Do you know who that was? That was Adolpho Escobar, the little czarovitch himself. And he put his stinking hand on my ass, the pigfucker. You're not going to kill him. I've got first dibs. . . . How much?"

"Half a million dollars. And a million in gold. Down payment on six million."

"You could finance a small war."

"A very small war. They pay hundreds of U.S. Customs men a million a year each for similar concessions. I should have had my mother with me. She'd have gotten me a better deal. She's worked in the markets all her life."

"How does it feel, playing with fire?"

"You're playing with it too."

"I am insignificant."

"Listen, Mauricio, you ought to know me well enough by now not to try to shove crap down my throat. Your life is worth at least as much as mine. There is nothing insignificant about you, and you damn well know it, so spare me this line of shit, OK? Just don't think you're going to make any stupid sacrifices tomorrow night. You want to be a hero, be a hero over there, not here. We have enough fucking heroes of our own. . . . Well, I don't suppose they'll bother storming the house tonight. Maybe we can get some sleep."

Mauricio didn't reply. Julio couldn't tell if his words had pleased or offended him. And he was too tired to care.

He did not sleep well that night; he did not expect to. He went over everything in his mind again and again: what he would do in the morning, and what in the afternoon; what he would do at night; what could happen to fuck it up; what he would do then, what Mauricio would do; how it could end. So many variables. But in any case there was the morning and the afternoon. He had a meeting in Estelí, a clinic to visit in the mountains, a small pilgrimage to make. So if it ended for him before the next day's dawn, it ended, but he would at least have said goodbye.

When you are in combat, death becomes a side-kick, a buddy; you expect to see him, you get used to his sour breath. But during a time of peace you become estranged. He's like a relative who belches and farts during meals; you'd rather not invite him, you'd rather forget he exists.

He thought about that the next morning while he was being driven to Estelí in a big, comfortable, government-owned Mercedes, a jeep of soldiers behind, a jeep in front. How soft he'd become, even his body was becoming soft. By contrast, how hard Patrice's body had been. The bodies of combatants harden but their hearts get softer. They get sentimental, write love poems, weep over letters from home. He had kept the sentimentality but lost the strength. Old warriors can still weep long after they've lost the power to fire a gun.

Had he lost the power? Had Cuba broken him when even the Guardia could not? Had he kept his sense of honor and pride through years of whoring and street hustling, kept it through

125

ambush and air raid and battle and bullets and surgery with nothing for pain but a shot of rum and a stick to grind between his teeth, kept it through poverty and revolution only to lose it on the streets of Havana?

The streets were like a drug, a poison. You took it in because you had to, but in terror. Every step was terror, every movement, every look. You could so easily betray yourself, so easily be betrayed. Sixty thousand men confined to work camps, to prison. Getting the degenerate elements off the streets. The parasites. The faggots and the queers. And the places to meet, the places you were driven to, driven by your very nature, there, too, nothing but suspicion and terror. State Security infiltrated the underground in drag. Kiss and tell.

As Mauricio said, We *Cubanos* are the best. At everything.

Watch what you say, the faggots warned him, the queens defiant in their lipstick, the daring boys who wore tight jeans and let their hair grow just that bit too long. Watch how you dress, how you walk. Watch how you speak, watch where you look. Especially where you look. They watch your eyes.

You must have a girlfriend in Cuba, they told him, kissing him in the leafy darkness of that park that was itself watched, raided, infiltrated, penetrated, but where else could they go? You must eye the women, they whispered to him, dance with them, very close. You must be seen kissing them on benches, under the trees, in the shadows of your street. Otherwise someone will report you. There are rewards for reporting degenerates.

Sixty thousand homosexuals confined in prisons. Because it was a crime against nature and the state. Because it embarrassed the revolution to have queers roaming free on the streets of Havana. Because Fidel hated faggots as much as he hated imperialists. Maybe he hated them even more.

He was a hero of the revolution, yet he was not trusted in Cuba. A hero maybe, but of the *Nicaraguan* revolution. The whole Island was a sort of prison, or a fortress under siege. Anyone from outside was suspect. But of all *Cubanos*, the ones who had most reason to fear him were the only ones who took him into their trust. Into their mouths, into their bodies, into their hearts. Knelt before him burning with desire, hero or no, revolutionary or no, *Cubano* or no, what did it matter? He was a man. That was enough.

And it was enough to punish them. Enough to imprison them. And then SIDA came, and then forced testing, and then quarantine. Finally Fidel was given an excuse to do what he had always done without excuse. Finally he was justified. By nature and by nature's God.

You are like this country, his last lover but one had said to him. *Very small, very poor. Beautiful, yes, in places. But your heart is not one of those places, Julio. It is not a green mountain, a fertile valley. No, your heart is the black earth and the volcano. Your heart is Momotombo. I cannot touch it.*

And after that one, Patrice, who now appeared to him like La Siguanaba, the beauty who turns into a hag, who leaves men who gaze on her face paralyzed, impotent, mad. Did he think a letter would bring him back? Was he such a fool?

There was a poem Patrice had recited for him. By a dead Salvadoran *guerrillero*. Patrice, of course, remembered it all; he himself had only bits of it left. *I'm nobody's friend.* That's how it started. *And I'm not a poet. I don't give a damn if nobody remembers me. I carry myself to San Salvador in my pocket.* (Patrice had loved that line.) *And talk to people who don't know each other and don't know me. I don't care if a door slams in Nicaragua, if a girl declares her love in Santiago, if a dove flies over the Yang-tse. It doesn't bother me. I'm empty, as alone as a winter overcoat.*

Lying in bed in Patrice's arms, tranquil, satisfied, he had let the lines wash over him, as though they were words without meaning. But now this one came back to him. Now he heard Patrice's voice saying the poem to him. It was Patrice himself speaking to him. It was about Patrice's life and it was about his own. It was not only about the life of a *guerrillero*. It was about the lives of queers and faggots and degenerates. It was about men whose hearts were like scorched black earth, like dead mountains, like soil that cannot give or nourish life. *I'm nobody's friend and I'm not a poet. I don't give a damn if nobody remembers me.*

I'm empty, Patrice. Alone as a winter overcoat. And you, where are you today? Will she know where you are? And if I ask, will she tell me? But will I ask her, Patrice? Why in God's name would I want to know?

Ileana was waiting for him in her garden. He hesitated in the gateway, not wishing to disturb her, wanting to take in this picture: the bright red hibiscus in full flower, the deep purple blossoms of the bougainvillea draping down along the wall, the dark woman in white sitting with a book in her hand, the dappled light on the tiles, the cat stretched out asleep in a patch of shade. Tranquillity.

She looked up, surprised. "Julio!" She rose with outstretched arms but there was concern on her face. "Come and sit down. Have you been ill?"

"No. Do I appear ill?"

She held him in her arms. "Your face is all eyes and your body is all bones. You've lost weight since I saw you last."

"Ah, perhaps I have. But I am well enough, and I can't stay long, Ileana. I'm sorry."

"Which means you want no inquiries about your life or your health, no lunch and no dilly-dallying, correct? Very well, *compañero*, let's get down to business."

"The business is as unpleasant as ever, I'm afraid."

"Economic, military or political?"

"The national plebiscite. The final vote of confidence."

"Do I detect a decrease in enthusiasm in you since we spoke of this last?"

"It is indicative of my state of mind. Well, we are caught in a rip tide now and there's no way back to shore unless we first allow the current to carry us all the way out. Ileana, I have come to ask something of you I have no right to ask, but must."

He took the chair she gestured to, though he would have preferred to stand. To pace and smoke and talk to her as though he were talking to himself. If it were only like battle—you point the SA-14 into the sky, the aircraft comes into range, you fire, hit or miss, live or die, all over in minutes. In politics nothing happened in minutes, everything was stretched out like a slow interrogation, stretched out for so long you forgot what the goal was, you were so bruised, so broken and battered, so starved, so hurt, you couldn't even remember what the question was whose answer you were slowly dying to protect.

"This mobilization of the Frente, Ileana. It poses a grave threat to us here. You know there are two tendencies among us, and the militant tendency has always encouraged Vladimir. But there has been a shift, toward reconciliation, toward compromise, if you will. The Accords . . . they bind us now and we will abide by them. So I must appeal to you to use your influence with your husband on our behalf. An offensive in Salvador at this time is in no one's best interest. Let's continue to negotiate. All of us, in good faith. Because once the Americans take it into their heads to invade us, Ileana, we will never see peace come again in our lifetimes."

She sat in her chair with her eyes closed. He felt as though he was appealing to one of those gods carved into stone at Palenque, at Copán, the ones you look upon without being able to tell whether their spirit is one of peace or of war.

"Negotiation and reconciliation. I have heard those words before. I have heard them for ten years. You are clutching at a very small hope, Julio. My husband has seen that hope die many times. You cannot blame him from learning the lessons of history. And do you know what that lesson is? The strong never bend to the will of the weak. Why should they? Only when there is no stronger, no weaker, when both are equal, Julio, only then will you have a negotiated peace, not before. So, one puts one's hope not in empty words and empty promises, but in arms, in strength, in the struggle if not for ascendancy, at least for parity. That is what this is, Julio. It is a means of checking on the balance of power, to see if the scales have tipped."

"And what if this exercise in weights and measures tips the scales in Nicaragua? What if because of this little exercise of his, we lose everything? Then where will he look for succor, Ileana? Where will he come to lick his wounds? Where will he send his paraplegics and his amputees and his saboteurs going through confinement and the children whose parents were slaughtered in front of them and have been driven mad by grief? Where will he come for money when he's broke, for bullets when he's out of shells, for intelligence when he finds his own people no longer know if the ill wind is blowing from the north or the east? Where will he hide his wife and children, Ileana, when we are gone?"

"It's too late, Julio. Even if I were willing to support your position, the die has been cast. The first piece has been played. The commando has been sent."

"What commando are you referring to?"

"That one who took your fancy in July, remember? The gringo. Patrice."

His body took in this news: he felt it in the dilation of his pupils, the rush of blood to his fingertips, he felt it in his sex. But he kept his voice completely even.

"Ah, yes. And he is going to assassinate another general, I suppose. That will bring Salvador to its knees no doubt."

"Not at all. He is not going into Salvador. Now I will tell you something even your intelligence cadre does not already know. Whatever it is, it is happening in Honduras. This is bigger than you imagine. And it cannot be stopped."

"Vladimir is operating commandos in Honduras now? Without consultation with us? Without even our knowledge?" Anger came as a great relief, like a purgative, cleansing him. "Our allies desert us, our friends deceive us, next the people will betray us. This is not the world I want to live in, Ileana."

"I am afraid there is no other."

"And I suppose Patrice is beyond recall?"

"Only Vladimir could find him now. But don't despair of victory yet, Julio. Nothing is written in stone."

No, he thought grimly. Only the names on graves.

The name of his friend was written in stone, not on his grave, but on the boulder beside the stream where he died. Of course Stephen would have objected to his friends laboring at carving his name into the stone. *But it was a labor of love, Stephen. It was a way for them to mourn you. It was all they had to give you, my friend. Their labor is all they have.*

It always seemed like a sort of pilgrimage, the journey up here from Managua. Traveling deeper and deeper into the countryside, the roads getting progressively narrower until they turned into dirt tracks, and then arriving at the spot and being struck again by the contrast between the absolute peacefulness of the spot and the murder that had occurred here. It served to remind him that places open only temporarily to make room for lives, and close up again afterwards, like the ripples that first spread across and then vanish from the surface of a pond. It was always consoling to him to think that he was merely passing across these landscapes, geographic, historical, political, just passing across them like a ripple across a pond.

And then too the place brought him back to himself, to the doctor inside him, buried deep down under the veneers of politician, administrator, party member, combatant, back to face a self-image he had found here, one that Stephen had nurtured in him, and made honorable in his eyes. A country doctor, with nothing more than his training, his medical bag, and gentle hands. With Stephen he had delivered babies and set broken bones here. Together they had chosen this site for a rural clinic and together they had brought it to light, given birth to it like fathers of the same son. But he had been called back to Managua, to a position in the Ministry, and thereafter he practiced medicine by proxy, by way of Stephen's letters and by way of dreams. He used to dream of birthings, of holding tiny, slippery, big-eyed babies in his hands. It had been years now since he had delivered a child. He half suspected he had forgotten how.

Stephen had been his friend, not his lover. He had never in his life had both together in one man, never once a lover who was also a friend. Some equality, some mutual respect, something to share besides the body alone, some mating of the soul. . .never, except those few days with Patrice. In Patrice he had seen a promise of something, and he had let himself hope. His hope had been like the tiny center of green in the *quintuplo*. So the fact that Patrice would choose the struggle over personal happiness, that he would turn his back on personal happiness like Stephen had, like he himself had, like all his friends had, the honorable ones, the ones who would rather die than surrender . . . isn't that exactly what he would expect of someone he would call friend? Why then was Ileana's news breaking his heart?

He never replied.

No, Julio. He is a *guerrillero*. He's nobody's friend. He carries himself in his pocket. He doesn't need anyone or want anyone. He's empty, Julio. Don't love him. Don't even try.

He stayed by Stephen's stream for a short while and then drove into Santo Tomás to visit the clinic. He had brought medicines with him, like a black marketeer with his car trunk filled with vitamins and antibiotics, surgical kits and morphine. They needed morphine more than anything. They weren't doing simple rural medicine in Santo Tomás. They were living inside a war zone.

He stayed only one hour at the clinic before heading back to the capital. People came to speak to him and he listened to them for as long as he could. He saw precisely what he feared he would see: a group of people suffering from a weariness of soul, or in more clinical terms, from grief and the anger that accompanies it, or from more overt symptoms of anxiety and depression.

He talked and he listened, but at the end of an hour they told him very politely that it was time for him to leave. Otherwise it would be dark before he was out of the district and it was dangerous to travel after dark because of the possibility of ambush or mines set in the roads.

He rode back to Managua thinking that perhaps a government that was unable to protect its own people from being murdered by mercenaries of a foreign power on their own district roads had no business being in power.

And perhaps in a few months' time that would be exactly what the people would decide.

FIFTEEN

The two cars pulled into the parking lot beside the single-story, turquoise-washed hotel off the airport road. It was in one of those lakefront areas completely flattened by the earthquake, overgrown foundations and open fields all around it, except directly across the highway where a shanty-town had sprung up, and fanned outward away from the lake.

Two taxis were waiting there. Men got out of one of them and approached Julio's car.

"Get into the second cab," one of the men said. "You two and two of your men."

"We agreed on six. Six bodyguards on each side. That was the agreement."

"Six? Armed? Who agreed to that?"

"Your boss. Escobar. And it's six men or nothing." The man hesitated. "Look, my friend," Julio said, "I don't go to the shitter without two bodyguards. You think I'm going with you to meet Adolpho Escobar with less than six then you're crazy. Start the car, Mauricio."

"No. Wait. All right. Get into the taxis. It's going to be tight."

"A few will have to ride with you then," Julio said. He got out on one side, Mauricio got out on the other. He locked the doors. "Not that it will do much good around here."

"There will be someone keeping an eye on it, don't worry," the man said. "Come on. Let's go."

They drove for sometime, past the airport and into the country-side. It was very dark. Another twenty klicks and they took a sharp right off the highway onto dirt. Soon Julio saw headlights ahead and the taxi slowed and then stopped. They were going to exchange goods by the light of highbeams, like in an old gangster movie. A very imaginative bunch.

133

"Rules, *comandante*. You and your boyfriend get out and walk up there to Escobar. Your men stay here."

"No. My men are no fucking good to me back here. They come and stand with me, those are my rules. And it's by my rules or not at all."

"I'll talk to him."

"No. We all go up together. No fucking around. I want my gold and your boss wants what I have in my pocket. Now you don't want to annoy either one of us, do you?"

He didn't wait for a reply. He opened the car door and stepped out into the country night, dense with the sounds of cricket and frog, sweet smelling, star studded. Other doors opened, other men got out; they moved toward the lights.

There were a good dozen men standing around Adolpho Escobar. One set of headlights belonged to a dark van which Julio would drive back to the city. In it were the crates of gold bars, a million dollars in gold.

"Welcome, *comandante*," Escobar said. "I see you've brought a good size entourage. The beginnings of a private army, perhaps?"

"I can fancy myself a *caudillo* if I choose, Escobar."

"Of course. I see 'Raul' did not fool you for long."

"Nobody fools me for long. Where is the gold?"

Escobar gestured toward the van. "Want to inspect?"

Julio nodded to two of his men who followed one of Escobar's into the van.

"And the cash?"

"Right here, *comandante*." Another gesture brought a suitcase into the light. Mauricio took it and opened it. "Does your little boy know what half a million dollars looks like?"

"He does now. Put it in the van, Mauricio, and get in yourself. Is it all there, Geraldo?"

"Yes, *comandante*," Geraldo said, stepping out of the van. "All of it is there."

"Good. And now I suppose you want me to sign something in blood?"

"Ink will do. Our receipts are rather simple documents."

Julio took the clipboard and the pen offered to him and signed his name.

"We have photographed this encounter, so there is always other documentation."

"Of course."

"And now you have security clearance papers for us?"

This was the moment now and Julio wanted to savor it. Savor it for its perfection, yes; also for the fact that it could be one of his last. His senses were attuned to every leaf stirring, to the placement of every stone. Mauricio, sitting sideways in the driver's seat of the van, draped somewhat over the wheel, a bit behind Escobar's left flank, but, of course, he was only Julio's boy. Geraldo and his partner directly to Escobar's left. He in front; the remaining four in position behind. Then Escobar's own dozen, thirteen in all, pistols tucked in their belts, M-16's on their shoulders.

Julio said, "Better than security papers, Escobar. I have Security itself."

Quick, smooth, clean, six rifles and a pistol, drawn and aimed. Precision work, accomplished before Escobar knew what was happening. One of his men fumbled; Geraldo fired. Simultaneously Mauricio moved like a cat and fired his pistol, not at the fumbler but at his chief, Escobar, whose fall was finally a simple return for the insult of stroking the wrong man's ass.

"Drop weapons or you're all dead," Mauricio shouted, and weapons fell. Sixty seconds; it was over.

One of the Security men called in for assistance. By the time a van and a medical unit arrived, Julio had already seen to the fallen men. Both of them were dead.

"Two less assholes in the world," Paco Ruiz said, shrugging. He had come in with the back-up, was standing around kicking the dirt while his people dealt with the eleven survivors. He'd have been just as happy if the proportion of prisoners to stiffs had been reversed.

Julio gestured Mauricio over from the step of the van where he was sitting, smoking. He came, flicking the cigarette away. His gait was different, more upright, more correct, now that he no longer had to pretend to be something he was not.

"Paco, I'd like to present my friend, whom you may have heard me refer to as Mauricio, but whose name in fact is Capitán Alberto Rodriguez, Special Division, Cuban Ministry of Interior."

He lit a cigarette and watched these two shake hands. He watched them closely, trying to imagine how they might weigh each other, the Nicaraguan and his Cuban counterpart, the one who had just scored a major victory, the other on whose territory the victory had been scored. Paco had played hard ball himself; Julio doubted it was the Cubans' idea to have Alberto Rodriguez play the role of *maricón* for two months before the game even got off the ground. But Alberto had settled the score, redeemed his manhood, shot the pig who had taken such liberties with his ass.

As for the damage to his own reputation, what did it matter? Certain things he'd live down and certain things he wouldn't. They could go to the press, of course, reveal Alberto's true identity, let the people think Nicaraguan Interior couldn't even deal with its own problems. . . . No, he didn't think such a revelation was necessary at this time in their history. Better people should think Julio Ibarra Cruz had made a fool out of himself for a boy than that the government couldn't handle its own affairs without bringing in help from the Island. Paco could get all the credit, Alberto could get a medal in secret, and he himself, maybe he could start getting some sleep.

Not that it was likely. The future reared up before him like a book whose pages he could read. His heart felt tight and hard inside him, and his mind ached like Cassandra's must have, for like her he could see into the future but had no power to stop what he saw from happening.

The Greeks claimed that suffering made men wise. What they neglected to mention was the irony that wisdom only made men suffer more.

He got into his car, but he didn't drive it home. It was past midnight. He drove to the precincts of the cathedral, parked down by the lake, and walked up to the cathedral square. There was the monument to Carlos Fonseca with its eternal flame and the little gazebo, one of his best pick-up places when he was working this square, and the little pond with the alligator they used to torture. The cathedral itself was cordoned off, not that the cordon kept anyone out, but he didn't really want to go in. He walked around the building instead and listened to the night. The place seemed deserted, it always did this time of night, but underneath the quiet he could detect activity.

He walked a bit into the stubble and burnt grasses behind the shell of that once magnificent church. Someone emerged from the shadows and fell into step beside him. A boy, ragged, skinny. There was the usual exchange of words. A small sum was mentioned. A million and a half in gold and dollars had passed through his hands an hour before. The boy wanted a few thousand *córdobas*, about fifty cents.

This was the way his life had started. This was the way it would end. All that had changed was that he was the buyer now, but buyer, seller, what difference did it make? It was the exchange itself, the time, the place, the feel of it, forbidden and exciting, furtive, dangerous . . . and squalid and shameful and empty. It was the emptiness of it, empty place, empty time, empty act. This was his life. He saw it there on the littoral of Lake Managua in the midst of burnt and burning grasses, and it was a revelation to him: dead, poisoned lake, dead, poisoned city, and his own dead, poisoned life, the desolation of it, thirty years of desolation. No matter what he had ever done or ever would do, this was the essence of him. Sodomites running forever across burning sands—Dante's vision of hell and his own.

The boy was waiting for his answer. And then, humbly, "Is it too much? I could do it for less."

"No," he said, "It's not too much."

And he thought, You don't know it, but you are an angel sent to me. You are the only joy there is.

He had come full circle. He had become one of those men he had once despised.

137

Days of the Dead

November and December 1989

SIXTEEN

Tegucigalpa, Honduras

He sat in the hotel bar smoking, nursing a beer, watching assorted members of the United States Army pick up women. Except for the specific Central American touches, the cowhides on the seat cushions and on the walls, the sound of running water from the fountain on the patio, the Indian features buried beneath layers of powder and rouge, except for those things the bar could be in any American-occupied zone on any continent where GI's could afford to buy native women and native women had no choice but to be bought.

He watched, detached but attentive. They were very young, these GI's. Young, more of them black than white, all of them, like himself, the size of giants compared to the women, twice their size, three times their weight. The strong have a natural right to tyrannize over the weak. A powerful argument, one brilliantly articulated by the Marquis de Sade.

He was just trying to occupy his mind with trivia. He'd already read the newspaper. Twice.

Except for the bartenders there were no local men to be seen. A few North American civilians like himself, yes. But this was the American sector of Goose City and this was a GI pick-up bar. The women were here for one reason only; no self-respecting Honduran man would show his face here unless he had a plastic explosive on him.

He ordered another beer. One of the girls took it from the waitress's tray and brought it over to him. She was wearing a yellow stretch tank top and a skin-tight mini-skirt of imitation leather. Her hair was beautiful, though, dark brown, long and thick, and her face was Indian, with that Asian cast to the eyes, those high cheekbones. She slid onto the leather cushion beside him and placed the glass of beer on the table in front of him.

"A cigarette, please, sir," she said in English. No one spoke Spanish here. This was the American sector.

He shook one from his pack and offered it to her along with a light. "Can I buy you a drink?"

"Please. A beer would be very nice."

He nodded to the waitress and ordered another. The girl moved closer to him so her thigh pressed against his. She was wearing a sweet perfume, bright red lipstick, bright pink nail polish. Her yellow tank top was stretched tight over her breasts, gathered between them so their contours were revealed, even the nipples, waiting to be sucked. All this for the asking and a few dollars. He might not even have to ask.

"What's your name?" He asked that much.

She put her arm around his neck and her mouth very close to his ear. "Victoria," she whispered. Her mouth was almost touching his ear. It made him smile.

"Mine is Edward. Edward Stillwell."

"You are a tourist?"

"More or less."

"Is there anything you wish to see? Perhaps I could show you." She smiled up at him. The waitress put another beer on the table. He asked for a check.

"I don't know if I can afford a private guide. But there are some places I haven't been to yet."

"I am sure I am familiar with those places."

"I'm sure you are," he said.

As they left she slipped her arm around him and pressed her body against his. Even in high heels she was the size of a child beside him, a girl-child. The GI's watched them walk out together. One less whore in the bar, but there were plenty more where she came from.

She gave the cabbie directions. They wove their way in a zig-zag through the hilly American sector, past the American Embassy, the National Museum, the Presidential Palace and across the Choluteca into Comayaguela. The barrios here were the worst he had ever seen, a whole city of homeless people living in cardboard boxes on top of garbage dumps. Several times the taxi nearly got bogged down in mud. Children stared out at the car from half-built shacks, children who had the look of the chronically malnourished.

"Are we nearly there?" he asked. She nodded. Meanwhile the evening gathered into twilight, half the sky still lit, but the darkness moving in, too swiftly, catching him unaware.

Her house was not in these slums. They came around again back toward the river and stopped in front of a small stucco house with a heavily barred entrance.

"Why the grand tour?" he asked her.

"I wanted you to see it all."

"Thanks so much."

Inside the garrison door there was a small courtyard filled with flowers, a sanctuary. In Goose City people barricaded beauty in, imprisoned it behind walls like dragons imprisoned virgins and gold. Everything about this city sickened him. It was the worst place he had ever been. It was not a place in which he wanted to die.

"Would you like to see your room? Come with me."

She led him across the courtyard to a corridor and a steep staircase. Upstairs there was a bedroom, very small, with a tiny barred window that looked north to Mount El Picacho. But he only glanced at the view. He kept his eyes on the woman. She went to the desk and opened the top drawer, took out a brown cardboard box, offered it to him. Inside, beneath rumpled newspaper, was an S and W 469.

"I also have final instructions for you, Eduardo."

"Good."

"Would you like a drink?"

"Please."

"It is tomorrow."

"Yes. Rum and coke if you have it."

"You will stay here tonight." She slipped her arms around him and held him. "You will stay here with me, OK?"

"Are those orders?"

"Yes."

He put the box and the gun down on the desk and took her in his arms. She was so small, only a girl. Everything he had refused himself for four years came rushing back to him, desires rushing through him like a drug. The strong have the natural right to tyrannize over the weak. He had the natural right, his body gave it to him, he had it by right of birth. It was time to assert his genetic rights: he could hear Alejandro laughing inside his head, in that beautiful place inside his mind where they still laughed together and held each other in the night. *If I may quote the Marquis de Sade....*

"Victoria," he said, "didn't they warn you about me? I don't take orders well."

"Then let's say it is a request."

"Let's say we'll see what happens."

She smiled up at him. "Very well then, *compañero*. There is a shower through that door and clothes in the closet. Try on the suit to be sure it fits. I will bring the rum for you now."

"And the papers?"

"I have everything. Don't worry."

He sat down on the bed. From there all he could see out the window was the very summit of El Picacho and a slice of midnight blue sky where Venus herself was rising through the space between the bars.

When she returned she was wearing a simple white cotton shift embroidered with the deep purple, blue and green geometric designs of the weavers of Zunil, a highland village just outside the city of Xela, which the Spanish named Quetzaltenango. She had removed all her make-up, even the garish pink nail polish had disappeared. She could have been the sister of those women who made him meals and sewed his clothing and cared for him when he was ill, but whom he could never touch because they were also the wives, sisters or daughters of his friends. He might have chosen one of those women for himself, but he could have promised her nothing. This woman understood that he had nothing, nothing at all, not even another night.

She took him downstairs where a table was set under the verandah at the edge of the courtyard, where they ate and drank by candlelight, where they went over the plan again, though he knew it already by rote. The next day was the Day of the Dead. There would be a ceremony in the old cemetery. A film crew would be present, North Americans. Also local TV. It would be a media event.

"Security will be discreet," she said.

"I don't think discretion will stop them."

"There will be too many people in the way. Too many North Americans. Too many journalists. If you surrender, they will not shoot you."

He smiled and lit a cigarette. "The meal was very good. Thank you. Now all we need is a good movie. *Casablanca* would be nice. I'd like to spend the rest of the evening on a different continent in a different war."

"I'm afraid the TV isn't working. I'm sorry."

"That's all right. Tell me something. The women in that bar, are many of them involved in the struggle here?"

"No. Most of them are supporting their families. Only a few of us are part of the cadre."

"Do you find it difficult?"

"Do you find what you do difficult?"

"Very difficult, yes. And I was once sent on a mission which required I do work similar to yours, and I found it extremely difficult."

"It is not the act that matters, but the intention behind the act."

"Sounds like Peter Abelard."

145

"Yes? Who is that?"

"A twelfth-century philosopher. He said the same thing you did. The act is not good or bad in itself, only the intention matters. It was declared a heresy."

"The Church doesn't think too highly of us either."

"True. Abelard was a fascinating man. He was a logician and a poet. He wrote one of the most beautiful poems I've ever heard. It's called 'David's Lament for Jonathan.' He had a very public and passionate affair with one of his students and she had his child. Then her uncle had Abelard castrated. A lovely little tale, isn't it?"

"Men do not change much. Tell me this poem you say is so beautiful."

"I know it in English. I'm not so sure I can do it justice in an instantaneous Spanish translation. But we'll see." He heard the poem in his mind, translated it as best he could, the first few lines anyway: *Low in thy grave with thee, happy to lie. Since there is no greater thing left love to do, and to live after thee is but to die, for with half a soul what can life do? So share thy victory or else thy grave. . . .* "I've forgotten the rest," he said.

A breeze came in from the courtyard, cool, rain-laden. Of course he hadn't forgotten the rest. He hadn't forgotten anything. It wouldn't be the same grave, but it would be the same sort of death.

"You feel quite prepared, Eduardo? There is nothing else you need?"

"No. Nothing."

"The pistol is satisfactory? You have checked it?"

"As well as I can without shooting it, yes."

"I range tested it myself. It is in perfect operating condition."

"Then we're in business," he said.

He sighed and glanced at his watch. This was the worst part, getting through the night. At least there was the courtyard. He could sit outside, find his spot, align himself with the four directions, watch the moon, count the stars.

"It is getting late," she said. "Do you want to go to bed now?"

"I'm not tired."

"You don't have to be tired," she said, smiling at him.

"Listen, Victoria. I'm very grateful to you, but. . . ."

"But what?"

"I don't want you to feel obliged. . . ."

"It would wound your pride if I were obliged? Are you such a romantic?"

"I suppose so, yes."

"Listen yourself, Eduardo. We are two people in the same struggle and tomorrow you are going to do something that is very dangerous and may have certain unpleasant consequences, you understand? And so tonight you are going to live with me and enjoy yourself and it will make me happy to give you pleasure. It is like this meal I prepared for you. Now did you look at this meal and say, I am very sorry, Victoria, but I can't eat it because I feel you are acting under an obligation to feed me and I don't want you to feel obliged—"

He laughed. "I don't believe it is exactly an analogous situation, but I am not going to argue logic with you."

She stood up and he went over to her. He felt power, but it wasn't tyranny. He felt strong, but it was a good strength, or anyway he intended it to be a good strength. He bent over her and kissed her throat. Her arms around him felt like a child's arms, her body also, light, frail. Like a child, but she wasn't a child, he wasn't raping a child. He felt such fear, though. As though what he was about to do was wrong, as though it were forbidden, taboo.

He hadn't been with a woman in so long he could hardly remember. How long . . . before Alejandro. Ten years was it? Ten years since he'd been with a woman, six of those years because he'd made his choice and didn't regret it, and four because he didn't have a choice, and now it was already a third of his life and he could barely remember, as though it had happened in a dream, as though he were still a virgin, he would do everything wrong, be too brutal or clumsy or quick, or maybe he wouldn't be able to get it up at all, maybe once you chose, you chose forever, maybe he was gay now, a homosexual, irrevocably, no turning back.

"Eduardo," she whispered.

"Call me by my real name."

147

"I am not supposed to know your real name. In case I am captured, it is best that I don't know."

Yes, he thought, but after tomorrow my name won't matter to anyone.

"If we are going to make love, you are going to have to call me by my name."

"Are we going to make love, Eduardo?"

He took her face between his hands, stopped thinking, let his body take over for him. All he said was, "My name is Patrice."

They climbed the stairs to the bedroom carrying candles. She laughed at him, he laughed at himself, but he wanted romance and he was willing to stoop to candlelight to have it.

In the bedroom he searched his jacket pocket.

"What are you doing?" she asked him.

He smiled at her. "It's funny. I just bought these this morning. I figured no good CIA agent should be caught without condoms in his pocket."

"You have children, Patrice?"

"Regrettably, no."

She slipped her dress over her head. Under it she was naked, smooth, copper skin dappled by candlelight. He felt stunned, looking at her. He had forgotten the beauty of a woman's body, so different from the beauty of a man's. He had forgotten and now he just wanted to look at her and remember. He wanted everything to be slow, he wanted the night to last, every moment of it to stretch out into eternity.

"Give them to me," she said. He turned the package of condoms over to her since she was clearly experienced at this, and began undressing. There was a cool breeze that caressed each part of him as he exposed it to the air. He felt his body as body, warm, alive, strong. He felt a certain pity for it, a certain regret, and then he saw her at the window, the tiny window with its bars, and he watched the condoms in her hand disappear through the bars into the night.

"You are going into battle tomorrow," she said. "Tonight we don't use those things. If you give me a child, I will be proud to bear it, Patrice, and I don't want to hear any arguments."

"But you don't even know me," he said.

"I know you. I am Maya. My family are refugees from Atitlan. We know who you are, Patrice. We know, but also *they* know. If once they learn your name—"

"They will never learn it," he said. "Come here."

Out in the courtyard where they drank their morning coffee there were birds singing. The sound of their song was sweet, as sweet as the coffee he was drinking, as sweet as the night had been, as sweet as his body felt right now, tuned in, receptive, content. They sat beside each other and listened to the birdsong and as he listened he began to feel himself clutching at time, as though he had just become aware of it and of its passing, as though he had to hold on to this moment before it fled away from him. And just as he thought it, she said, "Patrice. Eduardo. You must get ready now."

He reached over and pulled her up and onto his lap. "You are so beautiful."

She put her hand on the nape of his neck and kissed his mouth. "You are beautiful, too."

"Liar. I'm big and ugly and I'm going to eat you for breakfast."

"The time, Eduardo. Now listen to me. This is the plan. I will drive you to the designated place and continue on to La Paz. You will join me there later."

"Thank you, Victoria. Thank you for last night. Thank you for everything. But, truly, I don't think I will be joining you in La Paz."

"You are too pessimistic about the outcome of this action."

"No. I have no preconceptions. The cause can never predict the effect, or God would never have created the world."

"That is certainly heresy."

"Abelard's yes. God had the best of intentions, no doubt, but. . . . Give me a cigarette and one more kiss and then we'll get out of here. Theological discussion to be continued."

"That's better," she said, smiling at him, kissing him. But he closed his eyes and held her and wished, with the desperation of a man caught on a mountain top with a blizzard coming in, that he had the power to change what had been written for him.

He checked himself out in the mirror. The suit was right; it was, after all, a day of mourning. The short haircut made him look remarkably like his father; he could be a lawyer in this get-up. What little hair he had left was dark brown now, graying at the temples. No long blond ringlets: he wasn't trying for the surfer look this time; he was CIA. It might fool State Security, but he wouldn't put money on it. ID's in his wallet, the nine millimeter, light and loaded. What was he missing? A quetzal feather and a small stone.

She was wearing a red and white polka dot dress with short sleeves and a white belt, white heels, white pocket book. Her thick hair was pulled back with combs. A tiny gold cross around her neck. Sunglasses. The model bourgeoisie.

"Ready?" she asked him.

"Ready," he replied.

She stopped the car on a side street near the church of El Calvario. They sat in silence for some time, staring out the window as though fascinated by the two boys playing baseball with an old stick for a bat. He took a final draw on his cigarette and flicked it out the window. Instantly a small, ragged boy ran over, scooped it up from the street, darted away. He turned to her. He felt as though he was losing himself in a well of pity, deep and profound, from which he could not pull himself. This was not Guatemala. He did not hate this man that he was going to kill. If there was any tenderness in her now, if she showed him the least bit of tenderness, he would drown in compassion, he would never be able to act.

She looked at him but all he saw was his own face reflected in her sunglasses.

"Good luck, Eduardo," she said.

"Safe journey, Victoria."

He opened the car door and stepped out into the street.

There was no greater thing love could do. Poor Peter Abelard. Now his life would begin to pass before his eyes, now he would remember all those old texts as he enacted his own: the just war argument, the proof for the predicate calculus, Russell's paradoxes. Presenting yourself to the Creator, it helps to have a good text on your lips. But did he know which text? Had they bothered to teach him that?

They had taught him everything else, Vladimir's cadre. A new life, the life of Edward Stillwell. How to talk like him. How to think like him. They taught him how to harden his mind, how to make himself into nothing but will. They even gave him a taste of the torture the Hondurans would be likely to use on him, if it came to that. The only thing they didn't teach him was how to aim and shoot and hit a target. That much he already knew.

It surprised him, the size of the crowd gathered behind the old cathedral in the churchyard where Gabriel Aguilar would soon lay a wreath of flowers on his family tomb on this second day of November, the Day of the Dead. Aguilar had not yet arrived, but his security detail had, some of it anyway. They had cleared a space between the crowd and the tomb about three meters deep running the width of the cemetery. Aguilar would enter from the south gate; the street had already been closed to traffic. Patrick watched the detail attentively: like Mexican bank guards, they didn't rely on subtlety. They carried pistols in their belts and rifles on their backs and several were holding shotguns, cradling them like babies. Half of these were Aguilar's men, half secretly in the pay of the generals. A small piece of intelligence, for whatever it was worth.

The first row across the cleared space was filled with TV cameras and photographers, all wearing picture ID's around their necks. The North American film crew that had been following Aguilar around all week had set up on the angle so they could shoot his arrival and then pan to the wreath-laying. A portion of the crowd was probably there more out of curiosity about the gringo filmmakers than out of devotion to Aguilar. There were more kids than adults, pushy little buggers, hanging around the cameras, selling fruit, *refrescos*, begging cigarettes. The smell of roasting meat from the street stalls was strong and the smoke from the vendors' fires wafted into the cemetery, thickening the air. There was smoke from burning candles; in the highlands there would also be the smoke from burning incense, which in Spanish was called *copal*, and in Mayan, *pom*. He let the words play in his mind, all the different words, the sound of them. Soon languages would pass before him too, all the words he knew, all the words he would never need again. And all around him people were eating, waiting. All around him, as he made his way through. And then he was seen and targeted: the street kids discovered his presence the minute he began to weave his way forward. Soon he was sur- rounded by a herd of them, hawking garish holy pictures, votive candles, plastic crucifixes, *chicles*, slices of pineapple, sugar cane, and, because it was the Day of the Dead, *calaveras*, little candies shaped like skulls. No, he said, and pushed his way through. Behind his back they swore at him, thinking he didn't understand. *Pubic hair. Needle prick. Faggot.* The adults watched him coldly, saying nothing. He made his way through.

Ten meters from the security cordon he stopped. He was standing beside a tomb, long and flat, the length of a man. Half a dozen candles burned around it and several little girls in pretty dresses were sprawled on top, sucking sugar cane, dangling their bare legs. He hadn't sucked on sugar cane in a long time; in a place without dentists it wasn't a wise practice. The thought of dentists sent a chill through him, the thought of pain. He gestured to one of the ragged urchins and bought a stick of cane for the asking price, a price inflated ten times over, the gringo price. He paid without argument, allowed the kid this small victory, not even letting on he knew he'd been had. A real sucker, he thought, sucking on the sugar. Nothing more to do now but wait.

Latino time: nothing starts when it should. He expected no one to speak to him and no one did. Good. They thought he was an embassy man or a spy from Palmerola, AID or CIA. They thought he was what he was. The enemy.

He waited and measured the distance, measured height. The 469 was extremely accurate up to fifteen meters. He couldn't afford the distance, though. Too many people in the way, too risky. He'd have to get closer. Later, when Aguilar arrived and everyone moved in closer, he would move in too. Not until then. Until then he stayed put.

Aguilar was the most popular politician in Honduras. He was spoken about on the streets, in the newspapers, on the radio. He was the one ray of hope people had for peace, and everything he said sounded like peace was all he wanted, peace with neighboring countries, Nicaragua in particular, demilitarization, disengagement from the United States. He was a liberal, a social democrat, his political rhetoric was aimed at a resurgence of national pride, independence from the empire, and economic justice.

And all the rhetoric was lies.

Unless Vladimir's intelligence was incorrect.

Or unless it was in Vladimir's interest to keep Honduras on the brink of civil war.

Or unless Vladimir thought Aguilar's death would improve the Frente's chances of victory. Because if that were the case, it wouldn't matter to Vladimir whether Aguilar was a drug trafficker and fascist or another Che, he would have to die. He, Patrick, would have to kill him.

Because the end justifies the means.

Because it is the natural right of the strong to tyrannize over the weak.

Because the revolution is love.

He could feel the sugar working away at his teeth, finding every cavity, every hole. Bad teeth was a national trait, an occupational hazard. He hadn't even seen real toothpaste since he was in Estelí.

He had meant to think about all this last night, but he hadn't had time last night to think about anything.

He was trusting Vladimir with everything. His life, his honor. It wasn't the way Vladimir had described it, not at all. "I am trusting you with everything," he had said. But that wasn't true. It was the other way around.

What if everything Vladimir had told him was a lie? What if Aguilar wasn't in the pay of the generals and the cartel? What if he was about to kill a good man?

A good man. Or at least not an evil man. Where had the information about him come from anyway? Who was the source? How did he know it wasn't someone like Emilio Castillo, who could stand smiling beside a genocidal murderer, who could eat at his table, help him procure boys, and then sell him to the Frente—for what? So they would kill off his business competition? What if he was about to kill a man he didn't even know on the word of someone like that? Was this what he had become after all, an enforcer for the likes of Emilio Castillo?

He had never once doubted the righteousness of killing Garcia Fuentes. He had seen Garcia's handiwork with his own eyes. In Guatemala everything was clear, everything was known, the bodies were hung in trees, the killers left their marks proudly, so any fool could read them. Down here, lies were laid on top of lies, family feuds were fought out in the political arena, money and power corrupted everyone, there was nothing to hold onto anywhere except what you knew absolutely to be true. Down here, the only truth he knew was Julio; the rest was bullshit.

But he had said he would do it, he had given his word. That also was true.

People began to move forward. The cars had arrived.

Within minutes a clutch of men in dark suits encircled by guards in white shirts made their appearance in the cordoned space. Photographers flocked around them, were pushed back by the white-shirts. Pockets of people began to clap and cheer; others stood stock-still and watched. From the cathedral side of the crowd came the beginning of a chant: A-gui-lar! A-gui-lar! The chant caught on, the volume increased. A-gui-lar! A-gui-lar! *El aguila! El aguila!* And Aguilar, the Eagle himself, graying, debonaire, patrician, moved out of the clutch surrounding him, moved toward the crowd, his arms opened as though to embrace them.

As Aguilar moved forward, Patrick strode up to meet him. Eight meters, six meters. Aguilar raised his arms, Patrick raised his arm, the 469 small and dark in his hand.

He didn't see the video camera panning the crowd, he didn't see the men in white shirts or the children, the mothers with babies in their arms, the *campesinos* in straw hats. Everything blurred into the smoke, into the chant, everything except Gabriel Aguilar raising his arms, and his dark blue tie against the white cloth of his shirt, four meters away, the spot where the bullet would hit.

But he didn't shoot. Something behind Aguilar caught his eye, a face, a look. His attention shifted to the right, he lost the moment. Everyone around him was moving—Aguilar himself, his squadron of guards, the cheering people—but this one face was perfectly still, this one face was frozen as in a photograph, staring right out at him, knowing him, expecting him. His whole body felt penetrated by that look, his whole body knew it, the way the body knows when it's been bitten by a rattler and the venom is already in the blood.

He pressed the trigger. Once.

And then, fighting every instinct he had, fighting everything his mind and body knew, he did what he had been ordered to do. He stood still, palmed the pistol, raised his hands.

Spattered with blood, Aguilar fell forward, into the crowd. He was caught, steadied, surrounded instantly by his guards.

Behind him another, heavier body had already fallen to the ground, a single bullet through the heart.

Emilio Castillo, Patrick said. Fuck you.

Then Aguilar's security men, pushing through the crowd, got to him, twisted the pistol out of his hand, gripped him by the arms.

155

One of them raised a rifle and hit him hard. After that first blow there were others, but he was already down and sending his mind into the dark.

SEVENTEEN

Carlos met with his captains inside one of the shelters of the San Isidro market. The situation across the river in Tegucigalpa was reviewed: a dozen civilians reported dead or wounded, demonstrators in front of the U.S. Embassy, occasionally breaking bottles against the embassy walls, tensions high. Both the United States and the Honduran governments were sticking to the story that the attempted assassination of Gabriel Aguilar was not the work of the CIA, but the assassin had not confessed his true identity. The government spokesman assured the people his statement would be forthcoming within the hour. Every hour he made the same assurance. Meanwhile North Americans were warned to stay off the streets.

The commandos were dressed in close-fitting black, their hair blackened and their faces, their equipment attached to belts around their waists. Carlos had been as cautious as possible, letting them filter into the capital over days dressed as *campesinos*. Filtering in too, in the backs of farmers' pick-up trucks and the baskets of market women: flotation devices, rock climbing gear, explosives, AK-47s. Now he reviewed the plan of attack and said the final words. They were ready.

The river's edge. Directly across the Choluteca the Presidential Palace stood like a fortress prison, a replica of a Moorish castle of the Middle Ages, replete with turrets and battlements. Somewhere inside it tonight the president and his ministers and generals were eating and drinking from tables gleaming with crystal and silver, laughing, completely secure. And somewhere deep inside it, in those damp subterranean dungeons along the river's edge, other men were torturing Patrice.

The moon was dark, the river inky black. Normally they illuminated the building for the tourists, but tonight the power had

157

failed. A small explosion and this whole section of the city was plunged into darkness. And the generals were thinking: That's all those Marxist dogs are capable of, forcing us to eat by candlelight. But the electrodes run on batteries and candlelight can be very romantic. When he confesses, the generator can power the radio transmission. They were laughing about it even now. Carlos knew they were.

There were battery-operated searchlights, too, sweeping back and forth over the walls and grounds. There were guards and dogs patrolling around the building; the front gates were impenetrable. But tonight demonstrators were outside the gates, banging on pots and pans, more amusement for the generals. Carlos hoped that before the night was out they would be more appropriately entertained.

This was his operation. He had requested it, demanded it. Vladimir had wanted him in Salvador, but he kept asking, What about Patrice? Who's getting him out? Cinchoneros? Since when did Cinchoneros turn into trained commandos? What miracle is this?

No, the truth was Vladimir wasn't planning to send anybody. But he had planned without Carlos.

Down at the river's edge the commando were barely visible. Five men in each raft, five rafts afloat on the rippling black water. Across the river, the retaining wall, and beyond it, monstrous in shape and size, the dark form of the fortress, weirdly lit by the sweep of the searchlights. Carlos was aware of other presences on the bank too, river rats, the size of cats, fearless. There would be rats in the dungeons too. Hold on, Patrice, he thought. Just hold on a little longer.

What had Vladimir envisioned anyway? That Patrice would be shot down on the street? That he wouldn't be captured at all but blown away right there on the spot? Had Vladimir set it up that way? He had people everywhere, probably right on Aguilar's own security squad. But he, Carlos, had friends too. The Cinchoneros owed him for a few shipments of guns; it was only a matter of calling in his chips. So he would sacrifice the honor of taking San Salvador and save his own honor instead. And— who knew?—if all went well he and Patrice might be waiting on the steps of the National Palace to welcome Vladimir into San Salvador.

He watched the operation proceed through night vision goggles, U.S. Army issue; he could see in the dark. They had a REMBASS system in place in Palmerola but not here. Here they were still in the Dark Ages. No one had imagined an assault like this on such a pile of stones. No one had envisioned it, so no one had prepared for it. The commandos would not be detected by body heat or sound and no one but he would witness them scaling the walls.

He wished with all his heart that he was scaling them himself. Sitting here watching, worrying, was a kind of hell.

It seemed to take an eternity for the rafts to reach the other side of the river, for the lead man in each raft to scale the retaining wall, for the others to climb up the rope and disappear like shadows over the side into the yard below, for the last man to hoist the raft up and over with him to conceal it from the view of army boats patrolling the river.

Time was creeping by. He could not trust his sense of it anymore. He had to count out the seconds, the minutes; for his own sanity he had to count the time it took them to fan out across the yard, take out the guards, begin their climb. He found he was holding his breath, waiting for the one sound that would signal disaster, the firing of the first shot.

But there was no shot, no sound. Instead he saw the men begin to ascend. The Ninja, Patrice called them.

The first five scaled the wall as though they were climbing a mountain of stone, placing their camming devices, the 'friends', every twenty feet, securing the rope, climbing twenty more. He watched them move up the building, monitoring the sweep of the searchlights, avoiding their paths. This rock was crannied, not the smooth rock face they had trained on, easier to climb. Before long they were hoisting themselves through the merlins, securing the ropes fast around the crenels of the battlements. Then one by one the others scaled the wall, the last man on each team pausing every twenty feet to plant a directional charge and seal it in the masonry.

Now Carlos watched carefully. This was his work, this display of pyrotechnics, this opening of the walls, like blasting a tunnel through rock, but with more delicacy, more precision, more like blasting inside a mine to open a vein of gold.

The last man on each team had reached the battlement and raised his hand as a signal. The ropes were pulled up. The men moved left and right across to the turrets and rope-climbed to the roofs above in case his calculations were wrong and the entire wall collapsed.

Another signal and detonation. Carlos watched this impregnable fortress of dictators rock to its foundations and burst open like a rotten fruit, like a pomegranate spilling blood-red seeds.

Vladimir had told him he was crazy, wasting men, time, energy. There was a difference, he said, between a diversion and a second front. When argument failed he simply forbade Carlos from leaving Salvador with the commandos; they were needed for the offensive. Then Carlos had to become diplomatic, clever. You want a diversion, Commander? Let me take a squad of commandos into Honduras. Twenty-five men, and I'll give you a fucking son of a bitch diversion and be back in Salvador in time to take the capital. And when Vladimir understood that Carlos was not going to be moved, he had no choice but to agree.

He was professionally gratified to see that his reading of the architect's drawings was accurate: the walls opened but the supports remained intact and with them the roof. That was, of course, only one level of his gratification. He watched through the goggles as the commandos descended through the clouds of dust and falling rubble from the turret roofs to the battlements and slid down the ropes, swinging themselves in through the gaping holes in the wall. Soon there would be gunfire, but this gunfire would signal their victory, not their defeat.

And Carlos knew that the sound of the explosions had carried to the people in the street and down the two blocks to the central square, Plaza Morazan, and to the United States Embassy, the sound had spilled over the river to the barrios of the poor and up into the hills and that Patrice had heard it too, and for everyone who heard it meant the same thing: liberation.

He gripped his machine gun, took hold of the last raft, and went down to the river.

"So, *señores*, it seems we have disturbed your meal. And now, regrettably, we are going to have to disturb you a little more. If you wish to live, that is."

Carlos had rarely felt such pleasure. A room filled with stoolies of the North Americans, the grand puppets—he could almost see the strings—arrogant, self-satisfied, now struck dumb with terror. They had had it easy, these Honduran pigs. Washington's money all these years to turn their country into a Pentagon theme park, to buy new jets for their new air force and new high-tech weaponry for their new army and no dues to pay for any of it. Well, the piper had just shown up, bill in hand. Scared shitless, aren't you, assholes?

"We don't want to kill you," Carlos said, as though he almost meant it. "Our demands for your release are quite reasonable and straightforward. Comply with them and no one will get hurt."

A *compa* at his shoulder. "Commander. . . ."

He turned and saw two commandos holding up a bloodied soldier. "Well?"

"He is not here," the soldier gasped. "I swear."

Carlos was in no mood for this. He nodded to the commando who took a knife from his belt.

"I swear it! Stillwell is not here. The Americans took him."

"Where?"

The soldier mumbled, didn't know. Carlos turned to the table. "Where is that motherfucker Stillwell? Where are you hiding him from the people's justice?"

One of the puppet-generals laughed or barked, made some canine sound, and hearing it Carlos knew. It had been snatched from his hands, all of it: victory, gratification, honor itself.

"Your so-called people's justice has been well served without you, *cinchonero*," the puppet said, an idiot grin on his face. "Stillwell is dead."

161

EIGHTEEN

There were three interrogators, two Honduran, one North American. The Hondurans had their names on their uniforms; the North American was in mufti and had no name but *jefe*, boss. They had been at this for fourteen hours now, fourteen hours shackled to a chair. He kept passing out, they kept slapping him awake. His eyes were nearly swollen shut. His head was bleeding, outside and in, or felt like it was bleeding in, swollen up and in a vise. There were whole areas of his body he couldn't feel at all, or only felt as deep throbs. He'd been holding his focus all this time, but he couldn't hold it anymore. He was done holding anything.

For the thousandth time they asked him who he was. For the thousandth time he said Stillwell. Still well. I am still well. Some joke.

The boss was a flinty career man in his late thirties, Special Forces. A Green Beret just like the ones who trained the Kaibiles, who came up with slogans like, "Be a patriot, kill a priest," and drill chants like

What does a Kaibile eat?
Flesh.
What kind of flesh?
Human flesh.
What kind of human flesh?
Communist.

Now the boss ordered the Hondurans out. They'd been pretty useless anyway. And it was time to deal.

"I'm just about ready to give you to them, Ed, if that's your name. Just about ready."

He closed his eyes and floated into a dream. In the dream he had a ticket with numbers written on it. The numbers didn't mean anything to him. Something was starting at three o'clock. But it was already three o'clock and he didn't know where he was supposed to be. . . .

"Ever sit down the hall from a room where they're interrogating, Ed? Butchering pigs, that's what it sounds like. Oh, they're animals, Ed. Ever see what's left of a man when they're done? Not a pretty sight, Ed. Now all I have to do is walk out that door and you're one more piece of meat for the butchers. You're gonna be one unhappy son of a bitch in five minutes, Ed. Unless you deal."

"What deal?"

"One simple statement, Ed. You just admit the communists paid you to shoot Aguilar. Period. You say that, you sign your name, and we'll send you home on the next plane. You're a U.S. national, Ed, one of us. You're just a little confused that's all, a little stressed out. You need some down time, Ed, maybe a few months in a hospital 'til all this dies down, then you're a free man. A good deal, Ed. And see, it's that or you're just another Honduran abortion. Take your pick."

"I work for Tudor."

"Like hell you work for Tudor. Man's never heard of you."

"Tudor knows me."

"Not any more he doesn't. Man, I don't know if you're telling the truth or if you're lying through your teeth, but if I were you I'd get the hell out of this shit now. 'Cause in three minutes you're not gonna have any choices left."

"You better talk to Tudor."

"No, Ed. You better talk to me. Now. Because look at it this way. You were shooting at Aguilar, but you didn't hit him. That means no matter who you were working for, you fucked up. Now you fuck up with us, we reassign you, right? You fuck up with them, you end up in a ditch. And since you fucked up with them, man, you'd better talk to me. Because I'm the only son of a bitch alive at this moment in time that can save your ass."

A curtain kept falling over his eyes. It was black, swirling, everything kept fading out. He didn't even care anymore. He was leaving his body anyway. He was stepping out of it. All he needed to do before he let go entirely was to say one last word. *No.*

163

The North American was at the door. Then he walked through it. The Hondurans came back in. One was holding a black hood in one hand, a rope in the other. So, he thought, it begins.

He didn't know where he was or how much time had passed. They had moved him somewhere by van. It was on the floor of the van that he stopped remembering. Somebody's boot on his head and nothing after that.

This place was underground. Damp like a cellar, dark, floor and walls concrete. A door with a small rectangular hole, barred and covered with mesh. His hands were shackled and the chain was attached to a ring in the floor. Enough chain so he could sit but not stand. Not enough chain to hang himself.

Some time later the door opened and two different men came in. One of them unchained him, the other put the rubber hood over his head. It was tight and suffocating and smelt of other men's sweat. The pressure of it made his head feel like it was collapsing in on him. He could barely breathe.

They pulled him up and half dragged, half carried him along with them. Then hands were working on his clothes, peeling them off him. He was pushed onto a cold, metallic surface. His arms and legs were strapped down, spread eagle. Someone emptied a bucket of water over him; hands felt him over, deciding where to start. The mechanism was cool on his wet skin, cool for an instant until the current cut into him and the world turned into fire.

He knew sounds were coming from him, but he couldn't stop them. All bodies contort, he'd been told, all mouths scream. It was an automatic response.

They cut the current. Everything in him felt torn open and burnt. Through the hood, muffled by it, he heard a voice. He had to strain to hear it, there was such a pounding in his head.

What is your name?
For whom are you working?
Who ordered you to shoot Aguilar?
No answer but the scream.

164

Eventually he was thrown back into the cell.

His body was out of his control, kept going into spasms. He couldn't swallow; his mouth was burnt dry.

Later they came and hosed him down. The water was so cold it hurt. They left him lying in a puddle. He licked some of the water from the floor to wet his mouth.

The room again. The cold surface. Voices without faces. He heard something about an ignition switch, a distributor cap. Car trouble. Clamping an electrode to his balls, talking about fixing their cars. Maybe it's the starter or the solenoid.

He imagined himself opening the hood, looking down at the engine. Check the water in the battery? Who knows, maybe all it needed was a jump. . . . And then somebody turned on the current and everything in his mind dissolved.

It was the Tempter's voice, the voice that had the power to dissolve the world. And the voice said:

What is your name?

Who hired you to kill Aguilar?

The communists, wasn't it?

The Frente, wasn't it?

And now do you expect them to come for you?

They've forgotten all about you.

They've forgotten you exist.

Just tell me who it was.

Just start with your name.

We've been easy on you, Anglo.

We've been very kind.

This time we stop being kind.

They stuck something cold up his ass. The current jolted all the way through him. Nothing was connected, everything was split apart, nerves split, cells split. His body arched away from the table; the straps on his ankles and wrists held him down. The spasm didn't end, even when he knew they had cut the juice, it was still inside him, crackling, sizzling, a slow burn.

165

Name! You tell us now. Because after a few more hours you will not know it anymore.

"Water." His lips moved, but no sound came out.

They put a drop of water on his tongue.

"More."

A cold rim by his lips and he drank, a swallow to loosen his tongue, to bring it back to life. He chose a number, number eight, infinity, and he gripped it in his mind like a hand, like a drowning man grips onto a hand, and then he said, though his voice sounded like the croaking of some insect, not like a voice at all: "Call me Ishmael and fuck your mother."

Over the next period of infinity they had to stop and wait once in a while to let his body cool. While they waited, they talked about soccer.

It had been more than three days. Many more than three days. He kept count by the plates of beans and the two cups of water, by the number of times they put him on the wire. There was a science to it; it could only be done once a day. Three had passed long ago. He couldn't keep numbers in his head any more than he could keep beans in his stomach, but three was long gone.

It was dark in the cell, cold, like being in a grave. Cold House in Xibalba, the underworld, hell.

He wondered now and then, when he could wonder at all, what they were keeping him alive for. He had shot the wrong man. Aguilar was still alive. There hadn't been an uprising. Whatever was supposed to have happened, hadn't. So why did they still want to know his name? Why not just kill him and get it over with?

He could make up names. Every day he could give them another name. But you cannot say a word to them, not a word. You cannot break the silence. They electrocute you, but you don't die. They wait for your body to cool, electrocute you again. You still don't die. Always dying, but never dead. You have become nothing but will. All you are is will, unbreakable will.

In hell and no exit.

But there is an exit, Patrick.

It sounded like another voice.

He studied the darkness. There seemed to be something there, some form. But he had seen things in the darkness before.

You promised him three days. He promised to get you out. He broke the contract. You are not bound by it anymore. So get yourself out. Tell them what they want to know.

It was Lucia's voice, Lucia's face. Her hair was cut short, as it had been in Guatemala. He remembered her better with long hair. Yes, like that, he thought, as she changed into a long-haired woman, younger, but with the same dark, lambent eyes.

"It's time to go home," she said. She said it the same way she'd say it at parties, pressing against him in a hallway or bending over him, whispering in his ear, so sexy, so seductive, *It's time to go home.*

"I don't have a home."

"You could make a home for yourself. Go back to Boston and make a home. Marry, have children. . . . Only imagine it, Patrick. A warm house, a woman who loves you, children. You always wanted children, little brown children, all different shades—"

"Stop it!"

"Why? Why do you refuse to look at this? Is there something else you'd rather see? The other choice . . . do you want to see that?"

He couldn't help himself. He saw a man fifty, fifty-five years old. His face was caved in under the eyes, in the cheeks, the skin lined, aged. It was a sad face, defeated. He was meticulously dressed and there was something wearily effete about the way he moved his hands, as though he had yielded to something as one yields to fatigue. He only barely recognized Julio Ibarra in this man, beautiful Julio.

"That isn't who he is."

"Not now. That's what he'll become."

"Twenty years from now maybe. And only after twenty years of loneliness, Lucia. That's the face of someone who's spent a lifetime without love."

167

"All right, Patrick. You want to play the savior. Go ahead. Save him from a lifetime without love. You still have to get yourself out of here first. You have to do that yourself. . . ."

But he stopped listening to her voice. He saw Julio as he had been in Estelí, as he was now, in the present, young and happy and strong. He held onto that memory the way he had held onto Julio's body in Estelí. Nothing could erase that image from his mind. He would hold onto it on the wire, under the knife, no matter what they did to him. If he died with Julio's image in his mind he might die happy, and if he lived—

The sharp sound of the key in the lock startled him. They were back again. It was the beginning of another day.

Time didn't exist. Night, day, neither existed. He was in Razor House in the land of the dead. He hadn't found the doorway out.

He didn't sleep or wake. He was sometimes conscious, sometimes not. When he was conscious all he was conscious of was pain. When he was not conscious he didn't know anything at all.

They came in and out. He only knew one by name: Jesús, the young one. Baby Jesús. They brought food he couldn't eat, and water. Sometimes they came to hose him down, sometimes to beat him with blackjacks, sometimes dispassionately as though only obeying orders, other times as though inflamed with hatred. But they weren't ready to kill him yet. The wire left no marks; that's why they used it. If they weren't wary of leaving marks they could break him easily enough. But it seemed they were still unsure and they didn't want to risk sending the CIA back one of its agents without his balls.

He could just sit up. Jesús came in and went out again. He left something behind him. The stink was very bad. They had left something dead in his cell.

The smell was a presence, like another being in the confined space with him. It had a texture, a heat. It made him nauseous, dizzy; he could taste it, something bloated and oozing, something in full decay. They say you can hear the maggots moving in the flesh. They say that, but they are crazy. They go crazy in these cells and then they are let loose, some of them, to tell stories so that when other people are captured they will remember the stories and lose their nerve, become paralyzed with fear.

The Sandinistas had stayed sane. Some of them had spent years blindfolded, chained to the walls of cells, but they stayed sane. One of them, he had been told, planted trees all over Nicaragua. He had the map of his country fixed in his mind and during nine years imprisonment he traveled around it planting trees. But there were others, men he had met, broken men, driven mad by dead animals and drugs.

The stench of death oozed across the cement floor, crept toward him. He pressed his face against the wall and tried to breathe through it. There was no air that was not polluted.

He felt hot, feverish. He was out of Cold House but not out of hell. This was Jaguar House where there were dead animal bones. But before the bones were left, the animal had to turn to liquid, to crawling things, then to buzzing things. They would leave nothing but bones behind; they would come after him too. The maggots were coming already.

He could feel maggots crawling on his skin, into all the openings of his body. *Fuck you! I'm not dead yet!*

The animal stirred. He could see it now, white with maggots, teeming with them, radiating a yellow-green light. A dog. It lifted what was left of its head; a single eye ogled at him, Dali-esque. It was so repulsive, that eye hanging out of rotting flesh. But the eye was fixed on him, the eye watched him longingly. It wanted another body. It wanted his.

"It is true, my friend," the dog said. "You are no different from me."

He turned his face back to the wall, pressed against it as hard as he could. Cement, hard enough to break a human skull. Maybe that was the door. Maybe it was time to take that doorway out

169

before he became more demented, while he still had some small remnant of sanity left.

"Ah, *caballero*, are you surprised? All this time watching you—well, I had to speak at last. I will tell you a secret, *caballero*, just between you and me. It's true what they say about dogs. We are dead guerrillas. No, don't laugh at me. It's true. I was a guerrilla, like you, a combatant. They killed me and left me for the dogs, so I grabbed one and ran off. But even poor miserable dogs catch theirs, those bastards shoot at anything. So, take a look. Come on, don't be squeamish. Take a good look. I am what becomes of us. I am what you will become.

"Ah, you say no? No? But yes, my *caballero*, oh yes, yes indeed, yes, yes and again yes! There's nothing else but this. That young body of yours that you love so dearly, your strong hands, strong limbs, that sex of yours, that big cock you get such pleasure from—food for worms! A slab of rotting meat. You turn into them, those little worms. They eat you, my friend. That's what you have to look forward to.

"But I see you are a cultivated gentleman, a philosopher. Well, think what you like. Amuse yourself. But I'll tell you, if you're counting on immortality I feel sorry for you. You will disappear into nothing. We are material, chemicals, just a bunch of chemicals. You were a scientist, weren't you? Don't you know anything? Chemicals make you what you are. There's no mystery to it. You are deceiving yourself."

"What do you want from me?"

"Want from you? Nothing. What can you possibly give to me, you poor idiot? Wisdom perhaps?" The dog laughed. "Very wise, you are. At least I died with a gun in my hand. You—you're going to die with a rat up your ass. Stupid gringo. No, I don't want anything from you. I'm here on a mission of mercy. I'm going to do you a favor and give you some advice. If you'll take advice from a dog."

"Go ahead."

"Go ahead, he says! Thank you very much, *vaquero*. So put your fine philosophy away for a minute and listen to a little common sense. Survival. That's what I advise. Survival at any cost. Keep yourself together, my cowboy. Listen to me. They'll take you apart soon. I know these bastards. They like to dismember men. You'll see yourself minus important pieces soon. Those two eggs of yours, for instance, those balls—cut right off. Shears they use, big ones. Or maybe they'll start with ears, tongue, eyes. Hurts like hell to lose your eyes. They bring the bits home with them and put them in jars. You'll be all over this district, *vaquero*, pieces of you in glass jars all over the damn place. Show them to their friends. To poets. The poets write poems about it, about seeing bits of human bodies in glass jars after dinner. Very nice. You like poetry? I bet you do. There's a poem I heard once about the spirits of guerrillas passing into the bodies of dogs. Amusing poem, unless it happens to you, of course. . . . Well, that's what I have to say to you, cowboy. Stay alive."

"And that's all that matters, staying alive?"

"Well, I'll tell you this much—nothing matters at all when you're dead. Common sense, *caballero*. Nothing matters for shit then. Yes, I'm telling you, stay alive! Become *caradura*, be a bastard, but keep your balls and your life. That's what I say."

"And honor?"

"Honor? You're a fine one to talk to me about honor. Weren't you supposed to kill The Eagle, *vaquero*? Didn't you give them your word, weren't they counting on you? So what did you do? Saw someone you'd rather put a bullet through, and just went ahead and did it, didn't you? Just to satisfy your own personal vendetta. . . . Ah, *caballero*, the Frente will not be too pleased about that. They'll leave you here to die, is what they'll do. They'll abandon you in this hole. Not that they'd have done anything different anyway, no matter who you put that bullet through. They have no honor either. As for Castillo, the man was a snake, no doubt about it, but so are most men. The point is, your word was given, wasn't it? You are a *guerrillero* . . . or you were. You are bound by honor to follow orders. But never mind, *vaquero*. Honor is a joke, that's all it is. What the fuck difference does honor make when you're dead? They forget you, honorable or not. They forget you the same, hero or villain. Maybe they remember the villains better. But you won't know, will you? You'll be dead and you

171

won't know anything. Finished, *amigo*. Done for. You go out, you're gone. What's wrong with you? Did they burn your brains out of your head? A dead hero is the same as a dead dog. You've been dreaming all your life, man. Wake up!"

"And love? What about love?"

"Ah, yes. I knew you'd ask about that. Well the sad truth is there's no more fucking when you're dead. If you're a Muslim, man, I got bad news for you. There are no cunts and no holes where you're going. Even if there were, you'd have no meat to stick in them."

"No. I mean real love."

"*Real* love? Did I miss something? Since they blew my head off did something change in the universe? *Real* love? Whoa, *vaquero*. What kind of wet dreams have you been having in here? You want me to explain love to you in words you can understand? Poetic and philosophical, my *caballero*? Let's see if a dog can help you out. That's my job, to help you out. My mission, *vaquero*. A mission of mercy. So. There are four things we call love. One is lust. I don't have to explain that to you. Then there's vanity, pride. You think you love someone, but really you are just loving yourself. Then there is power, domination over someone. You know these three, all three of them. What satisfies the cock, what satisfies the ego, what satisfies the desire to possess and command another. You have experienced all these. You call this love? Yes, self-love, all of them. Then, my friend, there is fear. You don't want to be alone. You want companionship, someone to act as a witness to your life. And if a greater fear strikes you, you create a fiction and call it God and love that fiction because it protects you from the truth. And it does, until the end. This is love, *vaquero*. Real love. The only real love is love for yourself. Face it. The rest is bullshit."

"There is a love you haven't named."

"What? What love have I neglected to name?"

"The love you had when you became a guerrilla. The love you gave your life for. Selfless love. Love for others. Why else did you lay down your life?"

172

"I was wrong. I was a fool, like you. I defy you, *vaquero*, to show me this love. I defy you to show it to me!"

"I don't know how to show it to you."

"No, because it doesn't exist. No, the truth is before you. I am a witness. We dissolve. We dissolve into liquid like I am dissolving before your eyes. When these worms have done their work, when my brain becomes liquid, the matter that was I will no longer exist in a form that can hold memory. Memory will dissolve and with it everything I was. Stench is speaking to you now. The thickness in the air you breathe, the heat of my decay, that alone holds the memory of me. I am form with its substance in flux. My self decays as I speak to you, my self turns away from me, creeps toward you. . . . Take me! dog-man that I am, forgetting everything, tree, leaf, sun, mountains, the sweet earth. Take me, if there is such love as you claim! Take me if there is love, my brother! Take me into your mouth, your eyes, hold yourself out to me. I do not want to disappear. Look at me, how I fade. . . ."

In horror he saw the form struggling up from the carcass, struggling up, so hideous, dog-man, flesh alive with wiggling white worms. He felt dizzy, sick, his whole body in revolt against this creature he had to will himself to embrace. *If this were Alejandro*, he thought, and the thought was like a command. . . . *If this were Alejandro*, and he swallowed the sickness down and inched closer to the dog until the chain holding him was pulled taut. He stretched out his hand into the darkness; it met something mushy, slimy, cold. He moved his hand along the dog's form until it reached what must have been the skull. He was so dry he could only croak out the words, just sounds, into the darkness. *Come into me, then,* compañero, *if it will help you.*

But nothing happened. It was only a dog after all, a poor, dead dog. He was lucid again, lucid enough to try to brush the maggots off his hand, lucid enough to know how little time he had left.

The spasms that shook his body after a stint on the wire lasted longer and longer. He felt blackened, burnt, he felt as though there

173

was nothing left of him but one long, exposed nerve and charred bones.

They took the dogbody out of his cell, but they added a new torment: after they dumped him back in his cell they didn't bother to remove the hood.

Bat House. The hood tried to make him mad. He wouldn't let it. He told himself he was hiding in a dark secret room in a cellar and the darkness was his friend. And whenever he felt himself balancing on the edge, whenever it came too close, whenever he was face to face with the abyss, buried alive, whenever he felt buried alive, he would revert to logic, to valid well-formed formulas of propositional calculus, like the first DeMorgan Law: *Both p and q if and only if neither not-p nor not-q.* The formulas, because they were wordless, pictorial, appeared in his mind like a film that he could watch, knowing it so intimately, frame by frame; yet they could also be recited like a litany, a chant, a mantra to sanity: *p is equivalent to p; p is equivalent to not not-p; p or not-p.*

Still it would close in on him. Anxiety, intense, like madness, so near, like some bat-like creature, beating around his head. Never get out. Never, never get out.

They would come and force liquid down his throat. They couldn't make him eat, but they could make him drink. Hold him down, three or four of them, and force it down his throat. Not that they needed quite so much man-power as all that. He was so weak, they could do anything to him they wanted. But he always put up a struggle. Once he stopped struggling they would know it was over with him. Then it would just be a question of the *coup de grace.*

Let Gamma be a set of formulas of propositional logic. He used to know this. Alejandro would recite the Upanishads; he would answer with the Completeness Proof. *Assume that Gamma is consistent, that is, there is no formula, Phi, such that both Phi and its negation can be derived from Gamma. Now show that Gamma has a model if and only if Gamma is consistent.*

It took eternity, this proof. It took an eternity of will. The lines turned to gibberish. It took an eternity to right them. He envisioned the proof, repeated it over and over, the sheer elegance of it, the sheer perfection, the simplicity and the beauty of it. *The rules of proof are truth preserving. Phi and not-Phi can never be true together, so no model can make it true. Contradiction.* When he finally got that far he felt that he had pushed the abyss back, like it was an object that he could move if he were strong enough. And he was strong enough. He pushed it back, way back. He wasn't going to let the damn hood make him crazy. He could lie down in shit, half frozen, burnt, bruised, starved, with the damn hood over his head, but he would lie down sane, and sleep.

Second proof. If Gamma is consistent then Gamma has a model.
He couldn't remember when he'd eaten last.
Extending Gamma to a maximal consistent set Delta, let Delta sub zero equal Gamma. But something was missing. The imaginary page swam in front of him. *Deltas* and *Psis* and dancing *Upsilons*, hundreds and hundreds of dancing *Upsilons*, all swam like little sperm across his mind. Across his mind and into the abyss. He couldn't hold them, he couldn't place them on the page. He was missing half the proof. Where had it gone? *Suppose Phi, Psi are formulas of the propositional calculus and Beta is the assignment we are defining.* Assume that and then play music for all the dancing *Psi-Delta* couples. This completes the Completeness Proof.

He didn't bother to struggle anymore. He drank the water. Death would come soon enough. They had already stopped trying to force food into him. Too messy. But he wanted to tell them what he had remembered in this great black hole. He wanted them to listen. But they only held him down and made him swallow water. He wanted to tell them that he had surrendered, that there was victory in his surrender, that he had rediscovered something important to all of them. *Listen, brothers!* If he could only tell them. *Listen! For each sentence Psi of propositional logic, either Psi is a member of set Delta or it is not a member of set Delta, but of course it cannot be both a member and not a member!*

175

The dark closed in on him.

He had to accept that he was blind. This is how it is to be blind. He had to accept that.

Blind and without hands.

Blind and without feet.

Blind and demented.

An old man came to him. Even blind he could see him. It was Victor, his brother, coming to carry him out of this hell realm. But it was Victor grown old, frail and bent, white-haired. Had he been in this hole for fifty years then? Was it possible that he had spent his life inside this darkness, that their lives were over?

The old man smiled at him with Victor's smile and he spoke with Victor's voice. "Keep the day of today in your head. Find it and keep it. The Days will give themselves to you. But you must keep them. . . . The day of today is. . . ."

Pictures of the days passed through his mind. A wheel of fortune spinning: Maize, Snake, Death, Deer, Dog, Monkey, Grass, Cane, Jaguar, Eagle. . . But where to stop it? *The Days will only give themselves to him who keeps them.*

He thought this must be a dream and if it was a dream it was a message from the gods or from the dead. Victor would say that was the case. And if it was not the gods but only his own mind speaking to him, what was it telling him but that keeping the days might keep him sane a little longer. Because he could feel that nothing was right anymore, that he was on the verge of speaking to them now, that he would speak to them if they would only get him out of Bat House, tell them anything, give them anything. . . .

He had left Huehuetenango for Guatemala City during the night of May thirteenth. May thirteenth was a powerful day, 13 Thought. But there had been delays, problems with gassing up the jeep, with connections down below. They had left very late at night to make their beginning before the next dawn, the dawn of May fourteenth. The name of that day was 1 Knife, day of sacrifice, and it was the most unlucky day of the calendar, so unlucky that the parents of children born on that day would offer ceremonies and prayers to both Mayan gods and Christian saints to be given permission to change it.

So blind and demented he might be, but he could keep a day count from there.

May 14th. 1 Knife.

May 15th. 2 Rain.

May 16th. 3 Lord Sun.

May 17th. 4 Earth.

May 18th. 5 Wind.

He counted through the thirty-one days of May. Through the thirty days of June.

The night in July he killed Garcia Fuentes. 10 Death.

He looked at the day. He counted back again, forward again. It was not meant, Lords, he said. I did not intend to kill him on the day 10 Death.

He counted on through July. The day he left the Zone for Nicaragua was 5 Jaguar. A good day. The first night he made love to Julio, 2 Maize. A good day. The last night they spent together, however: 4 Death.

He counted through July, the days of travel with Victor and Carlos into the Zone. Slipping into sleep he held a day in his mind so when he woke he had a place to return to. August first, 2 Thought.

He counted through August. Confinement. September. Vladimir. He could not recall the date of their meeting. Not 13 Jaguar, his name day in its most potent manifestation, or surely he would not have ended up here in Xibalba. Perhaps it had been 1 Eagle. 2 Vulture. 3 Thought. 4 Knife. He didn't know. Counting on then through October to November second, to 4 Dog, the Day of the Dead.

He was out of time now, he had lost count here, he did not know the name of the day.

He was surrendering, but they didn't know it. Every time they came in to hurt him again he wanted to cry out to them, I have surrendered! But something kept him from speaking.

177

Once again the cell door opened. Someone came in, but quietly. He sensed this person was very close, but he did not sense anger or violence so he wasn't afraid. A hand touched his head. The touch was gentle. It sent a thrill down his spine, to be touched without hatred. And then a voice which was not angry said, "For today only," and hands unfastened the hood and lifted it off his head.

The release of the pressure, the onslaught of cool air, the brutal, knife-sharp stab of the light.

It was Baby Jesús, the young one. All this done by children, fifteen-year-olds, boy-soldiers. Jesús had a blanket in his hand and he laid it with a unsettling tenderness over Patrick's body. "A gift from my mother. For the Feast of the Virgin."

He touched the blanket with his hand. He had been naked all this time, sleeping naked, shivering in the dampness, never warm. Now this blanket. It was light brown wool, not rich brown, but camel, almost tan, and it felt so soft to his touch, the softest thing he had ever touched. Everything blurred. It was the brightness of the light, making his eyes tear.

"Please, thank your mother for me," he said. His voice was cracked, a raspy whisper. He hadn't spoken for a long time.

Another soldier came in with a bowl of something that smelt rich and thick and good. Jesús unfastened one of the manacles.

"Today, soup with meat in it."

He put his hand up to his face, to feel it, to cover it. He could not show emotion in front of these men. He could not show them how weak he was.

He had grown a beard; his face didn't even feel like his own face.

"Stillwell," Jesús said, "may Our Lady bless you today."

The voice was so gentle. He looked right at the boy. For a single moment their eyes met. Too much was revealed.

He sat on the floor of his cell wrapped in the blanket he had been given. Everything was burnt out of him. He was a desert. There was nothing left in him at all.

They were drinking hard. He heard them, loud, rowdy. Feast of the Virgin, so they have rum.

Feast of the Virgin, December 8th. He counted from November second. The name of this day was 1 Death. A terrible day. The Mayas calculated that the Crucifixion had occurred on a day named 1 Death. A terrible, evil day.

You still expect them to come for you? They've forgotten all about you. . . .

His hands were gripping the blanket. Hot soup and a soft blanket—it didn't take much to break a man. A cigarette. A piece of chocolate. Suddenly everything human becomes a need. You can't go back to not having a blanket. That's how they do it. Now he can't give the blanket up. He tried throwing it out of reach. He couldn't bring himself to do it.

What did they promise you, you dumb faggot? That they'd rescue you? That they'd bribe us to let you out? And you believed them?

His throat was tight. When he swallowed his ears creaked. He felt it in his neck, shoulders, back, chest, his heart pounding too hard, too fast. His whole body felt it, even what was left of his sex. Panic.

After all, he had shot the wrong man.

You're disappeared, gringo. Nobody knows where you are and nobody gives a shit.

He couldn't breathe, couldn't catch his breath. He knew they were coming. He could almost hear the sound of their boots through the floor, feel the power of their bodies like some unstoppable natural force, a pack of wild dogs, violence unleashed, coming right at him. Now they were outside the door, in the corridor, nothing separating them but a single lock on a single door. Knowing the date, it was like an announcing. And he had

179

spoken to them today. Never speak to them. It was a mistake to speak.

The door of the cell opened. He looked up at them, but they were back-lit by the bare lightbulb shining in the hall. All he could see were legs and boots and hands holding bottles and blackjacks. One of the hands pulled the blanket off him and one of the boots kicked him hard in the side, kicked him again and again until he turned away, kicked him over on his stomach, kicked at his legs until he was on his knees. *You first, Jesús. Here's the hole. Come on, let's see what kind of man you are. Let's see how good you can fuck this hole.*

Fuck him like a cunt, Jesús.

He'll scream for you. You'll be hot as the wire, right up his ass.

He heard them pushing Jesús forward, but he couldn't see. He was pinned against the floor, held down by hands and a boot on the back of his neck. He felt a man's weight come down on him and a cock being shoved into him. It took his breath away, how much it hurt. He tried to relax, tried not to fight it, but it felt like he was being ripped apart, and the only way he could keep himself from screaming was biting down hard on his lip until his mouth tasted like blood. Jesús was thrusting fast and deep, pounding him hard against the cement. The cock inside him didn't feel like it belonged to a man at all, felt more like a weapon boring in. He swallowed, gagged on blood.

Jesús shot, pulled out, but the boot came down on his neck again like a clamp. They weren't through with him yet.

Sometime during that night he must have prayed to Death. And Death heard him and came.

It was ugliness itself with its skull head and exposed spine, all the bones visible whenever it turned its back. The rest of it was dark, though he could see the yellow dots on its stomach and legs. It twirled in front of him, illuminated bones and florescent yellow dots. A Day-Glo god. Just what he needed. First a good long gang bang and then to cap it off a visit from a dancing Day-Glo god. His ass was bleeding and his face. Lying in shit and blood and now this.

First I sent to you my own wife, Xtabai, to whom you would not listen. Wise of you, Jaguar, since she is a deceiver. Then I sent to you my own dog, Tz'i, who would have been your guide to me. Now I have come myself, I, Death, Lord of Xibalba.

The stench of Death was overwhelming. He was nearly overcome by the smell alone, and by terror. He was shaking with terror. Or maybe he was shaking with laughter. That was what terrified him the most, that he didn't know whether to be afraid or amused, he didn't know whether he was really in hell or just hallucinating, whether what he was seeing and smelling and hearing was real or just his brain gone berserk. And then he thought that it was the same either way, either he was really damned or really insane, what difference? Like a bad trip, it didn't matter what caused it, it was happening and you had to deal with it. And now Death was multiplying before his eyes: One Death, Seven Death, Blood Gatherer, Pus Monster, Jaundice Monster, Bone Scepter, Skull Scepter, Bloody Teeth, Bloody Claws. All the faces of death. They spoke to him in stereo, the words coming at him from all directions, ricocheting off the cement walls, deafening.

Ah Balanke, Ah Kin, Lord Day, Jaguar Sun, what do you have to fear? That I know your name? Does that frighten you? That I know you, Balam Kin, Balanke, Jaguar Day. . . . Their laughs were hideous, scroll mouths laughing, goggle eyes rolling in skull heads, twirling all of them in skirts dotted with yellow eyes, death eyes. *Swimmer, warrior, protector of life, Ah Kin, here am I, Death! Look at me!*

He looked. Ten deaths danced before him, yellow dots swirling in the darkness, luminous skeletons, the rattling of bones, and the stench of Xibalba, an assault on all his senses. The yellow dots moved closer and closer, low down now, at his level, on the cement floor with him. They were the eyes of animals.

Ah, Balanke, Lord Jaguar Day, you will be our sacrifice. We eat the body of the god to become the god. We eat your body and your heart. Lord Day disappears at night and comes to us, Jaguar. By morning we shall have picked your bones clean.

The animals were gathered close now. One brazen one nuzzled his ribs with its nose, another scratched his leg with its teeth. He twitched his body, kicked them away, but others appeared, many others. One climbed onto his stomach, and then another and another. He felt cold feet on his skin, cold, naked tails. Rats.

He pulled himself up to a squat and pushed the rats off him, hitting them with his shackle and banging the chain as hard as he could against the wall. The sudden movement and the sound had only a slight effect on them; like an incoming tide, they moved back, then in closer. And it seemed that there were hundreds of them, that the cell was stuffed full of hungry, yellow-eyed rats, that it was on their very bodies that the ten Deaths danced, now changing shape again, heads growing on top of heads, distorted, cross-eyed, fanged, beaked. And their voices filled the cell with a din, echoing off the cement. . .How could the guards not hear this noise? Why didn't they come, force open the door, or did they want this, want him to die eaten alive by rats?

Submit, Jaguar. Surrender. There is no other choice for you. Two opportunities were given to you, Lord Day, to heal yourself, Master of Cures, and two times you refused. Now you are mine. You are in the well's mouth, you are consigned to hell. Isn't this what you want, Jaguar? You desire horror, and horror is given to you. When you refuse everything else, this is what remains.

The rats pushed closer. One scrambled under him. He kicked it away, but another took its place. Drawn to the blood. *At least I died with a gun in my hand. You . . . you'll die with a rat up your ass. . . .*

He closed his eyes and opened his mouth. He had no voice left at all, only a whisper. "Heart of Sky, Heart of Earth, Maker-Modeler, Bearer-Begetter, Mother-Father, Plumed Serpent, look at me! Listen to me! Don't let me fall, don't cast me aside. Tepeucucumatz, give me courage, give me strength . . . Creator, take my heart in your hand, don't let it fail me. . . ."

182

The power of the prayer created a space around him. The air sweetened, the stench of death faded away, and when he opened his eyes both the rats and the faces of Death had disappeared.

But what if he was really dead, dead and in hell? What if he was here forever, wherever this was, what if it never ended, what if this was all there was, this cell, these demons, this madness and pain and loss, alone forever, demented forever? What if there was no one outside the door to let him out, what if there was no other human being here, what if he called to them at last and no one answered, what if he was absolutely alone?

They went in for him as usual in the early hours, around dawn. They'd heard about what had happened during the night—who hadn't? There were jokes about it, but nobody was laughing. It was all taking too long, the colonel was angry, the Americans were putting on the pressure, they wanted results now or they'd get some themselves.

Today, man, they said to each other. *No more screwing around. We're done playing with this faggot. Today he'll talk to us. We'll break his balls. By the time we're finished with him, he'll beg us to let him talk.*

NINETEEN

Managua, Nicaragua

The *campesinas*, all of them wearing the *quintuplo*, sat in the waiting room of the Ministry of Health and drank sweet fruit *refrescos* from colored plastic cups. The drinks had been served to them by the Minister's secretary who apologized for the lack of coffee, the lack of canned soda, the lack even of ice. But the way things were this month. . . . And the women waved the apologies away with thanks. This month everything was different. They understood.

Everything non-military had ground to a halt. The army was mobilized, the ceasefire with the contra rescinded, troops and supplies rushed to the Honduran border. Lack of coffee was the least of anybody's worries.

While she waited, Martha read newspapers. She had a copy of *Barricada* for the official news and a two-day-old *New York Times*. In both papers she read about the Frente's offensive in Salvador, the aerial bombing of poor neighborhoods by the Salvadoran government under the direction of their American "advisors." She read about the Salvadoran army's massacre of six Jesuits at the University of Central America, men she had known well, men who had been her friends. She read about the arrest by the military of a young North American church worker, accused of hiding guns for the Frente. She read these articles and wept.

She read about the crumbling of the Berlin Wall, massive demonstrations in Eastern Europe, portents of profound political changes, perhaps signifying the end of Soviet power in the world.

She read that the Nicaraguan government was supplying the Frente with anti-aircraft missiles to assist them in defending themselves against continued aerial bombardment like that which had flattened whole sections of San Salvador. Sending the FMLN two

184

dozen SAM-7s was a Sandinista strategy, the *Times* declared, intended to force the disarming of the contra army in Honduras.

Below that article, a photograph of Eden Pastora, hero of the Nicaraguan Revolution, campaigning in Managua for the contra-supported opposition party.

Anything could be believed. Anything could be true.

But nowhere, not in *Barricada*, not in the *Times*, was there a single word about the attempted assassination of Gabriel Aguilar, the fate of Patrick Day or of the generals a group of Cinchoneros were holding as hostages at the Presidential Palace in Tegucigalpa, or the negotiations in progress for their release. It was as though this other news —war in Salvador, street fighting in Poland— had wiped Honduras off the map the way the North American propaganda station wiped Radio Sandino off the dial. That, or the curtain had purposefully been drawn. News blackouts were not the exception in this part of the world, of course, but the rule.

They were waiting here in this room for Julio Ibarra to return from that place that seemed no longer to exist. He was negotiating in Tegucigalpa, as he had been for weeks.

For weeks now she had been mourning and she had prayed. For the murdered priests and their housekeeper and her child, for friends who had fallen in combat, and all her friends in Salvador, so many of them now dead or disappeared, but mostly for Patrick, though it was a part of her grief that when she prayed for him she did not know whether to pray for the repose of his soul or the preservation of his life, or for a swift and merciful end to his suffering. It was inconceivable that only five months had passed since she had seen him last, so much had happened to all of them since July, so much had happened to the world.

She had left Estelí the day after the Victory celebration and traveled north to Santo Tomás, a small village near the Honduran border. By late afternoon she was deep in the mountains, walking down a dirt road between green fields.

185

It was a land that appeared blessed, yet the heaviest fighting of the terrorist war was occurring right in those very mountains. Children were killed there, farmers, teachers. The contra came down from Honduras and savaged the people, struck at everything the Revolution had built, struck down the engineers Managua had sent to them, the doctors, struck down her own son.

When his friends found him, his body was lying half in a stream. He had died beside it, kneeling beside it, and had fallen so that his head rested in the water and his blood mingled with the stream.

So she became something she never dreamt she would become: a mother who had buried a son.

It was July then too, but it did not rain. She remembered that. She remembered every detail of that terrible day: being embraced by sobbing women she did not know; passing the street sign in Matagalpa, *Avenue of Heroes and Martyrs*; walking down that street behind the coffin along with hundreds of others, and the President of the Republic walking beside her, holding her by the arm; the flowers and the music and everyone standing at attention while they played the Nicaraguan National Anthem, everyone in tears; and the final moment when they lowered the wooden coffin into the ground and the priest called out his name and hundreds of voices shouted back the response: *Presente!* He had been loved by many people, Stephen, and those who had not known him personally loved him for what he represented, a gringo who had come to live among them and accept everything that living among them implied, including dying among them. He had proven his love for them, not that they had asked him for proof.

That first night in Santo Tomás she ate dinner with her friend Javier at a small table outside his house while a fat moon rose over the mountains and the music of Radio Sandino echoed down the length of the street. Javier was bright-eyed, white-bearded, cherubic, missing several front teeth. When they spoke together they were like lovers, their conversation was that intimate. They were old enough not to fear being critical, but wise enough to be critical only between themselves. "About this revolution, I am like your son," he would smile at her. "He always said that what he liked best were the little things."

"I want you to come for a walk with me tonight, Marta," he said after they had finished dinner. "You have been away and things have happened here in your absence. There is a meeting tonight that will be of interest to you."

They left the table and walked down the dirt street. People greeted them from open doorways where they sat resting in the cool of the evening. The moon was low over the hills.

They took a road that climbed gradually, winding up between fields and woods. They walked in silence, listening to the breeze stir and whisper in the leaves. Contra patrols might well be somewhere in the vicinity, their own soldiers also. But one could not live always in fear.

Twenty minutes later they emerged from the path into a clearing. People were there, sitting on the ground. Martha was embraced and kissed. There were young people and older ones, though she might well have been the oldest. She had celebrated her sixtieth birthday in this village; no one could believe it was true.They thought she had the gift of eternal youth. They could not understand that children of the empire had twice as many years to live as they, that living to sixty, seventy, eighty years was not a miracle to her people, but an expectation. That to die at fifty was to die young. They had carried her around the village on their shoulders that night celebrating her long life. Later she had cried herself to sleep.

This night they were sitting in a circle holding each other's hands. Their prayer was a song to the Spirit, that it might descend on them. As the song rose she looked up at the sky, not to where the moon hung swollen, but into the darker part. May they speak with the voice of the Spirit, they prayed. May they understand its will. She gazed up and saw a single star streak across the blackness, a single falling star.

A woman began to speak.

"I was walking down the road from San Sebastián when I saw her. She was sitting on a rock by the side of the road, my sisters. She was weeping by the side of the road, my brothers. In her arms there was a child. Then she spoke to me. She said, 'Mercedes, my child is dying.' I said, 'There is a clinic in Santo Tomás. I am going there. Come walk with me.' She said, 'There is no medicine that can cure my child. He dies over and over again. Again and again he must die, like your children die, because men will not stop hating, will not learn to love.' And then I knew her, Mother of Sorrows. I knew her, my sisters, Mother of Life, and her child, he who suffers, he who dies, he who is to return. I knelt down and buried my face in the dust. I was full of fear. And then I heard her call me. 'Mercedes, when the land is seeped in blood it will never give forth good fruit, it will give only the fruit of death. Tell the people this: Plant in love and forgiveness will flower. But plant in hate and there will be ruin. The peacemakers are the children of life. Tell them.' And when I looked up again, she was gone."

Another woman in the circle spoke.

"My sisters, my brothers, I met her coming along the road near San Martín where the road crosses the river. She was walking toward me, walking quickly, carrying a baby in her arms. . . ."

Two appearances. Three. Four. In that circle every woman who was a mother had spoken with this other Mother. All of them wept as they spoke. Martha listened and as she listened something struck her. It crept up on her, up the back of her spine, the nape of her neck. Didn't they realize it themselves? Didn't they see and understand? Who was it they met on the road, by the brook? Whose child was dying and in whose arms? For each of these women had lost a child in the war, Mercedes' son on the road to San Sebastián, Maria Antonia's on the bridge at San Martín. Was it happening everywhere, all over the country? Were mothers meeting themselves and their dead children on every road in the land?

And the first angel sounded the trumpet and there followed hail and fire mingling with blood and it was cast upon the earth and the third part of the earth was burnt up and the third part of the trees and all green grass.

She looked up and another star fell and another. The stars were falling. It was the sign of the third trumpet.

In the silence they were waiting for her to speak.

"What will you do?" she asked them.

"We will lay down our weapons," Mercedes said to her. "We will tell everyone to lay down their guns."

"The killing must end."

"We will not fight any longer. Our war is over. We will have peace."

"Or die," said Mercedes.

It was this, and other encounters like it, that they had come here to explain to Julio Ibarra. It was why they sat patiently waiting day after day.

Faith was a terrible thing. It persevered even in the face of futility. One clutched onto it as onto a life raft in the ocean, clung to it, a single article of faith in an enormous, wild, inhuman sea.

Anyone can love his friends. Jesus understood that. That was natural, he said. I want you to do the unnatural. I want you to love your enemies. What he does not say, the secret he keeps, is that once you love your enemy, truly love him, he is your enemy no longer.

She glanced around at the women sitting silently in the room with her. It was their faith that had brought them to Azul. It was their faith that would convince him, not hers.

In the middle of the afternoon the secretary informed them that the Minister had just returned and would be happy to see them, though their interview would have to be short.

The office into which they were led was spacious but simple. There was a large desk, a conference table, chairs, bookshelves. At another desk over against a wall was a computer, monitor and keyboard. It was a utilitarian space, made personal only by a dozen or so framed photographs hanging on one wall and a large, brightly colored straw tapestry on another, the sort Indian women sold in the market in Masaya. Noticeable by their absence were the ubiquitous portraits of Sandino and Fonseca; in fact there was nothing in the least political anywhere in the room, not on the walls or the shelves, not even the Ministry's own propaganda posters, the smiling children, newly vaccinated, or the smiling young man reminding his *compañeros* to love safely and use a condom.

The Minister greeted her warmly, as the mother of one of his dearest friends. He reminded her that they had met once before, at Stephen's funeral, but he did not expect that she remembered him from that sad occasion. In fact she remembered him very well; of all the mourners she had spoken to that day she recalled him as the only one whose grief appeared to be as deeply felt as her own. Clearly it was only because of her relationship to Stephen that he was granting them this interview.

They sat in a semi-circle around the table and told their stories to him. Nine women with nine stories to tell. "I saw her on the road to San Sebastián." "We are to be her witnesses." "The Virgin told me that if peace does not come. . . ."

She watched him as he listened. He was a handsome man as many Nicaraguans are, with the dark handsomeness of the mestizo, that blend in feature of Indian softness and Spanish angularity. But he was far too bony, too thin. They were saying he was sick, dying of SIDA. They were saying that as Azul dies, so will die the Revolution, eaten away by a virus within. Inflation had hit 25,000%; hungry people will repeat anything.

Gabriela, one of the younger *campesinas*, was speaking. She was explaining the harassment they had experienced, the warnings not to speak in churches, not to speak out in community meetings, not to speak at all. The accusations that they were contra sympathizers, in the pay of the opposition, threats from Sandinista Youth, from the army. "But it is not true, *comandante*," she said. "It is only that we have been told by the Virgin herself to speak." Then she looked directly at him, all earnestness, all trust. "But we are afraid."

"I understand," he said. "Now, Gabriela, tell me this. The message that you bring to the people, what is it exactly? What is it that you would say to me, for example, if I asked you now what meaning the Virgin's words held for me?"

"That we must have peace, *comandante*."

"Only that?"

"Yes. Only that. No more fighting, she says. No more bloodshed. We must vote, not kill. We must listen to our hearts and then cast our votes."

"Well, *compañera*, if the army and the Sandinista Youth think that message is counterrevolutionary, then I myself must be a contra, since that is exactly what I have been saying all over this country for the past months. And the president himself is as guilty as I. So. I am glad you came to me today, that you trusted me with this problem. Now you will tell me exactly who it was who threatened you and I will see to it that it does not happen again. This is a free country. Many brave men and women gave their lives to make it so and there is no place here for fear. So, if you will tell me the names. . . ."

Names. The accumulation of names. Names of the living, names of the dead. There never seemed to be an end to it, names and lives weighing him down like those collars they once put on slaves, made out of stone.

He called friends in Interior, the army. Passing on the information, obtaining assurances, reminding them of their duty, the need to remain watchful of abuses of power, respectful, diligent. A lot to ask men who were being paid the equivalent of a week's wages for a month's labor. So he added, remembering the fear on Gabriela's face, See to it or there will be hell to pay.

There was already hell to pay.

Unstoppable. Only two months ago he had promised the priest he would put his body on the line to stop their tanks. But when it came to it, he voted with the majority. He did not raise his voice in protest. No, he wanted to go with the planes, go with the arms they were sending to Salvador, go and fight. The man he had made that promise to had been dragged from his bed and had his brains blown out by Salvadoran government soldiers armed with American guns. Let the center hold; he would be damned before he would be part of it. The very next day they began shipping arms to Vladimir.

It was unstoppable now. Too much blood spilled for peace to come. The Virgin had appeared a few centuries too late.

There was really no hope that Patrice was alive.

Home at last, in his room, in his bed, he weighed this thought. He could not put it out of his mind.

December ninth. Thirty-seven days since the attempted assassination of Gabriel Aguilar. Thirty-seven days without any word. No news from their intelligence sources. No statement from the Honduran government. No confession.

So Paco Ruiz must have been right after all when he said that Patrice had died within hours of his capture. That first blow to the head, the one they showed inadvertently on TV, that blow alone, followed by how many others, Julio. . . . That's what Paco said to him. But so far as his heart was concerned Patrice was not dead; he was disappeared. And like anyone who loves a disappeared, he had to suffer through the agony of not knowing, of never being able to give up hope and never being able to hope too strongly, of never being able to mourn and never being able to stop mourning. Memories of Patrice would rise in his mind, so clear, so intense. Listening to another voice and Patrice's would come back to him, an expression, a usage, a tone of voice, or seeing a gesture, the way someone lit a cigarette or pushed the hair back from his forehead and Patrice's image would return to him, the way he moved or smiled. Everyday he would remember more, and so it seemed to him that Patrice must be gone from the earth, only memories of him left, glowing now in the minds of those who had known him like the last embers before the fire dies.

It was nearly dawn when the phone rang. Paco Ruiz, with news. Because he had promised to inform him immediately if he heard anything about Patrice. . . .

Paco arrived twenty minutes later wearing the look of a man who had been awake too long. He didn't mince his words, blurted it out before he even took a seat on Julio's couch: Patrice was alive. The Hondurans knew his name and were contacting intelligence sources for information on him. Even if he wasn't talking to them himself—which he probably was, given their methods— they'd find out about him from somewhere else. G-2, for example. G-2 probably had a dossier on him a foot thick.

"All right," Julio said, forcing his voice to stay even, his mind to stay clear. "Now we can stop looking for him and start bargaining for him. What will they want?"

"It's not so simple, Julio."

"Of course it's simple. They know who he is. The Frente can't continue to deny its involvement."

"Of course they can. They can say his admissions were coerced, which they were. The Hondurans will have to produce him and they won't be able to do that for awhile, you can imagine what shape he's in. And until they produce him there's no reason to confirm our involvement. The minute we make a move to bargain for him, we are confirming it loud and clear. Besides, he's not our man anyway. He's Vladimir's."

"A dead man can't retract a confession. His life is in more danger now than it was before."

Paco sat for a moment perfectly still staring at his clasped hands. Very slowly he took a cigarette out of the pack in his shirt pocket and lit it. With growing irritation, Julio watched him inhale the smoke, shake the match, and exhale. It was like watching a man in slow motion. If Paco didn't speak in another second he would have to lift him up off the couch and shake him. Finally Paco cleared his throat and began.

"Listen, Julio. We've been friends for a long time. Now there's something I have to tell you that you're not going to like.

I'm sorry I have to be the one to tell you, but it's my job. Look at it, man. Don't you understand? Patrice Day didn't kill Aguilar. He killed Emilio Castillo."

"What is there to understand? He shot at Aguilar and he missed."

"He's a trained commando. He doesn't miss. And Castillo was shot through the heart."

"So you're suggesting that Patrice meant to shoot Castillo?"

"I'm not suggesting it. Vladimir is. In fact, Vladimir is insisting that it's true. He's saying that if the Frente got hold of Patrice now, they'd put a bullet in his head and consider it a kindness. Turns out Castillo was one of the Frente's most important intelligence sources. He was a big man in the ARENA party, had the confidence of people like Ponce and D'Aubuisson, moved easily in all those government circles, military, political, diplomatic. Not to mention the fact that he knew every element doing business in Central America, from coffee growers to arms dealers to the cartel. Naturally, his relationship to the Frente was secret. A very big secret. Only Vladimir and the senior members of his intelligence cadre had this information. Yet Patrice knew it. And he knew that Castillo would attend that ceremony with Aguilar. He had his own orders, Julio, and they didn't come from Vladimir."

"Vladimir told you all this?"

"Yes, I met with him last week and he told me. He told me about Castillo and other things about Patrice too."

"And what does he think Patrice is then? CIA?"

"Or SOF, more likely."

"Special Forces. I see. Tell me everything Vladimir said, please. Exactly."

Paco looked at Julio with an expression he was probably too tired to disguise, a mixture of exasperation and sympathy, just the sort of patronizing regard that set Julio's teeth on edge.

"He said that we should stop making inquiries, stop wasting time. That he had proof that Patrice Day was an infiltrator, that he was dangerous man, and that it would be just as well if he died in Honduras. At other hands than ours, is what he said, exactly. That's when he told me about Castillo. Then he said that it was good that he had discovered the truth now because Patrice had accumulated far too much power in the highlands, and posed a threat to the insurgency and the leadership there. That he had to die anyway, and that therefore his capture was for the best. . . . For the best, Julio. Which when spoken by a man like Vladimir just means that the fuck-up wasn't a mistake, that it was all planned. They needed to flesh him out and they did. Too bad Castillo died in the process, but it forced Patrice's hand, and so now Vladimir knows the truth. And so do we. He's a dead man, Julio. Even if he were released tomorrow, Vladimir wouldn't let him live, certainly not long enough to get back to the highlands. Because no matter what we know or how much proof we have, those Indians love him. And from what I hear, they can get real nasty when they're roused."

"And Vladimir's proof for all this is that Patrice shot the wrong man in Tegucigalpa? Is that all he has?"

"He thinks it's enough."

"And what do you think? Tell me truly, Paco. Would that satisfy you? This isn't a rhetorical question, my friend. I really want to know."

"If his bullet had gone wild, or if he had hit anyone else, I'd give him the benefit of the doubt. But hitting Castillo in the heart. . . . How much more overt can it be?"

"Exactly," Julio said. "It couldn't be more obvious, and yet, according to Vladimir, for four years Patrice has been totally discreet. Why would killing Castillo be that important to him? Then compare what he did that day with what he was supposed to have done. I questioned Carlos closely about this. Patrice followed the original plan exactly, a single bullet through the heart and then surrender, except he put the bullet in the wrong man's heart. But you know what I think, Paco? I think he shot the right man. I think he shot the man he was told to shoot. I think he was following Vladimir's orders. And that's what I'll continue to think until I talk to him and hear from him what happened in that cemetery. Because if it's a choice between believing Vladimir or believing Patrice—"

"Julio, I have to go to the Minister with this."

195

"And I expect you to. What you do is Interior's business. What I do is my own."

Julio drove himself to his office. On the way he passed by the shacks of the barrios and the skeleton of the cathedral, the two settings which formed the backdrop to all his nightmares. How surreal it was to live and dream in the same landscape, to have only that thin border of wakefulness between one reality and the other. Like the thin border he was struggling to maintain between rationality and madness.

He rejected entirely the notion that Patrice could be SOF.

The only alternative then was that Vladimir had changed Patrice's orders, making Castillo, not Aguilar, the target. He had done it to rid himself of Castillo, for whatever reason, but also to destroy Patrice. He had set it up so that there was no way he could lose and no way Patrice could win: Patrice would either be killed by Aguilar's security guards or by Honduran interrogators or, if by some miracle he survived that, murdered by the Frente itself for being an American spy.

Yet it seemed like an overly elaborate scheme for disposing of a man one didn't trust. Easier by far for Vladimir to disappear Patrice himself than to set in motion something as complex and potentially explosive as this. Why would Vladimir do it?

He didn't know the answer. He had many questions he did not know the answers to, and he wasn't a man who enjoyed being kept in the dark.

He couldn't ask Interior to help him on this. He would have to ask someone else.

On the way to his own office, he stopped at his secretary's desk and scribbled a name and number on a piece of paper. "Phones working today?" he asked. She shrugged. "Do the best you can. If you have to, tell them it's an emergency."

She smiled at that. An emergency—as though everything else wasn't.

An hour later, she came to the door. "Your call is through to the Island, *comandante,*" she said.

He picked up the phone. "To whom am I speaking?" he said.

"Good morning, Julio! It's Alberto Rodriguez. I'm the one you wanted, right?"

"Yes, Alberto," he said. "You're the one I want."

Days passed, ten of them. During those days negotiations resumed and broke off. Heavy fighting continued in Salvador. Brutal contra attacks occurred in the mountain regions of the north and on the Atlantic coast. In Guatemala the bodies of students and university professors were found mutilated. And then, in the early hours of the morning of December 20th Julio was awakened by another phone call. Nightmare repetition. It was the voice of the President. The North Americans had invaded Panama.

TWENTY

Honduras

He was sitting on a chair facing lights. The lights were hot and blinding and he couldn't see beyond them. He kept wanting to get up from the chair, but he was attached to it somehow and couldn't move. But he had to get out of the chair, he had to get up and move, he couldn't sit still any longer, he was beginning to shake, sweat and shake and soon he would start to scream.

He had told them his name. Only that. Name. He didn't have a rank or a serial number. All he had was his name.

She had told him that would be enough. Years ago, it seemed. Victoria. She had said, If once they learn your name. . . .

And he had boasted that they would never learn it.

They had both been wrong.

Days under the lights.

It didn't matter now what he told them, what lies he told them or what truths. He lied when he thought of it, though sometimes he couldn't think of any lie to tell. Sometimes he lied just because it hurt too much to tell the truth. It hurt like they liked to hurt him. They felt so entitled to hurt him, to put their cigarettes out on his hands, to beat him. They had nothing else to do, and it was nearly Christmas, after all. They needed some enjoyment to go with the season.

As soon as the lights went out, he started to dream. Or at least, he thought he was dreaming. They would come then in the darkness and speak to him and he would speak to them. The two boys would come, blowguns in their hands, whispering to him. The old man,

198

the daykeeper. Sometimes soldiers would come, sometimes faces would simply appear over him, once he thought they had sent him a priest. He never knew what language he was speaking to them, or what the words meant. He knew he was floating over the world and words were like bits of cloud, mist, smoke, floating around him, beneath him. They had no substance.

Sometimes they asked him questions so gently that he answered them. It was the least he could do, because they were being kind to him. They were solicitous about his feelings, they understood how it felt to be abandoned by everyone. One in particular, very handsome, very soft-spoken. He would always ask how it felt to be abandoned. There was such sincerity in his voice. And so he wanted to tell him the truth, but it got caught in his throat, how it felt, how it hurt. He couldn't talk about any of that yet.

It was the drugs they were giving him that were making him soft. He knew it, but there was nothing he could do about it. They were stronger than he was; they got the needle into his arm and then he got soft. There was nothing he could do.

"How did Vladimir find out Castillo was working for the Americans?" they would ask him. Or "What was Castillo's involvement with the poppy harvest in Guatemala?"

He said he didn't know anything about that. Castillo. The CIA. The Guatemalan poppy harvest. Supplying the bases. The drug route through Guatemala to Mexico. Nothing. He knew nothing.

When the drugs wore off, as they did more and more quickly, they left him more and more empty. No more words. He couldn't summon any more words. He was fading. It was something like sinking into a white fog. First he couldn't see, then he couldn't hear. Nothing hurt anymore. He floated over hurt. Noticed it, but from a place very far away. He was fading, becoming transparent, he could see through himself, sometimes he could look down and see himself bleeding on the floor of his cell, sometimes he could almost see through the wall into a courtyard, into a village, into the hills and then into the high mountains, sometimes he could fly with the hawk, slipping between smoking volcanoes, looking down at the dead zone, Xibalba risen from beneath the earth, all the land burnt black and bones spread on the fields like seed, flying next to the eagle, dressed in black woolen clothes decorated with quetzal feathers and golden suns embroidered into the wool, noticing the detail, the iridescent blue-green of the feathers, the red threads woven into the black.

Now they did not try to question him. The young one came to give him water to drink, but he was too tired to swallow water. He was tottering on the edge of a great sleep, some oceanic dream into which he would sink, into which he would fade like a streamer of mist.

There were men gathered near a *barranco*, candlelight and burning *pom*, a sacrificed cock. He was led along a path lit by candles to the *barranco's* edge. Clouds above him turned silver, then red and gold; below him those clouds held in the valleys rose upward toward him like *copal* smoke. Then it was dark. Night.

In the darkness there was a thicker darkness, textured, moving. He saw its form and knew what it was, a black puma, two meters away, watching him. But not for long. No, it moved quickly, covering the distance between them in a single spring, great head and paws coming out of the dark, a blackness he could not see but only feel, the air rushing toward him and then the weight of the animal's body, like the weight of a man, pinning him to the earth. Its mouth was just above him, it could rip out his throat with a single bite. But for some reason it didn't frighten him. He put his arms around it, white skin against black fur, and its mouth came down onto his and he found himself kissing it and it was not a cat's mouth but a man's, not a cat's body but a man's, and he heard words in his ear: You remember me, Jaguar? Listen. Everything leaves a path behind it. Everything that passes, remains. No matter how you try, you cannot erase time.

He was surrounded by dancing monkey men, eagle men, deer men, jaguar men. Hunahpu and Xbalanque danced in front of him, opening each other's chests with obsidian blades, taking out each other's hearts, spinning them in the air like balls, returning them to their bodies. The skull of One Death sprouted corn ears, quetzal wings, serpent fangs, Ah Mun's gentle smile. Then transforming into an old man, One Death reached out his hand.

They were standing under the roof comb of a high pyramid. Hundreds of steep steps below them, people waited, children and their parents, old men and women. Above them in the sky, light hung suspended, many different kinds of light, the crisp light of diamond-pointed stars, and the steady, brilliant light of planets, the blurs of galaxies and the broad pathway of moonlight. They stood there, he and One Death, suspended between light and the children of light, and he felt his heart stretched between the two, heart below, heart above, Heart of Earth, Heart of Sky, his own heart like a ladder on which the two could meet, the people climbing up his heart, the light descending through it. And One Death said to him: Now do you understand why?

He was an old *campesino* with a hawk nose and an AK47 over his shoulder. He was the Lord of Life and Death.

"Do you see now? There is only one proof, Patrice, and it is that you die for us. Not until you are dead and your body buried in our soil will we know that you have become one of us, because you have sacrificed your own life for the good of the people. That is the only test. That is also the only immortality. You will never be forgotten by us so long as there is light. It is what you wanted from me, Patrice. How can you blame me for giving you what you wanted?"

Was this what I wanted, he wondered. Did I want this death?

Now the roofcomb expanded into a stage or into a room, but a room filled with light. One Death disappeared; Ah Mun, Lord Maize, was smiling at him. He was as beautiful as One Death had been ugly, as beautiful as spring itself, of which he was the god, young and healthy, the epitome of life and growth. His long hair was gathered into two lengths, a single row of seashells and polished seeds braided into each length. His forehead was sloped, his nose long, his lips sculpted, his eyes the shape of almonds.

The candles had grown to the size of Easter candles, six feet tall. Their light was like torchlight, and in that light Ah Mun glowed. He felt a fierce joy rush through him, a crazy, hot, fierce joy which he recalled as desire, he felt his sex stir, try desperately

201

to stir, he felt blood come out of him, a knife in his arm, he felt himself press the knife into his arm so that he could make himself bleed. *Stay! Here is my blood sacrifice. You must stay!*

But Ah Mun put his hand on the wound and pressed it closed. "No, don't bleed for me, *querido*! I never wanted you to bleed for me. What is the good of all this blood, all this pain?"

"It was my fault, Alejandro," he said as Ah Mun transformed from a Mayan god into his dead lover. "That night . . . the night you died . . . I didn't go with you . . . I let you go alone. . . ."

"But I never asked to go with me, *querido*. If I had, you would never have refused. None of it is your fault, Patrick. I would forgive you gladly if there were anything to forgive, but there's nothing. I only want you to be happy. I only want to hear your voice again. Recite for me, 'It is not for the sake of the husband, my beloved, that the husband is dear. . . .' Please, Patrick. Recite for me."

"It is not for the sake of the husband, my beloved, that the husband is dear, but for the sake of the Self."

"Tell me more, my beloved."

"It is not for the sake of the gods, my beloved, that the gods are worshipped, but for the sake of the Self."

"Let the Brachman ignore him who thinks the Brachman is different from the Self."

He was holding Alejandro in his arms. He was home in his own bed and Alejandro was in his arms. They were falling asleep, reciting this litany. After making love, a dose of the Upanishads. He was so happy, he couldn't remember ever being so happy.

"Let the gods ignore him who thinks that the gods are different from the Self."

Alejandro stretched against him, he could feel his whole body, warm, strong, every muscle, every rib, his sex against him. "This is it, my beloved," Alejandro sighed, "that I wanted to tell you. THAT ART THOU."

He awoke from this dream. He was still in the cell, he was still alive. Nothing had changed. What did he have to do to die? He couldn't believe it was taking so long, that he could still be breathing, that his heart could still be beating, he couldn't believe that he could not simply will himself dead. He felt he would weep from rage, from the tedium of pain, from the pitiful loss of his own death. His hands ached, and his mouth and throat, his skin hurt all over either from burns or bruises or cuts or the punctures of the needles, so that he felt as though worms were crawling all over him, or maybe that was from the drugs, or maybe he was dead, in the ground, feeling the worms eat him. And he could feel the anxiety of withdrawal building up in him, he could feel the need for the drug begin again, need that would bring him to the edge but wouldn't push him over it. If only it would make him crazy enough so they would kill him out of irritation, or out of boredom, or because they were entitled to pieces of his body to bring home in glass jars.

Once in the dark he looked up and saw the boys, smiling at him, and that cheered him. They came quite often after that, the two boys, one with the tail of a jaguar, one with the scales of a fish, beautiful, naked boys with long Mayan foreheads, blowguns in their hands. They came and gave him water to drink. Sometimes they played the flute for him. He assumed he was dreaming this, but then when the others came, the men in uniforms, the ones with deep voices who spoke nonsense, they didn't seem any more or less real than the Twins, and so he didn't know really what was dream and what was reality, if there was any reality in this realm at all.

This time the drug hit him in waves, waves of pain, one after the other. Different drug this time. Fucking with his head: some made you feel nothing, some made you feel everything. They were asking about Castillo again. The handsome young one was holding his hand. Why was he holding his hand? Holding his index finger, and then he heard the snap, and felt the bone break. And the young one looked him right in the eye. *Castillo?* he said. And then he took the middle finger between his own and rubbed it slightly, in preparation. *Who informed Vladimir that Castillo was working with the CIA?*

The waves hit him. Castillo was working with the CIA. Castillo was providing intelligence to the Frente and Castillo was pals with General Garcia Fuentes, and now even dead, he was so powerful he could cause these waves of nausea and agony.

Emilio Castillo, may you rot in hell.

All he had to do was close his eyes and he saw the Twins dancing before the lords of Death. The lords were big men, ghostly white, dressed up as doctors or in business suits. The Twins were going to show the lords of Death a new trick, something they'd never seen before. Watch!

"Watch! This is the sacrifice of Hunahpu by Xbalanque. One by one his legs, his arms were spread wide. His head came off first, rolling far away outside. Then his heart was dug out of his chest and smothered in a leaf. All the Xibalbans went crazy at the sight. Now there was only one of them dancing there: Xbalanque."

He saw Xbalanque dancing. He was naked with long black hair gathered behind his back. He had jaguar ears and paws and tail, but his face was Mayan and his eyes burned. Jubilantly he cried out to Hunahpu: Get up!

He saw Hunahpu get up. He was so excited by this he almost leapt up out of his dream. Then he felt the longings of the lords of Death. Oh how he felt that longing. To die and to be brought back to life again! Yes, to have the bliss of death and the greater bliss of return.

"Do it to us! Sacrifice us!" One and Seven Death said to Hunahpu and Xbalanque.

But would they do it? Would they? Yes, of course, for such great lords, how could they refuse?

So they were sacrificed, the rulers of Xibalba. But the clever Twins did not bring them back to life.

"Such was their defeat. The boys accomplished it only through wonders, only through self-transformation."

They stood together before the lords of Death, big white men, defeated men. Only two boys, but they had won. They had conquered Death. He looked at Hunahpu and Hunahpu smiled at him. He could hardly believe it. They had defeated Death. They had won the war. It was over and they had won. The generals were done for. The capital was liberated. The war was over. He was filled with such joy he couldn't stay still, he couldn't stand with dignity, he had to jump up and cry out. He had to jump on his jaguar paws and laugh and dance with joy. And he did jump up, he did jump. . . .

"Why did you shoot him then?" the handsome one asked him in his soft, solicitous voice. "Why, Patrick? Why did you kill him? You didn't miss, did you? You didn't aim for Aguilar and miss? You wouldn't miss a target like that, would you?"

"No," he said. "I wouldn't miss."

"Why then? Why did you do it?"

He tried to remember. He had to remember. Something was forcing him to, forcing him back to that morning, that graveyard, to Emilio Castillo, Lord of Death, standing directly in front of him, just behind and to the right of Gabriel Aguilar. He saw Castillo and at the same moment Castillo saw him, his eyes penetrating into him as though looking for something in him, some knowledge he ought to possess but didn't. And in that split second, words, an image, the truth, whole and entire, pierced through him like the current of the wire soon would, forcing the knowledge Castillo feared he possessed out of his subconscious, like night lightning illuminating a black sky, revealing only blackness and still more blackness, but intensified now, absolute, certain, sure.

A dear boy, Alejandro. How much pleasure he must have given you over the years. . . .

He saw it all, the whole picture, everything. Once it might have paralyzed him, but not now. He had the instincts of a *guerrillero* now. He knew what to do.

He pressed the trigger.

He didn't even have to think twice.

The handsome one was still there, waiting. Waiting like a friend waits. Like a friend, like a lover, holding your hand, waiting for you to tell him the truth.

"I shot Castillo," he said, "because he was a son of a bitch."

Because everything leaves a trail behind it, Emilio. Because no matter how you try, you cannot erase time.

But he had become so soft, he had become nothing but emotion, ache, all he could do was think of Alejandro and weep.

They moved him while he was unconscious. He woke up one day, and he was in a room, above ground. There was light in the room and he was in a bed with sheets and blankets and an IV tube in his arm and instead of soldiers there were men in white, pretending to be doctors. He wasn't fooled. He closed his eyes, but instead of fading back into darkness he found his brain was working again. He found he wasn't sedated, drugged or dying; he found he could think.

After a few days, they got him into a wheelchair. They didn't offer to tell him what was wrong with him or where he was; he didn't ask. They wheeled him down a short hallway and into a room, up to a table. The room was empty except for the table and a few chairs.

It wasn't as bad as it could be. It wasn't a dental chair. It wasn't a surgery.

On the table were pitchers of water, several glasses. A tape recorder. A pad and pens. A briefcase. Benign objects. He noticed these objects before he looked at the man sitting across the table from him. He had entered other rooms where there were other objects on the table: syringes and surgical instruments, electrodes, bits of wire, blackjacks. The objects could clue you in on what the session was going to be about; the men, on the other hand, were always the same.

This one was North American. Early forties. Big, fair, mid-westerner, probably. Army in civilian drag. Come to cut a deal. Live free or die.

The North American opened the briefcase and took out a file folder.

"Patrick Day. Your dossier," he said, pushing the file across the table toward Patrick with his index finger. "Compliments of G-2. You are fairly well known in Guatemala, it seems, and the honor of your presence is requested there. I understand there are a few questions they'd like to ask you. And there is the small matter of the murder of a certain General Garcia."

Patrick sat very still. He knew this was coming. It was only a matter of time, though he had hoped that he might die in that time. He had nearly succeeded in dying. Alejandro had come for him, had taken him in his arms, but as much as he had wanted to leave, some evil karma held him back, wouldn't let him go.

"Yes, the Guatemalans want you real bad, Day. They have a bonafide murder to charge you with, and you can imagine how many of your friends they'd like to get to know. Then there's this little matter right here, with Castillo. We're damned interested in knowing how the Frente discovered Castillo's relationship with us, and how many more of our operatives your people have targeted, and when you're going to hit them. So it's really been difficult negotiating your release, Patrick. Damned difficult. But it's done. Seems you have another identity, your CO in Palmerola remembers you after all. So you're a free man. You can walk out of here . . . oh, next week. Yes, by next week I'd say you can walk right out this door. I just don't know where the fuck you're gonna go."

He knew the rest. His brain was back on line again at least. He said, "So I'm going to get to be the first openly gay Green Beret? Fabulous. And what rank are you going to give me?"

The North American hesitated for a second, just a beat. Then he went on. It was a canned speech, after all. They got training in how to fuck over people's heads. "High enough so that when they kill you, we'll have a good enough reason to go after them. After all, counterinsurgency is the hardest work we do down here. And we're going to tell them that you've been working deep cover for four years. Thanks to you we know every move the Frente's going to make and everything the Unity's up to, everybody involved, the whole ballgame. You're a hero, Day, and it's gonna be real sad when those shit bangers shoot you down. Or, who knows, maybe they'll do a slow job on you. Your own *compas*. Your own friends. Life's full of little ironies, isn't it?"

"You really think they're going to believe this bullshit?"

"Oh, yes. I think they'll believe it. I think we can make it reasonably credible. Plant a few stories here and there. Pass the information on to certain people who will pass it on to the right intelligence sources among the leftists. Reliable sources. Then, Day, you're a dead man. We just clean you up a little, drive you into town, drop you on a street corner. How long before they find you? You're out on your own. You got no friends here, no place to go. You won't even be able to get out of the country. And what if you managed to cross the border. To get where? Nicaragua? Guatemala? Salvador? Nobody's gonna help you anywhere, not us, not them. They'll hunt you down wherever you go. You're dead on arrival."

The American sat back in his chair. Smug. They had kept pounding the message in: nobody's coming for you, nobody gives a shit. Made him soft and planted all those seeds: they used you and fucked you over, Day. Do you think Vladimir cares what happens to you? They forgot you already. They forgot you exist.

"On the other hand," the big white man continued, "your life could be real different. Your life could be good. You could get out of this mess with all your faculties intact and money in the bank. You could go home, put it all behind you, get on with your life. That's what it's all about, Patrick. Getting on with your life. You say the word, cooperate with us, and we'll take good care of you. Otherwise, we let the word out tomorrow morning. In two days, your life won't be worth dog shit."

The American stopped talking. Patrick stared down at his hands. They were broken, bruised, burnt. He hadn't really looked at them in a long time. He wasn't going to be able to do much with them after this. But then it didn't seem likely he'd be using a gun again.

"I'll tell you the truth," he said. His voice sounded strange to him, too gentle to be his voice, too melodious. Maybe it was speaking English that made him sound this way. "I'm done here anyway. There's nothing more I need to do here. So as far as I'm concerned, you're doing me a favor. If I were you, I'd make it all real simple and put a bullet in my head right here and now. But if you don't have the balls to do that, and you want my *compas* to do it for you, fine. If they think I need to die for the sake of this revolution, they'll kill me and I'll die. I was willing to die for them before and I'm still willing."

"They'll hunt you down like an animal. You'll die in the gutter. For what?"

"People die on this planet," he said softly. "Everybody dies. All you can do is exit as well as you can."

"You dumb fuck," the American said, and got up and left the room.

The Green Path

January 1990

TWENTY ONE

Concepcion walked down the cobblestone street from the old convent with her basket filled with soiled linen. It was early in the morning on this New Year's Eve, the sun just rising over the mountains. Angela would have brought the water, poured it into the pot, set it on the fire to heat. She hoped Angela had done this. They would spend the morning washing, scrubbing these sheets, hanging them up to dry in the sun, folding them, returning them by late afternoon. And so this decade would come to an end.

She thought these thoughts as she walked, but she was feeling something else. The thoughts covered the feelings. The words of the thoughts concealed the flow of feeling. Because she could not spend any time feeling fear. It was useless to feel fear, even to give it a moment's time. Better to watch the sun rising. The sun in the east; Copán in the west; herself walking along cobblestones between the two.

Angela was in the yard, just standing there in the dirt, but not standing like herself. She was holding her body stiffly, eyes big as plates, arms hanging straight by her sides, fingers pointed down. Oh Mother of Sorrows! But she did not run, she did not hesitate. It was either the one thing or the other. She entered the yard, put her basket down. Angela, seeing her mother, began to shake, tremble like a young tree in the breeze.

"Inside," she whispered.

"All right. Stay right here. Mind the clothes."

She went to the doorway. The man was standing by her table. Only one small man. And he was Indian.

Relief rose in her like the sun.

"Good morning," she said.

"And good morning to you, *compañera*," the man replied.

213

Despite what she had been told, Angela had trailed into the room behind her mother. "This disobedient child is my daughter," she said. "Angela, since you are so nosy, go prepare some food for our guest. Bring him something to drink." She gestured for the man to sit down.

"I received your message through Copán, Concepcion. Thank you."

"He may not be the one you seek."

"When did they arrive here?"

"On Christmas Eve. They came to the old convent. Several cars, two vans and a truck. The one they had on a stretcher, one of my brothers was working on the repair of the wall and saw him for a minute. Only a minute. He said he was a gringo."

"And you go there every day?"

"Yes. They needed a laundress and the *padre* recommended me. They leave the baskets for me in the courtyard. The place is heavily guarded, *compañero*."

"Tonight you said they will be going to San Pedro?"

"For the New Year Celebration. There will only be six guards on duty, but tonight they will be drunk."

"There is a celebration in the village as well?"

"Yes."

"There may be shooting so be sure people stay away from the convent tonight. You will have to draw me a picture of the buildings."

"And what am I to tell the child about you?"

"A relative of yours perhaps?"

She considered this. There was Indian in her, too, in all Hondurans. "My mother's cousin, perhaps. From Ocotepeque."

"That will do," he said, but already he was staring down the lane toward the convent, making his plans.

Many visitors came to the village that day for the celebration so it was easy for him to walk several times along the street in front of the convent and study it without drawing any attention to himself.

They had not secured it very well. Even if the wall itself was studded with glass and topped with barbed wire, there was a tree beside the wall from which he could easily drop directly into the courtyard. If on top of it the guards were drunk, it would be child's play to get inside.

Concepcion drew him a plan of the convent, pointing out to him the cellar stairs and the location of the kitchen where the guards usually spent their evenings.

"And only you alone, *compañero?* You will go in alone?"

"Don't worry," he replied. "Don't even think any more about it."

The three men moved in the darkness like animals of the night. In the village square there was music, dancing. Many lights had been strung around the plaza and that area of light and movement was the focus of all eyes. They moved away from the light, into the dark, over the convent wall. From the shadows of the banyon, they crossed the convent's courtyard to the corridor.

From the plaza came the sound of firecrackers, sharp and distinct as gun fire.

They fanned out across the courtyard toward the light coming from within the building, from the kitchen where from the sounds, several guards and some women from the village were drinking.

As Concepcion had said, there were two kitchen doors.

One of the *compas* approached the side entrance while two waited at the front.

A skyrocket shot up into the night.

The *compa* at the side entrance ran forward and hurled a canister through the door.

The skyrocket and the bomb exploded at once. There was a flash of light in the kitchen and a woman screamed.

Two women followed by two men in uniform ran into the courtyard through the main kitchen door. The women kept running, the guards were stopped by a spray of bullets. Nothing, however, stopped the flames.

The air along the corridor began to fill with smoke.

215

He left his *compas* to deal with the remaining guards and took the stairs down. The cellar of the convent had at one time been honey-combed with storage cells, each with its own set of locks. Most of these rooms were empty now, as abandoned as the convent itself had been. He padded silently down the corridor between the cells, the tiny spot of light from his hand torch his only guide in the darkness. Every door he passed was off its hinges, the locks rusted, the entrances curtained over by silvery cobwebs, some shaped ornately, like spiders' webs, others as long and delicate as angel hair. Even along the corridor itself webs clung to his face as he walked along. No one had passed through those dust tapestries for many months.

He turned on his heel and made his way back to the staircase, back up above ground. The *compas* were exchanging gunfire with guards in the courtyard. The fire that had started in the kitchen was spreading upward. He released the safety on his pistol and ran up the stairs.

Patrick didn't ever really believe they were going to let him go. New Year's Day, they'd told him. You're DOA, they'd told him. Happy New Year.

He didn't believe it.

But he wasn't drugged any more, and he wasn't beaten every day. They didn't break any more fingers. They took him off the IV and brought him real food, bland, soft food, which he could eat and keep down. He wasn't chained to the wall anymore. Every day someone in a white jacket would come and help him get up, support him while he walked the few steps from one wall of the cell to the other, from the wall to the door. He hadn't realized how weak he was. They washed him and gave him clean clothes to wear. Every day they changed the sheets on his bed. There was even a little window in the cell, and a little light.

He didn't believe they were going to let him go, but then it seemed that after all they might.

And he'd walk outside and see the sky and the sun again.

It almost seemed too much to hope for. Even if it only lasted an hour, it still seemed too much.

If they were telling the truth, this would be his last night in a cell.

He heard the firecrackers coming from the celebration in the plaza. Then it seemed the firecrackers were going off right in the courtyard below his window. That close by. He could even smell the gunpowder.

And then he smelt the smoke.

He heard it coming toward the cell, eating its way toward him. It might already be inside the wall of the cell. He could almost feel it burning up through the floor, burning the corridor outside the door. It was roaring toward him, but it wouldn't be the fire that would kill him. It would be the smoke.

No way out of this cell. He'd tried before. He'd spent his life, it seemed, trying to get out of cells.

Unless the fire ate a hole in the wall for him before the smoke got him.

There was nothing to do but sit and wait.

Wait and pray.

The Twins went into the oven. Jumped in holding each other's hands. "Don't you think we know our own deaths, you lords?"

Don't you think I know my own death? he said to the empty cell.

This isn't it, he said to the cell.

More firecrackers went off right under his window.

The air was filling with smoke.

He didn't want to get down on the floor and listen to the fire eat its way through the joists.

Death by fire and smoke.

Dido on her pyre above Carthage, setting herself aflame as Aeneas' ship sailed toward Rome.

Hindu wives burnt alive on the same pyres as their dead husbands.

Heretics burnt at the stake. The *auto da fé*. The act of faith.

The smoke was so thick now. A few more minutes and there would be nothing left to breathe.

Beads of sweat collecting on his forehead, sweat streaming down his face like tears.

Alejandro, he said, is this it now? Will you open the door now and take me out of this awful place?

But when the door banged open, it wasn't Alejandro. It was his real death he saw, his traitor's death. A man standing in the doorway, a kerchief pulled up over his mouth and nose. Smoke all around him, but he stood poised under the bulb in the ceiling they never turned off, the light that was always burning, and Patrick saw him clearly and distinctly, a *guerrillero* in shooting stance, pistol in hand, aiming right at his heart.

TWENTY TWO

Managua, Nicaragua

It wasn't easy for them to arrange a meeting. Like everything in Managua now, even so simple, so ordinary a thing as meeting a friend for a few drinks and conversation had became an enormous task, Herculean. On days there was water, the phones were out. On days the phones worked, the electricity went off. People seemed dazed by it all, unable to concentrate on any task. It was as though the optimism and blind faith that had propped up the revolution for ten years, despite the shortages, the outages, the bombings, the deaths, that balloon of faith had suddenly popped. One day it was there; the next it was gone. People looked at each other amazed, as though coming out of a dream, looking at reality for the first time. Reality in Managua was a harsh and brutal thing to see. No wonder it was proving very nearly impossible to meet a man for a drink.

They couldn't meet at his house or at the Ministry, or at any other government building, any cantina or bar where either of them were known, any public place where they could be recognized. He didn't want to involve any of his friends by using their homes, or go to the extreme length of renting a hotel room for the occasion. Finally on the morning of New Year's Day, exhausted and at the end of his patience, he simply arranged for his companion to wait for him on a certain corner. He would drive them in his own car as far out into the country as he could get on the little gas he had left. To someplace that was no place, a parched landscape with a dead volcano for backdrop. A desolation, a wasteland. He was carrying himself in his pocket, like a good *guerrillero*. Cigarettes and a bottle of Flor de Caña, some gas, that's all he needed.

He swung his car around the corner by the National Library and there, ebony black and beautiful, though with his hair neatly trimmed and his jeans no longer skin tight, was Alberto Rodriguez, leaning against a lamp post, waiting for him.

They drove out of the city into the parched land.

Julio parked in a bit of shade on a dirt road, poured them each a glass of rum and lit a cigarette.

Alberto was smiling.

"So, *comandante*, is it time for my report? Very interesting work, snooping around this country. Everybody talks, you know. There are no secrets."

"Yes, I know," Julio said.

"Unfortunately there's nothing much to learn here. Everything I got came from Honduras or Salvador. It took a little longer there, but our people came up with the information you wanted." He grinned at Julio. "We *Cubanos* are the best. At detective work as well as everything else."

"Good," he said, trying not to be distracted by the proximity of Alberto's body, his arm casually draped over the seatback behind him, the sexual energy between them that he knew he alone was feeling, or would admit to. "What do you have for me?"

"You wanted to know why Vladimir would want Emilio Castillo dead. The consensus in Salvador is that he wouldn't. Castillo was rather unimportant himself, not in any position where killing him would be either necessary or useful. But he was a rich man with a lot of business interests and a lot of enemies, and he made a practice of ratting on them to the Frente in exchange for . . . oh, let's say personal satisfaction and let it go at that."

"Interesting. So Castillo worked for intelligence."

"Everybody's intelligence. He was on the CIA payroll, too. His information to the Frente was always reliable. Reliable and trivial. Of a sexual nature mostly. He was a notorious pedophile himself and had the inside scoop on most of the other sexual perverts in the region. And he wasn't above using the information when it suited his purposes. Whatever they were."

"I see," Julio said, and lit another cigarette. "So Vladimir had no reason to kill Castillo. So why is Castillo dead?"

"Don't jump the gun on me, Julio. I'm not done."

"So there's more?"

"I told you I got you what you wanted, didn't I? Once I realized I was going nowhere with Castillo, I remembered that you said you couldn't understand why the Frente would assassinate a man like Aguilar in the first place. Well, I asked the same question. Why kill Aguilar? Now Aguilar is a very popular man, but so are a lot of bastards. So I went to Honduras myself and started digging around. Guess what I found?"

"Please, just tell me, Alberto. Without the drama, OK. Just tell me."

"No drama? No foreplay? Just in and out, huh? All you want from me is an afternoon quickie?" Julio scowled at him and Alberto put his head back and laughed. "OK, *hombre*, here it is. Aguilar is everything they say he is. A good patriot and honest, probably because he's too rich and too proud not to be. He may well win the election and he can't be bought. So a lot of powerful elements want him out of the way, and you know which they are: the military and business interests, or in other words, the cartel.

"Turns out—no surprises here—that Castillo's business interests in Honduras are all with the cartel. He's got heavy investments like a lot of people. But their success in Honduras depends on keeping the trade routes clear to the American bases and keeping the traffickers happy. OK, now, about six, seven months ago, right before I came here to work with you, I got a call from an assistant of Aguilar's. He wanted to set up a meeting between us and Aguilar to discuss coordinating our respective drug interdiction policies should Aguilar win the election. He said Aguilar was fed up with the Americans, didn't like their attitude, didn't trust them. He wanted a different model, and he wanted our assistance in developing his own plans to stop the drug trade through Honduras. That meeting is still planned. You see where this is heading, Julio?"

"Yes, I see very clearly. It's not Vladimir who wants Aguilar to disappear, it's Castillo. So he gives the Frente bogus information and they act on it. But it's ridiculous, Alberto. Vladimir would never order the assassination of a man of Aguilar's position on such flimsy evidence, especially provided by a third-rate source like Castillo. He would need proof."

"You don't think that the cartel can manufacture proof? It would be the simplest thing in the world, Julio. And the information could easily be confirmed. Castillo and his business partners weren't the only elements a strict drug enforcement policy would hurt. The Americans would like Aguilar out of the way too, for obvious reasons. I suspect that anywhere Vladimir looked for confirmation, he'd find it. And, you know, a strong Social Democrat in power in Honduras is no big boon for the Frente in any event. The better he is at keeping the people happy, the less likely they'll be to join an armed insurrection. And that's what Vladimir wants ultimately, isn't it? He's still dreaming about the big revolution, the overthrow of the oligarchy, the destruction of national borders, Central American unity, the utopian state. He's still thinking of the People's Republic of Mesoamerica, Julio. He goes to sleep at night clutching that dream to him like a man clutches the dream of the woman he loves, and he won't let go of it no matter how old he gets, how old the dream gets, how old the woman gets. . . . He'd kill Aguilar for no damn reason except to get people on the streets blowing holes in each other, so if he has a reason, any reason, don't you think he'd take it? At this point in his history, what the fuck does he have to lose?"

"But his assassin killed Castillo, not Aguilar."

"Exactly. Which is why nobody believes Day was *his* assassin. The word is that Patrick Day was a high ranking officer in Special Forces. And this is leaked from the top. The very top. They're either neutralizing him in a very efficient and professional manner, or it's true."

"Let's say it's not true."

"OK. Let's. Then Gabriel Aguilar owes his life to that man, but I can't figure out how or why it happened. I talked to Vladimir and he denies up and down that he changed Day's orders. And I believe him because if Vladimir had learn he'd been lied to and decided to kill Castillo at the last minute there'd be no reason to deny it now. Before, yes, he'd have to stick to the story that Day was Stillwell, CIA agent. So long as his man kept quiet, there was no reason for Vladimir to spill the beans, right? But after the Hondurans released his identity and it was confirmed by his family, Jesus, why keep up the pretense any longer? Get the poor son of a bitch out of there. But no. He didn't. He told me that he had ordered Day to kill Aguilar, not Castillo. He insisted that by killing Castillo, Day had proven himself to be an infiltrator, an American operative, just as he had suspected all along. It's hard to argue with his logic, Julio, since the Americans are confirming this themselves."

"So there's agreement on all sides that Castillo was killed on orders from the Americans and that Vladimir's assassin was actually a member of Special Forces. Everyone agrees that this is the case."

"That's right. Everyone but you, I take it."

"I can't be the only one. What does the Unity say?"

"I didn't ask the Unity. You didn't say anything about—"

"OK. So we don't know what the Unity says. What about you, Alberto? I trust your judgment of men. What do you think?"

Alberto tossed his cigarette out the window and turned to face Julio. His expression was uncharacteristically solemn. "I think you're in love with this man," he said.

"You are a detective then, aren't you?"

"You are not so hard to read, my friend. And I lived with you myself, remember. As to the facts, what I learned, what I feel, it's only this. It is very clear to me that Vladimir never trusted this man. He sent him on a mission to assassinate Aguilar on the basis of false and incomplete information, which he believed to be true. Let's say Day discovered the truth in Tegucigalpa and could not reestablish contact with Vladimir. Let's say at the same time he learned that Castillo was an informant for the CIA. You or I might have aborted the mission; he shot Castillo instead. Vladimir, who did not trust him to begin with, would never give him the benefit of the doubt as someone might who knew him as an honorable man. Then the Americans got hold of him and decided that rather than kill him and turn him into a martyr, they'd neutralize him by identifying him as one of their own. No one would ever trust him again, and in fact someone might decide to terminate him, relieving the Americans of having to do it themselves.

"This makes sense to me, Julio, but I can't prove it. The only one who could have told you the truth about why Castillo is a dead man and Aguilar isn't would have been the commando himself. We'll never know now."

"How is that?" Julio asked, feeling his heart suddenly contract.

Alberto took Julio's hand and held it tight, so tight he felt it was his hand not his heart that was about to break. "Because he's dead, Julio. I'm sorry. Until this moment I didn't know . . . how it was between you. He died last night. In a fire. The place they were holding him burnt down. They couldn't get him out."

Alberto picked up the bottle from the floor and poured a finger of dark rum into each of their glasses. "To the dead," he said, and drained his glass. Julio drank his down too. He couldn't think about this now, he couldn't let himself feel it. He couldn't even say his lover's name out loud, the syllables wouldn't form in his mind. All he wanted was to close his eyes and sleep. He wanted to sleep until a new world came into existence, a world he could live in without a broken heart.

TWENTY THREE

Copán, Honduras

It was nearly dawn on the first day of the new year, the dawn of a new decade, the last before the millennium . . . according to the European calendar. But for the people waiting in Copán it was still the year 3 Wind, the day 12 Dog, and according to the Mayan Long Count, there were still another twenty-three years until the end of the thirteenth *baktun*, the thirteenth cycle of four centuries, and by some accounts, the end of this cycle of creation. On that day, by European count, December 23, 2012, the Long Count would return to the beginning, to day zero, 13.0.0.0.0. This present *baktun*, spanning the last four hundred years, had nöt been good for the Maya. So, though no one believed that the end of the thirteenth baktun would herald the end of this world and a new creation by the gods, daykeepers were aware of portents and signs, of greater dangers now that the *baktun* was coming to an end, and there were always rumors of spirits of the dead returning, of gods returning, power returning, though of these things the daykeepers would not speak.

Except one, the daykeeper who had spoken to Victor Zapeta. *He will pass through all the Houses and go into the oven. They will spread out his limbs for sacrifice. Fire will pass through his body but the fire will turn into fiery splendor and he will rise from the river into which they throw his bones. For I name him Xbalanque, the Jaguar Sun. . . .*

On the upper floor of the old convent, the gunman stood poised in a doorway, squinting into the smoke. Standing there, framed in fire, everything burning around him, behind him, above him, he was magnificent, a gunman of the apocalypse. Patrick stood up to greet his death, but as he did the gunman stepped forward and reached out his hand.

"Patrice!" he said. "Come quickly. This oven is getting a little too hot."

The *guerrilleros* drove their old battered pick-up down the road to Copán, two up front, four in the back. Driving down the bumpy dirt road to Copán as the east grew light, welcoming the new day.

Patrick lay stretched out in the back, watching the stars fade from the sky. Stars again. Sky. They had only just made it out of the convent. Only just made it out of that cell. The moment he passed through the doorway, one of the ceiling timbers fell burning across the floor behind him.

"Nice to see you, Victor," he had managed before the smoke got to him and, choking, he had stumbled down the stairs, across the courtyard and out into the fresh, clean air. The pick-up was waiting and they had veered away from the burning convent while skyrockets exploded over their heads.

Victor, on one side of him, Anselmo on the other, the stars fading in the sky. Patrick let himself feel this joy, this great, oceanic joy. Freedom. Life. Going home to Copán.

The great city of the Mayas, abandoned twelve hundred years before, was occupied by Indians again. It had happened quietly, without fanfare. When the first handful of *guerrilleros* stopped in the village of Copán during their sweep down from the Guatemalan border in search of Patrice, the villagers advised them to set up camp among the ruins of the temples. Since the attack on the Presidential Palace no tourists were visiting Copán, no archeologists or park guides were working in the ruins, and what better place for warriors to sleep than among the temples and courtyards of the Acropolis? They took this advice as a sign and set up permanent camp in the city. From that camp the *compañeros* spread out over northern Honduras following every lead in search of Patrice. But while they were gone, as though word had gone out that the time had come at last, Indians from the border region began filtering into the ancient city, gathering in the Central Court, on the terraces, in the Great Plaza, in the shade of the pyramids. Many of them were armed.

Every time Victor returned to Copán, more Indians were there to greet him. When he asked them why they had come, the men in cowboy hats, the women wearing colorful *huipiles*, they would say they were between harvest and spring planting or there was no work or they had simply come to meet real *guerrilleros* from Guatemala or for news or because they had heard something . . . . But what had they heard?

There were more Indians in the city now, not only Mayas from Copán itself and Ocotepeque, but from Zacapa and Chiquimula, across the border, and some from as far away as Atitlan, Xela, even the highlands. Victor could tell this from the women's huipiles and from the voices of the men speaking in Cakchiquel, Kekchi, Ixil, Tzotzil and Mam as well as Quiché. Many of them were refugees from the repression in Guatemala, threatened by death squads, unable to ever return to their own villages. Something had drawn them to Copán, back to the ruins from which their ancestors had dispersed. And here they were waiting. But for what?

They arrived in Copán just after the dawn broke and helped Patrice walk to the great ceiba, the sacred world-tree, where they covered him with blankets and urged him to rest. The *curandero* was called and women warmed *atole* for him and the *guerrilleros* gathered to greet him. Victor watched everything, but he was also aware of other activities in the city. He knew the questions that were being asked in the Ball Court and in the Great Plaza and all along the pyramids, from terrace to terrace, and even across the fields into the jungles and up into the hills: *Who is this man they have brought here?* And he also heard the answer like the sound of the wind in the leaves . . . but whose answer? whose words? from what place inside the city had this answer come? *Our brother, Xbalanque of Huehuetenango.*

Around noon scouts returned, reporting that an army convoy was approaching Copán from the east. Four vehicles, a company of fifty, sixty·men. "There are twenty armed combatants here," Victor said. "We should be able to handle them."

He spoke without consulting with the others; immediately he noticed that his *compañeros* looked at him strangely, that Anselmo, his second in command, shook his head as though at a man who has drunk too much and so cannot be held accountable for the foolish things that he says.

"Victor," Anselmo said to him, taking him by the shoulders, turning him around so that he was no longer looking at the Temple but down at the Central Court, "do you see there? There are not twenty of us, but two hundred. Look!"

There were indeed two hundred armed men in the Central Court, and not armed with machetes either, but with rifles.

"A new international unity, Victor," Anselmo said. "We made a little visit into the Zone, some of us and a squad of Cinchoneros. And we received gifts from our Soviet comrades by way of Cuba, Nicaragua and finally the Frente, some very ancient Kalashnikovs, but they still work."

"So we have guns. You suggest we use them against the Honduran army?"

"I suggest we defend this city."

"I agree. We defend this city. We, the twenty of us. Not those people out there. Because, Anselmo, we will disappear into the mountains when it's over. They will not."

"They don't want to disappear into the mountains. They want to reclaim their land. Here."

228

"Yes. But not today. We are going to intercept this convoy on the road from Santa Rosa. If there is going to be fighting it is going to happen far from these people, far from this place."

"Victor, the reason the army is coming to Copán is because they have heard the Maya are gathering here. Ambushing them twenty kilometers away is not going to divert them for long."

"Who speaks for the people down there? Is there a *chuchkahau* among them, a mother-father or a shaman? Is there a union leader or the elected representative of a cooperative? Is there anyone down there who has some claim to speak for these people? They should at least be consulted and agree to be slaughtered, Anselmo. They should know what will happen to them if they participate in an armed engagement with the army. And not just to them here, but to Indians all over this country. Who has the authority down there to make that decision? Because I don't have it and I won't accept it. I am a Guatemalan, a Quiché Maya. I do not know who these people are, but they are not of my lineage and I have no authority among them."

He said these words but his mind was thinking others, words that had been buried in his belly: But what if this is how it begins? What if the rising of the Maya begins right here in the ancient city of Copán?

"There are no leaders down there," Anselmo said to him. "But they will listen to you."

They had been walking back and forth in front of the Temple of Meditation. No one else seemed to be up on the acropolis except for the *curandero* and the women nursing Patrice and several *compas* who without being ordered or even asked had taken up position near the ceiba tree as guards. Victor's glance traveled to the tree. Anselmo saw and said in a low voice, "If he is going to die here, wouldn't it be fitting to offer sacrifices for his ascent in the old way, with the blood of our enemies?"

Anselmo had fought in Patrice's squad for several years. All the *compas* who had volunteered to come down from the highlands on this search mission were veterans of one of Patrice's squads. Two months ago the Honduran army had meant nothing to them; now the Hondurans were like the Kaibiles, blood enemies to whom no quarter would be granted.

"He looks worse than he is. He is not going to die here," Victor said. "But this is what we will do. We will wait for them here and we will fight them here, and by 'we' I mean you and I and the eighteen others of the squad. I do not want anyone else to be seen. They will conceal themselves up in the hills or here in the catacombs under the pyramids and temples of the Acropolis, and they will not engage in fighting unless we are killed and they must defend their lives. If we succeed, those we don't kill will escape to report that there are only a handful of subversives here, nothing to bother with. We'll let most of them run away this time so they won't have to exaggerate our numbers. Then by the time they come back we'll have given these greenhorns some training. You can give a man a rifle, Anselmo, but all he may do with it is shoot off his own foot."

Anselmo took Victor's arms and pressed them. This solution satisfied him, would satisfy the others. Victor watched him cross the courtyard on his way to the ceiba tree to speak with the *curandero* and to see Patrice. From where he stood now Victor could see both centers of energy: the Central Court with the people gathered, their make-shift shelters, their cooking fires, their horses grazing peaceably, their chickens pecking about the ground, the women and girls watching children, preparing food, the men talking, smoking, waiting; and a level higher, here on the terrace, the ceiba tree and those few gathered beneath it tending to Patrice.

The Maya had fought losing battles before; every battle fought by an indigenous people seemed to turn out to be a losing battle. Yet he knew his history. A hundred years before in the Yucatan the Maya had fought a full scale war and had nearly reconquered the peninsula. When they could no longer hold the territory they retreated into Quintana Roo, and there they established an independent state and defended it until 1929. A mere sixty years ago there had been an autonomous Mayan state; there could be one again.

The afternoon was hot. Birds and monkeys moved about under the canopy where the forest edged the central court, spreading out in all directions around the ruin. But here in the spaciousness of the city with its broad stairways and wide courtyards, its plazas and low, squat pyramids, there was a sense of human presence, civilized human presence, peace and serenity and security and strength. It made him glad that in the midst of these carved stones, these temples and hieroglyphic staircases, the sacred *yaxche* tree grew, huge, sturdy, giving the people its shade along with its blessing. For the *yaxche*, the ceiba tree, grew at the center of the world, its roots in the underworld, its bole on the earth, its branches in the sky, and from it sprang the four directions and the four paths, red to the east, yellow to the south, black to the west, blue to the north, while its own path, the Green Path, remained there in the center, leading from the underworld, through the earth and up into the sky.

And now Patrice, Xbalanque, Jaguar Sun, would sleep under the green tree in the center of the four directions in the cool shade and shelter of the tree of life until he got up.

Until he got up. The words rang inside him; his whole body began to vibrate with the sound of them. *"Get up, Hunahpu!" Xbalanque said, and Hunahpu came back to life. The two were overjoyed by this. . . .*

They would hold a dawn ceremony for Patrice. They would recite prayers all night, keep him warm, hold his spirit to the earth, beg, entice, cajole his spirit to remain with them and to grow strong again. And then the army would be defeated, the city would be victorious. For this time, for these days, these gods would rejoice with them once more.

The next day was a lucky one, *Oxlahuh Batz'*, 13 Monkey. When Victor learned that the Hondurans were stopping for the night in Santa Rosa, he felt good, gladdened by the knowledge that the coming day was an auspicious and powerful thirteen. The delay itself showed how lucky the day was going to be for them.

Though it normally took only four hours to drive from San Pedro to Copán, the army was taking its time: the scouts' initial report would have put the convoy in Copán by early afternoon of New Year's Day, but it wasn't until late the following morning that their informants reported the convoy leaving Santa Rosa and at its current crawl it wouldn't be likely to roll into Copán village until mid-afternoon. Anselmo had already determined the best defensive strategy for holding the archeological park, and they were counting on the army's arrogance and the mestizo's notorious disdain for Indians who as everyone knew were mentally deficient and genetically inferior. The twenty defenders were experienced combat veterans and well armed; Victor was confident they'd scare the Hondurans shitless. And then to confirm his faith, as a sort of announcement, a prophecy of victory, just after dawn, as the ceremony was coming to an end, a quetzal settled on the branch over Patrice's head. The quetzal, so rare it was thought to be almost extinct, had come to bless them, to announce that Patrice's spirit would stay with them, that he had indeed broken out of the chamber of death, burst out like Jaguar Sun from the ninth house of the underworld after traveling in dreams through Xibalba all through the long night.

The army had come to Copán at its leisure to eject Indian trespassers from the Archeological Park, one of the country's few national treasures and tourist attractions. They expected perhaps to massacre some worthless *indios*. They did not expect what they received.

It was their arrogance, that they drove in, jumped out of their jeeps and troop carrier, M-60s in hand, and ran into the Central Court. But no *indios* were in the Central Court waiting like dumb animals for the slaughter. There was nothing in the Central Court at all, no sign that anything ever had been. The soldiers stood around stupidly, sheep-like, waiting for new orders, stood right out in the open, scratching their balls . . . when from behind the stelae, from the Ball Court, from the temple steps appeared the guardians of Copán. They were naked except for feathers and leaves, their faces were painted red and blue, but they had kept up with technology and had abandoned their blow-guns for assault rifles. In the burst of bullets that followed a dozen soldiers fell while the other forty turned tail and ran, but there were more guardians waiting for them among the trees by the entrance, and more soldiers fell there and still more trying to climb into their vehicles and several died when a jeep went out of control and plowed into a stela at the park gates. It was the first blood sacrifice the stones of Copán had received in twelve hundred years.

The Hondurans had not even returned fire.

"We cut them in half," Anselmo said, counting up bodies. "They won't attempt another attack tonight. They'll wait for reinforcements. A battalion."

People were emerging from the catacombs, and from their hiding places in the pyramids, and running down the footpaths from the hills. No one had gone far; everybody wanted to see the battle. They wanted to use their guns.

"Now let them all look at these dead men and then I want to speak to everybody," Victor said. "We killed too many. They'll want revenge."

He went to find a drink of water. What he wanted to do was radio to Atanasio Tzul for orders, but Atanasio was dead these six months, fallen at Nebaj, and now he was the one to give orders, he or someone just like him, another field commander just like himself. Until the Unity could elect a new leadership, they were all of them on their own.

When he returned the bodies were laid out in the Great Plaza and people were walking around, looking at them. It was such a hot day; he was so thirsty. The wounded were in the shade; there wasn't much they could do for them. He watched the people move around the corpses, the men in their jeans and straw hats, the women in their long, colorful skirts, their beautiful woven and embroidered blouses and scarfs, babies on their backs.

He knew too much, that was the problem. He knew they could not possibly succeed.

It was the first time he had ever called them together to address them formally as a group. He said that they had already been through battle together, they as witnesses, but present nevertheless, so they were already *compañeros*. He told them that they had shown great courage in remaining in Copán. Then he told them that it would also take courage to leave. He told them the army would send many more men with heavy weaponry, maybe planes. He told them that it was not possible to defend Copán with so few experienced fighters, that his advice was to leave immediately while there was still time.

Then he told them that if, on the other hand, they chose to stay, he and his *compañeros* from the Unity would stay also. "Consult with your families, consult with each other—"

A young man stood up and shouted out in Chorti: "I have consulted with my heart. I am Maya. And I am staying right here." Other young men raised their rifles, laughing a little, because they had only seen this done by others and never expected to be doing it themselves. Some girls giggled. The older women nodded their heads, gathered their things and went back to the Great Plaza to set up their shelters again and re-light their cooking fires. The men went off to comment on the bodies and smoke. Victor could read what was before his eyes: nobody was leaving Copán.

So be it. He turned to Anselmo and gave his orders.

"Get on the radio, talk in the clear, announce what we've done here. The Maya have seized Copán. Tell them. Tell everyone: Unity, Frente, Voice of America, Radio Sandino, everybody. The more people who know, the less likely that they'll send bombers in. This is after all a cultural monument. What would the gringo archeologists do without Copán? So they need to be informed. As soon as we hear from the village, we'll bring these dead and wounded in. And I'm going to call the newspapers. Let's see if we can get through to Tegucigalpa."

It was not their style, to announce war strategy. It went against the grain. But Victor knew he was dancing right on the edge of the volcano's cone; he couldn't afford to slip up now. What had occurred to him all through Patrice's ordeal: why didn't the Frente try to save him by contacting the media, by playing on his ethnicity, by arousing the emotions of his countrymen, whose emotions, when it came to one of their own held captive in other people's countries, was not hard to arouse? Of course it was not in

Vladimir's interest to save Patrice that way or any other. But the idea . . . to exploit every tactical advantage even the non-military one, even the one that you might ordinarily scorn. Didn't the ancient Quiché once win their greatest battle by deceiving their enemies with mannikins and then setting traps for them using gourds filled with bees and wasps?

They could not defeat the Honduran army and strategically it was suicide for *guerrilleros* to be cornered like this in a siege. But they had this advantage: they were on sacred land, sacred to the Honduran people, sacred to the Tourist Board, sacred to the Ministry of Finance, sacred to archeologists and other gringos who otherwise wouldn't give a shit about a bunch of Mayas massacred on a village street. But it wouldn't help them if nobody knew they were there until the bombs had already dropped.

So he left the mopping up to the squad and went into the visitor's center to use the phone. He called the newspapers in Tegucigalpa, he called the TV stations, he called the University, and the National Institute of Anthropology, all the time facing a wall covered with artists' renditions of life in ancient Copán, all the time staring at his ancestors, his brothers, warriors painted like himself, and like himself wearing only loin cloths and feathers, though with the added decoration of earplugs and nose rings. As he talked to the journalists and the news announcers, nearly stark naked but holding the telephone receiver in his hand, he nearly laughed out loud, staring at these pictures of men just like himself slaughtering their defeated enemies by cutting out their hearts.

Anselmo spoke with their Copán village contact, a ten-year-old who came accompanied by two dozen or more other kids, all eager and ready to play war. The soldiers had gone, they told him, had driven right through the village, hadn't even stopped. Anselmo knew the villagers themselves had taken the very sane precaution of leaving their homes for the day to visit relatives in other towns in the district. See no evil; hear no evil. Only the kids had hung around to watch and bring information to the *guerrilleros*. They

235

were so excited to see the bodies of dead soldiers piled up all over that they wanted to join up and move in. Anselmo had to be stern with them; he doled out a handful of *centavos* and told them there was more money in it for them if they would agree to act as a Unity intelligence cadre. And their first assignment was to bring someone with a pick-up to take away the wounded and their dead companions. Maybe the priest.

They had kept a guard posted near the ceiba tree to protect Patrice. Now Anselmo left the boys and the bodies with the medicos and went up the broad hieroglyphic stairway from the Central Court to the terrace to see him. It still didn't seem real to him, that Patrice was present with them again, but so inconspicuously present, so invisible. He needed to go and touch him to make sure, and to look at him very carefully because with his beard he didn't look right, not like the same man. And he was so bony, emaciated, and cut and bruised. But whole, they said, the *curanderos*. Still a whole man, thank God.

Patrice was lying curled up on his side. They had covered him in the morning with a light blanket, but now in the heat of the day he had either pushed it off or someone had removed it. It would seem that on this day 13 Monkey every warrior had to be naked in Copán. The *curanderos* had sprinkled petals of dried roses around his sleeping mat and all night had burned *pom* so the whole of the terrace was still heavy with the fragrance of the smoke. All night long burning candles, keeping watch, chanting to the gods: *Oh World God, Heart of Earth, King Quiché, Tecún Umán, Leader and General of our Maya-Quiché race, holy ruins of Copán, guardians of Copán, hear us, help us. . . .* They had drunk *balche* and sacrificed a cock and the *curanderos* had kept chanting: *Heart of Sky, hold him. Heart of Earth, protect him. Blessed souls of the dead, walk with him, blessed ones, strengthen him, speak for him. . . .* And while the Dawn Ceremony continued, he and the other *compas* had paced and smoked and worried, and none of them had slept, but it had been good for them, made them wrathful by morning, murderous, tigers themselves, jaguars, thirsty for blood.

Patrice moved in his sleep, rolled over onto his back, reached for the covering with his swollen, broken hand. His whole body was bruised, the skin cut, blistered, but all wounds that would soon heal. A miracle, really, that he was saved.

Now he was lying on his back with his eyes closed, but he was awake, smiling a little. "Is it still 13 Monkey?"

"Yes, Patrice."

"How long a day is, Anselmo." His voice was raspy, cracked.

"How is it with you this day?"

"I'm alive. Bet I don't look it."

Anselmo smiled and poured some water into a glass for him. "Can you sit up a little?" He squatted down and helped Patrice sit up and drink. It was like holding up a skeleton. His fingers were so swollen and misshapen he couldn't even grasp the cup in his hand. "You may not look it today, no, but they tell us you're going to live."

"So I hear. I haven't thanked you yet, Anselmo. I owe you one again."

"I think we're even, Patrice. And if not, I give this one to you as a gift."

Patrice lay down again and closed his eyes, but he was still smiling. "Is there some reason why you're wearing war paint? Or am I seeing things again?"

"To scare the shit out of a company of assholes."

"That's what that shooting was about? Didn't seem to take you too long."

"Fucking cowards."

"What's going to happen next?"

"Victor is making announcements. He thinks the army won't bomb us if he tells the newspapers we're here."

"Excellent idea."

"Enrique is in charge of supplies. There's water here. So long as they come by vehicle we can engage them at the gate or wait for them inside. They have to cross the Great Plaza, which is all open space, except for a few stelae which we would man with our best marksmen and then they have to cross the Central Court, and again

237

they have no cover and we have our people up in the bleach-
ers. . . ."

He stopped because he had the overwhelming feeling that
Patrice was no longer present, a sudden withdrawal as though he
had simply closed his eyes and died. Frightened he went to shake
him until he noticed that it was only that Patrice had fallen asleep.

Two long-haired Indian boys, naked except for loin cloths of
jaguar skin, wristbands and anklets, holding blow guns in their
hands, emerge onto the ball court. They set down their blow guns
and begin to play. But when the ball is dropped it is the head of one
of them that falls. From the stands the voices of the Xibalbans, big,
white men dressed in camouflage, roar out, "We've won! You're
done! Give up! You lost!" But the head cries out, "Punt me,
Xbalanque! Punt my head as though it was a ball!" He stares down
at Hunahpu's head. It terrifies him that his head is just lolling there
on the ground. Hit the head? Yes, all right. He hits the head hard
and it flies out of the court into the trees. But as it flies it turns into
a squash! When he turns around there is Hunahpu with his head
back on his shoulders! They dance around with joy. The Xibalbans
cry out, "Have we been seeing things?" The squash flies back
through the air and he catches it, twirls it on his finger like a
basketball and laughs. His fingers work again, he has his hands
back, and Hunahpu's head is back on his shoulders. Then he
smashes the squash-ball onto the ground like he was spiking a
football after making a touchdown, and again he feels such incred-
ible happiness, seeing the seeds spill out of the squash, seeds all
over Xibalba's dead ground. "See us!" he shouts up to the lords of
Death. "We haven't died. We haven't been defeated. We have
succeeded through self-transformation. There will be no more
blood for you, Xibalbans. None of those born in the light, begotten
in the light, shall ever again be yours!"

Two days passed, 1 Grass, 2 Cane. The army seemed to have abandoned the district, but it was only the tide going out: the farther out it goes the more powerful its return to shore. In the two days of hiatus, people scurried around the area gathering food, corn meal and vegetables, chickens and pigs, wood for fires, gasoline, bottles, tools. Water was hauled up from the river, bullets were counted out, children were bundled off to relatives, those whose mothers chose to stay. Many women chose to stay.

Informants reported movement of troops from San Pedro, halting at Santa Rosa. Not a battalion, no, but a large company, about two hundred men. And not men alone, but tanks, bazookas, mortars, grenade launchers, and a limitless supply of bullets.

One of Victor's men, Juan Pech, experienced with explosives, began a Molotov cocktail assembly line. It worked on Somoza's Guardia, he said grinning at the boys sitting around the table with him. It'll work on these motherfuckers too.

1 Grass, 2 Cane. Each night the squad met under the ceiba tree to eat together and worry together. To scheme. To plan. They had to be ready for battle or for a long siege. They had to be prepared for aerial bombardment, for rocket-launched grenades. For casualties.

And they had to talk to Patrice, who as he got stronger became more demanding for news. They had to give him the history of the last two months because he knew nothing at all, nothing about the hostage crisis in Tegucigalpa or the offensive in Salvador or the Yankee invasion of Panama. They had come to terms with so much, but for him it was all news, and still unacceptable, still enraging. The murder of the six Jesuits in San Salvador, the aerial bombardment of the poor neighborhoods there and in Panama City, the capture of the Presidential Palace in Tegucigalpa—and the deaths of so many combatants in Salvador, the almost prodigal loss of life during that uprising, the shock of all this old news on Patrice reminded them of how truly shocking it was. The only amusing part was the story of how a handful of combatants from the FMLN captured the Sheraton Hotel in San Salvador with

239

twelve Green Berets inside, and the bravado with which they held it for days while the Americans negotiated with them, how the TV cameras were there when the twelve men were finally released and provided footage of the pride of the American military, those heroes of the Special Forces, running for their lives . . . and how the *guerrilleros* got clean away. That was the extent of the good news.

And the negotiations with the Hondurans dragging on and on and the elections in Nicaragua coming in February and the contra refusing to lay down their arms.

"Maybe we should be at that negotiating table, too, Victor," Patrice said one night just before he fell asleep. "After all we're holding a hostage too. The ruins of Copán. If they don't meet our demands we'll blow the damn thing off the face of the earth."

"But, Patrice," Esteban said, the youngest, the baby of the squad, "we would never do such a thing."

"But, Esteban, my child," Patrice said, fading into sleep, "they don't know that."

1 Grass, **2** Cane. And then on the morning of the fifth of January, **3** Jaguar, scouts reported the army company leaving Santa Rosa. On that same morning Patrice got up.

His skin was deathly white except for his hands which were still swollen and bruised black; his face was all beard and bone and above the beard and bone, two eyes of piercing, vivid green. To Victor he looked like some prophet from the Bible, John the Baptist coming off the desert. But he was up and on his feet.

"Give me a rifle," he said.

"You can't hold a rifle, Patrice. Your hands."

"Well I'm not going to just stand around here and watch."

"Listen. I've been thinking. About what you said last night. Can you get through to the Frente by radio from here? See if anybody in the Zone is in contact with Carlos. See if they can contact him in Tegucigalpa and tell him we need assistance here. We want to be part of these negotiations, too. Tell them anything you want. We have surface-to-air missiles, we have dynamite. Tell them we'll blow the place to smithereens if they attack us. Or blow their planes out of the sky. Whatever you want. But get us some time, Patrice."

"Who exactly is on this negotiating team? Do you know?"

"Besides Carlos there's only one who could help us, Patrice. A Sandinista."

"A Sandinista? Well then I'd forget the Frente, Victor. Just go through the Nicaraguans. Call the Embassy in Tegucigalpa, tell them you need to speak to their negotiator. They'll get you through. Shit, in the whole world now there's only one legitimate government on our side. We might as well use it while it's still around."

"I will try that then, if you advise it."

Patrice sat down on one of the stones of the temple as though suddenly overcome with fatigue. He didn't look up at Victor, but down at his hands. "Soon, Victor, we're going to have to talk, you and I. There are things I have to tell you."

"And things I must tell to you, Patrice. Discuss with you. Your place with us now—"

"I don't think I have a place with you now, Victor. I don't think I can have one."

"Then you are the only man in Copán with such doubts. No, Patrice, your place is with us up there. It is there waiting for you. The daykeeper saw it first. Now even I have seen it. But we won't talk of these things now. After, OK?"

Patrice looked up at him. His face was inscrutable, like one of those ancient kings of Copán, an image carved in stone.

Noon on the day 3 Jaguar. The army squadrons took up positions on the road between the village of Copán and the ruins. From the Acropolis, high on the tops of the pyramids, look-outs reported their movements: the troops off-loaded their weaponry from the trucks, but they were clearly waiting for orders, didn't seem to have much idea about what to do next; the officers moved their headquarters into the only hotel in town where there were real beds and real sheets. Meanwhile some of the boys peeking out from the temple tops were already plotting how to make a night raid to liberate some of the grenade launchers. It was beginning to occur to everyone inside Copán that these soldiers were fish swimming in the wrong waters, surrounded by young, hungry sharks.

And Victor had gotten through first to the Nicaraguan embassy, then to the Nicaraguan negotiator himself. Things were beginning to move.

But not noticeably. The Hondurans blocked the road and settled in. The defenders guarded the outside walls. Inside women made tortillas, cooked meals, life went on as though two hundred infantrymen were not gathered outside the city ready to begin a bombardment . . . except that all along the steps of the Jaguar Staircase hundreds of Molotov cocktails were lined up at the ready and in the western court men and boys were being given rudimentary training in how to load their rifles, how to aim, how to shoot. And Victor, in the visitors center now Unity headquarters, waited for a call from Tegucigalpa.

Twilight, 3 Jaguar. A young man ran into the visitors center. He was from Copán village, had climbed up the citadel from the river, had great and exciting news. He had heard it on the radio. It was on the radio, *comandante!* A small band of *guerrilleros* had seized the ruins of Copán, supported by some Indians from the area (the boy smirked a little, yes, some few hundred, *comandante*, but this was what was on the news), the army had them surrounded (though not quite, *comandante*, since, as you see, I got in from the river side), but in order to protect this national monument, the army would not attempt to retake the archeological park but would offer to negotiate for the *guerrilleros'* removal. The boy grinned; the phone rang. It was Julio Ibarra Cruz.

Victor emerged from the visitors center into a cool evening. The moon was in its first quarter; in a week it would be full. Full moon at Copán, it would be a good thing to see.

242

There were guards on the wall, guards on top of every pyramid and temple. He crossed the Great Plaza, a stadium as big as four football fields, stopped to watch some boys finishing a soccer game. Then he walked into the Central Court. For safety in the event of an attack non-combatants had been assigned places in the catacombs, but it was dinner time now and everyone was out in the grassy plaza eating their meals, either near their fires or sitting up on the ball court or on the Jaguar Steps. Soon gasoline torches would be lit so there would be light. There had been music on other nights, maybe there would be music tonight. Then with sentries posted, with combatants on the alert, the people would sleep. Children would cry a little, fuss, dogs would bark, roosters crow. And in the morning they would rise up from sleep and greet a new day, 4 Eagle. The city was inhabited, alive again. They were keeping the calendar, keeping the days. Time had been renewed; Copán had been reborn.

It was not yet time to talk with Patrice, but he was sure that here in this city he had found the true meaning of daykeeper's words. He understood everything now, the plan was complete before his eyes, the pattern emerging just as the daykeeper had said Patrice himself would emerge like the moon into its full splendor.

TWENTY FOUR

Tegucigalpa, Honduras

Julio Ibarra was standing at a podium arrayed with dozens of microphones, in front of TV cameras and lights and eager men and women holding tape recorders and pads and pens. There was excitement in the room, anticipation. He was reminded of an experience he had had only a week before when he had stood on a flatbed truck in Masaya facing a crowd of shouting, waving, jubilant people. But just as today he could not bring himself to share in their euphoria. He was not announcing a victory. Instead he was saying words he only half-believed, words that said only half the truth, to people who wanted to hear that half and that half only, and though he was tempted to speak the whole truth, he would not.

If he could only say, These words I am speaking are being spoken because the world is ruled by terrible gods who soak up irony like a dry milpa soaks up rain. If he could only say, And blood, too, they soak up blood, and these are words of blood I am speaking to you, words that come directly out of my veins. If he could say only that much then maybe it would not seem to him that he was half-dead, already dying and hearing the death rattle in his throat.

His voice in Masaya, in Matagalpa, in León, had broken over the words Peace, Reconciliation, Dialogue. Because he knew the rest, which no one else would admit and which even he didn't have the balls to say: Peace at any price. Reconciliation with those who have murdered your children. Dialogue with the empire, but only if you are willing to carry on the conversation while on your knees.

And when he was faced with those delirious crowds, he had to force himself not to remember other crowds, cheering, dancing, laughing, crying with joy, crowds that had surrounded him after the Triumph, the energy like orgasm, liberation at last, victory at

244

last, the people joined together in ecstasy, the people to whom they had promised so much, in their innocence, and been able to give so little.

He straightened himself and began to read the statement of agreement that had taken them months to reach: the Frente agrees to the release of the members of the Honduran government detained during the taking of the Presidential Palace and to withdraw its forces into an expanded Zone of Control whose Honduran border is hereby fixed and recognized; the Frente agrees to begin negotiations for a political settlement in El Salvador in exchange for a cease fire agreement with the Salvadoran government; the Honduran government agrees to lift the siege at Copán and to negotiate with Guatemalan Unity over the disposition of the Mayan archeological ruins now occupied by Unity forces; the North Americans agree to facilitate the disbanding of the contra troops and the closing of contra military camps along the Nicaraguan-Honduran frontier after certifying that the Nicaraguan elections scheduled to take place in February are free and fair; the President of Honduras grants a general amnesty to all Frente and Unity combatants engaged in recent military activity.

There were the usual questions from the press which he answered carefully but without enthusiasm. One North American reporter asked him if he supported the plan to have international observers at the polls in Nicaragua to insure that the elections would be free and fair. He was tempted to reply that he would support such a plan if all the other democracies on the continent welcomed similar teams of observers to monitor their elections. Or if only the ARENA government in Salvador would agree to such monitoring. He resisted the temptation, but ended the news conference soon after. He was not as strong as he used to be and certain temptations were becoming harder and harder to resist.

Back in his suite he collected his papers, prepared for his departure home. He was there and not there, as he tended to become when his feelings turned chaotic, refused to be named or placed, no longer carried with them appropriate rules for expression. There was a way to rejoice and there was a way to mourn. But he was at sea, waiting for the ship to go down, knowing that it would but being unable to save either himself or anyone else on board. But he was crazy, of course. No one else thought they would be defeated. No one else was in the least concerned. Defeat, he was told, was *impossible.*

Yet he seemed always to be on the verge of entering a room filled with coffins. The coffins were draped in black and red flags. Standing around were old men in suits, the leaders of the opposition, and young killers calling themselves Freedom Fighters, and big, self-satisfied North Americans with attaché cases filled with dollars. Every room he entered threatened to become that room; he was beginning to feel that he might be losing his mind.

He had been an arrogant fool, saying to Ileana, We are better than Fidel. Fidel will not let go of his children, but we are better than that.

These last few days at the negotiating table: the cathedral again. He was fourteen, skinny, poor, still on his knees, begging for crumbs.

His assistant knocked at his door. Did he have a few minutes to see Carlos? Of course.

He could feel Carlos coming through the sitting room like a tidal wave, the pressure building in front of him, stride by stride. The wrath of God.

"I won't keep you long," he said, closing the door behind him with his body.

"I have plenty of time, Carlos. Please, sit down."

"No. I just want to congratulate you on the close of the negotiations."

"I hardly think there is anything to congratulate me about."

They were half a meter apart, Carlos towering over him, burly, a guerrilla still in uniform. The brother of Alejandro Martínez. Looking at Carlos he couldn't imagine this brother whom Patrice

246

had loved. Yet he was almost deranged enough to say, Let's forget all this political bullshit. Talk to me about your brother and Patrice. Tell me where they lived and what they did and how they were together.

"Well, I'm glad you recognize that at least. And I am curious, *comandante*, about what you got out of it. How much does a revolution sell for these days?"

"Sit down, Carlos. Take a drink with me and we'll talk, OK?"

Carlos stared at the chair Julio offered him like it was something vile, but he sat on it. Julio poured them each a few fingers of rum.

"So, Carlos, tell me what you are thinking. Here, drink this first. I think we can both use it."

Carlos took the glass, spun it between his fingers. Pondering something. Then he lifted it slightly. "*Salud.*"

A concession. So they wouldn't be killing each other this afternoon anyway. Julio swallowed the rum; it went down like water.

"OK. You want to know what I'm thinking? I'm thinking that you cut a deal with the Americans. You got something big. I'd just like to know what it is."

"What we got is what's in the agreement: the disbanding of the contra no matter who wins the election."

"Forgive me if I say I don't believe you."

Carlos took the bottle and refilled their glasses.

"I'll tell you the truth, Carlos. I wish I could say we had gotten more. But with a Yankee invasionary force on our doorstep we were hardly in a position to play hard ball with them."

"Correct me if I'm wrong, but wasn't it you who persuaded the leadership to agree to these elections in the first place—on the imperialists' terms? And wasn't it you who argued against sending military support to us during the insurrection? And wasn't it you who set the campaign strategy around peace and reconciliation with the contra and the ARENA government? Wasn't that your work? So when the Hondurans ask you to be on the negotiating team, is it so odd that we should suspect collusion, *comandante?* Are we to be taken for such fools, to think you of all people would

247

represent our interests? Clearly not. The document speaks for itself."

"Frente representatives sat at that table, too, Carlos. They had every opportunity to speak, and they did speak. And at the end not one compromise was made without the Frente being consulted. Nothing in that document can come as a surprise to you. Why are you so angry now?"

He filled their glasses again. A few more shots and it would all blur into nothingness.

"Look at the world, Carlos. Open your eyes and look at it. It isn't the same world anymore. The romance is over."

"If you had supported us in November—"

" . . . it would have been Salvador that was invaded, not Panama. Don't you understand? They have no enemy left now but us. We are down and there is no one left to stop them from finishing us off. Now maybe you want to die for nothing, but you have a responsibility as a leader to all those who don't."

"Well, it is clear to me now why Patrice loved you. He always was drawn to the weak."

As though Carlos's fist had hit him in the gut.

"All that time, and you did nothing to save him. Tell me this, *comandante*. Is it pleasant to drink cocktails with the same men who are torturing your lover? Or was he just one of so many that—"

"Take care, Carlos. You are cutting too close. As for Patrice, he was a Frente combatant on active duty. It was not my responsibility to speak for him, it was yours. We had nothing to offer for him. You had everything. You had hostages you could have exchanged for him. Instead, what did you get? A few miles of Honduran territory and recognition of a border that doesn't mean shit to anybody. But you couldn't negotiate for him, could you? Vladimir wanted him dead. Vladimir set him up, and Vladimir killed him. None of you bastards ever once spoke for him, never once defended his honor against those fucking Americans and their fucking lies." He stopped. He had to control himself, force himself to remain calm. This was not the time to feel that rage.

Maybe it would kill him to feel it. Or maybe if he let himself feel it, there would be other men it would kill.

"Look, Carlos," he said as calmly as he could. "Neither of us could do anything. We both knew exactly what was going to happen, but neither of us could do a damn thing to stop it."

Carlos drained his glass and stood up. "Well, I have a message for you from the other side. He asked me to deliver it so I am delivering it. In case he didn't make it back, he said. He thanks you for your letter and regrets he could not respond. He says he loved you and he wishes you happiness. He hopes you will remember him. There. For myself, I'm glad he's dead. I'm glad he died before he saw this. The dead ones are lucky, the ones who died thinking they were giving their lives for something. You are going to lose those damn elections, Ibarra. You Sandinistas, you got power hungry, didn't you? Well now you're going to lose everything and they'll return—the CIA, the Embassy slugs, the death squads, the lists, the disappearances. Guatemala, Chile—you learned nothing. All those corpses and you learned nothing. Well just wait. Nicaragua will be a colony again. Yes, I thank God he's dead. I only wish you were in the grave with him."

The last word he spit out at the door. "*Maricón!*"

Twilight. Shadows gathered in the corners of the room. His plane was leaving at ten, but he already knew he wasn't going to be on it. He couldn't face Managua tonight.

He had said it himself: the romance was over. That David could slay Goliath. That the meek would inherit the earth. That power would somehow not beget more power, nor greed more greed. That there was some magical strength conferred on them because they were pure of heart, Jaguar Knights, Eagle Knights. All stories. All lies. Power came in the form of 2,000-pound "smart" bombs and laser-guided missiles, in the form of B-52s and F-111s, in the form of dollars with which the rich of the world bought the bodies of the poor, and sometimes even their souls. Maybe this time in his own country dollars would buy their souls.

249

Carlos still didn't see this, but Vladimir knew. Vladimir was changing his rhetoric even now, even now talking about reconciliation and negotiation as though he had been saying those words all his life. "Two armies in Salvador only means twice as much misery for the Salvadoran people. The goal of the Frente is to negotiate both armies out of existence." Yes, my friend, when your pocket or your armory is empty you find your tongue quickly enough, begin spinning out stories, cons, anything to save your ass. But better talk sweet and better talk fast because once the Soviets begin showing their running sores to the world, show their impotence, ah, then you will see such power unleashed on the world, the new American empire, the new *conquistadores*, nothing to stop them, no other power on earth to stop them, and nothing inside them to cause them even a momentary pause, a twitch of conscience, a sense of either guilt or shame.

In the bedroom he switched on the TV and played with the remote. So many channels here. Flipping through, avoiding the news, lingering on MTV. And there was John Lennon, singing "Imagine" into the camera as though he was still alive, looking alive, sounding alive.

It came back to him with the music, exactly where he was the first time he ever heard that song. In the square outside the cathedral. Between tricks. Tired, hungry, but happy enough, smoking a butt and drinking a Coke, sitting on a bench with the lake stretched out before him, the green of the mountains across the water, tranquil, like a dream. Almost his fifteenth birthday, 1974.

And some gringos, hippies, sitting on the bench near him had a transistor radio and were singing along. A girl smiling at him, translating the words for him, singing the words in Spanish so he could understand, so he could imagine it, too, a place where there was no country, no killing or dying, no hunger, no war. It was the same place he saw in his own dreams, where nobody owned anything, but everybody had all they needed, all they wanted. It was so easy to imagine it: all the people sharing the whole world, living together as brothers, happy and free.

The memory was so clear, so intense, it dwarfed every other memory from those years. That bench, that cigarette, that gringa singing to him, that song—they had made him what he was, they had made him himself. But were the words all lies after all, was the sun a lie, the peacefulness of the lake a lie, the friendliness of the Americans a lie? Because behind him was the cathedral and he was between tricks and nothing was different afterwards, he still had to turn around and go back into the dark. But something had changed for him because later when the Sandinista came he was willing to say yes.

His eyes were burning, his throat tightening up. It was over, everything. John Lennon was dead, Patrice was dead, maybe the Revolution itself was also dead. All he had left were these dirges to hope, these empty messages from the other side of death.

He had fallen asleep with the TV on. Except for that eerie light, the room was in darkness. But he woke knowing there was someone else there.

His pistol was near his pillow, so was the switch for the light. It wasn't as though he wasn't expecting this, though it had come curiously late. Unless it was not to be an act of provocation but an act of revenge.

He pressed the light switch and sat up with the pistol in his hand. He was stunned by what he saw, though nothing should stun him now, he should be beyond being surprised by anything. Except this, that the man standing at the foot of his bed was Maya.

The Indian raised his hands above his head. He was unarmed.

"What are you doing here?" Julio said, having to first clear his throat, still half-asleep. Not to kill me, he thought, or you most certainly would have done it already.

"Excuse me for disturbing you like this," the man said. "I have tried to make an appointment to see you, but they have told

me you were too busy, and I have a message to deliver to you."
His Spanish was hesitant, uncomfortable on his tongue.

"Give me the letter then," he said. "And tell me your name."

"I am Esteban Ixchajchal of Guatemalan Unity. The letter is
here," he said, pointing to his temple with his forefinger. "With
permission, I am going to say the message to you."

"Please," Julio said, and put his pistol down on the night table.
The man lowered his arms and stepped closer into the circle of
light. He was young, sixteen maybe. His eye caught the package of
cigarettes on the table; Julio offered him one. His smile was a
small delight in the dreadfulness of everything, a boy's smile,
bright, easy.

"Thank you. First the message," he said. "It comes to you
from Copán." He straightened up and closed his eyes, centered his
body, and then began to recite, slowly, carefully, with an accent as
melodious as the gentle rise and fall of a glass-smooth sea. "To my
esteemed *compañero* and dear friend, Julio Ibarra. I wish to tell
you that I think of you with great affection and thank you with all
my heart for that short time we spent together last year. In all my
hardship and difficulties during these last months memories of
those days many times saved me from despair. May you walk in
the blessing of heaven and earth and may your life flower with
every joy. Until we meet again, I embrace you. Patrice."

The boy opened his eyes and looked directly at Julio. For a
moment he seemed frightened by what he saw, but Julio did not
even try to control whatever emotion was on his face. Whatever it
was, it must be appalling, terrible hope or terrible joy or some
awful desire sweeping over his features. But he was finished
trying to disguise himself. Enough disguises. He took two cigarettes out of his pack. His hand was shaking. He handed them both
to Esteban. "Light one for me," he said. "Then sit and tell me
about Patrice. They said he died in prison, in a fire. What happened?"

"The *compas* rescued him from that prison. There was a fire,
yes. But the *compas* got him out."

"And how is he?"

"He is stronger every day, *comandante*. He is well."

"Is there a doctor there for him?"

"We have been under siege. No one can come in or go out. Too dangerous."

"You did it."

"Yes," he said and he flashed his bright smile at Julio. "I am Maya. The doctor is ladino. Big difference."

"What happens to your wounded?"

"We have our *curanderos, comandante*. And they are making Patrice well. They are taking good care of him."

"I must thank you, Esteban, for delivering this message to me."

"It's nothing. But truly it is we who must thank you for what you did for us today. You did not abandon us there at that table, you did not forget us. When we had nothing to offer you, you still protected our honor. You have our respect and gratitude now for as long as the light lasts."

"I think that before the Unity leaves, I would like to go and see Copán. Now that the siege is over and it is no longer so dangerous to come and go." He smiled at Esteban. He felt very happy, suddenly very, very happy.

TWENTY FIVE

Copán, Honduras

Only six weeks until the election, no one in Managua was going to take too kindly to his gallivanting off to Copán, especially when it became clear that he could not travel the next day as he wished to. And not for the lack of the government's cooperation. No, the Honduran government would be more than happy to provide the *comandante* with a helicopter, anything he wanted if it would expedite the removal of the Maya from Copán.

The Maya, on the other hand, were not so willing to cooperate. Victor Zapeta was all gratitude, then all apologies, but he would not be moved. It was an unlucky day for such a trip. 12 Night-House. A day of darkness. An evil day. The following day, however, 13 Lord Maize, was very propitious, dedicated to Ah Mun, god of youth, abundance, long-life, happiness, a very powerful day, a good day. Come tomorrow, *comandante*. It will be a great honor for us.

There was nothing he could do but agree.

It gave him a day to think. To calm down. To look at the situation. There was nothing to decide yet. One couldn't decide matters of the heart alone, unilaterally. Only a fascist thought like that. He would go, he would see Patrice, together they would know. It had been half a year, after all. Maybe Patrice only wanted his friendship now, nothing more.

And if that was the case, then he would return to Managua and face the election and what would happen after, more work or exile or civil war, whatever, face it with nothing in his heart at all, like a guerrilla, empty and alone as a winter overcoat.

By evening what had begun as a personal visit to Copán had developed into a political roadshow and media event. The Minister's agenda for the day was suddenly filled with meetings and press conferences. He was lunching with the Honduran military command headquartered in Copán village; he was then meeting with the guerrillas in the hope of determining a schedule for their withdrawal (or "removal," depending upon who was defining the terms). Reporters and TV newsmen were lining up to join the entourage, which now included a few Honduran vice-ministers, a general, a squad of security men, and Ibarra's new young Indian boyfriend whom he was passing off as a "Mayan interpreter." They were flying into Copán in helicopters graciously lent to them by the United States Army Special Operations Forces in Palmerola. When he heard this, Julio almost canceled the entire trip. Then he realized that it was only one more irony to add to the rest; that for him there would be no escape from irony; that even with Patrice now he should be prepared for the worst. Fair warning.

He made Esteban sit beside him at the well-laid table in the dining room of the only hotel in the town of Copán. While they ate, they had to listen to a general praise the restraint of his officers, who resisted every provocation on the part of the Indian subversives inside the park, and to the company commander discuss at length the ease with which his men could have forcibly removed the Indians. Of course such a task was completely beneath him and his crack unit, all trained, like the great Kaibiles of Guatemala, by U.S. Special Forces trainers, Green Berets, "the best for the best." Yes, though it was an honor to serve his country and his government, and to obey his general, he had to admit that it was also a bit insulting to be sent to put down a little Indian trouble up here at the frontier, so it was just as well that the Minister had negotiated their removal. The park might have been damaged in an assault, more damaged than it no doubt already was. "You'll see the mess

255

they've made of the place this afternoon, Doctor Ibarra. Them and their animals . . . well between an Indian and an animal, what is the difference. . . . "

Julio had to put his hand on Esteban's knee and press hard.

"So," one of the vice ministers said as they were leaving the table, "you will return tonight with a firm date by which the Indian subversives will leave Copán?"

"I can't promise anything," he said. "Negotiations are open. Now what are you prepared to offer them?"

"Amnesty. Freedom to leave unmolested. What more do they want?"

"I don't know. But I would suspect a good deal more than that." And then he named some things he thought Patrice and Victor and Esteban and the others might appreciate: the establishment of a legal and binding trust directed entirely by Mayas that would have physical and cultural control over the ruins; a declaration by the government that Copán belonged by right to the Mayan people; government funding for the establishment of Mayan language schools; the incorporation of Mayan culture and history in the national educational curriculum. He enjoyed the look of bewilderment and horror on the vice minister's face, but not so much as he enjoyed seeing Esteban smile.

After lunch there was a press conference and then, finally, they got into a government jeep and were driven down the dirt road to the gates of the archeological park of Copán. Just to the gates. Copán city was still under the control of the Unity and there were well-armed Indians standing all along the outer wall to prove it. The only invited guest was Comandante Azul; the general and the vice ministers stayed at the hotel to wait, and Julio hoped, to fret. But the press requested permission to come in and that permission was granted. Another delay to his meeting with Patrice.

Once inside Copán Esteban came into his own. It was he who presented the Unity combatants to Julio: Victor Zapeta himself, Anselmo Xec, Martín Azitzip, Juan Pech, Andres Tzampop, and the fourteen others, the defenders of Copán. As different from Patrice as men could be, short and compact while he was lanky and tall, with small hands and feet while his were big, black-haired while he was blond, brown-skinned while he was white, with broad Indian features, prominent cheekbones and slanted eyes. Trailed by the press, Esteban then led Julio on a tour of the city so he could meet and speak with the people, Julio greeted everywhere with respect, gratitude, affection . . . Esteban glowing . . . Already late afternoon. When was he ever going to see Patrice?

Soon the press was escorted out and preparations for the fiesta began. The Great Plaza would be ablaze with torches. Long make-shift tables were set up there so everyone could sit down and hear the music and the speeches and eat as much food as they desired, and toast and drink and toast and drink some more. This was a celebration of victory and of the Lord Maize, of abundance and long life. The city smelt of roasting pig and turkey and the rich scent of tobacco coming from the town's drying sheds nearby. There was bustle and excitement. The women were wearing their best, most beautiful *huipiles*; the men were polishing their speeches and their boots.

Julio took Victor by the arm and led him away from the others.

"Yes, I understand," Victor said before Julio could say anything to him at all. "Time is passing. We must talk about the negotiations. But this is a very special night for us. We'll do it, *comandante*. We'll sit down and do it, believe me."

"I want to see Patrice," he said.

"Yes," Victor said. And then Julio waited, but Victor didn't say anything else.

"Will he be here for the fiesta?"

"Yes, of course."

"And now, do you know where he is now?"

There was another pause, as though Victor were listening to a voice but one so faint nobody but he could hear it. "If you walk past the Ball Court and up the Hieroglyphic Stairs and across the first terrace you'll see a ceiba tree growing in the courtyard there. He'll be somewhere near that tree."

257

Victor spoke with complete detachment, complete indifference. Julio did not believe it, not for a single moment. Yet Victor was pointing the way to Patrice, the physical way. That was enough to be thankful for. And he did thank him and he meant it, but Victor only nodded and turned away.

Night. The torches were lit and the pig, roasting all day, was declared ready to eat. There were huge platters of turkey meat, maize dumplings and squash on the tables, and jars of *aguardiente*. In the torchlight, under the waning moon, two hundred Mayas prepared to sit down to feast.

Julio, trailed by Esteban, whose rifle was comfortably back on his shoulder, climbed the wide stone staircase and made his way alone across the terrace. Torches had been placed here and there among the ruins, stuck into the rocks of the pyramids, illuminating some spaces, leaving others in darkness. The courtyard where the ceiba tree stood, for example, was well lit around the periphery, but in the center the tree overshadowed everything, sky, stars, lamps, and there under the boughs everything was in deep shadow. He stood still, trying to see into the darkness. But the movement came from the temple, someone stepping out from a space hidden by the stones, someone who at first glance frightened him, tall, light-haired, bearded, haggard, angular, whose skin against his black clothing was white as death itself. A conquistador's ghost. Esteban had not prepared him for this, for seeing Lazarus after he had come forth from the grave.

"Patrice!" he called and opened his arms.

In his embrace, Patrice's body, even under the thick wool of his clothing, felt like nothing but bone. They held each other like brothers, kissed each other on the cheeks, like brothers kiss.

"I hardly recognized you," Patrice said, releasing him, gently but abruptly, and far too soon. "For a minute I wondered what such a handsome ladino was doing here. And I bet you thought, Who's that hungry ghost coming at me?"

They were standing close together, but awkwardly, and it seemed to Julio that Patrice was confused, disoriented, and still very ill. "Would you like to sit down?" he asked.

"I just want to look at you. I just want to be near you and look at you. It's hard for me to believe you're really here."

Julio felt he was going to explode with joy, or fear, or sorrow, he wasn't sure which. He had to go very slowly, and it wasn't his nature to go slowly. He wanted to say everything at once, to do everything at once, make love, make plans, make everything clear between them. Time was fleeting, time was flying by, every moment was precious and all he could do was stand still and let the moments fall around him like stars falling, like sparks from a roman candle, like notes of music falling, like tears.

They sat next to each other on a stone slab. Julio took Patrice's face in his hands and kissed him and kept kissing him. He couldn't speak, there was nothing at all he could say.

A few moments later the bell rang calling them to the feast.

They sat near each other at dinner, but not next to each other. Victor was on one side of Julio and his second in command, Anselmo, was on the other. Across from them were men from the district, and one man who had joined the occupation quite early, a refugee from Guatemala. Patrice was halfway down the table on the other side; they could see each other but they weren't close enough to speak. He noticed that, except for Victor and Anselmo, the Unity combatants weren't sitting together in a special place of honor, but were spread out among the people. And Victor and Anselmo were sitting next to him specifically so they could not only eat but also talk.

He made it easy for them, because he didn't want to agonize over anything else, not ever. He made suggestions, gave them options, tried to be reasonably accurate about what they could demand, but also what they could expect to get. They were amazingly agreeable; he had the distinct feeling that all any of them wanted to do was resolve the whole question of Copán and go home.

"And if I can get a commitment from them," Julio said, himself wanting to be done with solving the problems of the world and getting on to solving his own, "would you agree to withdraw the occupation forces from this site in two weeks time? Let's see, two weeks from today . . . January 29th?"

Victor shrugged and then stood up and called down the table, "Xbalanque, January 29th . . . what is the name of the day?"

The table went quiet, everyone stopped speaking and listened. And Patrice closed his eyes a moment and then said, "The day is 1 Knife, Victor."

"Thank you." And then as activity resumed, Victor sat down and said, "No. Choose another day. The thirty-first is a good day. We'll leave Copán on the thirty-first." And then he smiled at Julio. "A great mathematician, Patrice, you know? A professor of logic. What do we have him doing here? Keeping the days. *Comandante,* I know you are also a doctor. Perhaps later, before you leave, you might look at his hands."

They walked from the Great Plaza to the Central Court, retracing their path. Up the Hieroglyphic Stairway, a pyramid whose sixty three steps, Patrice told him, were each carved with hieroglyphs, each block of stone inscribed with a glyph, twenty-five hundred of them in all. But the archeological workers who restored the stairway had put the stones back any which way, so whatever text had been recorded in the stones was lost. And there were stelae, great slabs of stone from which the perfectly sculpted faces of men and gods seemed to be struggling to emerge and upon which the history of the city was recorded. And there was the Temple of Inscriptions, shaded by the ceiba tree, and then another pyramid, another set of terraces, and now they were on the citadel, the Acropolis, and there were the Jaguar Stairs, Patrice pointing out the jaguars, and there the Temple of Meditation whose entrance was shaped like the gaping mouth of a two-headed serpent and flanked by figures kneeling on skulls. Julio began to feel that he was on a guided tour.

But the stars were like diamonds, filling the entire sky, and the torchlight dappled the terraces and the stones, filling the ruins with flickering shadows, glyphs of shadow and light, mystery, placing them outside of time, or else at its very center. And they were alone here, and his heart was so full inside him, full as the sky was with stars. Once again he felt he might burst with joy or fear, anxiety or passion, again he could not name the exact emotion. . . . And all the while Patrice was pointing out this stone and that, talking about the ancient Maya, their obsession with the cycles of time, with the intersection of time and space, how they filled all their spaces, could not bear empty space anywhere, filled it all, and the air was filled too, with the sound of insects and frogs from the river below them, with the night calls of monkey and bird, with fragrance and a velvet-soft breeze. He had lived in a city too long and all this moved him greatly. And Patrice walked beside him but did not touch him.

"The ceiba tree again," Patrice said, presenting the tree as some archeological find. "But if we turn here, we can walk some more."

"I don't want to walk anymore," Julio said. He stopped and turned to Patrice, that tall ghostly form hovering beside him like something unreal, made of cloud and mist. "I want to touch you, Patrice. I want to lie down with you and hold you again."

Sounds from below carried up to them: laughter and music, trumpets, flutes, a turtledrum, guitars. The smell of tobacco leaf was strong, and the smell of wood burning, cooking fires going out, and a heavier, sweeter smell like incense. But they were standing above that world, above all that activity, alone among the stones inside the night, and time had stopped for them and was still, waiting as he waited for Patrice to reply.

"I can't, Julio. I can't make love to you."

He had expected this.

"I understand. You have been hurt, and you aren't healed yet, you aren't strong as you were. But don't worry. You don't have to perform for me, Patrice. We'll stay together tonight, we'll make each other happy. Just trust me a little."

They were standing so close, they were almost breathing against each other. Julio put his arms around him, and pressed close to him and Patrice bent down and kissed him. A gentle kiss, sweet, tender, but without passion.

"I didn't expect you to come here," he said, carefully disengaging himself from Julio's embrace. "And you're right, I'm very weak, and very . . . hurt. Too weak and too hurt for a one night stand, Julio. Even in this place. Maybe especially in this place."

"It would not have to be just one night, Patrice."

"One night, two nights. How many did we have last time? Three? I can't love you like that. Don't ask me to, Julio. Please."

"I came here to make you a proposition, Patrice. I came to tell you I love you. And that I want to be with you."

He said the words and then his knees buckled under him and he sat down hard on the stone slab behind him.

"Sit with me," he said. "I don't think I can stand up right now."

Patrice sat next to him; only their shoulders were touching. This was going to be harder than he had imagined. Perhaps this was going to be the hardest thing he ever did in his life. Living through this night, accepting whatever came. Surrendering to it as to one's fate.

"I love you, too," Patrice said very gently. "But I'm not in a position to consider your proposal. I can't even hear it now, Julio." He stopped speaking, but Julio couldn't respond. He couldn't find words, that was it. There were no words in his mind, only a deep, profound emptiness. When Patrice touched him with his broken hand, the gesture seemed more eloquent than anything he himself could possibly say. "I told them everything they wanted to know in the end," he said. His voice was soft, low, without expression. "I would have given them Guatemala if they had asked me. I would have given them the whole Unity. Everything. Fortunately they didn't ask. They thought I knew about poppies and the drug trade and the insurgency in Honduras, and they questioned me extensively about Salvador. Well, I don't know shit about poppies or Honduras, but I know a lot about Salvador. They brought in North American interrogators, asking about munitions dumps and arms suppliers and supply routes, and base locations, informers, communication networks. I tried to lie, but I don't know if I lied or told the truth."

"Patrice, when a combatant is captured, the leadership can't expect him to withstand interrogation. They make adjustments, they protect those who may be exposed. Don't you think Vladimir understood this risk when he sent you in?"

"There's more, Julio. I broke and that's bad enough, but even if they could let that pass, there's something worse. My orders were to shoot Aguilar. Maybe they think I aimed at Aguilar and missed. But I didn't miss. I meant to shoot Castillo."

Julio took Patrice's hand as gently as he could, held it as carefully as he could. Some part of his brain was wondering if it would be a good idea to re-break and set the bones and how that could be done, when and where; some other part of his brain was practicing patience, holding still, waiting.

"I was collecting on a private debt, but that's not something we're supposed to do in war, is it? Not honorable, not something Vladimir would approve of. I disobeyed orders and killed a man for personal reasons. I think in any army that's considered a capital offense.

"I haven't said anything to Victor about this yet. I didn't see any point if we were all going to die here anyway. But now I'll have to tell him. I don't know exactly what they do to combatants who disobey orders. Shoot us I guess. That seems the most likely thing, doesn't it?"

"They won't shoot you, Patrice."

"No, Victor won't, I'm sure of that. But Vladimir will want to. For one thing, he thinks I'm a fucking Green Beret. Probably everybody does, except you and the Unity. Some people in the Unity might think so by now too. So basically I'm pretty useless to everyone. I don't think I have much of a future down here anymore."

"I agree the situation right now is difficult. But fortunately you are officially dead, Patrice. You died in a fire in a little village in northern Honduras. Vladimir wanted you dead and buried, and so you are. If you should return from the dead, next year, say, or the year after, with a different *nom de guerre*, after the Americans admit you were never one of their officers, after Aguilar wins his election and turns out to be a successful leader, after all the dust has settled, do you think Vladimir will wish to embarrass himself any more with this ugly little incident? No, Patrice, no one is ever going to try you for disobeying orders. Killing Castillo was the best thing you could have done. For everyone. And now it's all over."

"They told me that Castillo was an informant for the CIA."

"Yes. I learned this too."

"They told me during the interrogation. They thought that's why I shot him. They thought the Frente had a line on all their operatives. But that's bullshit. I would have shot Aguilar, I would have followed orders. It's just that I saw Castillo standing right there, looking out at me. . . . And I recognized him. I knew who he was, Julio. I had met him before."

Julio sat still on the cool stone. Patrice had withdrawn his hand, even shifted his body slightly away, so that there was no longer any physical contact between them. Now it seemed that he was withdrawing from Julio completely, leaving him sitting alone in a dark, ruinous place, surrounded by tombs. *Don't leave me, Patrice!* he wanted to cry out to him. But he didn't cry out. He didn't speak at all. He ordered himself to be patient, to wait.

He had met Emilio Castillo before. How had he forgotten?

They had actually done him a great favor, his interrogators. They had forced him to put the pieces together, to make a whole out of all the parts, and then they had forced him to look right at it, the fruit of all his labor, what his body had done, his trigger finger had done, instinctively, without prior consent of his brain.

He hadn't realized how much his grief had erased.

Lying in bed, naked, watching Alejandro dress. A white room, Alejandro dressing in black. Black pants, black t-shirt. Covering his body in black, for the streets, for night in San Miguel. In the soft lamplight, watching Alejandro dress, watching him squeeze water out of his hair, comb it, pull it back. Six years together and still he loved watching Alejandro emerge from the shower, squeezing water out of his hair. Talking about the friends he was meeting for a drink: Silvio, Juan . . . how hard their lives were, being gay men in Salvador. . . . "They think you're French, you know, because I call you Patrice. . . . My French lover from the States . . . *very* romantic. If they ever saw you, they'd die of envy. So it's better that tonight I go alone. Besides, I didn't tell you, Emilio telephoned earlier. He wants me to drop in and see him later. He said he's been ill. Afraid he's going to die with too much on his conscience, the old bastard. But he practically begged me to come, so I guess I will. He's a miserable son of a bitch, but maybe it's time for me to forgive him."

"Is that what he wants? Forgiveness?"

"I don't know if that's what he wants. But that's all he's getting."

Their conversation moving on, vacation plans, when they had to confirm their flights, those last words that neither of them suspected were the last words. The last kiss. The last embrace.

Then that nagging anxiety in the middle of the night, waking up to glance at the clock, waking again in the morning to an empty bed, the frantic phone calls, the onset of panic, searching everywhere for him, his friends' houses, the bars, the local authorities, the Treasury Police, the Embassy, everything else erased, travel plans, flight schedules, Emilio's name.

An eternity searching until they found him a week later, ruined, a mangled corpse in a ditch by the side of the road.

That memory passing over him again: the heat, men digging, maggots and flesh emerging together from the ground, so horrible it had blocked out everything else until the interrogators forced him to remember.

Emilio Castillo. A smooth man. Elegant. Not a thug. Not a brute. A smooth, elegant man, a patrician, a man of influence, power. An aristocrat in his perfect black suit, his perfectly shined black shoes, his black car waiting for him by the gravesite, his driver keeping the engine running. Emilio came to pay his respects, but he would not stay long.

"You have my sympathy, Patrice," he had said. "What a terrible loss for you. He was always a dear boy, Alejandro. How much pleasure he must have given you over the years."

Sarcasm and triumph. He had heard it then, too, but he had refused to comprehend it.

And when they told him who the members of the *escuadron de la muerte* were, and where he could find them, what cantina they drank at night, where they worked, when they mentioned the name Castillo, when they told him the killers worked as guards at Castillo's finca, he had refused to hear that too. He had shot them down; what difference what their day jobs were.

He had refused to understand. They had to dose him up with truth serum and break his fingers before he would understand.

Blindly he reached for Julio's hand in the dark.

"I'll tell you why I killed Emilio Castillo," he said. "I killed him because he murdered my lover."

Julio stroked Patrice's hand, his arm. He didn't want to rush him, he wanted him to say everything he needed to say, to relieve this burden on his heart. At the same time his own heart was slowly filling with emotion. There were stories of great loves; he had read about them. But he had been schooled on different stories, of men sacrificing their personal loves for the struggle, heroes of the Revolution who were honored for remaining silent while before their eyes their wives, their children, were tortured to death.

He could not imagine Patrice being such a man.

He could not even imagine Patrice honoring such a man.

But Patrice was someone who stood everything on its head. He could make political expediency seem shameful, find praise an insult and ideology a form of deceit. He could also transform a casual sexual encounter into a night of lovemaking. It didn't surprise him that Patrice would defy orders to avenge himself on a man like Emilio Castillo. What surprised him was his own response, the power these few words had to move his heart. "Please, Patrice, go on. Tell me more. It is Alejandro Martínez you're speaking of, Carlos's brother?"

"Yes. Emilio Castillo was Alejandro's uncle," Patrice said. His voice was low, raspy, as though he was forcing the words out from a place deep inside him. "Alejandro had a terrible childhood. He was the youngest. He was different, always different, unusual. His father rejected him. His brothers tormented him. . . . But his Uncle Emilio raped him. It went on for years. Alejandro was terrified of saying anything. Besides, who would believe him? So he endured it, and told no one. Except many years later, he told me. Anyway, that day in Tegucigalpa, I was in the graveyard waiting, Aguilar arrived. I realized I had no reason to kill him, and didn't want to kill him. I was standing there with the damn pistol in my hand thinking, Why am I here? Why am I doing this? And then, like some kind of answer, I saw Castillo standing right behind him. I didn't even have to think, Julio. I saw him and I just pulled the trigger.

"Even then I thought it was because of what he had done to Alejandro when he was a child. I couldn't admit the truth to myself. I knew it, but I couldn't admit it. But it was so obvious a kid could figure it out. Castillo was a good friend of D'Aubuisson, he was an important man in ARENA, he was the employer of the three thugs I killed, the members of the death squad, and Alejandro was his nephew. They would never have touched him without Castillo's approval. They would never have dared to for one thing. They also would never have thought to. What reason would they have? He wasn't political. He didn't even live in Salvador. I was told that it must have been to get at Carlos. As though it would matter to Carlos. As though Carlos would even care. See, it was right in front of me, but I couldn't see it. I needed it beaten out of me.

"I'll tell you, Julio, I'm beginning to believe that the brain will conjure up anything—metaphysical systems, religions, psychosis, anything—rather than lose its innocence. It will hang onto any fiction rather than deal with certain kinds of horror, certain contra-

267

dictions. Like the fact that a man could give his own nephew to the death squads . . . that Castillo could do that to Alejandro, of all people. . . . And for what? Spite? Pleasure? Revenge? Because he wanted something and he couldn't have it? Because he was used to having everything he wanted and this time someone said no to him?

"Well, I don't care why he did it. I'm just glad he's dead. I'm just glad I lived long enough to kill him."

A great love. Beside it his own for Patrice seemed even to himself to be small, impoverished, wanting. He felt enervated, overcome by weakness, as though he would never find the strength to move again. All he could say was, "You loved him very much."

Patrice stood up and walked the few steps to the edge of the shadow of the ceiba tree. "The leaves of the ceiba tree symbolize paradise," he said. "It's a sacred tree, so whenever they can the Kaibiles hang slaughtered bodies from it." When he turned back to face Julio, the torchlight on his face made him look white, even his beard, his hair seemed white. He was like an apparition standing there in the tree's shadow, or a man emerging from the darkness of a cave or a tomb. "I've lost my innocence, Julio. I'm trying to see things as they are now. I'm trying to deal with contradiction. You said you wanted to be with me. You said you loved me. All right. Say we agree that we love each other. Say I accept your proposal. What would we do then? Would I be welcome in Managua? Would you come to the highlands, to the middle of war zone?" He took the few steps back and sat down heavily beside Julio, leaning his body against the stone of the pyramid. "Maybe the only place we can love each other is here. Only here, only tonight. Maybe it's better that way. I don't think I'd make a good long term investment. I'm still not completely sure I'm alive. Sometimes I don't feel completely sane. Sometimes I have terrible dreams."

"Just come with me," Julio whispered, already feeling his strength return to him. "Just come, Patrice."

"You're a very brave man," he said, and for the first time he smiled.

"No. But I hear from your *compañero* that this day is ruled over by Ah Mun, a young and beautiful god. A good day to start a long love affair, Patrice."

Look at his hands, Victor had told him. He took one of Patrice's swollen hands and kissed it. And then the other. And then, feeling completely dauntless, feeling himself as powerful as that young god, he drew him along to the sleeping mat under the ceiba tree.

Patrick let himself be drawn, but his heart was beating so hard its sound seemed to echo off the stones of the stairways and the walls, off the pyramid steps, a beat like doom itself, terrifying. Besides his heart and its awful drumming, he didn't feel that he had a body at all. Perhaps he was orifices only, perhaps for Julio that was enough.

To be a hole.

What they called him while they were raping him: *Faggot. Hole.*

Down in the Plaza the marimba band was playing. There would be dancing tonight. How many babies would be conceived before dawn among the stones of Copán?

We are only borrowing the world.

But it was futile. He and Julio, all of them, they were living through the ruin of civilization. They were the end of it. Copán was a ruin; soon Nicaragua would be like Copán. Everything destroyed, the idea destroyed, and when they tried to reconstruct it, if they ever tried to reconstruct it, they would put the text back together wrong, all the words in the wrong order. Fifteen days they had had here, like Paris during the Commune, like the mythical Palmares, that free nation of escaped slaves, like heaven, even though they were under siege. Something had happened to them here. They had awakened from the nightmare of history and found themselves, all of them, living in that luminous space where men are friends and so have no need of justice.

Forgive us. We are only borrowing the world.

It couldn't last. It was momentary, fleeting as time. Soon Copán would be dead again, like Paris after the Commune was crushed or Palmares after the Portuguese invasion. What was left after all that? Two people embracing in the ruins. Nothing else.

The day is borrowed.
The light is borrowed.
The earth is borrowed.
The world is borrowed.
We are destined to die.
We are destined to disappear.
Forgive us.
We are only borrowing the world.

Julio, beginning to undress him, kissing his whole body, as though each kiss could heal a wound.

May there be no blame, obstacle, want or misery. Let no deceiver come behind us or before us. May we neither be snared nor wounded. Heart of Earth, Heart of Sky, Maker-Modeler, Bearer-Begetter, give us a sign, a word, as long as there is day, as long as there is light. Keep us on the Green Road, the Green Path. Give us a steady light, a level place, a good life, a good beginning.

TWENTY SIX

2 Rain. Victor and Patrick sat side by side on top of a pyramid overlooking the city of Copán. From this height, almost a hundred feet higher than the terraces of the Acropolis, it hardly seemed there was a city there at all, but only a lower canopy of the jungle over which birds flew and on top of which monkeys played. The city had returned to stillness, to history, to the state of nature. No one was camped out in the Central Court, no boys were playing ball in the Ball Court, there were no voices raised in argument or song, no gossiping, no chasing of children. There was nothing human left in Copán, only the ghosts of the dead.

"So," Victor said. "Tomorrow on 3 Lord Sun we abandon Copán. How is it with you?"

"I shall miss this place."

"Yes. I also. But our home is up there, Patrice."

"Yours, yes. Mine, I don't know. It's been an entire *tzolkin* since I left the highlands. Two hundred and sixty days, Victor, a complete cycle of time. A long time to be away."

"That is what a home is, Patrice. A place that waits for you, that is there when you return to it, no matter how long you are gone."

Patrick gazed out over the top of the Lilliputian canopy to the steep hills that rose up around Copán. The light this time of day, just before sunset, made him glad to be alive, glad to have his eyes, thankful that they didn't take out his eyes. Compared to what they could have done to him, they had done very little. He could still see the colors of the clouds change from white to pink to red-orange, and Venus appear alone there without rival in the pale azure before the sky began to darken into night.

"I would like a home like that. I'm just not sure it exists for me up there. I don't know if I could face going back into battle. I don't know if I have the heart for it anymore."

"And you think there's no other place for you among us except in a combat squad? Is that what you truly believe?"

"No, I guess I could make it as a guide in some Gringotenango. But besides that, what else am I good for?"

"Only look into your heart, Patrice. The answer is there. Look at your life among us. Look at it with clear sight."

He tried to look, but all he could see was the sky. No, he could see more. He could see himself walking from village to village, all through the dry season, all through the rainy season. While other men planted their fields and harvested their corn, fathered their children, lived their lives, he was a nomad, going from place to place with his rifle and his radio, with first this squad and then that one, sleeping every night on the ground, having no home, no family, always keeping vigil, tracking the enemy, trying to push him back whenever he came too close, as though he could hold back the sea with his own hands. And it was all futile after all. There was no holding back the sea.

"Yes, Patrice, you had a place among us before. You were *Balam*, Jaguar, guardian. But now there is another place among us for you. It is empty, waiting for you to take it. Remember what the daykeeper said to me about you? He said, 'You are his brother, his twin. You are one body. He will read your heart, you will understand his.' I have been thinking about these words, Patrice. Now I understand their meaning. Now it is white clarity. Now it is an announcing. Why do you fear what is hidden in your belly, hidden in your heart? Why do you fear what you know to be true?"

"There is something else hidden in my heart, Victor. Something you should know. I love Julio Ibarra. We love each other. Like men and women love each other, Victor. You understand?"

"Yes, Patrice. I have known this since Estelí. I was your appointed guardian in those days, remember? I had at least to know where you were."

It surprised him a little, but not so much. It would make sense that Victor would always know where he was. He might have slipped his leash with Carlos, but never with Victor.

"So you know," he said. "Then can you imagine Julio and me living together in a little village up in the Cuchumatanes? Because I can't."

"I don't think many of us are going to be living in little villages up in the Cuchumatanes, not for some time anyway. Things are changing, Patrice. Take Nicaragua, for example. Just look at how it is there. The Sandinistas are holding an election in a country under siege. They've had to mobilize in the middle of the campaign, the Americans bomb Panama as an object lesson to the people, and the opposition is funded by the empire. Tell me, how can they hope to win an election under such conditions?"

"Then even Nicaragua will be gone," he said. "Everything will be over."

"In that form, yes. So we must think new thoughts. We must begin to imagine again."

"Imagine. Or remember, Victor. I have been thinking about these words ever since we've been here. Listen:

And then they remembered what had been said about the east. This is when they remembered the instructions of their fathers. The ancient things received from their fathers were not lost. 'We're not dying. We're coming back,' they said when they went. Then they went through a great deal of pain and afflic-tion: it was a long time before they found their citadel. They stayed there and they settled. They tested their fiery splendor there. They were of just one mind: there was no evil for them, nor were there difficulties. Their reign was all in calm: there were no quarrels for them and no disturbances. Their hearts were filled with steady light: there was nothing of stupidity and nothing of envy in what they did. And they tested them-selves. They did it as a sign of their sovereignty. It was a sign of their fiery splendor and a sign of their greatness. There was only happiness in their hearts. What they did was no small feat. Such was the beginning and the growth of Quiché."

"Ah, that was very long ago," Victor said.

"I don't think so. I think it happened right here. These past weeks, Victor. Didn't you feel it? I did. And look at daykeepers like your father and Oxib Tz'i, and all the weavers and all the *curanderos* like the ones who cured me. That's not long ago. That's right now."

"Perhaps. Yes, perhaps."

They sat, Victor smoked, time passed, the sky transformed itself, turning from azure to pink to blood red and brilliant gold, the expanse of sky becoming luminosity itself.

"I have never believed that military victory was possible," Patrick said softly. "Have you?"

Victor had smoked his cigarette down to his fingers. He took a final draw and flipped the butt out into the air, watched it drop down into the gathering dark.

"Given the historical situation we are living in," he said, "no."

"All along it's seemed to me that all we've been doing up there is holding ground. Dying on our feet at least. But that's about the best we can do. Then there was this . . . hope. This city, Victor. Didn't you feel the hope here, the joy? And still it was all makeshift, it was a community under siege. Imagine what we could create if we could only get a place and some peace and some time. But how do we get that place without fighting all our lives for it? How do we get it before we're all dead? And then I think of Nicaragua, and it's heartbreaking, Victor. To have fought and won and struggled for ten years and then to lose it all. If they're defeated in the election, I don't know how Julio is going to bear it."

Thinking of Julio made his heart ache. It had been left in his hands, to say yes or no. No was the easier response. No had only one meaning. But what did yes mean? Yes, try to get from Managua to Guatemala alive. Yes, try to find me again, without anyone to guide you, passing through roadblocks and firefights, traveling along hidden, dusty, narrow mountain roads up into the highlands. Yes, try to find me, Julio, and then try to love me. With the Sandinista government about to fall, a civil war about to start, with

American planes poised on the border to bomb them and, in Guatemala, Kaibiles in troop carriers sweeping up to Quiché from the capital, that yes was a joke. If they ever saw each other again it would be a miracle, and they both knew it.

"You know, Patrice," Victor began in his gentlest, most melodious voice, "there is your place among us now that we still must discuss. Because, you see, there was more the daykeeper said that I did not tell you. He used ancient words. He spoke of the fulfillment of prophecies. He foretold that fire would pass through your body but that it would turn to fiery splendor. Fiery splendor, Patrice, is the sign of the ancient lords. And it seems that everyone knows that these words were spoken about you. To us now you are no longer *Balam* but Xbalanque, no longer Jaguar but Jaguar Sun. The people need leadership now, Patrice. Can't you see what a singular and unique position you are in?"

Victor's voice was like a caress. He felt it on his skin, thrilling, like a lover's hand working its way down his spine. It made his head light, and his sex hard, fiery splendor centering in his groin, that heat, that desire. It was Victor's voice, as seductive as a lover's, the closeness of their bodies, the sweetness of the night. On such a night, Julio would offer him sex, but Victor offered power. Over and over, the same offer, the same temptation. How many times would he be tempted, how many times would they test him, or maybe this was the final test, or maybe it was the final offer. And the thought came to him then that perhaps he had misjudged the situation all along, that he had no place among them except in this role that they expected of him, that he didn't know Victor at all, hadn't heard what he was really saying all this time or seen what he was really doing. He had thought it was a form of friendship, of love, that had made Victor come for him, but maybe it was something else, some larger plan into which he fit, some use they had for him, that all along Victor had some use in mind for him just as everyone else had.

The bats were coming out now, dark shadows flitting above their heads. He remembered Bat House, being hooded, Jesús bringing him the blanket, the despair of that long night, how he had prayed, how utterly alone he had felt. They had come for him

275

at last, though, for whatever reason. They had saved him, and now he owed them something, the truth, or what little of the truth he knew.

Down the steps, in the shadows below them, he could almost sense other presences. He felt them everywhere in the city; they still visited him in his dreams. In prison the Twins, the old daykeeper, Alejandro in the form of Ah Mun, even Death himself had come to him, but here in Copán only the two boys, Hunahpu and Xbalanque. He'd glance into a tree and see them with their blowguns hiding in the leaves. He'd cross the Ball Court and feel the rush of air as they passed by, chasing the ball. If they had become his spirit-familiars, he would be glad to have them around, keeping an eye on him, those daredevils who went down into Xibalba to avenge the murder of their fathers and made fools of Death. Their weapons were cleverness and skill at playing ball and dancing; their vengeance had taken the form of laughter and mockery. They didn't die there, they weren't defeated, they succeeded through self-transformation. Well, he had gone into hell, too, to avenge a death, and he hadn't died there either, he hadn't been defeated—not entirely. Maybe like the Twins he had succeeded through self-transformation, but it hadn't made him into the man Victor wanted him to be.

"I do see the position I'm in," he said. "I see it very clearly. I'm trusted by no one but you and Julio Ibarra. I haven't got enough strength in my hands to hold a pistol no less pull the trigger. I haven't got a passport or a penny to my name. I don't know where my next meal is coming from or even where I'll be when the sun sets tomorrow. But it's OK, Victor. Because I don't have any anger left, either. No rage, no guilt, no blood lust, no delusions. For the first time in four years I feel completely free. So there's no point talking to me about Cucumatz and Quetzalcoatl and prophecies and gods returning. I've told you before, I'm not that man. I'm not that . . . being. I'm not, and I won't pretend to be. Not even for you. If that's what you want from me, the answer is no."

"So," Victor said softly, "you have no desire to be king?"

Patrick stared at him, dumbstruck. A bat flew close by, squeaking just above their heads. Then he saw that Victor was smiling at him, and he knew he had made a terrible error. He had blundered badly and nearly missed Victor's irony on top of it. But Victor was laughing at him for it. The joke, after all, was on him. He put his head back and laughed.

"It's true, Patrice, there was a moment or two when I hoped that the daykeeper's words could be taken to mean exactly what they said. There is always a desire in men to be aided by the gods in this realm as well as in the others. If a lord returned to lead us, that would be very good. But you're right, of course. Military victory is impossible now. So we have to fight a different kind of war.

"Now I want you to look at yourself through my eyes, not your own. To me this is who you are: you are neither Quiché nor Jakaltek nor Yucatec nor Mam. You are neither Guatemalan nor Mexican nor Honduran. But you are a Maya, Patrice. You have shed your blood for us. You speak our languages. You are my brother, as though we have the same parents, the same blood in our veins. And the people accept you, love you for who you are. Not only because your coming was announced, but long before that, when you were just living with us, just fighting with us. You have earned this place of respect, Patrice. Now if you speak, everyone will listen to what you say. Wherever you go you will be known. If you stay in the highlands and talk about war, men will come, boys, to fight beside you. But if instead you were to go to Chiapas, to the refugee camps, and talk about political organization and economic justice, about resettlement, about people returning home to the communities in resistance, about other ways of forging alliances, about unity, Patrice, Mayan unity. . . ."

Patrick was watching the golden sky over the river. Then it seemed he was hanging in the sky there like a hawk, high in the sky, and from there he could see all of Guatemala, the lowlands, the highlands, the communities in resistance up in the Cuchumatanes, even into Mexico, the Yucatan, Quintana Roo, and the sprawling refugee camps in Chiapas. Mayan land, all of it, though none of it in Mayan hands.

"That is where we need your leadership now, Patrice, and all the skills you have. This government cannot last forever. When it is time for us to return, we must be ready. We must be united and strong, courageous. We must have help, too. The world must know about us, especially that part of the world that you come from, Patrice. And someone must speak to that world on our behalf. Someone must be our voice, our *Ah Tzic Uinac*, he whom the ancients called the Lord Crier to the People. All this the daykeeper was saying to me, though the fullness of the announcing stayed dark until this day."

Patrick gazed down. There, below him, he saw the Green Path. But for once it was not just a narrow, overgrown track snaking through the cloud forest, not just a steep ascent, but it was a road, smooth and broad that stretched out beyond the limits of his sight. He could step on it here in Honduras, in the great city of Copán, follow it to Guatemala, to the *altiplano*, take it from there to Mexico and into the camps. He knew he was on it now and no matter where he set his foot down he would be on it still. *You are to go,* the daykeeper had said to him. *You are to wander. Do not turn back. Something you will achieve. Something the Lord of the Universe will assign to you.*

"I have been to Chiapas," Victor said, "Our people in the camps need everything. There are very few medical workers, for example. If a doctor were to go there, how much good he could accomplish, Patrice, how the people would welcome him."

Victor lit another cigarette and smoked in silence for a few moments. In those moments Patrick allowed himself to imagine what it might be like to be happy.

The name of the next day was 3 Lord Sun, an auspicious day. For the days were gods, each day a god, precious, unique, each one having its own presence, its energy for good or evil. Right after the election a new year began, a new count of days. He had promised Julio an answer for the new year.

They sat shoulder to shoulder watching without speaking while the intensity of color faded in the west and darkness nestled and thickened down below them and the sounds of the forest rose up all around them. Then Victor started to laugh and threw his arm around Patrick's shoulders. "Gringotenango," he said, still laughing, trying to catch his breath. "That's a good one, Patrice. Yes, they'd take you for that. All we carry inside ourselves, such depths, such distances, like the universe out there, the same inside us. And yet I can be taken for a dirty animal, a subversive, and you for a tourist from Antigua or Atitlan. Then we spin around, transform ourselves like the Twins, my brother, defeat them in their arrogance, dance together for joy, through all of time dancing with each other's hearts."

3 Lord Sun. The Honduran army waited outside the gate of Copán for its occupiers to leave the city. As arranged through long and hard negotiations, a Nicaraguan helicopter was waiting to transport the Unity *guerrilleros* from Copán to an undisclosed location in the Guatemalan highlands. As an additional protection, the negotiators had arranged for a delegation of international diplomats to attend the ceremony which temporarily transferred the archeological park from control of the Unity back to the directors of the National Institute of Anthropology and History. And of course along with the diplomats, scholars, archeologists and generals of the armed forces, came the press. The Unity commandos walked out of Copán into the arms of recorded history.

There was a gringo with the Indians, too, a long-haired, bearded hippie gone native, but nobody looked at him twice.

Nobody except Julio Ibarra. But the gringo stayed in the background, and disappeared quickly into the copter that was waiting to take them north. It was Victor, shaking hands with the negotiators before getting into the copter himself, who gave Patrick's message to Julio, like one of those skyrockets the Maya send up as messengers to the gods, a streak of fire that bursts into a giant stream of light.

3 Lord Sun. Julio stood on the ground, close enough to feel the wind from the propeller, and watched the copter lift off, watched it

ascend into a sky in which both the sun and the moon were shining, noticing with a certain pleasure the Nicaraguan flag on the side of the copter.

Then from close by, shaking the very air, stopping his heart, came a loud boom, a long swish, and then another, and another. He kept his eyes fixed on the hovering copter as the air erupted with the sound of bombs exploding, followed by a barrage like bullets. It was the skyrockets, the firecrackers, a madness without which no Mayan celebration was complete. But though he had been informed this part of the ceremony was coming, though it was expected, his whole body felt the shock of the sound, the horror of the image it evoked in him, the copter being shot down out of the sky.

Soon, within a month perhaps or two, they would be together again under the canopy of the cloud forest, while in Managua his *compañeros* would either be celebrating victory in the elections or attempting to comprehend defeat. Everything in the world was in flux, governments, revolutions, frontiers, but what was written in their hearts was fixed.

But there was still the war. Helicopters were blown out of the sky. Men were shot dead on village streets.

Behind him, around him, people were singing. The music of the song spread through the crowd, voices swelling all around him. It was not a song whose melody he knew, but he could predict what the lyrics would be, another song about struggle and victory. The words didn't matter to him. No words mattered except the ones Victor had spoken to him: Patrice sends his greetings, *comandante*, and, regarding the proposal you made to him in Copán, wishes me to tell you that he accepts.

So many voices were singing now, with such conviction, such strength, but all he could hear was his own heartbeat drowning out the words. He was in the grip of terror, but terror of what? Then he recognized it. It was an ancient memory, ten and a half years old now, riding into Managua on a tank with the victorious army, seized by this same emotion which then too he had mistaken for terror but which was only the first rush of hope after years of hopelessness, that terrible rush of love by which you are utterly and forever bound to the fate of other men.

The song rose up all around him. In the midst of the singing people, he stood perfectly still, eyes fixed on the helicopter, watching it grow more and more distant until it disappeared finally into the hills.

Author's Note

Although *Days of the Dead* is a work of fiction, the world it describes—the war against the Maya in Guatemala, the fall of the Sandinista government in Nicaragua, the subversive activities of the United States military and the drug cartel in the region, and the homophobic policies of the Cuban Revolution—exists, unfortunately, not in fiction but in fact.

I would like to acknowledge the help I received in writing this novel, particularly the generosity of my Central American friends and acquaintances, who shared with me their personal histories, their political experience, and their frank appraisals of the evolving situations in their countries, and whose courage and steadfastness inspired the creation of many of the characters who inhabit the pages of this book. However, many of these people are still active in the struggles going on in their respective countries and the politics described in the novel do not necessarily reflect their own positions, opinions or beliefs. To avoid creating any difficulty for them, I will not name them here, but I do want them to know that each of them has my deepest thanks and admiration. I have taken many liberties for the sake of Patrick's story, but I hope that even in doing so I have been able to preserve something of the truth.

I also relied on many written works, both testimonial and scholarly. For the Maya, *The Daykeeper* by Benjamin and Lore Colby (Harvard University Press, 1981), *Time Among the Maya* by Ronald Wright (Weidenfeld and Nicolson, 1989), *Testimony: Death of a Guatemalan Village* by Victor Montejo (Curbstone, 1987) and *Granddaughters of Corn* by Marilyn Anderson and Jonathan Garlock (Curbstone, 1988) were important sources. Dennis Tedlock's translation of the *Popol Vuh* (Simon and Schuster, 1985) along with his accompanying notes on the Quiché was vital to the conception of the novel. The most recent examination of the civil war in Guatemala and its effects on the Maya and their communities is *Unfinished Conquest: The Guatemalan Tragedy* by Victor Perera (University of California Press, 1993).

For information on the Nicaraguan Revolution, I am particularly indebted to Margaret Randall for her interviews with Nicaraguan women, *Sandino's Daughters* (New Star Books, 1981) and to Omar Cabezas for the story of his life as a *guerrillero*, published in English under the title *Fire From the Mountain* (Crown, 1985). Many thanks, too, to Adam Kufeld for his courageous photographs collected in the book *El Salvador* (W.W. Norton, 1990).

Although information on the situation of gays in Cuba is often contradictory and hard to obtain, I found the documentary film, *Improper Conduct*, by Nestor Alemendros and Orlando Jimenez Leal, to be a candid discussion of the Cuban government's homophobic policies. Another source for the persecution of gays in Cuba is the work of the late Reinaldo Arenas, particularly the novellas *Old Rosa and The Brightest Star*, (Grove, 1989) and his posthumous autobiography, *Before Night Falls*, (Viking, 1993).

Finally, I want to thank Jim Page for helping me out with the completeness proof, William Hernandez for teaching me how to swear in Salvadoran, Isaias Mata and Imelda for escaping with their lives and then going back again, and especially Ileana Rodríguez, for the gift of her friendship.

AGNES BUSHELL is the author of
three novels, including the political
thriller, *Local Deities*. She has
taught at the San Francisco Art
Institute and the Maine College of
Art, and currently lives in
Portland, Maine.

Also from **JOHN BROWN BOOKS**

The Taking of the Waters by John Shannon
402 pp. (quality paperback)
$13.00 plus $2.50 postage & handling

A gripping three-generation saga of the American Left. Maxi Trumbull, matriarch and muckraker, aids the embattled farmers of Owens Valley, California, in their struggle against L.A. powermongers. Maxi's son Gene, named for Eugene Debs, later organizes workers in a taut dramatization of the Flint sitdown strike. And Maxi's grandson Clay, a disaffected writer, confronts the fractured, demoralized America of the Reagan era as he seeks to return to his roots. Shannon limns these scenes with a sensibility worthy of Goya. His novel is part history, part mystery, part journalism, part social analysis, all told deftly and wittily while filling in holes in America's past and present.

Clancy Sigal calls it "a racy, ambitious edit of recent history" that has the "scope of a good road movie and the depth of a Gramsci text, without the dullness".

Mike Davis says it is "the most moving novel to come out of the experience of American radicalism".

For the *L.A. Times*, it "traces the deep, dusty channel where the American left once flowed," and does it "with a wry, almost anthropological detachment".

The *Maine Progressive*: "Sometimes a writer is so good he can reconstruct the past with such veracity that he grants us access to the lives of generations he never knew."

Violent Spring by Gary Phillips
275 pp. (quality paperback)
$9.00 plus $2.50 postage & handling

Los Angeles, 1993. The racial and class tensions that exploded on April 29, 1992, with the announcement of the Rodney King verdict, are still boiling beneath the surface of the City of the Angels when the body of a Korean merchant is discovered during a groundbreaking ceremony that is planned as part of the healing process. Black private eye Ivan Monk is hired to investigate the crime. Hounded by the FBI, dogged by street gangs, Monk rejects the easy out and follows his clues relentlessly until the murderer is revealed. With subtle humor and acute observations, Gary Phillips reveals a contemporary Los Angeles that doesn't always get into the newspapers, shatters the glib stereotypes by which most Americans navigate their cities, and suggests a solution to the troubles of a disintegrating society.

"As an examination of L.A.'s racial strife, it's quite enlightening." --Booklist

"Its political perspective is absolutely refreshing . . . . [Phillips] is hellbent on imbuing his story with hardline class analysis, and some important history, too."
--Quarterly Black Review of Books

"Tough, smart, and unabashedly political, Monk is a P.I. for the 90's." --Gar Anthony Haywood, author of *You Can Die Trying*

Send orders to:

JOHN BROWN BOOKS
P.O. Box 5683
Salem, Oregon 97304

John Brown Books publishes fiction that challenges the reader, and the status quo, offering unconventional views on contemporary and historical issues.